Pr...
THE L...

"*The Love Con* is a laugh-out-loud, tropetastic, sexy love-letter to fandom, women's geek culture, and everyone who's ever been unapologetically passionate about something. With friends-to-lovers, fake-dating, mutual pining, and the most delicious steam, this book makes for a fantastic read. I cannot wait for what Seressia Glass writes next!"

—Ali Hazelwood, #1 *New York Times* bestselling author of *Love, Theoretically*

"From pop-culture costume mashups to off-the-chart chemistry, Seressia Glass's *The Love Con* is a winner! Kenya is a body-positive, authentic woman following her dreams, no matter what anyone thinks."

—Julia London, *New York Times* bestselling author of *You Lucky Dog*

"Smart, sexy, and unputdownable. *The Love Con* will have pros and novices alike ready to don their favorite costumes and immerse themselves in this fun cosplay romance."

—Farrah Rochon, *USA Today* bestselling author of *The Dating Playbook*

"*The Love Con* is a laugh-out-loud delight! Seressia Glass takes the reader on a romantic ride full of intense emotions and high sexual chemistry. Even when the story is done, Kenya and Cam will still have a hold on your heart."

—K.M. Jackson, *USA Today* bestselling author of *How to Marry Keanu Reeves in 90 Days*

"Glass' sharp wit sparkles in *The Love Con* as we root for Kenya and Cameron in the finals of a reality cosplay competition. Fake relationship, check. Slow burn, check. A satisfying romance full of heart, heck yes! This fun romance is sure to enthrall geeks and non-geeks alike."

—Roselle Lim, author of *Sophie Go's Lonely Hearts Club*

"A charming and swoonworthy rom-com, *The Love Con* had me cheering for Kenya and Cam from the very first page. Set against the excitement of a cosplay reality show backdrop, their slow-burn romance was a perfect balance of laughter, heartwarming moments, and heat."

—Sara Desai, author of *The Singles Table*

"*The Love Con* is an unabashed love letter to geekdom and female fan culture, while also refusing to ignore the dark side of geek culture and the challenges female fans, especially female fans of color, must face. Friends-to-lovers is a difficult needle to thread as a trope, but Glass executes it with an abundance of steaminess and heart, proving that the best way to create an iconic duo is to be true to your heart."

—*Entertainment Weekly*

"If you're a fool for a friends-to-lovers trope and a slow-burn, hilarious romance, *The Love Con* won't disappoint."

—*The Augusta Chronicle*

"In this delightfully original tale, the fake-relationship trope gets new life in Glass' capable hands."

—Washington Independent Review of Books

TITLES BY SERESSIA GLASS

SUGAR AND SPICE NOVELS

Spice
Sugar

The Love Con
Game On

Game on

SERESSIA GLASS

Berkley Romance

New York

BERKLEY ROMANCE
Published by Berkley
An imprint of Penguin Random House LLC
penguinrandomhouse.com

Library of Congress Cataloging-in-Publication Data

Names: Glass, Seressia, author.
Title: Game on / Seressia Glass.
Description: First edition. | New York : Berkley Romance, 2023.
Identifiers: LCCN 2023013959 (print) | LCCN 2023013960 (ebook) |
ISBN 9780593199077 (trade paperback) | ISBN 9780593199084 (ebook)
Subjects: LCSH: Video gamers—Fiction. | Video games industry—Fiction. |
LCGFT: Romance fiction. | Novels.
Classification: LCC PS3557.L345 G36 2023 (print) |
LCC PS3557.L345 (ebook) | DDC 813/.54—dc23/eng/20230327
LC record available at https://lccn.loc.gov/2023013959
LC ebook record available at https://lccn.loc.gov/2023013960

First Edition: December 2023

Printed in the United States of America
1st Printing

Book design by Kristin del Rosario

To all the Blerds and nerds.
The world is a better place with you in it.

Game on

Chapter 1

"What the hell?"

Aron Galanis scrolled through his social media stream, his frown deepening. What had begun as a pleasant Saturday morning ritual quickly descended into chaos.

#LEGENDSFOUL was trending, and from what he could see, every post with the hashtag also tagged Artemis Games. *His* Artemis Games and *Legendsfall*, his flagship game. None of the posts were complimentary. Dozens of female gamers had latched on to the negative hashtag in relation to the depiction of women in gaming from working to playing, but by far the majority of the posts used another tag, #MISOGYNOIR.

His alarm and confusion deepened as he scrolled through post after post. He'd vaguely heard of the term before but couldn't remember the context. A quick search gave him the answer, but he couldn't believe it. Someone had accused Artemis Games of hating women in general and Black women in particular.

It made no sense. Aside from his brother, his mother was the most important person in his life. So important that he'd named his company Artemis to honor her. His goal from the time he'd developed his first game was to make games for everyone. To that end, he wanted his company to be a safe space for anyone and everyone regardless of who they were. As long as they had the talent and the desire and the motivation to help him with his vision, they could have a place on his team.

The company's vision statement held a prominent place on the website and in the break room at the office. He did his best to walk the walk. He couldn't understand why someone would accuse Artemis of something so heinous and then blast it all over social media. A viral complaint against Artemis Games was the last thing he needed. Not when he was this close to sealing an agreement on a partnership with WeCAN, the World Consortium on Autism and Neurodiversity.

While many called it a CEO's passion project, he called the certification process the culmination of three years of hard work to move his plan of making gaming even more accessible from idea to reality. These charges of discrimination could very well doom the certification and torpedo the promise he'd made to the board of directors. He couldn't allow that to happen.

He placed a call to the company's public relations head, speaking as soon as it was answered. "Mark. Who's monitoring our social media platforms today?"

"Give me a moment." Mark paused. "Should be one of our junior assistants, Paul, I think."

"Pull them off immediately and put someone with more experience on it instead."

"Did something happen?"

"The hashtag LegendsFoul happened. It's been trending for a while on every social media site. We need someone other than a junior assistant dealing with it."

"Let me take a look." A heavy sigh. "Dammit, this doesn't

look good for us and it's the last thing we need right now. I'll get the team on it immediately."

"Good. While they do that, I want you to craft a strategic response that can go out today. We also need people mining the hashtag on all platforms. Find out who started this, who they are, what they want."

"Probably some disgruntled former employee looking to create a fuss ahead of the certification. It will be my pleasure to ferret them out."

"Once you get that response drafted, send it to me for review. I'll contact the rest of the leadership team so that they're aware of what's going on and that we'll have a statement ready soon. Get Legal to take a look at it too."

"Of course."

"So, damage control this weekend, Mark. I don't want anyone thinking that we're ignoring this, or worse yet, unaware of the accusations. Then make sure your team is ready to launch an action plan Monday morning. I'll contact the WeCAN selection committee myself."

"I'll make sure the statement says something along the lines of us believing in equity and inclusion and taking these accusations very seriously," he said. "Once approved, we'll release a statement on our website and all platforms. If we're lucky, there will be some new celebrity scandal before the weekend's over and this will be a bad memory for us. Netizens have a short attention span."

"I'm not going to rely on luck when it comes to the bottom line for this company," Aron retorted. "Just like I don't care whether or not it's a former employee making these charges. Have you seen how many posts with this hashtag there have been in the last hour? And that's just one platform. If we do nothing, this could become a pile-on that gets picked up by all the tech sites and then breaks onto mainstream media outlets."

His stomach soured at the thought. "If these accusations have any grain of truth, I can't let it just blow over. I'll take action so that the public, our team, and our customers know how serious we—I—take this. I don't need something like this hanging over my head when I'm trying to win that accessibility certification."

"Understood."

He tightened his grip on his phone. "GamerCon is coming up. Even if the hashtag dies down now, it could easily be revived that weekend when the focus should be on our latest development and not social media accusations. If the certification committee hears about this before I can contact them . . ." All his plans would be ruined.

"I'll have a plan ready to go Monday morning."

He had no doubt that Mark would take care of it. He was good at his job. Aron was good at his too, and there was no way in hell that he was going to sit on his thumbs and do nothing while some unknown poster took potshots at the company. He'd worked too hard to lose everything over some sourminded social media posts. But if the accusations were true . . .

Pushing back from his desk, he made his way to the digital whiteboard that took up a large chunk of wall in his home office. He wasn't about to mount a defense without a strategy, and he wasn't going to wait for Mark and his team to produce results. He would do his own research, make a contingency plan, then turn his defense into offense. He would be the one to turn this around.

He quickly created a list of objectives: Find the originator of the hashtag. Do a deep dive on the OP—the original poster. Discover if any of their claims were true or an attempt to sabotage Artemis Games. Gather evidence to refute or prove the claims were valid. Praise or punish based on the outcome.

Mark sent the statement as Aron finished his initial plan. He reviewed it, made changes, then sent it back before revisiting his whiteboard. With the game plan in place, it was time to do the work. Returning to his desk, he turned his attention to his laptop. Most of the quote posts and replies were to an account named @ReyofSun.

Aron frowned. Why did that name sound familiar? The account's picture was of a Black Wonder Woman. No, that was Nubia, Wonder Woman's sister. Was the account holder really a Black woman or was it just a sock puppet?

The account name and profile picture remained consistent across most of the social media platforms. He scrolled back through the history on each platform but couldn't find an actual photo of the person behind the handle. All of the posts dealt with gaming in one way or another. She didn't appear in any of her video reviews or gaming live streams, instead using only audio to accompany her screenshots. No matter how long he searched, he couldn't find any identifiable information—not her legal name, location, nothing. If not for the voice in the audio, he'd think the accounts were fake.

So why did her handle sound familiar? Digging some more, he came across another hashtag frequently used by the account: #LiteThemUp.

That was it. ReyofSun used the LiteThemUp hashtag for game reviews, particularly for games and their creators that fell short in the diversity department. There was nothing wrong with campaigning for equality and access in gaming, but reviews with that hashtag were scorching. Now she'd apparently set her sights on Artemis Games.

Why? Was she trying to up her clout and follower count by taking on Artemis? He dug a little deeper. She didn't seem to be having any problems monetizing her streams, especially with her inclusion reviews of several games both online and off. Of course taking potshots at gaming companies would be profitable. Those "Lite Them Up" reviews got her the most attention, got her panel invites to numerous gaming conventions, and apparently, got her paid.

He frowned. He or Artemis reps had been to nearly all the cons she had mentioned in her posts, yet he had never seen her. Although he usually flew under the radar at cons, he hadn't heard reports from his conventions teams of being approached by ReyofSun. Maybe if she had, he wouldn't be dealing with a social media firestorm now.

A sense of dread rolled through him like an icy fog as he clicked on her review of Artemis Games' flagship first-person shooter game, *Legendsfall*.

"Hey everyone, ReyofSun here with a new review of *Legendsfall* by Artemis Games. It's been out for a minute and has been pretty successful since its release. I think Artemis Games said it was their best release to date."

It had been and still was. An interview from one of the tech sites popped up on-screen, highlighting the actual quote. ReyofSun obviously did her homework and backed her statements with proof. His foreboding grew.

"It's a very playable game, blending really intense maps with some that are low-pressure for experienced players. Overall I've liked each iteration even though the character offerings are not as robust or customizable as other games, and none of the cast of playable characters are a Black female. But now I have to light them up. *Legendsfall* is now *Legends-Foul*."

"What the hell," he muttered again as he looked at a Photoshopped copy of the *Legendsfall* cover art with her new, derogatory title. She'd liked the game initially but now wanted to trash it? *Why?*

"You're probably wondering why I changed my review. Remember how I said none of the playable characters were a Black female? That's true. But there is one non-playable Black female character, and she's in this urban warfare map. Surprised? I sure was. I cleared this level and never encountered this character. That's because it's an Easter egg. If you encounter this character, she gives you a gift to use on a later map and a key to clear the current map. As soon as she does, she gets killed, more graphically than any other character in this game. I'm talking a total fridge moment."

A screenshot of the character appeared. "Weirdly enough, no one has commented on this character in the months that this release has been out. Do you wonder why that is? I'll tell you why. That Easter egg wasn't meant for us to find. I'm talking general us, not just Black women us. Somebody deliberately programmed that scene into the game to satisfy a certain segment of gaming fans."

What was she talking about? Aron would never let anything like that fly. Neither would the head of the development team. There was no way—

An image of a message forum flashed on-screen behind her. "Someone tipped me off to this forum. I don't know how long this discussion will still be visible, but screenshots last forever. It's apparent from some of the comments that a certain segment of gamers were extremely happy to find this Easter egg."

The forum screen peeled away to the screenshot of the NPC, the non-playable character. "Let's recap. The only Black female character in this entire game is a non-playable character who is literally a Magical Negro. A no-name, unnecessary plot device that you don't even need to visit to complete the level? A forum of male gamers gleefully playing the map just for that scene? That, my friends, is misogynoir. A hatred of Black women built into a game."

Righteous anger burned through her voice. "That's why I had to light them up. This is worse than not being represented. I'm going to be charitable and say that I don't believe the Artemis Games execs know about this, but the questions need to be asked: How did this get past the gatekeepers at the company? How many people looked at this and said okay before its release? Either people knew about it and thought it was okay, or there's a rogue developer coding whatever the hell he wants—because let's be real, it certainly wasn't a female coder—into a game. Either way, Artemis Games, you have a problem."

The view changed to a split screen of the NPC and the two hashtags superimposed over the Artemis Games logo. "You need to fix this, Artemis Games. You know better. And now that you know better. Do. Better."

The video ended with **DO BETTER** in large white letters against a black background.

Aron sat back in his chair. What. The. Hell? There was no way *Legendsfall* had something like that in it. He'd played the game through several times before and after each update, and he'd never encountered that NPC.

If ReyofSun's claims were true, he had more than a trending hashtag to worry about. The claims weren't something he could leave to others to investigate; he'd have to do it himself. Even if it took the remainder of the weekend, he'd review every piece of code and uncover which of his developers had decided to have some fun with the company's reputation, which supervisor had signed off on the code.

If the claims were true, he'd have to publicly own it as the head of the company. He would do what he had to do even though he absolutely hated public appearances. That alone was reason enough for someone's head to roll.

The next event that Artemis was slated to attend was GamerCon, in two weeks. A quick check revealed that ReyofSun would also be there.

Perfect. Two weeks gave him enough time to create and implement an action plan. He'd present the plan to the WeCAN certification committee after his phone call with them on Monday. After he ensured that the certification was still on track, he'd refine the plan and focus on presenting it during the main Artemis Games panel at the con. Hopefully, that would be enough to take the steam out of ReyofSun's crusade before the Q and A.

But if this wasn't real, if it was something cooked up by a former employee or ReyofSun herself, she would have to own that. Fair was fair, after all. Her retraction needed to be as loud and public as her claims. If she refused . . . well, that's why he had lawyers.

Game on, ReyofSun. Game. On.

Chapter 2

"Congratulations! Your hashtag is trending!"

"Still?" Sam looked over Quinn's shoulder at her laptop screen. Sure enough, #LEGENDSFOUL was still going strong, and so was the debate. Multiple people had even reposted her "Lite Them Up" review of the game.

"I bet your mentions are trash," Max said, plopping down beside Quinn on their sofa, a bowl of popcorn in her hands.

"When aren't they?" The ReyofSun account always had a dumpster fire in its mentions, some good, most bad. Her Block-Fu was excellent, though, so at least her DMs were mostly unscathed.

"Let me see." Max patted the empty space beside her. "Get out your phone and sit beside me."

"Did you seriously bring a bowl of popcorn to my dumpster fire?" Sam asked.

"Girl, it's not like we don't know how this goes." Max rolled her eyes, then shifted to give Sam room on the couch. "You post a legitimate critique and include receipts. Reasonable people start a conversation, people are being civil. Then the rabid fans roll in because you dare to criticize their holy object, insert derogatory noun here. They shout you down for being wrong despite the receipts you have, claiming you're loud and angry and jealous when in reality they're the ones who are loud and angry and wrong. Then the concern trolling starts. It's like a movie we've already seen but we watch it again anyway because maybe this time things will turn out the way we want."

She tossed some popcorn into her mouth. "Frankly, I'm just here to see what Black social media has to say about it."

"They're doing what they do, and I am here for it." It was hard to preach a sermon without the choir backing you up. Thank goodness she was part of a great online network of fellow Blerds under the Nubia's Shield banner. "I don't think it would have gotten nearly the traction it has without other people chiming in with their stories."

Max snorted. "People trying to hijack your hashtag as always."

"The important thing is the visibility. The bosses at Artemis Games are so far removed from the development process that they let something like this slip in under the radar. That's what I'm going to believe. Just like I believe they'll do something about it."

"You're being too nice," Max said, then turned to Quinn. "Ain't she being too nice?"

"This is why she does the videos instead of you," Quinn said in her usual soothing tone. "You have anger management issues."

"Well, it's not like I don't have a hellified number of reasons to be angry," Max said as she put her popcorn on the coffee table, then pulled out her phone. "But that's what burner accounts are for."

"Max," Sam chided.

"What? Pissing off trolls is a great anger reliever. Especially when they're wrong. And stupid." She laughed as she called up her app. "Let's see who I can get banned today."

"Apparently, not all heroes wear capes." Quinn shook her head, then looked at Sam. "Do you think Artemis Games will respond?"

"From a social media and PR standpoint, they have to. They'll probably post some toothless statement about taking the claims seriously and an equally toothless promise to look into it." Sam snorted. "Then they'll issue another statement a couple of weeks from now that will be a rehash of the first one, hoping by that time that everyone's attention will have switched to something else."

"But GamerCon is coming up in like two weeks. Even if people forget, they will remember when it's con time."

Sam folded her arms. "They can try to forget all they want. I'll be there too, and I'm not going to let this slide. I'll sit front row at their panel, and I'll be ready with my questions. They need to answer about this character, and they need to tell us what they're going to do to fix it, and what their plan is to make sure that it never happens again."

"If you do that, you'll be putting yourself in the crosshairs for anyone to take potshots at you, or worse," Quinn pointed out. "Even in your con disguise, do you think that's the safest thing to do, especially now?"

"Unless someone in registration leaks my personal information, the only thing con-goers will know is my handle. Revealing anything else violates their own policy and makes them liable for whatever happens."

"I suppose we'll just have to hope that the con admins are

good people," Max said. "It's going to be bad enough with you walking around as ReyofSun."

"I know." Sam sighed. "I think that this is important enough for me to be at that panel, in the front row ready to question them if they don't address the issue."

"We'll be right there with you."

"I know you will." Knowing her friends had her back made it bearable. There were others out there doing the same call-outs, but it still felt lonely and it got to be too much at times. It wasn't like she needed the attention to further monetize her streams in an effort to become an influencer. Honestly, she really just wanted to sit around at home or online or hang out with her friends at Game and Flame, a local bar that specialized in games of all kinds and an extensive beer inventory. She wanted to go to Thursday Game Night embracing her love of gaming. Was it too much to ask that it love her back, or at least, not treat her like trash?

Max lowered her phone enough to rejoin the conversation. "I bet you could march into Artemis and set them straight. Your mother definitely could. They're in Atlanta just like we are."

"Without a doubt, Rise Consulting is good at what it does, and my mother is one of the best at helping companies shift their culture and mindset to be more inclusive. I'm proud to work with her and for her. As much as I love helping companies become more inclusive, I'm not doing this to get a consulting gig. I keep my gaming life and my professional life as separate as possible."

"Yeah, I know." Max sat back. "But it would be funny as hell if you got Artemis Games to do better by going to work for them."

"No!" Sam clapped her hand over Max's mouth. "Don't you dare speak that into existence! Can you imagine what that would be like, after calling them out? It would be like strolling into a melee with just an umbrella!"

Max broke free with a laugh. "I do believe you did just that in that *Coliseum Chaos* game, remember? You could totally stroll into Artemis Games, fix their issues, get revenge on Internet trolls and butthurt fanboys, and make bank doing it."

"That would be pretty funny," Quinn chimed in, then spread her hands as she looked skyward. "I can see it now. Samara Reynolds, ReyofSun, Bringer of the Fire, Snatcher of Edges, meeting the CEO of Artemis Games and after reading him for filth, gets offered a job. That would be perfect!"

"That would be ridiculous!" Sam jumped to her feet. "I don't know what you sweetened this tea with, but y'all need to stop putting that out into the universe. There's no way in hell I'd get offered a job changing Artemis's culture. Just like there's no way in hell I'd accept it."

The spot between her shoulder blades itched as she picked up her phone. Probably all those people commenting on her posts. Sure enough, the conversation had devolved into vague threats and less vague name-calling by accounts with numbers in the handle and no picture for the profile.

"Looks like it's scrub time," she announced, settling back on the couch. It was her least favorite pastime, clearing her notifications and scouring her mentions. It was the usual process whenever she posted about the lack of inclusion in games and gaming. She was used to it, and decompressing with Max and Quinn definitely helped. Some days, though . . .

Luckily, today was not one of those days. The filters she'd

created took care of most of the hateful comments, but some got through. Too many.

"How bad is it?" Quinn asked, her tone quiet.

Sam twisted her lips. "Could be worse. Most of these are probably fans and possibly employees of Artemis Games. And y'all think it would be hilarious to work with people who fixed their fingers to type out responses like these?"

She raised her hands to cut off their protests. "I know, I know. It's not fair to paint all Artemis employees with the same brush. I'm sure there are some very fine people working there."

Max spluttered into her tea. "I'm sure there are. You gotta look at it from both sides, after all."

Sam scrolled through her notifications. "Yeah, that would be a no. Not with these receipts."

The challenge to do better was out there. Artemis Games would either accept the challenge or not, and she'd give them her money in the future or not.

She'd go to GamerCon and see what Artemis Games was made of. Maybe she'd be surprised, but she doubted it.

• • •

"Are you sure you want to do this?"

Aron settled his glasses into place, then stepped back to assess his reflection. He'd done his best to look like every other male gamer at the con: jeans, sneakers, T-shirt, gray hoodie. The glasses and disheveled hair added to the image, a far cry from his corporate persona. Just as he intended.

He turned away from the mirror to look at Grayson, his personal assistant. "I don't have much choice. I need to gather data on what people really think before the presentation, and this is the fastest method."

"A follow-up question, then. Are you sure you can do this?"

That was the real question. He didn't like crowds and preferred to keep interactions in which he was the focus to a minimum. Some people called him standoffish, eccentric, or worse, but he didn't care. He much preferred to have his marketing and communications teams do the talking while he focused on making Artemis the best gaming company around. Having to be Aron Galanis, founder and CEO of Artemis Games, was exhausting at the best of times. In his mind, there was nothing wrong with preferring to have a lower profile, if not be completely anonymous.

Unfortunately for him, his anonymity would only last until Artemis Games' presentation later that afternoon, when he'd have to face the crowd in the auditorium and announce the results of his internal audit.

ReyofSun's claims had borne out. Yes, she'd shown evidence, or receipts as she'd called it. Yet he couldn't bring himself to accept her claims at face value. He'd needed to find proof himself.

And he had. It had taken the entire weekend, but he'd hunted down every detail and gathered the evidence himself. As Mark had predicted, by the following Monday the dumpster fire of a hashtag had died down, but Aron wasn't one to let things slide by that impacted the company that bore his mother's name. Before the day had ended, he'd sent three people off to search for other opportunities.

Today he would share that information with attendees. He would own up to the issues and he'd describe an action plan to prove that Artemis would do better. Not because he had to, but because he wanted to. Artemis Games couldn't pursue accessibility on one side while turning a blind eye to problematic portrayals on the other. That wasn't what Artemis Games was about. That wasn't what he was about.

"I'll do what I have to do," he finally said. "I can't do anything else."

Grayson nodded. "I know."

Even tone. Shoulders relaxed but hands clasped in front of him. Confident yet concerned. Aron assessed his assistant as he did everyone he had to interact with. It had helped him become better at social cues, which he missed more often than not and were another reason he'd rather be head down in code instead of talking to people. "You're going to tail me, aren't you?"

"Of course."

Grayson usually served as a buffer, running social interference. He was a master at creating graceful exits when Aron's social meter was full, a fact that Aron gratefully paid him well for.

"It shouldn't be overwhelming," Aron said to reassure them both. "I can talk games and gaming. Taking the pulse of my fellow gamers will be worth the discomfort."

"Even if one of those gamers is ReyofSun?"

Aron adjusted his glasses. "Especially if one of those gamers is ReyofSun."

Chapter 3

"And now, we'll open the floor up to questions," the panel moderator said. "Please raise your hand, and when we call on you, please stand up."

Samara looked out over the crowd. With her "Lite Them Up" reviews going viral, she hadn't been sure if their Diversity in Gaming panel would be packed with curiosity seekers, protestors, or allies. Despite her intentions not to, she'd examined each person that had entered the room, sorting them into friend, foe, or undecided categories. Being wary of people wasn't something she enjoyed doing, but some folks had issues with marginalized gamers and creators wanting inclusion and access in the gaming world. The world in general. Her inbox proved that.

As usual, she was at the con in "gamer mode," wearing a high-end wig of auburn and gold ringlets, red-framed glasses, and a red T-shirt with a sun on the front. It was so far from her IRL professional persona that no one could connect the two. At least no one had in the years since she'd started her game reviews.

Her scan of the crowd made it seem that she and the other panelists were largely preaching to the choir as usual. The people who needed to hear her message, game developers in general and Artemis Games in particular, were nowhere to be seen.

Not that she could recognize anyone from Artemis on sight, whether they were an executive or one of the trade show minions. She didn't know what the suits at Artemis looked like. She'd done a cursory scan of their corporate page and the board of directors, noting the mostly homogenous line of executives broken only by a female financial officer and a couple of East Asian men.

Aron Galanis, the head of the company, seemed to be a rarely seen boy genius, a relatively young man with swept-back dark brown hair and amber-brown eyes. She couldn't remember ever seeing him at any of the gaming conventions, but then she guessed that when you were the CEO, you paid other people to pimp your product or face the flak for you while you stayed safe in your cash-lined ivory tower.

Shortly after #LEGENDSFOUL blew up, Artemis Games had issued some lame-ass statement about taking diversity, equity, and inclusion seriously, pointed to their leadership in providing accessibility for all their games, then added a nebulous promise to do better. If they actually had an action plan in place to address their issues, they were certainly keeping it under wraps, probably hoping the noise would subside.

Not if she could help it.

Artemis had a big panel scheduled for later in the day, and Samara planned to park herself in the front row. Let them see her Black face staring back at them. Let them look her in the eye as they attempted to sugarcoat their issues and make toothless promises they'd forget about as soon as the next dustup went viral.

Samara had no intention of letting them forget. It didn't matter how much hate mail she'd received, how many threats she'd had to report across all of her social media accounts. She could deal with them all. Her parents hadn't raised her to be meek or powerless. She also had her friends who always had her back, who lifted her spirits when the trolls got to be too much.

Without them and her parents, she would have faltered in the fight long ago. Yet she couldn't give up, couldn't give in. She owed too much to Marquessa to back down now. Her late friend would never get the justice that she deserved, but Samara could raise her voice so that no other Black female gamers had to endure what she'd suffered.

One woman stood up. "What I want to know is, have you heard anything from Artemis Games after you called them out? Did they reach out to you in any way?"

"I didn't really expect them to, so I'm not disappointed that they haven't," Sam answered. "As a matter of fact, I don't need Artemis Games to contact me. I need them, and other game developers, to do better."

A polite smattering of applause greeted her answer. Two people later, an earnest young man posed the next question to her. "What do you say to those who say you should just not play the games if you dislike them, or make up your own game, if diversity is that important to you?"

Samara leaned forward and unzipped a smile. "I would tell them to come up with an original thought. I mean, really."

The audience tittered. "I'm not saying that to you, but let's get real. Marginalized creators are out here in these technology streets, building content and pushing envelopes. They're launching apps and games and other content left and right. If you haven't seen them, then maybe that means you need to expand your circle. The problem is, and always has been, breaking through the established power structure. Getting the visibility and the financial backing that cis, male, white developers do is like swimming against the current with a two-ton boulder strapped to your back."

She took a sip of water. "What's so wrong about people wanting to see themselves represented in the things they love? To be able to look through custom mods and see their skin color, their hairstyle? What's so wrong about wanting to see yourself in a game, and not as some wack stereotypical non-playable character that's so offensive it's not even laughable? What's so wrong about wanting a seat at the same table?"

She gestured to the crowd, frustration and hope duking it out inside her. "You—general cis, white, abled male you—don't have to ask those questions because your demographic is the standard. You're the one that gets catered to historically—catered to, listened to, and marketed to. And to that, I say the game developers need to get new marketing teams and ditch those outdated statistics. Gamers are browner. About forty-five percent of gamers are female. There are more neurodivergent gamers, more LGBTQ+ gamers than ever before. And while you can be anyone you want behind the comfort of your screen name, people still want to play characters who are an extension of them, who look like them, who are not a bland default. It's not giving in to social and societal pressures to make them feel welcome. It's just good business. The only color businesses should be concerned with is the color of money, and marginalized people have money."

Applause crashed through the room, startling her. She'd been so focused on making her point that she'd forgotten her audience. Several people nodded their heads in agreement. Now that the panel was almost over, she could relax, and she offered up a smile and a nod of thanks to everyone.

Even the white guy in the hoodie sitting by himself at the back of the room clapped and nodded. She'd been wary the moment she'd seen him enter the room, right before their panel started. Almost everyone at cons ran around at least in pairs, so a loner always pricked her radar. His seeming agreement made her lower her vigilance even more.

It was an automatic thing these days, to be on guard and identify any potential threats at cons since she'd started calling out game companies. Fanboys felt some type of way about their precious toys being meddled with, and while she hadn't had any physical altercations yet, it was better to be vigilant. She made sure she didn't go anywhere alone, even to the restroom. She certainly didn't go to her hotel room by herself, and the reservation wasn't in her name either.

Her parents worried about her and the crusade she'd picked up after Marquessa's death, yet they still understood and had given their blessing. The least she could do was take every step she could to protect herself when she went to conventions and other speaking engagements. She wouldn't back down, not now, not ever. Whenever she got tired, whenever she faltered, she would think of Marquessa. No one had stood up for her; no one had protected her until it was too late. Samara would stand for her now.

After a few more questions, the panel finally wrapped, and Samara joined her friends waiting for her in the front row. "You did great!" Quinn said, her wide smile revealing her braces as she draped an arm over Sam's shoulders. "You were unshakable!"

"I'm glad it seemed that way, because my stomach is still in knots. I need a Caramel Frappuccino like yesterday!"

Max threaded her arm. "Looks like we have some time before the next panel starts. Want to head to the food court for lunch?"

"Yes, please!"

Hoodie Guy stood up as they approached the exit. "Excuse me, ReyofSun?"

Sam paused, on instinctive alert. Max and Quinn immediately formed up in front of her, Max jerking up her chin. "Yeah?"

Hoodie Guy looked at both of them, gave a nod, then turned back to Sam. "I liked what you had to say on the panel. I was wondering if I could talk to you more about it."

Okay. Maybe Hoodie Guy was an ally. The golden-brown eyes certainly seemed earnest enough behind the wire-rimmed glasses. She glanced at his convention badge. No press credentials or other affiliations were attached to it, just a first name, Benjy. "Are you with a media site?"

He adjusted his glasses. "Just doing some research right now."

Hmm. That could mean anything or nothing at all. She didn't want to brush him off, especially since one more with her would be one less against her, but—

"Sa—ReyofSun gets paid for her time," Max cut in, "and right now it's time for lunch."

"What if I buy you lunch?" the guy said, holding up a placating hand. "All three of you lunch? I'd like to know more about your experiences in gaming. I want to understand where you're coming from and what you've been facing. If I can write something up that will help you, I'll do it."

She exchanged glances with Quinn and Max. All three of them had been gaming friends for years, hiding behind masculine versions of their names and generic profiles until they'd lost Marquessa.

"Okay, then, Hoodie Guy. We were planning to grab a bite at the food court." In such a packed public place, there was less likelihood of things going sideways. Besides, she had Max and Quinn with her.

"Sounds good." He drew in a breath, then stuck out a hand. "You can call me Benjy."

"All right. Benjy it is." His grip was warm and firm, and he maintained eye contact, something that Sam admired. Maybe he wasn't such a bad guy after all. It would be great to have another ally. A real ally, and not some bullshit performative ally that ghosted when things got hot. As frustrating as it was, sometimes people heard a message better if it came from someone in their same demographic.

So yeah, she'd talk to Hoodie Guy, convince him that the concerns were real and being more inclusive wouldn't hurt anyone. He said he'd help. She'd hold him to that.

Chapter 4

Aron would apologize to his younger brother for borrowing his name as soon as he saw him. Benjy probably wouldn't mind, but their mother would head bop him for sure.

The casualness of his dress, the glasses, and the alias were all a necessity. It wasn't like he could put on a suit and walk around the convention with a badge proclaiming him as Aron Galanis, Artemis Games CEO. Not unless he wanted to get mobbed by fans and critics alike. There would be plenty of time for that at the Artemis Games panel later that afternoon. There had been numerous requests for interviews from media outlets covering the convention, but he'd leave those to his PR team. After making his statement at the panel, he wanted no more questions about #LEGENDSFOUL.

He'd wanted, needed, a couple of days of anonymity and distance before his speech in the crowd of gamers as he took the pulse of the community, gathering data about what they were excited about, and to just be a fellow gamer and not the head of a tech company. Besides, he definitely needed to know how people felt about Artemis in case he and his team had to make any adjustments to the panel later.

Even though she'd been right, he'd attended ReyofSun's

panel, wanting to know more about her than what he could find through her video critiques. He'd been impressed by a woman with a sharp, data-driven mind, who quoted statistics and facts as if gathering diversity data was her career. The data and the reputable sources she used made him wonder what the hell his marketing team was doing. While Black women in gaming was her focus, she'd championed other marginalized communities, supplying her fellow panelists with the informative weapons they needed to drive their points home. Along with the data she'd presented, her passion and conviction shone through in every word she'd spoken, passion that had the audience nodding in agreement. Members of that diverse audience were his customers, potential customers. He knew then that the announcement he planned to make during his speech was not only the right one, but one that would also salvage Artemis Games' reputation. ReyofSun had the information he needed, information he couldn't acquire from randomly approaching gamers on the convention floor. He had to get that information to further his expansion plans for Artemis Games. First, though, he had to win ReyofSun over to his side. To do that, he had to understand hers.

Keeping his word, he accompanied them to the food court adjacent to the convention hall and paid for each of their lunches. They managed to find a relatively quiet area to sit, eat, and talk. Conscious of the time, he resisted the urge to dive right in, and focused on having a general conversation instead. He'd had to learn how to make small talk, had to learn how to act and react to people based on their body language. It was a difficult learning experience, and he much preferred to get right to the point, but some people took that as him being rude instead of direct. He didn't want ReyofSun or her friends to think of him as rude. Not when he needed their input, especially hers.

At the moment, each of them displayed cautious curiosity, with the one with the close-cropped curls eyeing him with deep suspicion. Given some of the comments he'd seen on the #LEGENDSFOUL post and their gaming streams, he understood her caution. He decided to begin with an innocuous question.

He dug into his hoodie pocket for his personal phone, then held it aloft. "Do any of you mind if I record our conversation?"

Rey exchanged a quick glance with the others, then turned back to him with a relaxed smile. "Sure, go ahead."

She probably thought he was recording an interview, which, he supposed, he was. He had a near eidetic memory, but it might prove useful to have a recording of their conversation. "Would you mind introducing me to your friends?"

"Of course," ReyofSun said after taking a sip of her drink. "The one in the blue shirt is MaximaCarnage and the one wearing the pink rainbow shirt is MannequinnSkywalker. You can call them Max and Quinn."

"Are those your gaming handles?"

"What's wrong with that?" MaximaCarnage rushed to her friend's defense. "You think we came here just to look pretty?"

"No, of course not," Aron replied, realizing that someone who gamed as MaximaCarnage was someone he had to be vigilant around the most, since being full of suspicion seemed to be a regular status update for her. "I know there's more to GamerCon than showcasing new games, so I was wondering."

"Yes, we do game," MaximaCarnage answered, her tone much softer now. "We have a team called Nubia's Shield."

"We named our team after Wonder Woman's sister, Nubia,"

ReyofSun added. "The shield part is because we always stand ready to compete and we defend our fellow Black girl gamers. We try to protect one another online as much as we can."

It was a good opening. "Based on what you said in your panel, is that something you have to do often?"

"Sometimes we get to play in peace," MannequinnSkywalker said after she swallowed a bite. "Most times when we stream, we and other marginalized people get hate-raided. Assholes coming out of the woodwork like the roaches they are."

"Hate raiding." He frowned, trying to remember where he'd heard that before, sure it was in connection with ReyofSun. "That sounds familiar."

"We touched on it a little in the panel," ReyofSun said. "It's when accounts bombard streamers' chats with what basically amounts to hate speech. That crap drowns out any legitimate chat, and no matter how thick your skin is or how you try to rise above it, sometimes it clings to you like an oily film."

"That's harsh. How often do you have to deal with that?"

All three of them looked at him with high levels of incredulity. "Every time we log on," MaximaCarnage told him. "Every. Single. Time."

It was difficult to comprehend. "Are you serious? Why?"

"That's a very good question." MannequinnSkywalker took a sip of her drink before continuing. "Because they think it's fun. Because they think marginalized groups are invading their territory and pushing them out. Maybe it's because they have the emotional level of a toddler. No offense to toddlers, of course."

"They do it because they want us to quit," ReyofSun added,

"but we're not going to give them the satisfaction. Whether we stream or not, we'll keep playing because we love it."

"I wouldn't want to give up playing either." Of course, he'd never had to face anything like what she and her friends dealt with. A few negative reviews or customer service complaints were mild in comparison.

Time to steer the conversation to Artemis. He chose his words carefully. "Did you get more of that after you posted your review of *Legendsfall*?"

She snorted. "Of course I did. I would have been surprised if I hadn't. *Legendsfall* is a pretty popular game, and it has a lot of fans."

"But they don't speak on behalf of Artemis," he pointed out.

"Of course they don't," she agreed. "All we've heard from Artemis Games is a statement that sounded as if it had been written by an intern who copied it from the 'oops, we messed up but can't admit it' playbook. Then again, maybe they were hoping that people would forget about it by the time Gamer-Con came around."

"It's only been two weeks," MaximaCarnage said. "There's no way they're that dense to think no one would ask them about it, especially with their big panel this afternoon."

Aron looked down at his barely touched sandwich. He should have ordered something else. Maybe a ginger ale to fight the acid bubbling in his stomach. Mark had been wrong about the scandal blowing over. Everyone he'd talked to at the con so far knew that ReyofSun and Artemis were both at the convention. They were eager to see a confrontation, something he most definitely did not want to be a part of.

"Do you think they owe you an apology or a thank-you?"

MaximaCarnage laughed, and he was pretty sure it was at him and not with him given how MannequinnSkywalker tried to hush her. Rey's expression telegraphed distaste, and he struggled to not get defensive. After all, he was just a regular gamer guy, not the Artemis CEO.

"No offense, but Artemis Games owes me nothing. I know I'm not the only one who emailed the customer service inbox with complaints. If anything, they owe their female gamers, especially their Black female gamers, better options and representation in their games."

"How would you fix the misogynoir in *Legendsfall*?"

"For one thing, I'd have more than one Black female character," she quickly answered. "Two, I'd make her a playable character. Three, her story wouldn't be a digital stereotype. Make her a person—I mean seriously, that NPC could have been a talking rock instead."

"Rey could write a dissertation on how to make *Legendsfall* more inclusive," MannequinnSkywalker told him. "But she wouldn't hand it over to Artemis Games without decent compensation. We don't labor for free."

Really? "What if they wanted to pay you for your labor now? Like have you do some consulting work with character development or something. Would you do it?"

A peculiar expression crossed Rey's face. MaximaCarnage snorted and MannequinnSkywalker smiled. He couldn't parse the meaning behind their reactions. "Did I say something wrong?"

"No!" Rey waved her hands at him. "I mean, no, you didn't. I doubt that would happen."

"Why not?"

"Why would they?" She laughed. "It's a ridiculous idea. They don't know me. To them I'm just some random gamer."

She was anything but a random gamer. Her trending hashtag proved that, as did the information he'd gathered about her in the last two weeks since her review had gone viral. Her criticisms and insights were sharp and on the mark. He'd found it impossible to find fault with any of her arguments. He needed to leverage her knowledge.

"Can a random gamer do what you did? I bet someone at Artemis Games noticed."

"Yes, well . . ." She gave him an uncomfortable smile. "I guess it would be a 'put up or shut up' moment, right? It would depend on a lot of different factors, and only one of those is monetary. If I truly believed I could make a difference, and if they truly made me a sincere offer, I'd give it serious consideration."

Yes! Aron buried his excitement. If he could bring Reyof-Sun on board as a consultant, it would be a PR win for the company. Not only that, having her on board would be the impetus he needed to implement changes at the company.

"Are you going to their panel later today?"

"Damn right I am. I plan to sit in the front row and be the first one to the microphone if they're brave enough to take questions."

Which would start a spectacle he wanted to avoid at all costs. Which meant it was time to come clean, if he could have a private conversation with her. He took a glance around the area and caught sight of his assistant failing miserably to blend in with the con-goers. He'd never seen Grayson in a pair of jeans. "Do you think I could talk to you for a moment?"

Her eyebrows scrunched. "Isn't that what we're doing now?"

"Yes, but there's something you—"

"Crap." MannequinnSkywalker stood up, staring at her phone. "Sam—I mean, Rey—we've got to go. We've got a meetup on the other side of the hall in ten minutes."

Aron stood when the rest of them did. He made a desperate Hail Mary as he picked up his phone. "Can I get your number, so I can text you before the Artemis panel? I really want to talk to you some more. You've got great ideas, and someone needs to know about them."

Surprise widened her eyes. "Umm . . . that's not something I usually do."

"Rey." MaximaCarnage grabbed Rey's sleeve in a not-so-subtle attempt to leave.

Aron raised his hands. "I swear, I only want to talk gaming. I'm harmless."

MaximaCarnage twisted her lips. "Anyone who claims they're harmless is usually anything but."

Desperation gripped him. He couldn't lose this chance. There wouldn't be another. "If you don't want to give me yours, I can give you mine," he quickly offered. "We can meet before the panel. Please?"

That plea must have worked, because she dipped her head with a soft smile. "Okay."

He quickly held out his phone, realized it was still recording, stopped it, then held his phone out again. "Here."

Never had he allowed anyone to touch his phone, business or personal. Not his mother, not Grayson. But for this woman, handing it over was not only easy, it was a relief.

Her fingers brushed his as she took his phone and . . . he let it happen. It didn't bother him at all. Not even when she input her number and called her phone, then touched his fingers again as she handed his phone back to him. "Here you go."

"Thank you. Seriously."

"You're welcome. Seriously," she said as one of her friends grabbed her by the arm again to pull her away. "See you later!"

Grayson approached him as Aron looked at Rey's contact information. Surprise rolled through him. She'd entered her name as Samara Reynolds. Was that her real name? Was it intentional or accidental? He'd keep her info to himself, of course, but he needed to immediately do a search using that name before his panel began.

"Did I see what I thought I saw?" Grayson asked.

Hearing the surprise in his assistant's voice, Aron tucked his phone away, then faced his assistant. "What? Did I make a mistake?"

Grayson shook his head. "Not only did you not look pressured talking to strangers, but you also looked like you were enjoying yourself."

"I did. She's an impressive woman, and the conversation kept me focused. I forgot about the crowd and the noise. It went better than I'd estimated."

"I suppose it did, since you *handed her your phone*."

"She used it to call her cell so we'd have each other's numbers. I need to text her before our panel starts." He studied Grayson's expression. "Are you surprised?"

"Of course I am. You used your personal phone."

"It didn't seem right to use the business phone with her."

With Rey gone, the sounds and crowd in the food court began to press in on him. Time to leave. "Let's go."

"Are you listening to yourself?" Grayson asked as they headed back to the main hall. "You not only used your personal phone, which has like three contacts in it, you actually let her touch it."

"Yes." Aron paused. "That's different."

"That's an understatement. You don't even allow me to touch that phone. Didn't it bother you?"

"No." Since his personal assistant helped him navigate social encounters, he provided more information. "Our hands touched. Twice."

Grayson jerked to a stop in the middle of the hallway. "You touched someone you don't know and you're all right?"

Aron rubbed his thumb over his fingertips. He could still feel the impression of Rey's touch, and it wasn't uncomfortable at all. Usually, Grayson or Janet, his administrative assistant, ran interference for him at public events because he didn't like to touch or be touched, didn't do small talk, and didn't like crowds unless it was incognito like this.

"I'm fine. Maybe it's because I had a clear objective and I achieved it." That was it. He'd needed her contact info. That overrode everything else.

"Did you tell her who you are?"

"No." An uncomfortable mix of regret and guilt crashed inside him. He should have told her his real identity, but he knew their parting wouldn't have been as friendly as it was. He wouldn't have gotten her honest opinion about Artemis Games and *Legendsfall*. He certainly wouldn't have gotten her phone number.

"I plan to," he assured his assistant, and himself. "That's another reason why I needed her number. I'll call her and ask for a private meeting. I'll tell her who I am then and explain my actions."

And then hope he'd get her understanding and agreement before she saw him take the stage at the Artemis Games panel.

• • •

"Girl." Quinn bumped her shoulder as they made their way to the auditorium that housed the Artemis Games panel. "I didn't get the chance to ask you earlier. What's up with you and Mr. Hoodie Guy?"

Sam glanced at her with surprise. "What do you mean? Nothing was up."

"Oh really?" Max bumped her other shoulder. "It certainly seemed like you were picking up what he was laying down."

Sam jerked back with a frown. "What the hell does that mean? I have no idea what you guys are trying to say. Both of you were sitting at the same table. You know exactly what we were talking about!"

"That's right, you and Hoodie Guy were talking."

So Max was running with the nickname too. "I'm not the only one he talked to."

"At the beginning," Quinn clarified, "just to be polite. When he got to the important stuff, he only had eyes for you. We might as well have been at another table. On the far side of the food court."

"That's what I'm saying." Max nodded. "I mean, it seemed like he wanted to do more than talk about gaming, if you know what I mean."

"Come on," Sam protested. "Don't you think you're reading too much into it?"

"Are we?" Max asked, raising her eyebrows. "After all, he didn't ask for our phone numbers, just yours."

"And you gave it to him!" Quinn added, eyes wide with surprise. "Do you know you did that?"

Sam slowed her steps. She had given him her number, hadn't she? Dialed it herself on his phone and everything. Without hesitation too. "I guess I did."

Quinn and Max stared at her with twin expressions of disbelief. "Why did you do that?"

"I don't know." She hunched her shoulders. Giving Hoodie Guy her number was a split-second decision. Not even a decision, just a spur-of-the-moment act that seemed as natural as talking to him did. Their discussion had been a good one, his questions spurring ideas, and she wanted it to continue.

"He's not the one you're supposed to be exchanging numbers with," Max told her. "Remember, your objective is Artemis."

She huffed. "Right, like anyone at Artemis is going to want to call me."

"All you have to do is talk to them like you talked to Hoodie Guy," Quinn suggested. "By the end of the discussion I bet they'll be throwing their phones at you."

"Or cease-and-desist orders." Sam swung her hair over her shoulder. "I doubt they'll be as easy to talk to as Hoodie Guy."

"I don't know if anyone is as easy for you to talk to as Hoodie Guy," Max said. "And giving him your number? That's not like you at all."

No, it wasn't. She was usually more cautious than that. "It seemed like a good idea at the time. I felt like we had a vibe going, you know? My instincts told me to trust him."

Max snorted. "I think your instincts are rusty."

"It's not a big deal. Besides, I think he might have some

follow-up questions I need to answer. He's texted me twice asking me to meet him, but we've been running since lunch, so I haven't had the chance."

"He really wants to talk to you again." Max frowned. "I don't know how to feel about that."

"Well, if he's a problem or a stalker or anything, I can always block him. Besides, he doesn't know my real name."

She had reasons to be cautious. They all did. But the more she'd talked to Benjy, the less worried she'd become. By the time they had to leave, it felt as if she were talking to a friend, maybe even a kindred spirit.

Not that she'd ever admit that to Max and Quinn. She didn't need them teasing her for the rest of the con. "Come on, let's go find some seats."

Dismay stopped her in her tracks as they rounded the corner for the auditorium. A line had formed for entry into the Artemis Games panel, wrapping around the corner. "Dammit."

Quinn surveyed the line. "I expected a crowd, but I didn't expect this."

"Everyone's looking for a face-off, which they're not going to get if we can't even make it into the room, Sam." Max turned to her. "What do you want to do?"

What could she do? Not getting into the room was a setback, not a defeat. "We can talk to one of the staff or door monitors, but it's not important that I'm in the room," she told her friends. "It's not about facing them. It's about their plans to make change. We should be able to listen from out here, and I can do a recap video later and share it across my accounts."

"Excuse me, are you ReyofSun?"

Sam turned to face a young man who seemed completely out of place wearing jeans with his tailored shirt and sweater-vest in the sea of jeans and T-shirts. Maybe he was a volunteer. "Yes?"

He looked at her badge to confirm, then smiled. "You and your friends have reserved seats for the panel."

"We do?"

"We do?" Max and Quinn echoed.

Dapper Dude stared at Max a little too long before answering. "You do."

She narrowed her eyes at him, a sudden suspicion striking her. "Did the con reserve the seats, or Artemis?"

He hesitated a moment, then said, "It was a special request of the CEO. I'm Grayson, his personal assistant. Mr. Galanis would like to meet with you after the panel to personally answer any questions you might have."

The CEO, huh? Of course. Someone must have told him about the crowd lined up outside the doors and he'd decided to . . . what? Make sure she got in? Sam looked at her friends. Both looked back, wide-eyed, then nodded. They'd follow her lead.

Grayson turned slightly, gesturing toward the auditorium's main entrance. "If you'll come with me?"

"Lead the way." She raised her chin. Artemis had made a power flex. If they thought that gave them an advantage or would make her look at them more favorably, she'd show them exactly how mistaken they were. She had a voice, and she intended to use it.

Game on, Artemis.

Chapter 5

Aron took his seat in the front row with other members of the Artemis executive team, his insides wound tight. The marketing team was already in place on the stage, ready to discuss the company's forthcoming releases. First, though, they had to confront the elephant in the room. He had to confront the elephant in the room.

It was make or break time for him, his company, and his plans for the future. He had to win the audience over.

He had to win ReyofSun over.

Their lunchtime discussion had reminded him of his early days of brainstorming when he'd just started out, talking to his father at the dining room table, refining his business plan in his father's office, coding that first version of *Legendsfall* in his bedroom. He'd felt the same excitement, the same lightning strike of possibility. Before lunch had ended, he'd known that he wanted Rey's help to steer Artemis in this new, inclusive direction.

It bothered him that he hadn't been able to talk to her again before the panel. Revealing his identity after approaching her and establishing a rapport had been a critical step two in his action plan for winning her over during this convention.

Informing her that Benjy was really the CEO of Artemis Games wasn't something that should be revealed via text—at least, that wasn't his way.

He looked down at his phone, his mind assessing and discarding possible scenarios. None of them went well. In fact, he could only conceive of two that would give him the outcome he wanted.

His phone buzzed with an incoming text. From Rey. He smiled despite his increasing tension as he read her message. **ARE YOU HERE?**

YES, he texted back. **DID YOU GET IN?**

He already knew the answer and resisted the urge to turn around and look three rows back to his left. **THE ARTEMIS CEO RESERVED SEATS FOR US. CAN YOU BELIEVE THAT?**

HE WANTS TO HEAR WHAT YOU HAVE TO SAY. He paused. **I'LL EXPLAIN EVERYTHING. DON'T BE TOO UPSET.**

WHAT??? WHAT ARE YOU GOING TO DO???

What was he going to do? His version of the right thing.

The auditorium lights dimmed until only the stage was illuminated. Mark, the VP of communications, stepped to the podium. "The Artemis Games team has a lot to share with you today, including previews of our upcoming releases. We'll also have some giveaways at the end of the session. Before we get started, our founder and chief executive officer would like to say a few words. Please welcome the CEO of Artemis Games, Aron Galanis."

Aron made his way to the stage amid a scattering of applause and a low hum of murmurs from the crowd. He thanked

Mark and turned to face the audience. The light made it difficult to see beyond the first couple of rows, but he didn't need to when he could feel the anticipatory weight of every audience member. What he said next, and how he said it, was critical.

"First, I'd like to thank you all for attending our session today. I think you'll like what Artemis Games has in store for you.

"Second, I'm here to address the elephant in the room. By now, I'm sure most of you know that Artemis Games was called out on social media two weeks ago for our depiction of a Black female non-playable character in *Legendsfall*. That led to charges of misogyny in general and misogynoir, dislike of Black women, in particular. It's a serious charge, and we took it seriously. I took it seriously."

He looked out over the crowd, hoping they heard the gravity in his words. Hoping Rey heard it. "I personally reviewed the game. Let me be perfectly clear: that character should not have made it out of development. She shouldn't have made it out of storyboarding. But she did, and as head of Artemis, that's on me. Today, I apologize to everyone offended and harmed by that character's depiction, and I want to thank the gamer with the handle ReyofSun for rightfully pointing out this problematic character. As the only Black female character in *Legendsfall*, she deserved better. We need to do better."

Another smattering of applause and the clicks of a few hundred phone cameras filled the silence. "You may be wondering what we're going to do now that we've verified this issue. An internal investigation identified the parties responsible, and they are no longer affiliated with Artemis Games.

We are going to upgrade that non-playable character. She will receive a name and a better backstory, and will become an actual player in *Legendsfall*. My team and I will launch a comprehensive review of our entire catalog to identify any other problematic characterizations and will take a deep dive into our design process with an eye toward equity and inclusion. The company as a whole will also undergo awareness training."

He stepped away from the podium to approach the edge of the stage. "Artemis Games wants to be the go-to game developer for everyone, both in the people we hire and the people who buy our products. To do that, we need to create games that everyone can enjoy. You have my promise and my pledge that goal will be top of mind with every project we launch going forward. We'll have more news in the next few days and weeks, so be sure to follow our social media accounts for updates. And with that, I'll turn it over to my team. I hope you enjoy the rest of the convention. Thank you."

• • •

Sam's mouth dropped open as the CEO of Artemis Games walked onstage and greeted the moderator and other panel members, basically his employees. No matter how much she blinked, her vision remained the same. Hoodie Guy, aka Benjy, was actually Aron Galanis, the CEO of Artemis Games. The guy who'd sat in on her panel, who'd bought her and her friends lunch, who'd listened to her bitch about misogynoir in the gaming world and call out Artemis in particular, owned the company.

He'd done a whole Superman thing too: no more glasses, hair slicked back, a light blue button-down instead of the gray hoodie. Those golden-brown eyes were unmistakable, especially when he looked in her direction, as if he knew where she sat. Of course he did. He'd sent his minion to get her, hadn't he?

"Oh my god, Sam," Quinn whispered. "Hoodie Guy is actually the CEO?!"

"Apparently so." She forced her jaw to unclench. Manifesting a migraine while dealing with this shocker was not what she needed to weather this panel and the aftermath.

"I knew I didn't like that guy," Max hissed. "He was too smooth while talking to us, conning us from the get-go."

That was the problem. That wasn't the sense she'd gotten from him. He'd seemed genuine, as if he really wanted to know about the issues she'd taken on as her mission. She'd warmed up to him faster than she had anyone else at the con and could have talked to him a lot longer. How could she have been so wrong?

No, she wasn't wrong. He'd taken the stage in front of everyone and apologized, thanked her for revealing the issue, and revealed an action plan to do better. He'd promised to do everything she'd wanted, yet she couldn't swallow the embarrassment and rage. It would have been easy to walk out, but she had nothing to be embarrassed about and a whole chest full of things to be enraged about. If he dared to stay behind after the session, she'd give him the earful he deserved.

A soft tap on her shoulder had her turning around. The same man who'd escorted them to their seats earlier now knelt beside hers. "Mr. Galanis would like the opportunity to talk to you after the panel."

I bet he would. "In private, I'm guessing."

Grayson made a sympathetic face, then nodded. "He would

very much like to continue the discussion you had at lunch without any other distractions."

She pressed her lips together so hard they went numb. Every fiber of her being urged her to go off on Aron Galanis and his company, to reveal the trickery that he'd subjected her to. Every cell phone in the room would record her diatribe. But being angry would win her no support and would probably cast her in a negative light, damaging her platform. That was the last thing she needed.

The first thing she needed was answers. No, first an apology and then answers. If she had to meet him in private to get them, so be it.

She turned to her friends. "I'm going to talk to him in private after this session."

Quinn frowned. "By yourself?"

"I'll be fine." She snorted. "I doubt Mr. CEO will do anything more than what he did today, but I'll record the conversation anyway. I'll meet you guys in the hotel lobby before dinner."

Doubt shaded Max's features, but she eventually nodded. "All right. You need backup, you text us." She leaned closer. "Don't go easy on him, either."

"You know it."

Sam snatched up her bag and stalked to the door, exerting effort to keep her expression bland and her anger banked. She could feel curious gazes following her, disappointed gazes, speculative gazes. So many had come in hopes of seeing a confrontation. She would have dashed their hopes regardless of who the Artemis speaker was. She had come to the session to ask for change, to determine their commitment to doing the right thing as they'd declared in their social media statements. She'd wanted a public promise so that she could hold them accountable. Their CEO had given it. The rest of the discussion didn't need an audience.

Probably needed a referee though.

She followed Grayson to a conference room filled with Artemis Games merchandise and promo materials to stock the booth they had in the exhibit hall. A long conference table sat in the middle of the room, surrounded by faux-leather swivel chairs. A drink and snack stand sat against the back wall.

"Would you like something to drink?" Grayson asked as he led her to the table.

"I'll get it myself, thank you." Sam tried and failed to leach the heat out of her voice. She wasn't angry with the assistant, and it wasn't fair to direct her irritation at him. At the moment, though, he was a proxy for his boss, and her upset needed an outlet.

"How long?"

Grayson grimaced as he glanced at his watch. How many people still wore traditional timepieces? "It shouldn't be long," he assured her, then gestured to a chair again. "If you'd like to take a seat, I'll be happy to find out for you."

"I prefer to stand, and I'll find out for myself. Don't worry," she added as alarm flashed across his features. "I'm not going to sprint back to the auditorium to make a scene. That would negatively impact my standing, and I'm sure your boss knows that."

She dug out her phone, called up her contacts, then typed out a text. **YOU HAVE TEN MINUTES BEFORE I WALK AND PUT YOU ON BLAST.**

After closing the messaging app, she called up the clock app and set a timer for ten minutes. She would see what he thought was more important—glad-handing his fanboys or dealing with the person he'd deceived and betrayed.

Anger refreshed, she stalked across the floor and back again, arms folded across her chest. Her mind whirred on an endless loop, testing what she would say and how she would say it. No matter how she thought it through, her mind returned to the same thing: Aron Galanis had lied to her, had pretended to be someone he wasn't, had faked his persona to get close to her and discover how she would fix his company's issues all for the price of a barely warm cheeseburger and limp fries.

Aron Galanis strode into the room in all his CEO glory at nine minutes, thirty-three seconds. She stopped the timer, then folded her arms across her chest, attitude rising. "Cutting it close there, aren't you, Mr. Galanis?"

He stopped short, then spoke to his assistant. "Thank you, Grayson. You can go now."

"Are you sure you don't want him to stay?"

He frowned in confusion. "Do we need him to stay?"

"I don't know, are you planning to do something that we need a witness or a referee for?" She reached into her pocket. "Either way, I do think you should know that I carry pepper spray."

He stared at her as if trying to gauge her seriousness, which was firmly pegged in the danger end of the range. Finally, he nodded, then stepped to the far side of the conference table and gestured for her to sit on the opposite side. "Grayson, please stay. Will this arrangement suffice?"

Suffice? Just further proof that this man wasn't a gamer named Benjy. "It will do."

He pointedly looked at her phone, then back to her. "If you would like to record our conversation, I'm fine with that. I would, however, ask that you not upload it or any video to the Internet."

"What? Don't want your lies and deceit spread on the web for all to see?" She splayed her hands on the conference table, too angry to sit. He hadn't sat down either. "I guess not, since it would contradict that pretty little speech you gave."

"It wasn't just a speech. I meant every word I said out there. I meant the promise I made, and I intend to implement the action plan. As for the recording, since we'll be discussing company business that isn't public knowledge yet, I'd like it to be a personal record for you. Of course I can't stop you from posting it; I just ask that you please don't."

"Aron."

He didn't turn Grayson's way but kept his gaze on her. "I want ReyofSun to trust me and what I have to say. Proving that starts now."

"Using our conversation as the jumping-off point?" Blood pounded in her ears. "You're a real piece of work, Mr. Galanis. No wonder you had employees hiding NPCs like that in your games."

He winced, and she almost felt sorry for him. Almost. Then he collected himself. She had to admit, the restraint was admirable. He probably didn't have anyone who talked to him the way she just had.

He took a step back to gather himself, his expression flattening. "I want to apologize for not making a better effort to tell you my identity."

"Better effort? How about no effort?" She began a slow clap. "I have to hand it to you, that was a phenomenal acting job. You fooled me, making me believe you really were just Hoodie Guy, a fellow gamer interested in my opinions."

"I understand that you're angry—"

"Angry?" she echoed. "I'm beyond angry. Since you like big-dollar words, I'll tell you I'm furious, awash with animosity at how you deceived me."

"I would like the chance to explain my reasoning, to apologize again, and to discuss my talk during the Artemis session. Will you hear me out?"

Staying angry took more effort than she wanted to expend. This wasn't worth her anger. *He* wasn't worth her anger. She'd told herself that she wanted an apology and an explanation. It seemed he was ready to give her both. The least she could do was display the manners her parents had taught her.

"All right." She finally sank into her chair, then folded her arms across her chest. "You have the floor."

"Again, I want to apologize to you. I'm sorry that I—"

"What? Lied about who you are? Buttered me up with small talk so you could deceive me and my friends? God!" She slammed her hands on the armrests. "I even defended you to my friends, telling them they had the wrong impression of you, that you were sincere!"

His expression blanched as he shoved his hands into his pockets. "I am sincere. I'm a gamer before I'm a CEO. I like to attend cons and listen to panels as a regular gamer, just like everyone else."

"You're not like everyone else, and you know it."

"I realize that. That's why I was incognito." He pulled his hands from his pockets, took a step closer. "I especially wanted to hear your panel because I wanted to see and hear you for myself. I sat in the back because I wanted to be just a guy listening to you and the others speak, and not be the CEO of

Artemis Games disrupting your panel with my presence. I have more respect for you than that."

She grudgingly admitted to herself that he had a point. If he'd come to their panel as himself, their panel would have devolved into chaos and their message would have been lost. "Point for you. But what about after the panel?"

He frowned in momentary confusion. "At lunch? That was an excellent conversation, don't you think? I haven't had a good gaming discussion like that in a long while. You have no idea how much I appreciated it."

The earnestness of his words smothered some of the anger burning through her. "If you enjoyed the conversation that much, why didn't you tell me who you were? I felt like a complete idiot when you got up onstage."

"I did try to tell you, but you had to leave for a meetup, and I didn't think that information was something that should be sent in a text, which is why I asked you to stay behind after the panel. So that I could explain."

"Explain what? How you used me?"

"I wasn't using you," he insisted. "I listened to you. You had a message to deliver. I wanted to hear it."

"By pretending to be some random dude in a hoodie?"

"Would you have been so open if I'd told you I was the CEO of Artemis Games?" he wondered. "Would you have been so frank about everything?"

Probably not, but she wasn't going to give him the satisfaction of acknowledging that. "Well, you're lucky. You got my opinion on how to fix your game for the price of a Happy Meal. I should send you an invoice for my labor, with a bonus for my emotional expense."

"You're right. You should be paid for your labor."

She drew back. "You're agreeing with me?"

"I'm doing more than agreeing with you," he told her. "I want you to work with me."

Her mouth dropped open. "What?"

Surprise and discomfort ran across his features. "What?"

"Did you just offer me a job?"

"Yes, I want you to work with me. The work you're doing—you could make a career of it. Since you're recording our conversation, I'll state that this is a serious offer that I won't rescind unless you refuse it."

She noted he said *with* instead of the expected *for* and took a moment to appreciate that distinction and that he was savvy enough to make it. Still, she eyed him, skeptical. "Work with you to what?"

"To do what you're already doing," he answered, his expression as sincere and earnest as his tone. "Keep calling us out, holding our feet to the fire on our response to do and be better. Help me fix the culture issues inside Artemis so we can make sure hashtag LegendsFoul never happens again."

"You're kidding, right?" She looked at his assistant, who seemed completely shell-shocked, before returning to him. "You don't know anything about me, yet you want my help with your action plan?"

"Yes. Also, I know something about you."

The matter-of-fact way he said that had her pausing. "A few videos and social media posts are not the full picture of who I am."

"I know that." His gaze held her in place. "I also know that you really do get paid for your labor, so hiring you is a sound business decision. You are Samara Reynolds, aged twenty-eight. You work at Rise Consulting. Your mother is the company's president and CEO. The firm specializes in helping companies create a more inclusive workplace. You do an excellent job of keeping your professional and personal lives separate."

"How did you—"

"You probably didn't realize that you put your number in my phone under your real name. I didn't realize it until I tried to text you before the panel. Then I searched under your real name, and the first result was your professional profile."

He smiled. "I have to say, your disguise is much better than mine."

Of course she didn't look the same. Gamer ReyofSun and consultant Samara Reynolds were separate identities. For safety's sake, she had never let one persona mix with the other. Until now. Until Aron Galanis. She had to hope the mistake wouldn't bite her in the ass later. "So now that you know who I am professionally, what are you going to do? Blackmail me?"

"What? No." He looked genuinely surprised and upset with the question. "You had your reasons for not revealing your identity and I had mine. I just wanted to point out that commonality."

"Do you want a gold star or something?"

"No, I want your help. Your professional expertise."

"This is unbelievable." She pressed her fingertips to her temples, forcing herself to stop allowing her emotions to hold sway when she needed to think clearly. "Of all the things I considered when I followed your assistant here, being offered a job wasn't even on the list. You really think you can pay me enough to help you?"

"I remember that you said that you don't work for free. I can afford more than an overpriced burger. The compensation package at Artemis Games is very competitive, but you'd be a special hire."

That stopped her. "Special how?"

"A consultant instead of an employee. I want to leverage your gaming knowledge and your professional skills. I want to bring you on to conduct an equity and inclusion review of our entire game catalog, but I also want to announce an updated expansion pack for *Legendsfall* before NexCon."

NexCon was a huge convention on par with E3, the massive trade show for video games. "You know NexCon is like three months away, right?"

"Five, actually." He nodded, an animated smile blossoming on his face. "I want to offer you a three-month contract with an option to extend. My team will handle NexCon. You and I have something bigger to do. That means we'll have to work really hard to get everything I want to do done in time. I will of course compensate you for your hard work."

"Is this for real?"

Her skepticism must have shone in her expression, because he moved until he could lean against the table beside her. "It's a real offer, and I can tell you more about my project after we agree on terms and you sign an NDA."

He raised his hand to halt her reply. "Not to put you on the spot, but you did say that you'd take the opportunity to fix things if Artemis asked. As the head of Artemis, I'm here asking. Help me make *Legendsfall* and our other games better for everyone."

He gave her a smile, half enthusiasm, a quarter conniving, and a quarter manic. "Now the hard part begins. Are you game?"

It was "put up or shut up" time. He'd offered her an unbelievable opportunity that included everything she could hope for. There was no way she could refuse to help, regardless of how their association began.

She returned his smile with one of her own. "That depends. How much are you offering for my labor?"

He told her. She blinked. "Say what now?"

Chapter 6

"Sam. Samara. Samara Nikole Reynolds, snap out of it right now!"

Sam blinked, half-surprised to find herself back in their hotel room. "Sorry."

Max clamped her hands to her hips. "You've been in a daze since we met up with you, and all you can say is sorry?"

"I guess I'm still in shock. I can't believe what just happened."

"Why are you acting like this?" Quinn asked with uncharacteristic heat. "When you left, you were ready for a fight. When we met you back here, you were staring off into space, shell-shocked."

"That's because I am." How could she not be, after that conversation?

"So what the hell happened between you and that guy to make you space out like this? Did you at least get an apology?"

"Yeah. Yes, I did." She'd gotten more than that. Much more. She began to laugh at the unbelievableness of it all.

Max gave her a shake. "For god's sake, will you snap out of it and tell us what happened, or do I need to call your father?"

The threat worked. "Okay." She licked her lips. "I'm sorry I'm acting like this. I'm getting it together. I'm just . . . still stunned. Do we have any more water in the mini fridge?"

She started to rise, but Max pushed her back down. "I'll get it. You just sit there and try to get your thoughts together."

Rubbing her forehead, Sam did as requested, trying to regroup and compose herself.

Her after-panel meeting with Aron Galanis hadn't gone as expected. While it had begun as she'd imagined it, it had turned sideways, then quickly gone off the rails after that. Was that how the man normally conducted business? Talk circles around his adversary, mention an eye-popping amount of money, then get them to agree to his scheme?

"Here," Max said, pressing a bottle of water into her hand.

"Thanks." Sam accepted the chilled bottle, then rolled it across her forehead. The cold contact brought clarity, and she took a swallow as she faced her friends' worried expressions.

"Okay. First of all, I swear all we did was talk. He just—he just blew my mind, and I'm still trying to deal with that. At least I recorded our conversation so I know I'm not dreaming."

"Deal with what?" Max threw her arms wide. "Blew your mind how? Girl, I swear, if you don't come clean right now, I'm going to call your dad out of spite."

"Are you out of your mind?" Sam questioned. "You know damn well if there's even a whiff of a problem at a con, he'll never let me go to another one without him as a bodyguard. It doesn't matter that I'm grown and out of his house."

"Then tell us everything that happened," Quinn urged. "You're worrying us."

"I'm sorry."

"Don't be sorry, be straightforward."

"Okay. Yes, he apologized for not telling us who he was. He said he didn't want to disrupt my panel."

"How generous of him," Max snorted, folding her arms.

"Can you blame him for being incognito?" Quinn, ever the levelheaded one, said. There was a reason why she was the tactician of their team matches. "Can you imagine how he would have been mobbed if he'd gone around as himself to your panel or on the convention floor?"

Sam knew that, and even sympathized. Didn't mean she was okay with it, though. "Dammit, why are you so logical? I'm still irked about that."

"And you have every right to be." Quinn sat down beside her. "No one can blame you for being pissed. But I don't think we can blame him for doing things the way he did either."

"He said he tried to tell me who he was at the end of lunch, but we rushed away."

"I guess that was my fault," Max said, her tone sheepish. "I thought he was putting the moves on you."

"Just the brain moves," Quinn said. "Gotta admit, I would have done it the same way, especially if I couldn't get in touch with you."

"Did he try though?" Max asked.

"Like I told him, I didn't hear anything from anyone related to Artemis." Sam blew out a breath. "Then again, there's a reason why my DMs aren't open."

"I know, believe me, I know," Max said, rummaging in their mini fridge for a soda. "I told you we should have ignored him and went on our way."

Sam rubbed at her forehead. Sometimes being between

Quinn and Max was like having an angel on one shoulder and a militant devil on the other. Then they'd switch places and Max was the straight and narrow angel while Quinn played the reasonable devil.

Which she did now. "So the CEO of Artemis Games talked to you as one gamer to another, gave you his phone number, got his assistant to give us primo seats at their panel, and then pulled you out of the panel to give you a private apology?"

"Better have apologized," Max said, popping the top on a can before passing it over to Quinn, then taking another for herself.

"No," Sam admitted. "I mean yes. He apologized for the subterfuge, and he apologized for not telling me before the panel. Then he said I should really be paid for my labor."

"He certainly has the pockets to do more than buy you lunch," Max said. "What did he offer?"

A laugh bubbled up again. "He offered me a job."

"What?" Quinn and Max said in unison.

Sam took another drink, wishing they had some rum to go with their cola. "He knows who I am. He knows about Rise Consulting. He asked me to do some consulting for him. For Artemis Games."

"Doing what?"

"Like he said during the panel, he wants to make *Legendsfall* and Artemis more inclusive. He wants me to help him to review all of their games, not just *Legendsfall*. Basically, do what I'm doing now, advocating for underrepresented communities, Black women in particular. But there's something else, something I'd have to sign a nondisclosure agreement for, if I accept his offer."

"Hell yeah, you better get paid to do it," Max retorted. "I'm sure the CEO of Artemis Games who personally and privately apologized to you for concealing his identity after attending your panel and picking your brain about his company that you called out is going to compensate you for your professional time. So just how willing is he to put his money where his mouth is?"

"Very willing."

"How much?"

When Sam named the number, Quinn and Max looked at each other, then back at her. "When do you start?"

"What?" Sam looked from one to the other. "Are y'all saying you want me to accept his offer, after everything he did?"

Quinn nodded. "With that potential payday, you're damn right you should accept his offer."

"You too, Max? I thought you'd be the first to say not just no, but hell no."

"Are you kidding?" Max pointed her soda at Sam. "In all this time, you've advocated for seats at the table for under-represented groups. Advocated for our voices being heard. Now you've got someone who not only is listening, he wants you on board and he's willing to pay for the privilege. Isn't this the goal you've always wanted?"

"Yes, but—" She broke off to glare at them. "This is y'all's fault, talking about how funny it would be if he gave me a job. I'm blaming this on both of y'all."

"Okay, then, so we manifested you a job," Quinn said, rubbing her hands together. "Now let's manifest you a date."

"No." Sam shook her head as vigorously as any GIF. "Not only no, but hell no. Don't start that up again."

"You're the one who said you had a vibe with him," Quinn pointed out.

"And handed over them digits," Max added.

Her thoughts returned to their lunch conversation. The way his eyes had lit up like sparklers behind his glasses, the passion in his voice and gestures, his love for games and gaming obvious and infectious. She couldn't deny that she'd gotten caught up in their interaction, how their thoughts and likes were so in sync that she wanted to talk to him more. Wanted to know more about him. Maybe that was why she'd subconsciously given him her real name.

She wanted to pinch herself, or better yet, ask them to pinch her, but they would follow through and leave her bruised. "Maybe he's pulling a prank. Maybe he just wants to be able to announce something to the public so they'll forget all about it. Maybe—"

Her phone chimed with a text. She looked at her friends, who looked back at her before breaking out into matching Cheshire-cat grins. "I bet that's him," Quinn whispered.

Max nudged her shoulder. "I bet he wants to seal the deal over dinner."

"Stop, just stop." Where was a freeze ray when a girl needed one? Instead, she reached for her phone.

"Is it him? Is it him?"

Of course it was. ROUGH DRAFT OF CONTRACT ATTACHED FOR REVIEW. THIS IS MY PERSONAL NUMBER. I'LL ANSWER ANY QUESTIONS YOU MAY HAVE. I LOOK FORWARD TO HEARING FROM YOU.

She frowned at the screen, trying to decide between being irritated or impressed. "He's sent me a contract already? This guy sure is determined."

"Knows what he wants and will do anything to get you—I mean it," Max said with an unrepentant grin.

"Since when did you become Team Artemis?"

"Since he threw you a contract with a payout that's way more than your annual salary," Max shot back.

"You guys are no help. No help at all." Sam looked at her phone. She needed a new name for him instead of Benjy Hoodie Guy. Artemis Asshole? Jerky McJerkface? The Man? Finally, she saved him under Aron Galanis, Artemis Games.

"What?" Quinn said, her tone all wide-eyed innocence. "Are we supposed to talk you out of an enormous payday doing what you love with a guy who obviously wants you? For your brain, I mean."

Sam released a sigh as she crossed to the desk. Her pique was now nothing more than hot air. He'd had this Pied Piper / Peter Pan vibe going when he'd asked her to join him. Irresistibly attractive in his hoodie or the tailored shirt, he'd all but won her over before he'd named a price.

"Instead of shipping me and the Artemis Games CEO, maybe you should think about what we should have for dinner. I need to call my parents."

She called her mom and switched to speaker. With a job offer and contract in hand, she'd need her mother's approval. Dr. Vanessa Reynolds was literally the boss, after all.

"Hey, baby girl, how's the convention going?"

"It's going. It's been a bit unbelievable here."

"Good unbelievable or bad unbelievable?"

"Probably depends on who you ask," Sam replied, looking at her friends eagerly eavesdropping on every word. "Maybe both?"

"Samara," her mother said, her tone laced with worry. "Are

you having problems there? What about Max and Quinn? Did something happen during your panel?"

"Actually, we had a higher attendance than I expected," Sam answered, fidgeting with the notepad on the desk. "I think a lot of people were expecting another tirade against Artemis Games, so they might have been disappointed that we talked about underrepresentation across a wide swath of games and platforms."

"Too bad. They need to know that it's not just one company, it's a systemic issue." Her mother paused. "No one's giving you a hard time, are they? You, Quinn, and Max are sticking together and watching out for one another, right?"

"Of course." Her mother worried about them traveling to cons in general, but that concern had shot into the stratosphere after Marquessa had died. "Don't worry, Mama. We're being safe."

"I know you are, but you know I can't help worrying."

"Yeah, I know." Just as Sam also knew how hard it was for her mother and father to sit back and watch her continue the work that made her a lightning rod for online trolls and haters. Speaking of work . . . "Mama, I need to get y'all's opinion on something. Your professional opinion and Daddy's gut check. Is Daddy there?"

"He is. Hold on, let me put this on speaker."

Muffled sounds, then, "Hey, sunshine, what's going on?"

"Hey, Daddy. I just need some advice." She gave them a general rundown of the convention so far. "There's this guy I talked to after my panel. I thought he was just a fellow gamer. Turns out that he's Aron Galanis, the founder and CEO of Artemis Games, the people who make *Legendsfall*."

"Wait," her mother interrupted. "You were telling the CEO

of the problematic game why his game was so problematic? To his face? And you didn't know?"

"No, I didn't. He called himself Benjy when we first met." Indignation returned. "I can't believe I got played like that. I mean, the pictures I'd seen of the CEO made him look more like a dudebro, not the nerdy guy I spent an entire lunch talking with."

"Did you ask him why he did that?" her mother wondered.

"Of course I did. He told me he didn't want to take the focus away from our panel by being there as the Artemis Games CEO, and he claimed he really wanted to get honest opinions from gamers on the convention floor."

"Well, that makes sense, doesn't it?" her father asked. "I mean, it's kinda sneaky, but understandable. It's the same reason why you don't tell people your real name. Did he apologize?" her father demanded. "I know he better apologize to my baby girl."

"He did. Profusely and sincerely." In hindsight, she could acknowledge that he could have just apologized once and been done with it. But the sincerity had surprised her, as if he wanted to make sure she had no doubts that he meant his apology. And everything before, and everything after.

Her mother interrupted her thoughts. "So what's the problem, baby? What do you need our advice about?"

Sam forwarded the attachment. "I'm sending you something I need you to take a look at, Mom. Dad, I want you to weigh in on this too."

"I have it." Her mother paused. "Why is this attachment named Rise contract?"

"Because after he apologized, he offered me a job."

"Samara." Reproach filled her father's tone. "You told him who you are?"

Guilt and embarrassment hunched her shoulders. "We had such a good talk that when I gave him my phone number, I used my real name. Google did the rest. Once he knew my professional background, he was more determined to work with me."

Her dad cleared his throat. "Work with him how?"

"He wants me to help him to make *Legendsfall* more inclusive. Apparently, there's another big project he's working on, important enough that he wants me to sign an NDA about it."

"If he's offering you a job, that means he wants to pay you for what you've been doing anyway," her mother pointed out. "But you already have a job."

"That project's winding down. I was going to set up a meeting with you to talk about the next one. I haven't decided anything yet because I need to run it by you, but he's already sent over an initial contract and consultation fee. That's what I just sent you."

"How much is he offering to pay you?"

Quinn and Max shouted the amount in unison. She waved them to silence, then said, "And there seems to be some bonuses tied into the NDA project."

"When do you start?"

"Dad!"

He laughed. "That's the advice you're asking for, isn't it? You want to know if we think you should take him up on this offer or not?"

She bit her lip, undecided. "Yes, I think?"

"Baby, haven't you always said you wanted an opportunity

to make real change with the people who can facilitate that change?" her mother asked. "You've got the ear of the CEO. That is a huge opportunity. He's obviously serious about working with you to change his company's culture."

"Yes, but—"

"But what? I'll review this contract and then we can talk about it when you get back. Bring Max and Quinn with you to Sunday dinner."

She ignored her friends high-fiving each other. "Yes, but—"

"If this is something you want to do and the contract looks good, then I have no problem with it," her mother added. "My primary concern would be this: Does Aron Galanis want ReyofSun to help him or Samara Reynolds of Rise Consulting? Both are newsworthy in their respective circles, but only one would be detrimental to you."

Trust her mother to go straight to the heart of the matter. "That's something I'm worried about, too."

"If you're leaning toward accepting the offer, I will stipulate that the contract is with Rise Consulting, and not Samara Reynolds who's known in the gaming community as Reyof-Sun. Any public communications and press releases would have to mention the company, not the individual. If Mr. Galanis is serious about addressing his company's issues, he should be concerned about making the PR about contracting with an award-winning firm to fix it, and not a person who works for the company. If he can't agree with that condition, we can't work with him."

Her shoulders relaxed, and Sam realized that had been an unconscious worry in considering the offer.

"I agree with your mother," her father added. "You're

grown, but you're still our baby girl—and your mother's employee. We'll make sure you're protected."

"I know, Dad. Thanks." She knew she could trust her parents to have her back, but the question was, if she agreed to take the contract, could she trust Aron Galanis?

Chapter 7

Aron quickly discovered that patience wasn't his strong suit.

It was the Wednesday after GamerCon, five whole days since he'd made Samara Reynolds a job offer. No, he hadn't expected acceptance of his offer during the convention, but he thought he'd have a response to his offer by Monday. An offer he thought she wouldn't refuse. An offer he thought she *couldn't* refuse.

What was taking so long for her to decide?

It wasn't that he was impulsive by nature. In fact, he was completely on the other end of the scale. Every major decision in his life had been made after careful consideration and a couple of decision trees. Yet once he decided, he was locked in and it was full throttle until the end.

His mission had been to get ReyofSun to agree to a partnership. Discovering that she worked for one of the most prestigious consulting firms on the East Coast only cemented his decision, and his opening contract bid was to show her just how serious he was about their collaboration.

Hiring her as a consultant would be positive publicity for Artemis Games, proving that he intended to deliver on the promises he'd made at GamerCon. It would benefit Ms. Reynolds and her platform too. It was a win-win.

So why hadn't she called him yet? He'd made her a competitive offer, but there was still room for negotiation, if she wanted that. All she had to do was call. This waiting game was making him lose his mind.

"Have you lost your mind?"

Aron looked up as Mark stormed in, with his admin Janet following. Of course his communications vice president would be the first team member to come to his office. The GamerCon recap email he'd sent to his executive team the night before had contained a review of the apology panel and his intention to bring Ms. Reynolds on as a consultant. He was sure it was the latter that had brought Mark stomping into his office.

"It's all right, Janet, thank you," he said to his administrative assistant, who knew he didn't like surprise visitors, even those that worked for him. Especially ones that bulldozed their way in.

He waited until Janet left, thoughtfully closing the door behind her, before turning his focus back to Mark. "Good morning. Thanks for waiting for me to sit down and take a sip of my coffee before barreling in." He gestured to the chair opposite his desk. "You want to sit down and talk, or do you want to keep pacing back and forth like a human version of *Pong*?"

"How could you do this without consulting me?" Mark demanded, finally throwing himself into the chair. "I thought you were going to let me handle this!"

"If you're talking about PR, you are handling that," Aron pointed out.

"Handling it?" Mark echoed. "You just hired her on your own without telling anyone. How am I supposed to spin that?"

Aron released a slow breath. He didn't want to argue with Mark, especially about this. "If it will settle your stomach, an offer has been extended; it hasn't been accepted yet," he said, trying not to grind his teeth. "Besides, I'm reasonably sure that personnel decisions outside of your department aren't among your list of job duties. But what do I know? I'm just the president and CEO around here."

He watched in a blend of amusement and irritation as Mark wrestled himself back into some semblance of professional decorum. Aron didn't like to pull rank, because everyone at Artemis Games worked to make the company the best, most profitable one it could be. Still, there were times like now when people needed the reminder that his name was at the top of the org chart.

"I offered a contract to Ms. Reynolds to consult with us regarding underrepresentation in our company's catalog, specifically in *Legendsfall*, among other things."

"Why?"

"Why?" Aron pushed back from his desk. "You know why. Who better to help correct our shortcomings than the person who criticized us in the first place? The preliminary discussion I had with her regarding possible improvements was enlightening."

He gestured between them, his irritation rising. "The press release practically writes itself. That being the case, I expect to see a draft before noon so that we can issue it as soon as Ms. Reynolds accepts the offer."

Mark didn't relent. "Does she have the experience to do this?"

Aron leaned forward. He'd known Mark would be the most vocal in his disagreement and had already prepared his talking points. "Does this mean that you didn't uncover the fact that she works for Rise Consulting, one of the leading DEIA consulting firms in the city, if not the country? Did you overlook the fact that she holds a bachelor's degree in management communication from Howard University and a Diversity, Equity, Inclusion, and Accessibility certification from Georgetown University and instead only focus on the negative reports of her gaming handle that you found online? The consulting gig I'm offering her is literally what she does professionally."

Red suffused Mark's face before the man spoke in a surprisingly measured tone. "I know the company is important to you, but isn't hiring her an overreaction to overcorrect a social media event that's already behind us?"

"Yes, my company is important to me. It's the most important thing to me after my family. As for Ms. Reynolds, I interviewed her myself at the convention. Based on her statements there and what I've seen and heard of her online critiques, she has a good eye for these things. Not just through her personal perspective, but also a professional one. Even if she does what ReyofSun normally does—plays games, reviews content, then notes the lack of equity—that's more than what we have in-house now."

Mark huffed. "You're really set on this course of action?"

Aron smiled. "I'm just waiting on her phone call."

His communications VP sat back in his chair with an air of disbelief. "You're really going to hire her."

Aron had reached his tipping point. "Do you think I would bring someone into my company if I didn't think they could do the job? Think carefully before you answer."

He watched the struggle on Mark's face, but the other man wisely remained silent. It had taken Aron a while to determine how to interact with Mark. It had taken time with everyone he'd brought into Artemis. He'd deliberated over each and every hire, focusing not only on the skills they'd bring to the company, but also on how they would fit with the people already here. He enjoyed energetic debates over the games but not confrontations. His own coping mechanism when irritation arose was to resort to stilted, formal speech to put up a defensive wall. It was a tell, and he certainly hated it being common knowledge, but if his tell got people to focus on the work and not the emotion, he was fine with it.

He decided to explain things to Mark one more time, then he'd be done with it. "If it makes you feel better, Ms. Reynolds will work with me in the capacity of a personal consultative assistant in one specific area. She will sign a special projects nondisclosure agreement before getting to work addressing some opportunities in the company. For one thing, it's painfully obvious that we don't have anyone on payroll either willing or capable to point out potentially problematic content. We need to change the atmosphere so that people feel encouraged to say something if they see something."

Mark huffed out a breath. "The company is fine."

"That way of thinking is when stagnation starts," Aron shot back, more than ready for the conversation to end. "Artemis Games is a future-forward company, always looking to do and be and offer better. That means we can't maintain the status quo just because it's what we've always done and it's comfortable. Being comfortable costs us the growth and innovation we need to survive."

He stood. "I made a promise at that convention. I promised that my company's process, products, and people will reflect society's diversity. I will get that accessibility certification. I will make our company and our games equitable. Anything less is not an option. If anyone is unable to buy into that, I'm happy to release them to seek employment elsewhere while maintaining the noncompete clause. Do you understand?"

"What if she doesn't accept the offer?"

"She will," Aron answered with every ounce of confidence he possessed. The offer was more than agreeable. Samara was just doing her due diligence. He could understand that.

Another long-suffering sigh from Mark. "Well, then. I see you're dead set on this course, so talking about it more is useless."

"I'm glad you understand." Aron picked up his tablet. "What other questions do you have?"

He used that question in every meeting to signal that discussion time had ended. Mark got the message and stood. "I'll have that release draft in your inbox before noon."

"Thank you." He watched his communications VP leave before retaking his seat, spinning his chair in a slow circle to help him process and soothe his irritation.

It bothered him that Mark had reacted so strongly to him bringing on Ms. Reynolds as a consultant. It made him wonder if other employees, especially his executive team, felt the way Mark did. None of them had spoken up when they'd discussed his plan of approaching her at the convention. It wouldn't do to have discord in the ranks, but change was needed and necessary. Maybe his communications VP had a problem with Samara, someone he hadn't even met yet. Samara. That was how he now thought of her in his head, although he'd call her Ms. Reynolds as she'd requested until she said otherwise. Thanks to the lively discussion that they'd had at the convention, talking to each other as equals, just Reyof-Sun and Benjy talking about their love of gaming, he'd felt as if they'd started a friendship. He wanted more discussions like that and hoped that those talks would continue even though they'd be in their roles of CEO and consultant.

Mark was being ridiculous. He and his executive team had weighed the pros and cons of him speaking with her during the convention, and it had ultimately been his decision on whether to approach her or not. They'd even discussed implementing some of her suggestions. Why would paying her for her ideas be a bad thing?

Mark hated to be wrong. So did he. His instinct told him that having Samara on board would benefit his company, and his instincts had yet to steer him awry.

His personal phone buzzed on his desk. He looked down and smiled. Mark was going to be so disappointed. He picked it up and answered it, sure his smile could be heard on the other end. "Aron Galanis."

Chapter 8

"Aron Galanis."

It really was him answering the phone, and not his assistant. That floored her. Still, she could play it cool. "Good morning, Mr. Galanis. This is Samara Reynolds."

"Ms. Reynolds." Warmth and excitement flowed through his voice, as if he was really happy to hear from her. He confirmed it when he said, "It's a pleasure to hear from you today."

Sam fought the urge to fidget. This tone definitely wasn't Hoodie Guy. It certainly wasn't warm and eager Benjy. No, this deep, self-assured, formal voice belonged to Aron Galanis, founder and chief executive officer of Artemis Games.

She had the Artemis Games CEO's personal phone number. She let that realization wash over her like a bucket of icy water, leaving her wide-eyed and shocked. "I honestly expected to get voice mail or your assistant."

"This is my personal phone, which means you have direct access to me," he explained. "Given the nature of the project, there's no need to have a screener between us."

That would have made sense except for the fact that they had exchanged phone numbers before he'd given her a job offer. She wouldn't remind him of that, though. That wouldn't be businesslike of her, and this call was all about business.

"Ms. Reynolds?" He called her name as if he'd said it more than once. "Have you given thought to my offer?"

"You weren't joking when you said you like to get to the point."

"When it comes to my company, no, I don't joke."

Good. That made it much easier to remain professional. "Then I'll get to my point. Rise Consulting has reviewed the initial contract that you sent over. We've given your offer some thought and made some changes."

"All right." He didn't sound upset that changes were made. Made sense. Negotiations were a normal part of business contracts.

"I just sent the contract back to you. After you and your people have had a chance to review it, I have some questions I'd like to discuss with you before I make a decision."

"Of course. I'm happy to answer any questions you might have. Would it be better to meet in person to discuss things? Or we could do a video call if you prefer."

"I think in person would be best."

Curiosity burned through her. She'd seen Hoodie Guy and the Khaki CEO. How was he when in his power center? Would he have an aura of command the way he'd exuded charisma at the Artemis panel and when he'd asked her to work with him? It was easy to imagine the man attached to this voice to be a business suit–wearing commander of the business he'd created and built with his own hands.

Then again, he had yet to do anything she'd expected. That button-down with the Artemis logo embroidered on it was probably as formal as the company got, which suggested that his office wasn't one of those massive command centers she'd seen in other companies. Seeing him in person would satisfy her curiosity and give her real-time observations of his demeanor as they negotiated.

"When would be a good time for you?" she finally asked. "Or should I talk to your assistant Grayson to schedule an appointment?"

"You're a special hire, Ms. Reynolds. Or soon-to-be hire," he said, his voice a peculiar mix of warmth and humor. "I'm handling this process personally, including scheduling our meeting. When would be best for you?"

"Shouldn't I be asking what your schedule is? I'm sure the schedule of the head of a company is fuller than mine."

"Your time is important to me, Ms. Reynolds, which is why I named an amount that I think your time is worth. I doubt the suggested changes you've made to the contract are insurmountable. Besides, I don't want you to have any reason to not accept the offer."

Oh, the man could be smooth when he wanted to be. There weren't many reasons to not accept the offer, but she did have concerns she wanted to address. "I'm free anytime this week after four thirty. When is a good time for you?"

He paused, probably checking his calendar. She fully expected him to be too busy today, so soon after returning home from the convention. So it surprised her when he said, "My schedule will be clear later today, so I'll be able to give you my full attention, uninterrupted."

Lord. She must have caught a cold or some other variety of con crud without realizing it. It was the only explanation for why she read flirtatious innuendos into everything he said. The man had just told her he didn't joke about his business.

She needed to remember that, and forget about the relationship jokes Max and Quinn had showered her with. "Thank you. Are your headquarters still north of Atlanta?"

"Yes. While most of my employees work remotely, Artemis Games has a small office space in the Concourse property near Perimeter Center."

She whistled silently. That square footage had to be pricey. "The King building, or the Queen?"

"The Queen," he answered. "There are plenty of restaurants nearby. After we finalize discussion on the contract, we can have dinner to celebrate."

She hesitated. That formal tone was so at odds with the picture of him that resided in her head. The assumptive confidence that she'd sign the contract later that day, the power flex of an office in that property. This version of Aron Galanis was the most intimidating yet. Luckily, she had experience dealing with those types. She was not the one to be intimidated.

"The presumptive close," she murmured. "That's very smooth of you."

His soft laugh sounded way too intimate to her ears. Yup, definitely con crud. "I presume nothing when it comes to you, Ms. Reynolds. In fact, I think I just showed my hand to you. I'm at your mercy."

Business, business, this is about business. "Dinner will depend on the outcome of our discussions," she warned him. "You might not have a reason to celebrate when we're done talking."

"The odds are even," he reminded her. "There's a fifty percent chance that you'll say yes. I intend to up those odds in my favor during our meeting this afternoon."

That confidence was amusing, awe-inspiring, and pushing her contrarian button. She almost rejected the gig right then, but that would be cutting off her nose to spite her face, and her parents didn't raise no fools. "I look forward to it."

"Same here, Ms. Reynolds. See you this afternoon."

Another tactic: end the conversation while you were ahead. "See you then, Mr. Galanis. Goodbye."

The rest of Samara's day passed in a blur. Her current contract was in its last days, and while Rise Consulting had several new contract opportunities, her mother had agreed that the Artemis contract was not only lucrative, but also would give Samara an opportunity to create the change she'd long dreamed of. The chance to work with one of the hottest gaming companies out there, directly with the CEO to correct issues of equity and inclusion, combined two of her passions in a way that she couldn't ignore.

She shook her head in wonderment as she got in her car to head to Silver Springs, just outside the Perimeter north of Atlanta. When she'd started the LegendsFoul hashtag against the game developer a few weeks back, she had no idea that this was where she would land. Honestly, if anyone had told her that Artemis would offer her a job, she'd have laughed at them and told them to stop using drugs. Now she was the one who had to pinch herself to make sure she wasn't dreaming.

There really wasn't a reason to not accept the contract. Her current contract work was winding down. Her nearest and dearest thought it was the perfect opportunity for her, so how could she refuse it? She'd asked herself that question many times since the convention, and she still didn't have an answer. So why was she hesitating?

Because she'd liked Benjy the Hoodie Guy, dammit. They'd

had a good conversation, and when the talk veered away from Artemis Games, they'd had a good vibe going. She had believed that she'd come away with a new friend, a new ally. Even though he'd seemed very open and honest during their phone call, she knew already that he would fudge the truth if it got him the result he wanted.

"Girl, get it together and get over yourself," she muttered. Manifesting lingering ill will toward the potential boss was not the way to go into a new job. She understood his reasoning for going undercover. In his place, she probably would have done the same. When someone was straight with you when explaining why they did what they did and apologized profusely, you were supposed to forgive and forget and figure out how to move forward, right?

Which was why she'd asked for the face-to-face meeting. She wanted to look him in the eyes while they discussed the contract. She needed to know if there was actual work involved or if she was just a publicity hire. The answer to that question, and whether he honestly answered or not, would determine whether she would work with him or not.

With traffic miraculously on her side, she arrived at Concourse Corporate Center fifteen minutes ahead of schedule. She parked, then navigated her way through the parking deck to the two office towers known officially as Concourse Corporate Center V and VI, but everyone called them the King and Queen buildings due to their white "crowns" that lit the skyline after dark. They made great landmarks to give direction by for people traveling on 285 or Georgia 400, sort of like the Big Chicken KFC in Marietta.

Sam entered the bustling Queen lobby, then consulted the

directory for Artemis Games. Nerves began to flutter in her belly as she crossed to the elevators, surreptitiously studying herself in the shiny facade of one of the lifts. Makeup perfect with a nude lipstick, braids gathered into a sophisticated updo, black dress trousers with a subtle pinstripe, with three-inch black red-bottom pumps. A string of pearls her parents had given her after college graduation draped the scoop neckline of her lilac blouse. A very muted yet professional appearance overall, a perfect first-impression look if she encountered anyone else from the company. The only standout was her red leather business tote, a present from her father after she'd gotten her business degree.

Take that, Mr. Galanis. I have an alter ego too.

It didn't take long for an elevator car to arrive, spilling out workers reminiscent of school letting out for the day. She wondered how many of them were Artemis Games employees and figured that those in business suits probably weren't. She stepped into the empty car, then punched the number. The butterflies in her belly increased, but the nerves were more of anticipation that fear. Aron Galanis wanted her on this project; as he'd said, that gave her an advantage in negotiation. Although as far as she was concerned, after her mother had reviewed the contract, there wasn't much to negotiate. That three-month contract paid more than her salary for the entire previous year.

Her stomach leapt as the elevator slowed, stopped, opened. She stepped out, and a crowd of people streamed past her in a rush to leave their workday behind. Several of them glanced at her in mild curiosity, and a couple of them outright stared. Probably Artemis executives, probably unhappy with her impending employment. She raised her chin. That was reason enough to accept the offer.

Knowing her worth, Samara turned right and strutted down the hall. The hallway opened into a reception area in muted earth tone colors. Behind the reception kiosk stood large glass doors emblazoned with **ARTEMIS GAMES** in big, bold type and the company's logo.

A young woman who looked fresh out of college stood as she approached. "Hello, welcome to Artemis Games," she said. "Are you Ms. Reynolds?"

As was foretold, she almost said, but the receptionist looked so serious she dialed her humor down. "Yes."

She reached for her phone. "I'll let Mr. Galanis know that you're here. Please have a seat."

Samara perched on the edge of one of the soft leatherlike chairs, her bag balanced on her knees. She wasn't sure what she'd expected of the Artemis Games corporate office, but she hadn't imagined something so . . . corporate-y. Just as she checked others' assumptions about her, sometimes she had to check herself.

Glancing at the glass doors again, she saw a man in glasses striding toward her, pale green dress shirt tucked into navy dress pants, with a navy tie with flecks of green around his neck. He smiled at her as he reached for the door handle, and she realized in a flash of shock that he was Aron Galanis.

"Ms. Reynolds, welcome." The wide grin lit his features. "I hope traffic wasn't too bothersome getting here."

He spoke in full-on CEO mode, his tone formal. The man must be a Gemini with all those personalities stuffed inside his brain. She stuck out her hand and he grasped it, his hold warm and firm. She tried to remember if they had shaken hands at the convention.

"No, it wasn't," she belatedly said. "The traffic gods were on my side today."

"Lucky for us. Why don't you come in and I'll give you a quick tour of our offices?"

"Thank you."

He led her through the doors to an open area of low-walled, bright white cubicles, the walls painted in the company's logo colors. "You saw our reception area. This area is where marketing and sales happen. The bulk of our customer service calls are handled by an off-site call center. Our designers and developers work in those two open areas to foster collaboration when they're in the office."

He pointed to two large rooms on either side of the hallway. They were light and airy, with sizable U-shaped pods filled with large monitors and docking stations. Posters of some of Artemis Games' most iconic characters graced the walls of each room, with only one, a male, with bronze skin. "I don't know if I mentioned it, but we encourage our employees to telework if they want. The executive team comes in a couple of times a week, but almost everyone's duties can be done remotely."

Remote work. Hmm. She had a decent enough setup at home, but her computer was in her bedroom. That was fine since she kept it dark when gaming and streaming, but she wasn't sure it would be appropriate for work meetings. She'd just have to work in the dining room or invest in better lighting and background screens.

There were a few people still working in both rooms, and

they stared at her with avid curiosity as she and Aron walked past. He didn't introduce her, and she supposed that he wouldn't until she was officially on board.

After the collaboration spaces, they passed what looked like a well-stocked and inviting lounge area complete with the company's top games cued up on four massive monitors. Pretty cool setup for the employees to take a break.

Past the lounge were a few glassed-in offices flanking the hallway. "These are the executive offices," he said, gesturing to them as they approached the end of the hallway. "And here's where I work."

"Here" was very similar to the reception area outside, but in soothing shades of gray and blue instead of earth tones. She'd expected a dynamic and energetic color scheme like the open work areas, then remembered that even though his company was about fun and gaming, Aron said he took his business very seriously. Here, in the power center of Artemis Games, that was fully apparent.

Grayson stood as they approached. "Hello, Ms. Reynolds. It's nice to see you again."

"You, too." He looked very dapper today in a navy blue sweater-vest over a pale blue dress shirt. Amazingly, he got the navy blue sweater to match the navy khakis. She nodded in appreciation. That took a special skill, but it wasn't the season for sweaters. Then again, since the ambient temperature in the office seemed to be set just above refrigerator level, she could understand his sartorial decision.

"Would you like something to drink, Ms. Reynolds?" Grayson asked. "We have just about everything."

"Green tea?"

"Hot or cold?"

"Hot with two Splendas would be great, thank you."

"Of course." He looked to Aron. "Boss?"

"I'll have the same."

Grayson looked momentarily surprised but quickly regained his composure. "I'll bring it in shortly."

Aron gestured to the glassed-in entrance to his office. "After you."

Chapter 9

Samara stepped through the open door into a spacious office. This was definitely an executive's domain, with two of the walls made entirely of windows offering a 180-degree view of the north Atlanta skyline. The soothing blue and gray decor continued, anchored by charcoal gray office-grade carpet. An oval conference table with twelve chairs ringing it sat closer to the door on the left. What looked like an interactive whiteboard hung on the wall behind it, with a conference phone and tech inputs embedded in the center of the table.

A leather sectional occupied the space in front of one of the glass walls, and by the other perched a sleek executive desk and low credenza. The other windowless wall held a progression of pictures documenting the history, present, and possible future of the company. Curious, she moved closer. The first picture showed a teenage version of Aron with a loose grin on his face. A tall man with dark brown hair graying at the temples stood beside him, one arm around Aron's shoulders. His grin matched Aron's, leaving no doubt as to their connection.

"That's me at sixteen," Aron said quietly. Pride echoed in his voice. "And that's my father, Alesandro. This photo was taken on the day I finished developing my first game, a birthday present for my brother, Benjy."

Ah, Sam thought. *So that's where the name Benjy comes from.*

"My father was so impressed, he helped me set up an LLC. I decided to call it Artemis Games, in honor of my mother and maternal grandmother."

He was going straight for the emotional jugular, hitting her directly in the feels. Any lingering animosity dissolved like suds going down a drain. How could she be mad at someone who created a game for his brother and named a company after his mother and grandmother?

She tried to distance herself from the emotion. "Alesandro, Artemis, and Aron. Why is your brother named Benjy?"

"Actually, his first name is Aristotle, and his middle name is Benjamin. He hated his first name, even when my mom shortened it to Ari. He likes being called Benjy, so Benjy it is."

He reached out, touched the picture frame, his expression brimming with sad reflection. "My mother took this picture because Dad was my first investor. That was the last summer we had with him."

Sam covered her mouth. Such an important photo marking the beginning of Artemis Games and the end of his time with his father. How difficult was it for him to come into his office every day, see this photo, and be reminded that he'd lost his father?

Aron cleared his throat. "I believe that is what's known as killing the mood."

"It's not," she protested. "I can see how proud your father was of you. Capturing that moment is precious and reminds you to live up to the promise your father saw in you when he helped you start your company."

"You're right." Warmth flooded his tone again, chasing the sadness away. "You can see how the company's life has unfolded. Our first official game launch. The first employee—second, if you count me as first—that we hired. The first million in sales. The first time we hit triple digits. Our IPO. Opening our headquarters here."

He stopped at the last picture, a road running straight into the sunrise. "And finally, the aspirational photo, showing that our future is bright as long as we keep driving forward."

She glanced up at him at the moment he turned to face her. She felt a little blip as their gazes met, locked. This guy was too good to be true. Yet she was getting swept up in his hopes and dreams and plans for the company. And dammit, she wanted to contribute to those hopes and dreams and plans.

"Sir. Ms. Reynolds." Grayson glided into the room, bearing a tray of steaming mugs. He placed it on the highly reflective surface of the table in front of the sectional. "Your tea is ready."

Aron cleared his throat again as his assistant nodded, then left. "I suppose that's the signal to return to the business at hand," he said, gesturing toward the sectional. "If you would . . . ?"

She preceded him to the sitting area, then waited for him to take his preferred seat so that she'd know where to sit. He again gestured, this time to the long part of the sectional facing the window. "Why don't you sit there? That way you can enjoy the view."

There was no part of the seating area—or the entire office—that blocked the astounding view. Still, she perched on the center seat while Aron sat on the corner part to her left.

She reached for her tea, noting that Grayson had brought

biscotti and shortbread cookies too. It was a thoughtful gesture, but she wasn't going to eat one. The last thing she needed was cookie crumbles on her dress pants or stuck in her teeth. Instead, she removed the tea bag from the mug closest to her, added the sweetener and gave it a swirl, then sat back.

Aron did the same. "When I'm in the office, I usually work until sunset. Not only is it beautiful from here, but I use the moment as an opportunity to examine everything I did that day, determine if my actions made the company better than the day it started."

"I don't think I can get any more impressed," she said, looking at him over the rim of her mug. "You don't have to keep laying it on so thick."

He frowned for a moment, then his expression blanked. "There's no need to be impressed, Ms. Reynolds. I'm the CEO. It's my job to conceive of ways to improve Artemis Games. I have a responsibility to the people who work with me and those that invest in us."

Then he smiled. "Hopefully, today I'll be able to say that signing you definitely made the company better."

"That's not subtle at all."

"It wasn't meant to be, and I'm not known for my subtlety in any form or fashion. I hope I can answer whatever questions you may have to your satisfaction. I am eager to close this deal today."

• • •

Aron blew across the rim of his mug before taking a careful sip. The green tea wasn't bad, but he usually preferred chai or a matcha blend. No idea why he'd impulsively mimicked her drink selection, but he seemed inclined to impulsive actions around her. Like trying this tea. He took another sip while covertly studying Samara.

She'd been striking in her con gear and copper-colored curls, appearing much younger than her actual age, but this business professional look knocked him back on his heels. Which version was the real Samara? Maybe they both were. It didn't matter. He'd told her the truth when he said he was eager to immediately sign the contract, bring her aboard, and officially kick off their collaboration. Hopefully, that didn't come across as too pushy.

He returned his mug to the table, ready to get started. "You said you had some questions for me. Feel free to ask me anything. I'll answer what I can."

"All right." She leaned forward to return her still-steaming mug to the table, then dug into her bright red bag to extract an equally bright red planner. She opened it, then pulled out a pen. "First, if I accept this position, will I be given company equipment to use?"

Easy question. Did that mean the questions got harder the further they went along? "Yes, you'll be given a company laptop with all the software you need. Our tech support team will set up your credentials and get you into our systems."

"Okay." She made a note, then looked up to ask her second question. "Would I be working here in the office, or working remotely?"

A harder question that needed a nuanced answer. Too bad he didn't do nuance. He'd just have to spit it out and deal with her reaction after. "Since we need to be in direct in-the-moment communication for this collaboration to work, you'll work in the office when I'm in the office. When I'm remote in my home office, you'll work there too."

He waited, studying her face, watching for an indication of her thoughts. Her expression flattened, her gaze hooded, her body still. Then she looked up at him, her eyes direct and assessing. "Alone?"

Ah. Understanding the quiet query, Aron shook his head. "No, Grayson is there eight to five, sometimes longer if there's a need. And there's a housekeeper, Mrs. Jeffries, who comes three times a week. It is an actual office, and while the view isn't as grand as this, I think it's spectacular in its own way."

Her gaze dropped to her planner as she considered his words. It probably seemed strange to her, wanting to work out of his home office. Although the scenery had changed, working there reminded him of the early days of Artemis Games, when it was just him, a laptop, and his dreams.

Truth be told, he'd partially instituted the telework policy because he hated coming to the office. Hated the traffic getting there, the crowd of people flooding into the building, the noise they generated. Sometimes he came in around six a.m. just to avoid the throngs. If it meant Samara would sign the contract, he'd swallow down his issues and come to the office every day. Earbuds and soothing music would probably blunt the bulk of it.

She clipped her pen back in her planner, then folded her hands atop it. That was a bad sign, wasn't it? When she spoke, her tone was coldly formal. "You do realize that any hint of impropriety will reflect negatively on me, not you, correct?"

No, he hadn't realized that, because the idea of impropriety never crossed his mind. "I understand your concerns, but rest assured, I have no intentions or desire to do anything other than work, Ms. Reynolds. This project and its outcome are too important to me—and to you, too, I'm sure—to allow anything to overshadow it. We had a good flow of ideas going, and you brought up some very good points. That's why I want to collaborate with you, and that's why I want to brainstorm in person."

"Okay, I can understand that."

"Also, it is entirely possible that after the first couple of weeks we'll have locked in our game plan and timeline, which means you won't need to collaborate with me face-to-face. Is that satisfactory?"

"Yes." She hesitated, then said, "I didn't intend to insult you. I just need to make sure that my side of the street is clean."

He had no idea what that meant but didn't ask her about it. "I'm not insulted. I simply want to make sure that the terms are agreeable."

"They are," she answered, nodding for emphasis. "Speaking of terms, I realize the compensation isn't based on an hourly rate. Are you expecting there to be any night or weekend work?"

"My weekends are reserved for my family," he answered. "We encourage a healthy work-life balance here. However, after you and Grayson leave for the day, I will probably continue working. Of course, I'll update you the next day so that we stay on the same page."

"That's fair." She pulled her pen free and made more notes. He had a sudden desire to take a peek, but that would negate all that he'd reassured her of up to this point.

"Do you have any other questions for me?"

"Just one." She closed her planner. "Why me?"

The soft question brought him up short. "Excuse me?"

She pulled her bottom lip between her teeth before clarifying. "Why did you pick me to help you with this?"

He leaned forward, dropping his elbows on his knees. "You impressed me with your panel. Our lunch conversation showed me that we had good knowledge exchange and better synergy on several topics. Your professional credentials are a necessary bonus. I like your enthusiasm and desire for change, and I think it matches my own. You believe passionately in the things that are important to you, same as I do. That passion, energy, and enthusiasm combined with your credentials are what I need to bring this project to life. If anyone can help me do that, I firmly believe you can."

She blinked, eyes wide. "Umm . . ."

He looked down to hide his smile, then looked up again. "You seem surprised by my answer."

"Well . . ." She spread her hands in a helpless gesture. "What you call passion and enthusiasm, other people would call anger and sarcasm."

He leaned forward, making sure he had her attention. "In this moment, do those other people matter?"

Wide eyes and parted lips denoted surprise. Leaning backward— rejection? Then leaning forward again. Agreement.

"No," she finally said, then gave him a smile that showed a dimple in her left cheek. "No, they don't."

"Good. Do you have any other questions for me?"

"You've answered the most important ones."

"Then have you come to a decision, or do you need more time?"

"Hmm." She returned her planner to her bright red bag. "No, I don't need more time."

He sat silent, trying to glean anything from her expression, her posture, her tone. Being able to read people was a vital part of his job as he interacted with employees, the public, and investors. Sitting here, waiting for her to give him her decision, he couldn't read her at all, and that fact made him anxious.

He smothered the anxiety down, as he smothered all difficult emotion. Whatever her answer was, he'd deal with it and move on.

"I've decided to accept the offer."

"Really?"

"Yes." She smiled. "I also enjoyed our conversation we had during that lunch. And I also want you to know that I understand why you went incognito during the con."

She understood. Did that mean she wasn't mad at him any longer? He decided to clarify. "So you're no longer upset?"

"If I was, I wouldn't accept the contract." Her smile slanted. "You had your reasons, very valid reasons. I respect that. Besides, our conversation was a good one, and we even did a little brainstorming. I like firing off ideas like that. To work with someone with the passion, talent, and resources to see them come to fruition, I definitely want that chance."

"Excellent." They were on the same page, just as he knew they would be. He allowed himself a small smile as excitement began to build. "Do you agree to the other terms in the contract?"

"I should be asking you that question," she told him. "Did you have the chance to review our stipulations?"

"I did. The contract is between Artemis Games and Rise Consulting. Any press releases from either party will reflect that. No mention of Samara Reynolds and especially no mention of ReyofSun in any official or unofficial communications."

He frowned. It was the only change to his initial contract offer. "Why?"

"It's a protective measure for both of us," she explained. "It will seem more like a business decision and less like a publicity stunt if you leverage Rise Consulting's standing in the local business community. The work should be the focus, not the person doing the consulting."

She was right, and it galled him that he hadn't considered that. "Based on your advocating efforts, I had thought it would be something you'd want to share."

"You mean shout my victory from the rooftops?" She shook her head. "No, given some of my more virulent detractors, gamer me and professional me need to stay separate."

Mark would be thrilled to revise the press release. "Tomorrow, I'll get Janet to prepare the final contract and the NDA to send over to Rise. Once everything's official, we can do a joint press release. When can you start? I'm assuming that you have to transition your current client to another consultant?"

"Monday."

Too soon and too far away. It would give him time to gather everything needed to get her up to speed. He extended his hand. "Welcome aboard, Ms. Reynolds. I look forward to working with you on this project."

"Thank you," she said, taking his hand. "I'm looking forward to it too."

Shaking hands was a necessary part of doing business, a part Aron usually gritted his teeth and endured for the few seconds it took. He didn't mind shaking her hand though. "Okay, then." He cleared his throat as Grayson returned. "Any final questions?"

"Is everyone who works for you addressed as Mr. or Ms.?"

"No. We're all on a first-name basis around here."

"Then why are you still calling me Ms. Reynolds?"

She sounded bothered. "That's how you told me to address you, when we talked after my panel at the convention."

"I did?" She frowned. "Oh! That was after I found out who you really were. I needed the distance then."

She looked away, flustered. "Since we're going to be working together, it's fine to call me Samara."

He already called her by her first name in his head, but it was nice to say it aloud. "Thank you. Samara it is."

She fell silent, as if waiting. Waiting for what? He looked over to Grayson, who made a gesture he couldn't interpret. He didn't like to be at a disadvantage, but he needed clarification. "Am I missing something?"

"Reciprocity," Samara said. "Can I call you Aron?"

Surprise and chagrin splashed through him. "Haven't you been calling me by my name already?"

"I called you Benjy and Hoodie Guy. In that conference room at the convention, it was Mr. Galanis."

"Oh. Well." He should have caught that. "Then I would appreciate it if you would call me Aron."

He was rewarded with a genuine smile that caused dimples to appear in both her cheeks. "Thank you, Aron. If you don't mind, I'll take a rain check on dinner so I can begin wrapping up my current project. I'll see you Monday."

It couldn't come fast enough.

Chapter 10

Samara eyed her GPS, sure it was giving her false information. There was no way that the bachelor CEO of a tech company lived in a gated community filled with McMansions. This place, with a guard at the gate, security patrolling in golf carts, huge houses hulking on tiny plots of land, was definitely #GOALS for many. Yet it made her wonder if she'd be meeting a Mrs. Aron Galanis when she rang the doorbell—or a Mr., for that matter. He hadn't mentioned a spouse, nor had any of the online bios referred to one. It seemed Aron kept his personal life on lock. Not that she blamed him.

Gripping her steering wheel like a life preserver, she distracted herself by contemplating what sort of spouse a man like Aron Galanis had or would have. Would they be a fellow gamer? If so, why hadn't they attended the convention with him? A spouse would have surely interjected when she'd given him a read after the Artemis Games summit. Grayson hadn't interrupted, and Aron had introduced him as his assistant.

Besides, Aron didn't give off a married vibe. She hadn't noticed a ring on his finger either. Not that she had looked for one intentionally. It was simply one of those cursory checks you made when meeting with someone cute.

Whoa, chile. Don't let Max and Quinn know you've got these thoughts in your head. Don't go into this job thinking of the boss as cute. You've got a job to do, important work for hella money. Do your job, get your coins, then get on with your life.

She circled through the lush green space slowly, thankful that she'd taken good care of her hybrid SUV. Even so, she felt completely out of place driving along the wide, silent, perfectly presented street. It didn't matter that her name had been on the visitors' list; anyone passing by would probably assume she was there to clean someone's house.

Finally, her GPS cheerfully pointed out the road that led to Aron's house. The homes here were just as large as those closer to the entrance but had more land around them, making them much more attractive in her opinion. Probably made them more expensive, too.

She pulled to a stop, then killed the engine after verifying the address, and gawked. Aron's home sat at the end of the cul-de-sac, which seemed to front a nature preserve. Forget the houses at the front of the enclave. These McMansions were impressive. His house certainly had the wow factor needed for a CEO, but she wondered again why a supposed bachelor chose a place like this instead of one of the downtown penthouses or high-rise condos with the million-dollar views.

She had to admit, the man piqued her curiosity. It was part of why she'd agreed to the contract and to come to his home to work, the other parts being he talked a good game and had deep pockets. It wasn't often that she was in spaces with executives. Most of her contract work had her in contact with managers or directors at the most, with a few vice presidents thrown in for good measure.

This guy, though . . . she was beginning to wonder which version of him was real. Hoodie Guy Benjy and CEO Aron were too different to be the same person.

She exited the car, then took a moment to settle herself and smooth down the front of her outfit. Just as she had the day before when she'd met him at his office on her first day of work, she'd gone with business professional with black stilettos, charcoal dress trousers with creases so sharp they could slice butter, and a seafoam-colored silk blouse tucked into the waistband. She'd pulled her braids back into a ponytail and finished her ensemble with simple gold jewelry at her ears and throat. She could be Corporate Barbie when she needed to be, but it would be great if they could go with business casual from now on. Still, she wanted to show that she was ready to work, and this outfit clearly said that.

Grabbing her bright red leather business tote, she shut the door, set the alarm (like there was danger of anyone taking her car in this neighborhood), and made her way carefully across the circular cobbled drive, up the three flagstone steps, past the large white columns, before stopping at the front door inset with an oval stained glass panel. Again, at odds with what she thought she knew of the man. Above her hung a massive light fixture that would have been called a chandelier if it were inside the house. She tried not to think of sword of Damocles similarities as she rang the doorbell.

The door opened before the melodious chime faded. Grayson, Aron's assistant, smiled at her. "Welcome, Ms. Reynolds," he greeted her, stepping back to allow her to enter before closing the door behind her. "Aron's on a call right now, but he should be done soon. Can I get you something to drink? We have coffee, water, or lemonade."

"Lemonade sounds great, thank you." She clasped the handle of her tote in both hands, waiting for Grayson to tell her where to go while trying not to gawk at the two-story marbled foyer with its appropriately sized metal and glass chandelier that looked more like an art piece than lighting. Then again, it was an executive's house.

"If you'll come this way, I'll show you where you can wait for Aron," his assistant said, guiding her past the grand staircase, what must have been the formal dining room, and on to what could only be called a great room. The open-concept area had high ceilings with exposed beams running from the sitting area over to an open kitchen any wannabe chef would love. The bright, crisp lines of the furniture, lighting, and window coverings looked straight out of *Architectural Digest*, their bright severity softened by a scattering of plants and a couple of trees flanking the fireplace.

For some reason, though, the decor didn't feel like Aron. He probably had an interior designer do it for him, since she didn't think he had any time to decorate himself. Still, the lack of any personality to the room made her wonder if he'd just rented the house, furniture and all.

"I'll be right back with your lemonade," Grayson said, gesturing to the seating area. "Please make yourself comfortable."

Sam doubted she'd feel comfortable in a place with a foyer as large as her bedroom and a coffee table that probably cost as much as her car. She supposed the CEO of Artemis Games needed the right space and place to entertain, and this house and its decor certainly fit the bill.

Grateful again that she'd dressed up for the occasion, Sam settled into one of the eggshell white leather club chairs, surprised at how inviting it was. She stared at the giant mirror above the marble-surround fireplace, wondering if it was one of those types that became a TV with the press of a button. That made her speculate whether or not the room had ever held a movie night, or if Aron had ever played video games there.

She sighed. Her thoughts were galloping off again. She should have spent her time reviewing her ideas, not pondering Aron's private life. *Remember why you're here. Do the work, make your coins, move on.*

"Samara. There you are. Thanks for coming."

She shot to her feet as Aron appeared from a short hallway. He looked much the same as he had when she'd met him at his office yesterday. Light gray khakis and a navy blue dress shirt, the sleeves rolled up. The only difference was his dark hair falling over his forehead in unruly waves, and his eyes smiling at her behind wire-rimmed glasses. This was her Hoodie Guy, and whether or not the reappearance was a deliberate choice on Aron's part, she was glad that he'd made it.

"Hi, Aron, it's good to see you again." She gave him a genuine smile as she stuck out her hand.

He took it, shook it, but didn't release it. "Let me give you a quick tour, then show you where we'll be working."

He was already moving, pulling her along, and she barely managed to snag her tote. "I'll take your lemonade to the office," Grayson called from the kitchen, seemingly okay with his boss dragging her around the house.

Aron led her back to the foyer. "Up the stairs are three bedroom suites, and over there is the formal dining room. There's a powder room here next to the door to the garage. You've seen the great room and the kitchen. Through here is my second-favorite spot of the entire house."

He led her through French doors and out to the patio, although "patio" was too small a word to describe the outdoor living area. The covered space was basically an outdoor room, three ceiling fans hanging overhead with a large dining set on one side and a seating area on the other, and a modest-sized fountain gurgling away. The dining area led to a fully furnished outdoor kitchen, and beyond that was a pool complete with a waterfall and slide. All against a backdrop of trees that acted as a buffer from the neighbors.

"I can see why this would be a favorite spot," she finally said. "It's so peaceful. I would work out here when the weather allowed it if it were up to me. And my father would drool over this outdoor kitchen. If he saw this, he'd immediately tear out his and start over."

"You can invite him over for the next company gathering," he suggested. It didn't sound like a fake invitation either. "I like the tranquility of it, and I like to work and think out here sometimes too. This area, the nature preserve at the back of the property, and the pool are a large part of the reason why I bought the house. My brother, Benjy, loves splashing water, and he took to the pool and the fountain right away."

She wanted to ask how old Benjy was, then pressed her lips together. His personal life was none of her business. He could share whatever he wanted at whatever level of detail he was comfortable with. She wouldn't probe deeper, even though she burned with the curiosity to learn more about him. She immediately broke that resolution by saying, "If this is your second-favorite, I can't wait to see number one."

Aron tugged on her hand, making her realize he still held it. She'd been so caught up in the tour that she hadn't realized it. Surprisingly, she didn't mind. He led her back into her dream kitchen, past Grayson, then down the short hallway he'd come from before. "The master suite's over there," he said, waving at a set of double doors at the end of the hall. He led her into another room, then released her hand. "And here's my first-favorite, the office where we'll be working most of the time."

The spacious room was organized chaos with dove gray walls, bright white trim, and furniture so dark brown it was almost black. A massive TV dominated one wall with a row of gaming chairs in front of it. Built-ins flanked the TV, showcasing an expansive collection of games, controllers, and consoles, some of which looked to be rare. On the wall behind the chairs ran a credenza holding a popcorn machine, a mini fridge, one of those gadgets that turned water into sodas, and a couple of arcade machines, one of *Galaga* and one of *Centipede*. A perfect play area.

"Oh my god." Sam stepped closer to one of the built-ins. "You have one of the 1990 Nintendo World Championship gold-edition cartridges? And a gold PS3? And holy fuck, an actual Sega Genesis *Tetris* game? There's only like ten of those around!"

She bit her lips after the curse word slipped out, but Aron laughed. "Figured you'd like my collection. I have just about every game and system known to man. Some of them took longer to track down than others, and some of them I probably overpaid for, but when you want what you want . . ."

"I understand." At that moment, Sam wanted nothing more than to plop down in one of the gaming chairs and play against him but reminded herself that this was about work, not pleasure. She reluctantly stepped away from his collection to examine the rest of his office.

The other side of the room held the business area. A custom-looking desk stood in front of the windows, wide and long enough for two people to work comfortably side by side or across from each other. Electrical outlets and charging ports were embedded in the surface at each end. There was still plenty of room even with picture frames, Aron's large dual monitors, and a laptop, tablet, and cell phone at the ready. Sticky notes and scribbles covered a whiteboard on the wall closest to the desk. "I knew it!"

Aron's eyes widened in surprise at her outburst, loud in the quiet room. "Knew what?"

"This is you, the real you." She made a slow circle, taking in the room again. "This part of your house is where you really live."

"You got me." He laughed, scrubbing a hand through his hair. "The front of the house is just camouflage. Other than the patio, I spend most of my time here."

"I don't blame you. I now fully understand why you prefer to work from home," Sam told him, looking from one side of the room to the other. "If it were me, I wouldn't want to go play in traffic either. You surprised me, though."

"Really." He focused on her in that way he had. "How did I surprise you?"

"I fully expected you to live in a condo near Buckhead or Midtown with a 360-degree view of the Atlanta skyline."

"God, no." He shuddered. "There's nothing for me down there."

That surprised her. "Not even the clubs and restaurants?"

Did he shudder again? "I have never done clubs. Too many people, too much noise, too much everything. And you don't have to be downtown to find a good place to enjoy a meal."

True. She occasionally went out with Max and Quinn, and they had a standing Game Night out, but work and streaming left little time for anything else.

"Actually, this house was supposed to be for my mother."

The quiet tone caught her attention. Greed for every tidbit she could glean rose to the surface. She carefully prodded him. "Really?"

He nodded. "After the first million in profit, I found this house, thought she'd love it, and bought it. But she wanted to stay in the house we grew up in, probably because it's filled with memories of Dad. So I updated the kitchen and bathrooms at home and was left with this."

Oh. "You decided not to sell it?"

A shrug lifted his shoulders. "Like I said, my brother likes the pool and the fountain. He stays over every other weekend, and I know he'd hate it if I were in a high-rise condo somewhere. Besides, it's a lot easier to have the team over here for company events than in a condo."

A chuff of embarrassment had him shaking his head. "To be honest, I prefer gadgets to people. I like having the buffer this place gives me. I like being able to hear myself think."

"I understand that. I have roommates—you met Quinn and Max—but sometimes I have to retreat to my bedroom and put my earbuds in and listen to something soothing and instrumental, just so that I'm the only one in my head."

"Yes." He gave her another genuine smile of understanding and commiseration. "That's it exactly."

She took a final look around the room before turning back to him. She'd love to live in a place like this, with an outdoor oasis like that, and a collection like his. She placed that wish on the imaginary shelf labeled "One Day."

Her mental picture of him began to sharpen in focus as she found more common ground with him, income disparity notwithstanding. His family seemed as important to him as hers was to her. He preferred silence and solitude to noise and gatherings. Although she loved to go to Game and Flame with her friends, sometimes she needed time away from them, time to herself.

She had the feeling their working styles would mesh well together too, and there was only one way to find out.

"Where do you want me?"

Chapter 11

Aron blinked at her in momentary confusion. "Excuse me?"

She held up her bag. "Where should I set up? At the desk over here, or the seating area over there?"

"Over there" was his well-broken-in thinking couch and a sturdy coffee table that Grayson used when they ran down the tasks and appointments for the day because he'd spread out too far on his desk. There was a good five feet between that seating area and his desk, but for some reason that felt too far away. "Grayson uses that space, so why don't you get set up on the end of the desk here? It will make it easier for us to brainstorm."

"Sure." He watched as she placed her bag on the desk, then opened it to remove a laptop, her phone, and a medium-sized binder that matched her bag. Although working here was his idea, it also made the space between his shoulder blades itch. Other than his family and Grayson, no one visited this part of his house. He even cleaned it himself. This was his personal domain, the area where his brain worked best, the area where he felt most himself. Now that he'd invited Samara Reynolds into this inner sanctum, he had to wonder what he had been thinking.

This Samara was not the one he'd met at con when he was just a gamer talking to a fellow gamer. Nor was she activist Samara, giving him a verbal beatdown after his panel. No, this Samara was all business, from her no-nonsense ponytail to her pointy-toed shoes. It relieved him that he'd chosen to put more effort into his clothing than he usually did when he worked from home. He felt self-conscious enough as it was.

He probably should have just continued meeting with her in the Perimeter office even though he disliked being there most of the time. If he had to be formal when he worked, it would be better to be there than here. He never wanted this space to be anything other than comfortable.

"Is something wrong with my outfit?"

He belatedly realized he'd been staring too long. "No. Why?"

"You're staring at my pants and frowning."

"Oh." He smoothed his features into something he hoped was more pleasant. "It's different from your con wear."

She laughed. "So's yours. Well, different from Hoodie Guy, anyway."

"I'm Hoodie Guy most of the time, except when I have to be CEO." He realized he might have insulted her earlier. "Not that you don't look nice this way. Very nice. But if you want to dress more casually when you're here, it's no problem."

A dimple appeared in her right cheek. Did that always happen? "You're just looking for an excuse to be more casual, aren't you?"

He raised his hands. "You got me. We don't enforce a dress code when working remotely. Even when we're in the office we go casual to business casual. I care more about how my team works than how they look."

"Brains over looks?" She gave him a thumbs-up. "Got it."

He blinked at her, unsure of how to take that or what to say next. Luckily, Grayson took that moment to appear in the doorway, bearing a tray with some snacks, three glasses, and a pitcher of lemonade. It gave him a much-needed moment to regroup. Why had he dragged her all over the house? Why had he blabbed about dress codes? More importantly, why was he so nervous with this woman, so much that he felt an uncharacteristic need to impress her?

He wanted the vibe of that incognito meeting to return. He still had a lot of ground to recover with Samara before they could get back to that easy camaraderie they'd had before she knew his identity. Grayson looked at the overburdened desk, then placed the tray on the coffee table. He poured lemonade into a glass, then handed it to Samara. "Here you are, Ms. Reynolds."

"Thank you. And please, call me Samara." She took a sip, then her eyes widened as she held up the glass. "Did you make this from scratch?"

Grayson shook his head. "Aron did."

She turned back to him. "You did?"

He crossed to the coffee table to fill his own glass. "Lemonade was the drink of choice in my family growing up. I spent a lot of afternoons juicing lemons for my mom. Some people run on caffeine. The Galanis family runs on lemonade."

"I can see why." She took another sip, her expression happy. "I'd drink this all the time if I could. Thank you for making this, Aron."

He shifted his feet, uncomfortable with her appreciation. "You're welcome. By the way, do you have any preferences for lunch? There's a little bit of everything nearby, and the kitchen is fully stocked too. Grayson will order it for us."

Samara waved her hand. "Oh no, you don't have to do that," she protested. "Grayson's supposed to be assisting you, not waiting on me. I'll go out and get something myself."

Grayson smiled. "I always order for myself and Aron, so it's no big deal to order for you."

"But—"

"Grayson's trying not to tell on me," Aron confessed, scrubbing at his hair again. "I have a bad habit of forgetting to take breaks or eat when I'm working. Grayson helps me stay on a schedule." He really needed to stop confessing all his flaws to her, even if she seemed to take them all in stride.

"All right, then. I'll just have whatever you two are having, Grayson. That will make it easy for everybody."

"Sounds good." He turned to Aron. "I'll work over here. Let me know if you need anything."

Aron heard the question in Grayson's tone and nodded. They had run through a couple of different scenarios in case things became awkward with Samara. Hopefully, he wouldn't need his assistant to referee or remind him to be social, and hopefully, Samara wouldn't run for the hills. "Thanks, Gray."

Samara took her place at the desk, then opened the red notebook and removed a pen from a loop. "I suppose we should get started, then."

Right. He crossed to his side of the desk, placing his glass onto a coaster bearing the Artemis Games logo. She was there to work, not socialize. Usually, he had little patience for small talk, but with Samara it seemed no conversation was a waste of time.

The day before had been easy. Mondays in the office followed a typical pattern, and there hadn't been much deviation aside from Samara and another Rise consultant walking him and his executive team through the expectations. The other consultant would partner with Human Resources on the culture shift while Samara worked with him on the special projects.

Now that he knew the activist, the gamer, and the professional sides of Samara, he wasn't sure how he should interact with her. It wasn't until he saw her glance at his games display case that an idea struck him.

"Before we get started, why don't we do an icebreaker like you did at yesterday's meeting?"

"What sort of icebreaker did you have in mind?"

"Would you like to play a game?" he asked, gesturing to the built-ins. "Visitor's choice."

Samara rose and crossed to the other side of the room faster than he'd anticipated to peruse his shelves and display cases. "I think, just to be fair, no Artemis Games properties should be used in this icebreaker."

"Understood and agreed."

"All right." She scanned his collection. *Eyes: bright. Smile: loose and delighted. Overall body language: confident yet restrained, the restraint easing by slow degrees.* "Any particular platform? Online or off?"

"You choose." It was his collection after all. He'd played all of them multiple times. It was assumed that he had the advantage.

She turned to look at him. "You're being so generous. Is that because you're that confident you'll win?"

"I mean, those are all my games. They're not for decoration."

"Okay, then." She picked a system and a fighting game, then handed him a controller. "Let's duel."

Grayson laughed. "I think I should make some popcorn for this."

Aron expected her to sit on the couch, but she surprised him by settling into one of the low-slung gaming chairs. And with that, she transformed from Samara Reynolds, consultant, to ReyofSun, gamer.

A challenging grin lit her face as she patted the chair next to her. "Come on down to my level, Mr. CEO."

It was the level he wanted to be on, so dropping into the seat was easy. Trying to win against her? That was harder. Based on what he'd seen in her streams, he knew she was good, but seeing was one thing; experiencing was another. It took his full focus, but he still lost the first round and barely won the second.

"You're as excellent a player as I thought," he said, putting down his controller. "But I noticed that you're not as talkative as you are in your streams."

"I'm entertaining as well as gaming when I stream," she answered. "And since we had that whole talk about needing quiet time, I figured you'd prefer silence during our match."

"I want you to be yourself, Ms. Reynolds," he said, holding out his hand to help her up. "I want you to be comfortable. I'm sure you find the working conditions uncomfortable enough."

She looked at him for a long moment before reaching out to grip his hand. "It's going to be difficult to establish a comfortable working routine if you keep calling me Ms. Reynolds. You called me Samara when you gave me the tour. Let's go with that."

"Okay." He tightened his grip, then pulled her up. Unfortunately, he used more force than he needed, and she crashed against him. He steadied her with his free hand, and suddenly they were nose to nose.

He froze, unsure what to say or do, conscious of Grayson staring at him with wide eyes. What had they been talking about? Oh yeah, making her feel comfortable.

"Samara, I . . . I think it's time to get to work, don't you?"

She broke away from him, then rubbed her hands together. "I think you're right. Can we revisit your objectives?"

"Of course." Work was comfortable. He crossed back to his desk, Samara following. "Like I mentioned when we discussed the contract, I have three goals I want to achieve. The third goal depends heavily on achieving the first two, and all have tight deadlines."

"Naturally," she said, scribbling notes. "Go on."

"The first is focusing on the next iteration of *Legendsfall*. I want your help to brainstorm characters for the update with a focus on equity and inclusion. Once we formulate a character list, I'll have a meeting with our design team. Given the timeline your colleague shared yesterday, this meeting will take place after a diversity workshop. I may or may not ask you to attend the design meeting, so be prepared."

"Sending David in to chat with Goliath. Got it."

"It won't be that bad." He hoped. He crossed to the whiteboard, uncapped a marker, and began making a goals list. "In between character concepts and development, I'd like for us to review the most popular games in the Artemis catalog for problematic content. Ten would be ideal, but five should be possible within our expected deadline. Given the blunder in *Legendsfall*, I'm resigned to the thought that some of our other games and all the *Legendsfall* iterations may have issues. If we find any, we flag them for the development team. I already know which games the former developer worked on, but I only have enough bandwidth to review one game's code, so I also have a couple of people reviewing every other game that my former employee touched. You and I can play through a few more. Hope you don't mind."

"Me, getting paid to play games?" She snorted. "Why would I mind going to heaven?"

"Good." He made a note on the board. He'd use the sticky notes for the finer details once they had the objectives mapped out, then add everything to a web-based board. "The last goal is part of my personal project and the reason you signed the NDA: obtaining an accessibility certification from WeCAN, an international body whose focus is on autism and neurodiversity. The certification will not only help with launching our educational lineup, but also with creating a workspace that accommodates the neurodiverse."

She whistled. "You're nothing if not ambitious, aren't you?"

"To borrow the analogy you used, I'm building a bigger table," he told her. "That's why your callout hit so hard and I had to act fast to fix it. Bringing you on board is very timely since I need to push my timeline forward. You and the hand-picked developers will get a bonus for bringing in *Legendsfall*'s new version on or ahead of time to showcase at NexCon. Reviewing our other games will take some time, so if we need to focus on creating review parameters, we can create an in-house team to review the games. The certification application needs to be submitted shortly after your contract ends. I want your help with that. It's a lot to do, and not a lot of time to do it."

"Apparently not." She made a few more notes in her planner before closing it with a snap, then folded her hands atop it. "Where do you want to start?"

He tapped the marker against the whiteboard. "With the most visible goal, *Legendsfall*. An update will go out soon to remove the problematic Easter egg. We had a good discussion to start at the convention, but it's time for a deeper dive. Tell me what you know of *Legendsfall*."

"Sure. *Legendsfall* is your company's flagship game. There are currently three iterations: the original *Spear Quest*, *Gladiator Games*, and *History's Heroes*. The vast majority of characters in *Spear Quest* are Eurocentric, straight out of Tolkien. And in *Gladiator Games*, even your urban futurescape maps are homogenous, except for that NPC."

"It's about time for us to begin conceptualizing the next version of *Legendsfall*. I think it's time to expand the world."

"If you're thinking of creating a new version, what about doing something that includes world myths? Africa, the Americas, and Asia also have a plethora of cultures with a wide variety of myths and folklore that can inspire characters for the new version."

"Hmm." A version of *Legendsfall* using myths from around the world. "We could call it *Legendsfall: Mythica*. It could incorporate myths and legends from around the world and bring back some of the popular characters from *History's Heroes* while bringing in new ones."

"Great idea." She reached for her laptop. "There are plenty of daring and badass Black women and men throughout history you could pull from for the hero characters' list."

"Like Harriet Tubman."

"She definitely qualifies as a badass." She nodded. "But have you heard of Stagecoach Mary?"

"Who?"

She pointed at him, giving him a wink. "Exactly. Let me tell you why Stagecoach Mary is a badass, and then we'll move on to Queen Amanirenas. And look at this."

She did a quick Internet search for the website she wanted to show him. "This artist did interpretations of the orishas, a group of gods from the Yoruba religion. You could certainly use these as inspiration for new characters for the *Mythica* expansion pack."

"These are great," Aron said, scrolling through the images. "That's a whole pantheon of inspiration."

"Exactly. And why you don't have Sekhmet, the Egyptian goddess of war, as a playable character, I don't know. You have Amazons, so why not have the warrior women of the Dahomey, who were an all-female military corps and often the last line of defense between enemy forces and the king? Sound familiar?"

"It sure does." He stepped back. "You're making my head spin, but in a good way."

"Then you should fasten your seat belt. I just want to point out that there's a vast world of legends and myths outside of Europe. From Pele, to Kali, to Oya. There are plenty of legends that Black and brown women would love to play, if given the chance."

"Wow." He shook his head in wonderment. "I'm standing at a whiteboard. Why didn't I write this down?"

She smiled. "Not necessary. I gathered these examples along with some statistics and artist links for a presentation I put together just in case I needed to present to your leadership team. I also included some gamer demographics and predictions based on trends with sources cited. I'll email it to you."

"You're good." He looked at her, then the laptop, then back again. "I knew you were good because Rise is good at what they do, but did you put this together over the weekend?"

"I like to be prepared." A smile of soft pride graced her lips. "Honestly, I've been thinking about this since I did that review."

Her eyes widened and her smile faltered. Surprise and uncertainty. He needed to reassure her. "I'm glad you did. Maybe 'glad' isn't the right word, but you did the right thing. Now that I know about it, I can continue to do the right thing. We'll make *Legendsfall: Mythica* better than the ones that came before it. It will be successful, and Artemis will get its certification. Are you with me?"

"I'm here, aren't I? Let's do this."

Chapter 12

Aron sent off an email with a list of items he wanted Janet to attend to, then stood and stretched. Sam continued to type away on her laptop, oblivious.

He took a moment to watch her, a habit he'd developed since they'd begun working together. Sometimes she wore glasses and sometimes she didn't. He had yet to determine a pattern to her wearing the glasses and now bet with himself each morning whether she would wear them or not.

That was probably going overboard. He'd talk to Grayson to see what he thought. Knowing Grayson, he'd say it was indeed too much and that Aron needed to get another hobby.

Aron didn't consider Samara a hobby. He studied her because he wanted to know more about her, her likes and dislikes. That knowledge grew every day. Maybe he did need to take a step back, or at least take a break.

Grayson closed his laptop, then stood. Per Aron's request, Grayson documented his interactions with Samara so they could debrief the following morning before she arrived. "If you don't need me for anything else, I'm done for the day."

"Nothing that can't wait until tomorrow." He turned to

Samara, who scribbled a note in her bright new planner. "Samara?"

She finally looked up. "Yes?"

Eyebrows scrunched, mouth in a flat line. She didn't appreciate the interruption. "You might want to wind things down since Grayson's about to leave."

The frown deepened. "Would it bother you if I worked a little late? I'm in a zone here and don't want to break my momentum."

"It won't bother me at all," he answered as she turned her attention back to her screen. "I don't have a set cutoff time. Working late night for others is just a normal workday for me."

Grayson made a cutting motion, and Aron realized he'd rambled on. As Grayson had already noted, it was part of his uncharacteristic desire to engage her in conversation even when they worked on separate tasks.

He cleared his throat. "Anyway, work as long as you need. I'm going to walk Grayson out."

She nodded, already engrossed in her work. He followed Grayson to the door. The other man stopped in the foyer. "Are you sure about this?"

"About what?"

"About being alone. With Samara. In your house."

Aron didn't understand the emphasis Grayson used. "Is that supposed to be a problem? She's not an employee working overtime, and she's not paid by the hour. I don't see the issue with her working as long as she wants. I'll work too."

"Since she seemed concerned enough to suggest leaving when I leave before, I suppose it means that she's comfortable with you now." Grayson pointed at him. "Don't mess that up."

He had no intention of messing anything up. "Don't worry. We'll continue as we already have. I'm not going to jeopardize our work by committing a social faux pas."

"All right." Grayson opened the door. "Call me if you need me."

"I won't." Aron pushed him over the threshold. "Go home. Go out. Just go."

Returning to the office, he found Samara still hard at work. He crossed to his desktop to do the same thing, catching up on the dozens of matters that needed his immediate attention. It wasn't long before his attention returned to Samara. She clenched her fountain pen between her lips as she furiously typed away. It didn't seem as if she'd wrap up anytime soon.

What was he supposed to do in situations like this? Other than his family, he'd never had anyone this late in his house. Even in the office he made sure Janet left on time, and Grayson only worked late when Aron had to attend some nighttime event. He was in uncharted territory.

What did other people do? He scraped his brain. Ah, that's right. Dinner. People working late usually ordered pizza or Chinese food or something like that. Given how long ago lunch was, Samara would probably appreciate something to eat.

He opened the delivery app and scrolled through previous orders. One favorite seemed to be a nearby Thai place. He reordered their usual, then continued working until the food arrived. Gathering everything they would need, he took his haul back to the office and set it up on the coffee table.

"I ordered some dinner," he announced. "Take a break and eat."

She looked up. "Thanks, but I'm gonna"—her stomach growled loudly—"come over there and have some dinner."

He arranged everything as Samara came over and sat down on the other side of the coffee table. He joined her on the floor and pointed to the bottled water. "Water or lemonade?"

"I'll grab a water." She reached for it before he could. "Thanks for ordering dinner. I didn't realize I was hungry until I smelled the food."

"Same here."

They dived into the food. He made a happy grunt at the first bite while she wriggled her bottom, then laughed. "Okay, I guess we both were really hungry."

"Mm-hmm." He belatedly realized that this was one of those social interactions Grayson had warned him about. But this was Samara, and if he made a gaffe, she'd probably call him on it and set him straight. "Can I ask you a question?"

"Sure, as long as I can ask you one in return."

He nodded. "Fair enough. Does ReyofSun have any special meaning or is it just a play on your last name?"

"Ah." She took a sip of water. "You're right. The Rey part is from my last name. The Sun part is because my dad always calls me 'sunshine.' I actually thought my name was Samara Sunshine until I started first grade."

She smiled softly. "My father introduced me to *World of Warcraft* when I was around seven, I think. He explained everything to me as I watched him play, then let me play under his account. After a while, he allowed me to set up my own profile and suggested ReyofSun because I was his 'little ray of sunshine.' I've been ReyofSun ever since."

What a great story, and it explained a lot about her. "The

handle suits you. You're warm like sunlight, but you also shine a light on issues in the gaming community. I can't think of anything better than that."

Her eyes widened, and he wondered if he'd made some sort of social blunder. "I'm so—"

He broke off his apology the moment she reached across the table to cover his hand. "There's no need to apologize. I haven't thought about my handle's origin story in a while, and reminiscing about it and sharing that with you makes me happy. I think it suits me too, which is why I haven't used another handle in the past twenty years."

To his intense disappointment, she pulled her hand away. He asked another question. "What about your group, Nubia's Shield? How did it come together?"

"It started with meeting my friends Max and Quinn at Game and Flame when we were playing *Pokémon GO*. Game and Flame is a gaming bar. You know, like a sports bar but this one is an e-sports bar."

She pointed her fork at him. "By the way, you should come out to a Game Night on Thursdays if you can. After all, almost everyone there is your target audience. You could probably even recruit a few gamers to be beta testers."

She was inviting him to come to her night out with her friends? The sudden warmth in his chest surprised him. "Would that be okay?"

"Of course. We can be low-key on your identity until you're comfortable with them. Mostly, if you love to game and you're not an ass, they'll welcome you."

He held up a hand. "I swear I won't be an ass."

She laughed. "I believe you. What was I saying? Oh yeah.

Quinn and Max and I became friends immediately, and when we started streaming our game play on Twitch, we organically gathered other Black female gamers. Aside from gaming online, members sometimes have local meets like we do at Game and Flame, and we meet up at cons so we can roam together. Any female gamers can hang with us at cons because we lessen the potential for harassment that way. Safety in numbers and all that."

Was it really that bad for female gamers? He wondered. Surely, convention organizers were guaranteeing the safety of their female guests. He was about to ask her when she waved her hand.

"That was two questions, Mr. Galanis," she teased him. "Don't think I didn't notice."

"You're right," he acknowledged, lifting his glass to toast her. "Obviously, I'm going to be fair and give you two questions back to back. Go ahead."

She sat forward. *Eyes bright, smiling, rubbing hands together. Eager.* He wondered what sort of question she'd ask.

"One thing you haven't told me about yet is the why behind the WeCAN certification. I heard your explanation about placing more seats at the table, but I also heard the passion in your voice about it, as if this is personal to you."

She'd noticed that, huh? He usually wasn't one to share personal things with anyone but Grayson outside of his immediate family. Yet he'd begun this by asking her a personal question. It was only fair to reciprocate.

"You're right, it is personal." He fiddled with his water bottle as he considered what to tell her, then froze, frowning. Why had he chosen water when the lemonade was right there?

"Is that too personal? Should I ask you something else?" She leaned forward. "These two questions don't count, by the way."

"No, it's not too personal. No, you don't have to ask something else. No, I won't count those questions."

He resolutely poured a glass of lemonade, deliberately ignoring the half-empty water bottle. "I told you that I developed my first game for my brother. He's also the reason why the WeCAN certification is my passion project. He's autistic, so I designed that game for his specific needs. Even after Artemis was formed and we created *Legendsfall* and other lucrative games, I never forgot my first game. While I have continued to personally develop games for Benjy and local centers, I still feel the need to do more for him and others who are neurodivergent. The WeCAN certification will give Artemis international recognition and allow me to move my agenda forward."

"Wow." She blinked, then reached out to cover his hand again. This time he turned his wrist until their hands clasped. "Wow, Aron, that drive, that passion—I can now see why you were so quick and thorough to fix the *Legendsfall* issue. You're amazing."

Discomfort slid through him. He didn't feel that he deserved that praise. Not yet. "Thank you for saying that, but I know there's still more to be done."

She gave his hand a squeeze, then let go with a wide, excited grin. "Good thing you have me."

Another sweep of discomfort blew through him. Not because her words made him uncomfortable. His reaction to those words did—a strange combination of happiness, pleasure, and hope.

Not knowing what his reaction meant, he decided to file it away to examine later, after she left. One thing he did know: if he continued to have strange emotional reactions during their conversations, working with Samara was going to be a very interesting experience.

Chapter 13

"Spill. How's it going?"

Thursday night meant Game Night at one of Samara's favorite places: Game and Flame. The bar and gaming hall boasted a long list of beer, wine, and spirits and an extensive menu, including the best flame-grilled burgers in the city, aside from her father's. It also had an impressive array of pool tables, darts, pinball machines, and even some cornhole games on the outdoor patio. But what Sam and her friends gathered for was the array of monitors and peripherals set up for online gaming.

Lately, though, Game Night might as well have been renamed to Weekly Work Update, and she was already over it. "How long are y'all going to keep this up? It's been three weeks already."

"It doesn't matter how long it's been," Max told her. "We still want to know what's going on with you and *Aron*."

"I don't know what you mean about what's going on, but thanks to the nondisclosure agreement, there's nothing I can tell you about the project, just that we're working hard to get it done."

Working with Aron meant working at a breakneck pace and using all her brain cells at maximum. She had to use her brain cells for gaming, but battling her way out of a level was far less stressful than brainstorming with the CEO of Artemis Games. Still, she enjoyed the process of working with him, enjoyed being stimulated and kept on her toes by all his plans and the information he wanted to make come to fruition. It was one of the best projects she'd ever worked on, and he was clearly the most fascinating client.

"Girl, you know we don't want the details of the project," Max scolded. "We want to know how you and Aron are getting along."

"Working with Aron has been pretty good so far," Sam told them. "I get to his house about eight and we start the day by playing one of the games the fired developer worked on, looking for any other issues. There are some other projects we're working on that I can't talk to y'all about, but he knows his stuff—I mean, of course he knows it, he's head of a gaming company—and he also has a brilliant mind. It's just awesome and awe-inspiring to watch his mind work, pushing me to do and think and perform better. The way he brainstorms and challenges and creates an entire process almost on the fly to determine if an idea not only has merit but if it's feasible enough to deploy. In fact, he—"

"Hold up." Max held up her hand. "Did you just say that you're working at his house, like you thought you could just gloss that over like it's nothing?"

"Because it isn't a big deal." At least it wasn't any longer. It was surprising how quickly she'd gotten used to working from Aron's home office. "Everyone at Artemis telecommutes. From what he says, Aron only goes into the Perimeter office a couple of times a week. His home office is unbelievable. I wouldn't want to work anywhere else either."

"How long have you been working from his house?"

She hadn't told them that? Of course she hadn't, because she hadn't wanted to deal with the reaction she was now getting. "From the start."

"Seriously?" Max and Quinn leaned closer. "You know you better spill the tea on this. What does his house look like? I'm sure you got the whole tour, since you're working with Aron, alone in his house together."

"Not the whole tour." She heard their emphasis on his name and tried to skate around the bait by giving them a general overview of the parts of the house she'd seen. "And we're not there alone. His personal assistant, Grayson—you remember the guy who gave us the primo seats at their panel?—is always there, and a housekeeper comes in too. Everything's legit."

She shifted in her seat. "Besides, we're working closely together on this project. I have to work wherever he works. The deadline is hellacious for everything he wants to implement."

Quinn sighed. "You and Aron working so closely together. At his house. Long hours."

Sam slapped Quinn's arm. "Will you please stop saying his name like that? You're making more of it than there is!"

"Are we?"

"You are. We work well together, and it's an exciting project. That's all there is."

"Okay." Max held up her hands. "We get it. All there is, is this great working relationship, this synergistic thing going on."

"It's the truth," Sam insisted. "I'm enjoying the work so far, and it doesn't even feel like work. We're just getting started though. Everything's gonna ramp up even more soon."

"Work, work, work." Quinn shook her head. "That's all it ever is with you."

"What else is there supposed to be?" Sam wondered. "You guys have got to stop with your rampant imaginations."

"What's wrong with imagining? Especially with someone who looks like him, and has deep pockets like him? Who knows what could happen once your contract with him is over."

"Forgive me for not being as mercenary as you guys," Sam retorted, knowing that she had to put this to bed, especially with Quinn. "Do I have to remind you of how many eyes are on this project since Aron announced it at the convention? There's a lot of pressure to not only pull this off, but also make it successful. Second, there's a lot of pressure for me to make a significant contribution for my mom's company. I don't want to do anything to jeopardize her company's reputation. And finally, can you imagine the fallout if people found out Samara Reynolds is ReyofSun? That could damage Artemis and Rise. So not only is it important that we—I—stay as clean and professional as possible for the duration of the project, I can't even have my name attached to it."

She pushed back so that she could see them both. "Can you imagine the negative buzz if that got out and someone wrote an article about it? The scandal would cause forums everywhere to self-implode. Our streams have just now quieted down to the usual amount of crap. I'd like to keep it that way. Because if this got out, you know they would come for me and not Aron."

"Oh." Quinn sat back with a disappointed sigh. "I didn't think of that, and I should have."

"It's okay," Sam reassured her, giving Quinn's shoulder a bump with her fist. "Just kick all those fantasies out of your head, okay? Now, are we gonna game or not?"

Just as she settled in, Sam's phone chimed with an incoming text. It was from Aron. For a hot minute, she debated answering, but decided that Aron wouldn't contact her unless it was something important.

ARE YOU AT GAME AND FLAME?

Hmm, maybe he was considering whether to interrupt her Game Night. **YES, BUT I CAN HELP IF THERE'S SOMETHING YOU NEED.**

A pause, then, **I'M OUTSIDE.**

Sam shot to her feet, drawing her friends' collective attention. Max and Quinn rose. "What's going on?"

Sam held up her phone. "He's here."

"Who's he—" Max's eyes bugged. "*He's here?*"

"Way to go, guys. You talked him up." She shoved her phone in her back pocket. "I'm gonna go get him."

"Why?" Max asked. "He's a grown-ass man."

Sam made a calm-down motion with her hands. "Just treat him like a normal guy and not the Artemis CEO, all right? I'll be right back."

She quickly threaded her way through booths, bodies, and barstools until she made it to the door. It took her a moment to recognize the guy in the green hoodie and gold-rimmed glasses as Aron. She grinned. He was going to blend in well with the other patrons.

Smiling, she walked up to him. "Benjy?"

He startled, then smiled as he recognized her. "Rey. Thanks for coming out."

"No problem. I'm surprised you decided to come here."

He scrubbed a hand over his hair. "Curiosity got the better of me, and I'm always up for gaming."

The move combined with his bashful smile was too cute. She stopped herself. *You can't think of him like that. You're collaborating with him. He's NOT cute.* But there was something about Hoodie Guy mode that was endearing. From what she'd seen, Aron was more relaxed and open this way than when he had to be "on" in CEO mode. She was sure her friends would give him the space and grace to continue.

"Should I introduce you as Aron or Benjy?"

He appeared to think about it. "Aron is fine, just not the whole 'CEO of Artemis Games' thing."

"Okay. I'm not going to mention your career, but if anyone recognizes you, I'll tell them you want to keep a low profile. Happy hour's over, so it's not as crowded now as it was earlier, which is why we like to come on Thursdays. If it gets to be too much, we'll leave, okay?"

"Thanks."

Aron followed Samara into the gaming bar, appreciating her tactfulness. It hadn't really been an impulsive decision to go out, but Grayson would say that the ten minutes Aron had used to decide to visit was too hasty.

He couldn't help his curiosity. Once Samara had described Game and Flame, he became inclined to check it out. He wanted to see the gaming bar in action and hang out with fellow gamers on a smaller scale, but more than that, he wanted to see Samara in a nonworking environment.

She led him over to a cordoned-off section of the bar with a full multiplayer setup occupied by a diverse group of people who watched their approach with avid curiosity. "Everyone, I'd like to introduce a new friend to you. This is Aron."

He froze. Did she just introduce him as her new friend? He quickly gathered himself. How else could she introduce him? He lifted a hand in a wave. "Hi."

Staying close to him, she pointed out each friend separately. "Don't worry if you don't remember names; we're a big group. These two are Kenya and Cameron Lassiter, who got famous for being on a reality cosplay competition show. Even though they were runners-up, they're now making small props and specialty costumes for the *Anubis Rising* series that's shot here in Atlanta."

He dipped his head in greeting. Although he didn't have much time for television, their accomplishment sounded impressive to his ears. "Congratulations."

"You know Max and Quinn already," Samara continued, "and that's Janelle and beside her is Dev. They're both computer engineers. We have other friends that come and go, but this is our core group. And this person is the reason we have VIP seating every Thursday. This is Rashad Avery, and they own Game and Flame."

"I know who you are, and I'm surprised you're here with our ReyofSun." The bar owner came closer. "Still, she brought you, so . . . pleased to have you grace my not-so-humble establishment, A—"

"Aron's a fellow gamer," Samara smoothly cut in. "When I told him about your place, he wanted to come and meet everyone and maybe play a couple of matches."

"Ah." Understanding lit their eyes. "Any friend of Rey's is

welcomed here. What do you want to drink? Your first round's on me."

"Thank you, Mr. Avery. I'll take bottled water."

"Call me Rashad like everybody else. Only grandpops gets called Mr. Avery."

Aron did his best to commit each person's name to memory. They were Samara's friends, which meant they were important to her. Just like Samara, they were gaming fiends. Watching their play with growing admiration, he couldn't believe that none of them were or had been professionals. He decided to ask Samara about it as everyone packed up and headed for the entrance.

"Why isn't there a Nubia's Shield professional team?" he wondered. "All of you certainly have the talent to do that."

Sam waved as everyone but Quinn and Max left. "We've talked about it, but it's too much of a hassle in many ways."

"How so?"

"As of right now, there are two professional teams in Atlanta playing in different gaming leagues. They have awesome rosters and no one's leaving either of those teams anytime soon. I'm sure they have a deep bench, too. Besides, Nubia's Shield would want to be its own team, not separate players joining other groups."

She shrugged. "We'd need sponsorships to play professionally. The majority of us have well-paying careers we love, so there's not a lot of incentive to go pro. Besides, we get enough grief just playing for fun."

"You know what would be great?" Rashad stepped closer. "If a certain local gaming company established a *Legendsfall* League with monetary prizes that modeled college basketball championships, maybe some local groups could make a good showing and earn money at the same time."

"Rashad!" Sam protested.

They threw up their hands. "I'm just saying."

"They have a good idea," Aron said. It was better than a good idea. It was a great idea. "I'd bet Artemis would be willing to consider it after they fix their current opportunities. Don't you think so, Samara? Maybe you should talk to them."

"I . . . umm, maybe I should?" She spoke slowly, uncertain if he was joking or not. He wasn't.

"I'm serious," he insisted. "I heard you have an in with the management. You should definitely bring this up."

She gave him a hard stare, then nodded. "All right, I will."

"Good." He leaned forward a bit. "Did you drive? May I take you home?"

"Oh. Umm, well . . ." She used her thumb to gesture over her shoulder. "I came here with Max and Quinn."

"Of course." There was no opportunity to spend more time with her, but there was an opportunity to take her hand. "Thank you for inviting me here. I enjoyed it."

"I'm glad you did." She gave him a genuine smile as she shook his hand. "You should come back anytime you want. I'll make sure no one tags Hoodie Guy as that CEO dude if they take pictures."

"I appreciate that." He reluctantly released her hand. "See you tomorrow."

"See you."

Sam felt her friends approach her as she watched Aron head to his car. *Three, two, one.*

"Just work, my ass."

She turned to face them. "I'm as surprised as you are, Max.

He's not a people person. It took a lot for him to come here. He must have really been interested in seeing Game and Flame."

"Sure." Quinn nodded. "Sure it was the bar and not a specific person in the bar."

Sometimes Quinn's sweet sarcasm hit harder than Max's did. Unfortunately, Samara didn't have a good retort at the ready. She'd been too surprised by Aron's arrival to fully question him. Did his statement about curiosity getting the better of him mean Game and Flame or her or both? What would she do if he meant her?

Chapter 14

Several days later, thoughts of Game Night still lingered in Samara's mind like those clingy white shipping pellets she couldn't shake loose. Her relationship with Aron Galanis was strictly professional. Outside of their gaming time, there were few moments in the workday in which he wasn't in full CEO mode managing the company's operations. She'd learned early that while Grayson was his personal assistant, a woman named Janet was his administrative assistant. He had two phones. Janet called him on one and apparently forwarded business calls to that line. The other phone was his private line, the one that stored her number. It didn't ring often, but when it did, he always left the room to answer it.

She'd thought there was a distinct line between business and personal, a line he held firm to. Which was fine with her. The work was too important to jeopardize with anything personal. In fact, before Game Night, the only time he wasn't formal and aloof was when they were gaming, eating, and brainstorming. In those moments he seemed more free, more warm, more attractive.

No, not attractive. That wasn't the right word, was it? Attractive wasn't one of the words she should use to describe her client. Not that he wasn't. He was a very good-looking man, and when he wore his glasses or got that light in his eyes . . .

Gurl, get a grip on yourself. Maybe she was working too hard. As she'd predicted to her friends, the workload on all three projects had increased significantly. Her workdays were longer, and lately she'd continuously outstayed Grayson, as she had today due to some prior engagement he had. His absence had left her and Aron at their respective devices, working silently and furiously.

Sam rubbed her forehead, trying and failing to massage her light-headedness and fatigue away. Maybe it was time to invest in some blue-tinted glasses to help with screen glare. Maybe she should have gone home two hours ago. They were at a critical point in character development, and they needed to wrap that up so that they could present them to the design and development teams next week. And she still needed to review her citations for the certification project. Then there was . . . something else.

"Samara."

She looked up to see Aron staring at her across the desk. "Yes?"

His brows scrunched in concern. "Are you all right?"

"I'm okay. I think I need a break, though." Deciding to get some air, she pushed back from the desk, then rose to her feet. The room wobbled, her head spun, and the edges of her vision grayed. Heart pounding, she flailed for the chair, trying to make it to the seat before her legs gave out. She failed, and knew she was going to miss the chair and hit the floor but couldn't call for Aron to help her.

"Samara!" Strong arms caught her as she dropped, stopping her fall. Those same arms half carried, half dragged her, depositing her on the couch. "This is not you being okay. Should I take you to the hospital or call 911?"

She blinked open her eyes to discover Aron hovering over her, his face filled with worry. "No, not 911," she managed to say, rubbing her forehead again. "Can you bring me my bag?"

He rushed over to the desk, grabbed her bag, then rushed back, setting the bag beside her. After helping her sit up, he sat on the edge of the coffee table. "What else can I do?"

Her hands shook despite her effort to steady them, giving her a good clue as to her problem. "I need to check my blood sugar. I'm pretty sure it's in the basement."

She fumbled into her purse, finally pulling out her glucose monitoring kit. He took it from her. "Your hands are shaking too much. Tell me what to do."

"Can you open an alcohol wipe? Run it over this finger, then your hands so you can pick out a test strip."

He did as instructed, loading a lancet into the lancing device, then carefully removing a test strip from its container to insert into the meter. She tried to hold her finger up for him to lance, but her trembling hands made that difficult.

Warm fingers wrapped around hers, gently pulling her hand down until it rested on his knee, holding it steady. She shook again, a reaction that had nothing to do with low blood sugar.

"I've got you," he said softly. "I'll prick you on three. One, two."

He lanced her finger before he counted to three, taking her by surprise and giving her no time to prepare. A wasted effort since she was distracted by him holding her hand. This time a tremor went through his fingers as he picked up the monitor and touched the strip to the dot of blood. "What should it say?"

"I'll take anything 80 and above."

He frowned, then turned the meter to her. "It says 68."

Crap. This was so not a good look to have with her client. "Okay, giving you permission to go into my purse again. Look for a container of glucose tablets."

"Okay." He rummaged through her bag, then held up a slender container. "It's empty."

Dammit. This couldn't get worse, could it? She tilted her head against the back of the couch, then closed her eyes to calibrate her brain and dispel the dizziness. "Do you still have any lemonade or juice? Orange or apple juice would be best. I need a sugar hit."

"Juice it is." He stood, then surprised her by lifting her legs so she lay on the couch. "I'll be right back."

Aron raced to the kitchen, adrenaline flooding his veins. Yanking open the refrigerator, he fumbled through the assortment of drinks until he found a carafe of orange juice. He quickly grabbed a glass from the cabinet, then made his way back to his office, only to pause outside the door.

Sam's condition was his fault. They had a brutal timeline, and while he took on the bulk of the work like the control freak he was, Samara was doing her fair share of the heavy lifting too. But just because he had a usual regimen of long work hours, short sleep cycles, and forgetting to eat didn't mean he should impose them on Samara. It would have been easy to say he'd forgotten because Grayson wasn't there, but he should have at least set a timer on his phone to remind her to eat something. Grayson would kick his ass once he found out.

He entered his office. Samara was still stretched out on the couch, one arm over her eyes. He mentally kicked himself again. So much for his powers of observation. How had he not noticed that she wasn't feeling well?

He placed the glass of juice on the coffee table, then sat beside her. "I'm sorry."

Sam tried to sit up, but he was able to push her back down with one hand on her shoulder. She frowned up at him. "Why are you apologizing?"

"I'm a bad host and a worse boss." He shook his head. "My schedule is normal for me but brutal for everyone else. I should have noticed the effect on you, and I didn't. I should have noticed you testing your blood sugar and made allowances for that."

"I'm a grown woman. I can handle myself." She gave a weak laugh. "Besides, you would have had to follow me to the bathroom to see me testing myself."

He didn't think the situation was funny as he slowly helped her upright. Her hands still shook, so he held the glass for her to drink. He needed to add straws to the grocery list. "Are you sure you don't need to go to the hospital or an urgent care? It happened during work, so of course I'll pay for it."

She waved a hand. "It's not your fault. I have type 2 diabetes, which is managed by medication. If I had checked my glucose earlier, I wouldn't be in this predicament now."

He would definitely put a couple of reminders into his personal phone. "Should I put this away or do you need it again?"

"Don't worry about throwing it out. Even when I test in the powder room, I take everything with me when I leave. I have a little baggie that I put all the used things in and dispose of it when I get home. I'll test again in a little bit. Soon as I get a reading in the good range, I'll clean all of this up, so don't worry."

"I'm not worried about this stuff. I'm worried about you." He leaned over her. "What else can I do for you? Are you hot, cold, still dizzy? What do you need from me?"

"The juice was enough. Give me a few minutes, and I'll test my blood sugar again. I'm sure I'll be fine in a bit."

"Okay." He grabbed the throw off the back of the couch, then spread it over her. "Drink more juice, take a rest, then retest when you're ready."

"I don't need—"

"You're on an official break," he ordered. "You don't want me to get in trouble with the Department of Labor, do you?"

He was rewarded with a slight smile. "No, sir. But I feel compelled to point out that I'm your consultant and you're my client. There's no boss-employee thing going on here. We're collaborators. Project partners."

"That's better." Deciding that she wouldn't rest if he hovered over her, Aron made his way back to the desk. Instead of reviewing the character backstory list, he reviewed his reaction to Sam.

Partners. He liked the sound of that. And it fit, really. They worked well together, and they also had a lot of the same work habits, being so focused that they lost track of time.

He'd been concerned when she'd been unsteady on her feet, but it wasn't until he caught her to prevent her from falling that alarm had swept through him. A real, visceral scare. He had to repeat to himself that she'd probably gone through moments like this before throughout her life, repeat to himself that she knew her body better than he could.

Her body. In those scant moments in which he'd carried her over to the couch, the imprint of her had branded his arms. And when she'd leaned against him to drink the juice. Even now he could feel her.

He rubbed his hands together, a slow movement. Normally, he didn't like touching others. Yet when she'd wobbled, he'd automatically reached for her. There had been other times, too, when he'd taken her hand without thinking. Somewhere during their brief association, Samara had transitioned from a professional acquaintance to something else, something he didn't know how to categorize. Someone whose contact information went into his personal phone. Then he realized with a start that she'd always been a personal contact from the moment they'd met.

There weren't many people who had his personal phone number. Only family and a few people he could call friends.

And he'd added Samara to that list. She was now someone he had more than a passing interest in. She was now one of his people, his inner circle. Not family, but more than a project partner. Friends. He considered her a friend now. And friends took care of friends.

Fifteen minutes later, he heard her stir and immediately crossed over to the couch. She didn't look as shaky as she had before as she pushed the blanket away to sit upright. "Is it time to check your levels again?"

She smoothed her braids back, then nodded. "Yeah."

"Do you want help, or should I leave you to it?"

"I can do it, but I appreciate you asking."

He backed off enough to not hover, but stayed close enough to help if she needed. "My numbers are much better," she told him, then began to gather her supplies back into her tote.

He resisted the urge to help her, knowing she could handle it and probably wouldn't appreciate his assistance. Still, he had to ask, "How are you feeling?"

"Embarrassed, which is another sign that levels have gotten into the normal range," she said ruefully. "That also means it's time to stick a fork in work tonight so I can head home and crash."

"All right. Let me get my wallet and keys." He crossed to his desk.

"You don't have to do that," she protested. "I can get myself home."

"The hell I don't," he retorted, surprising them both. Outbursts and curse words were not his usual reactions, but again, nothing was usual when he was around Samara. "You were dazed, shaking, and almost hit the floor when you stood up. Do you really think I'll let you drive like this, especially as late as it is?"

"I'm better now, though," she pointed out.

"Better, but not a hundred percent," he retorted. "And you still haven't eaten anything. So you've got two choices: you either allow me to take you home, or you sleep in one of the guest rooms upstairs."

Silence. She looked at him, and he wondered if his expression mirrored her shocked one.

"Did you just ask me to spend the night?" she asked.

"Well . . ." He hadn't, had he? "Perhaps you could consider it a suggestion instead of a request. I also gave you two options, but I'll add a third, a rideshare. I can order a car to pick you up tonight and bring you back tomorrow."

"You don't have to do that," she said again.

"I know I don't have to. I want to." Again, surprising them

both. Obviously, he needed food too. And more than four hours of sleep. He cleared his throat. "Which option do you choose?"

She looked down. "Do you mind taking me home? I know it's late, but it's not that far."

Did she avert her eyes out of embarrassment over the entire situation or because she hated to ask? "I'll be happy to. Shall I pack up your things too?"

"You've been through my bag. You might as well." She leaned forward, head hanging down. "This is so embarrassing."

"This isn't embarrassing." He tried for a joke to distract and reassure her. "Loudly farting in the middle of a board meeting? Now that's embarrassing."

Choked laughter filled the room. "You didn't!"

"I can neither confirm nor deny which board member dealt it, just that we all smelled it. Grayson won't confirm or deny either, so don't bother asking him."

Her smile was a reward he was glad to gain. "I won't. How about this? You never mention my embarrassing incident, and I never mention the alleged board incident. Deal?"

"Deal."

He added one more thing to the never-mention list. He wouldn't mention that their relationship had evolved into something new, something he wanted to examine more.

Chapter 15

"Can I ask you a question?"

Aron glanced up from his keyboard, removing his glasses to look at her. "Of course you can."

Sam dropped her gaze to her planner. Ever since the Low Blood Sugar Incident, the atmosphere between them was different, as if embarrassment had sanded down the client-consultant divide into something else, something warmer.

The weekend after her low-sugar event, he'd installed a medicine cabinet in the powder room complete with extra alcohol swabs, glucose tablets, and little blue glass bottles for her to use for disposal. He'd also changed up the office snacks by adding in some healthy, low-carb options, and set alarms on his phone for breaks. All those changes without being asked, without showing off, without wanting thanks, but doing them out of concern for her.

This level of attentiveness was . . . nice. His surprising thoughtfulness touched her, and over the course of the time she'd worked with him, she'd discovered that this was his default setting, and not the cold, formal version she'd seen in the con boardroom. Matter of fact, she only heard that stiffness when he was on a phone or video call about business.

That attentive thoughtfulness gave her the impetus to make her request. "There's an event for an organization called Girl Code, which provides outreach and training programs for middle and high school girls in STEM in general and coding in particular. The event is a combination fundraiser and awards ceremony. Would you like to go with me?"

Silence. Sam looked up to find Aron staring at her with a blank expression as if he was processing the meaning behind her words.

Finally, he blinked. "Go . . . with you?"

"Not go with me, go with me, like a date or anything. You could come with Grayson. I mean, I'm not a PR person, but I think it would look good if Artemis Games had representation there or made a donation. Of course, someone in your company may have already made a donation. Not that I'm trying to pressure you into donating, but—"

"Samara." He reached over to grip her hand. The surprise touch instantly stopped her babbling. "When is it?"

"Next Wednesday at eight p.m. at the Fernbank Museum." She twisted her lips. "That's probably too short notice, but—"

"Is it black tie?"

"No. People will probably be in business attire to cocktail dress. I'll be in professional mode, so a dress and heels for me."

"Okay."

"Okay?" she parroted.

"Okay." He emphasized his answer with a bob of his head.

"Are you sure?" she pressed. "There will be a lot of mixing and mingling going on beforehand since some of the participants have the opportunity to showcase projects they've been working on, but then we'll go into an auditorium where there will be a couple of guest speakers and then awards given out."

He tilted his head, studying her in that focused way that he had that fluttered her belly with excitement and apprehension. "Are you trying to dissuade me now that you've asked me to go?"

"No, I really want you to go, but I just remembered that you don't like crowds. I don't know what your limit is, but there will be at least a hundred or so people there, maybe more."

"Thank you for the warning." He looked down, and she realized their hands were still entwined. She quickly drew back. He frowned as if unhappy, then continued. "It's an event centered around coding and raising money. I'm proficient at both."

"I believe you." She relaxed. "Thank you."

Again, the long, assessing stare. "This must be an important organization for you."

"It is." She reached for her lemonade, needing to do something with her hands. "You know that Max, Quinn, and I are gamers, and we have other local friends who are too. A couple of them are computer engineers, and they have issues just like us gamers. People think Black women in tech don't exist, so they don't bother looking for them either. Or they assume people like my friends are unicorns—that just because there's one, there's no reason to look for another."

He made a face. "That's . . . There's really nothing I can say about that, since I have exactly zero female coders in my company. I don't even know if any have ever applied."

"I'm not going to hold yesterday against you. But this is part of why Girl Code is so important. They draw in a wide swath of girls interested in tech careers. They offer programs and courses to teach young girls how to code. Their work is important."

"I believe you." The warmth in his smile and his gaze spread through her like a tequila shot. "And I'll be—"

Grayson chose that moment to walk into the room. "Boss, Janet had a courier deliver those documents you needed. Once you sign them, I'll send them back."

"Of course." Aron sat back, retreating behind his glasses, and Sam wondered if he felt the same sudden awkwardness she did, as if they'd been caught doing something improper. As Aron's personal assistant, Grayson seemed at times to be his boss's shadow, always present. Lately, however, he seemed to have more business outside the office than in, leaving Sam to wonder if it was a circumstantial or intentional act, and if the latter, which one of the men was the instigator.

Aron took the envelope. "By the way, Samara has invited us to an event next Wednesday evening. I think we should go."

"Really?" Grayson looked to Aron, who gave him a nod, then he turned to Samara. "What kind of event?"

"It's for an organization called Girl Code, a nonprofit for girls wanting tech careers. It's going to be held at the Fernbank Museum."

Grayson pulled out his phone. "What sort of event is it?"

"It's a combination fundraising event and showcase," she answered. "Buying tickets is the fundraising part. Girls from around the city will have a chance to showcase their projects."

"Okay." Grayson made notes in his phone. At least that's what she assumed he was doing. Was he going to review and verify everything she'd said? Was he looking for a way for Aron to gracefully decline? "How many people are expected?"

Confusion curled through her. "Are all of these questions necessary? I don't know more than what I've already told

Aron, but I might be able to put you in touch with one of the organizers if it's that important."

"Ah, I'm sorry." A guilty flush suffused Grayson's cheeks as he darted a glance at Aron. "I was just—"

"He's doing it for me," Aron interrupted. "I prefer to know as much about an event and location as I can before agreeing to attend."

Certain she was missing something, she looked from one man to the other. "You scope out a place before you even decide to go? Are you afraid of being jumped or kidnapped for ransom? Ah, it's so you can figure out if you need extra bodyguards or something?"

She pointed to Grayson. "Isn't he your bodyguard masquerading as your assistant? He should be all you need, unless you're afraid of a bunch of middle-school girls peppering you with questions."

She expected them to laugh, but Aron didn't. "That sounds terrifying, actually."

The seriousness of his tone leached the humor out of hers. "So a group of girls peppering you with tech questions is worse than walking through a crowd of gamers?" A surprising twinge of hurt hit her. "What's the difference for you?"

"Samara." Aron stood enough to lean across the table and capture her hand. Why she didn't pull away, she didn't know. It probably had something to do with the earnestness of his expression. "Grayson's just doing his job, and it had nothing to do with gender. And it was you who worried about crowding me a few moments ago."

Geesh, she had done that. Sheepish, she slowly settled deeper into her chair, watching as Aron returned to his. "I apologize. I'm admittedly sensitive about things like this, and the last few years have made me more defensive. That's not an excuse, though, and I'm sorry for thinking the worst of you."

His grip on her hand loosened but didn't release. "I have my . . . quirks. If you try to understand me, I promise to try to understand you."

Well hell. All of her hurt and pique faded, and she squeezed his hand. "I thought one of your quirks was not liking to touch people."

"I like touching you."

I like touching you.

His blunt words careened through her skull as if playing a sped-up version of old-school *Pong*. She floundered and flailed, fighting to find something to say or do to keep her thoughts from flying in a direction they had no business going.

• • •

Aron couldn't understand why Samara gaped at him. Grayson coughed, causing Aron to immediately drop Samara's hand. He looked to his assistant. *What?*

The other man touched his lower lip. He'd said the wrong thing, then. "Ah. I'm sorry. I probably shouldn't have said that I like touching you. It could be misconstrued as harassment, or me conflating you with a pet—which I suppose could also be considered a form of harassment too, neither of which I was intending. I should have said that I like holding your hand"—Grayson ran the flat of his hand across his throat—"and I probably should have stopped talking several sentences ago."

"Probably."

Her even tone and neutral expression gave him no indication of what she thought of his bumbling admission. Why had he rambled on like that? He hadn't overexplained himself in years. And he was sure Grayson was already mentally creating a debrief after Samara left for the day. "See? Quirks."

"Run-on sentences and discomfort with crowds are your quirks, which poor Grayson tried to steer you away from." She didn't smile but she didn't frown either. He'd take neutral, especially when she added, "I'm not offended. But quirky doesn't feel like the right word to describe you."

He braced himself. "What word would you use?"

"You've got money. That makes you eccentric."

Was she teasing him? He could handle that from her. Tension lifted away. "I approved your contract, remember? If they're all like that, you're on your way to eccentric, too."

"Touché." She made a few taps on her tablet. "I don't want to keep Grayson from doing his job, so here's the website information, which also has photos from previous years. That should help you determine whether it's safe for you to attend or not. If you get there and decide that it's not your thing, feel free to bail. I won't tell anyone that you're coming, so it'll be easier for you to leave."

Her tone changed, throwing him off again. "Do you not want me to go?"

"I want you to do whatever makes you feel comfortable. If the thought of going to the Girl Code event makes you uncomfortable, of course you shouldn't go."

He studied her posture, parsed her tone. There was a hard edge to both, but he didn't know if it was because of the event talk or the touching her talk. Either way was because of him, so he had to make it right.

"It's a professional event. Any discomfort should be

minimal if I can limit small talk." He mentally winced at the formal words, forcing himself back to causal. "What do you think?"

She gave him a clearly assessing look. "Honestly?"

"Always."

"I think you should go," she told him. "I think it would be good for both you and Artemis Games. The price of the tickets is a donation, but if you go there as Aron Galanis, CEO of Artemis Games, it will underscore your commitment to diversity not only in your games, but also in a future workforce. Even if you don't attend in an official capacity, I believe it will be worth it for you to see what this organization is doing for marginalized girls who want tech careers."

"Then it's settled. We'll be there."

And hopefully able to keep his eccentricities to himself.

"Good." He stood when she rose to her feet again and reached for the small pouch that contained her testing kit. "I'll be right back."

He waited a few moments after she left before slumping back into his chair. "I suppose that could have gone better."

Grayson, used to debriefing Aron's social interactions, shook his head. "You said you like touching her. You said that with your outside voice, as blunt and plain as saying grass is green."

"Not my best moment," he admitted. "I did try to say it differently."

"Maybe you shouldn't have said it at all," Grayson suggested.

His bluntly truthful way of speaking was part of the reason he hated receptions and mixers. His response to "Nice weather we're having" was usually something along the lines of, "Not for those with seasonal allergies." Or the time the president of the chamber of commerce had suggested a golf outing to talk business and he'd replied with the fact that he didn't play golf and had no desire to start. He met personal questions with even more brusqueness because the people he discussed personal matters with could be counted on one hand with digits left over.

"She said I didn't like touching people. I wanted to correct her misstatement."

"She certainly knows it now."

He rewound his mental tape of the past several minutes, reviewing everything he'd said and how he'd said it, Samara's words, tone, and body language, leading up to the moment she left the room. "Do you think I upset her?"

"You can't tell?"

Aron shook his head. "She's very neutral. In fact, she reacted stronger about me attending the event. Maybe my clarification helped."

"Your clarification was to admit that you like holding her hand." An incredulous look crossed Grayson's face. "You don't like shaking hands with random people, much less holding one."

True. Not just because of germs, oil, and sweat and having no idea what that person had been doing with their hands; he didn't want to make that kind of connection with random people, even those he did business with.

"Samara isn't a random person." There was nothing random about how he'd learned of her, how they met, how they ended up working together. "I don't want her to be a random person."

"That's a given." Grayson glanced at the doorway before

leaning closer. "The speed with which you went from adversaries to collaborators is astonishing, especially for you."

"It's a connection. We clicked immediately."

"That's possible," Grayson conceded, "or are you just fixating on her?"

It was a question that needed to be asked. His tendency to fixate worked best when it came to problem-solving or developing, but it could quickly become a detriment if he spiraled too far and ignored everything else. He'd never fixated on a person before, though.

"I don't know yet," he finally answered, "and I'm not sure I can explain this properly. I like talking with her. I like working with her. I like gaming with her. And I like holding her hand. She's a good person. I like good people. She's either a puzzle I need to solve or a friend I'd like to have. Or both. I'll know for sure by the time the contract ends."

Chapter 16

"What is going on with you?"

Sam glanced at Max. "What do you mean? Nothing's going on."

"Right. Not only are you tapping that red-bottom stiletto like you want to dig a hole into this floor, but you're actually wearing a watch and you keep glancing at it every fifteen seconds."

Holding her wrist out to Max, she surreptitiously glanced at the dial again. Only five minutes had passed since she'd last looked. "It's jewelry and it matches my dress."

She'd chosen to wear a formfitting orange, white, and navy African print dress from one of her favorite online shops. Looking at the gold watch strapped to her wrist was less obvious than lighting up her phone screen instead of talking to Max and other guests who passed by them on Dinosaur Plaza on their way into the Fernbank Museum's great hall to look at the Girl Code exhibits.

"But you're keeping track of time, and I don't think you're counting down the seconds until the showcase starts," Max observed. "Does that mean we're waiting for your CEO boyfriend to show up?"

"He said he would show up and he doesn't lie, so—" She bit off her words as her brain finally registered Max's question. She cut her eyes at her friend. "Most importantly for the record, Aron is not my boyfriend. I expect that sort of thing from Quinn the Queen of Shipping, but not from you."

"Aren't our other nicknames Mischief and Mayhem?" Max laughed. "Quinn gave me explicit orders to tease you about him if there was a chance. Looks like there's a chance. I can't believe you invited him to this."

"Why wouldn't I invite him to this?"

Max gestured around the plaza teeming with people drinking and networking. The plaza, with its dinosaur display in the center, had been transformed into an open-air cocktail reception with several drink stations and cocktail tables scattered throughout. A light breeze filtered through the twilight spring air, making it a perfect night for the event. "Is this his usual type of thing? This isn't a con."

"I'm aware." Which was part of the reason she'd invited him. Aside from his only appearance at Game Night, she hadn't seen him outside of a con or work, and while this event could be considered work, it was more social.

"And he still plans to attend?"

"He said he would. That's all I know."

Max folded her arms. "Of course, this event gives him great PR brownie points, doesn't it? He'd be stupid not to come given his company's issues, and I don't believe the man is stupid."

"Aron's not like that. In fact, no one except for you and me knows that the Artemis Games CEO might show up."

"Then why?"

It was a valid question, and she gave Max all the reasonable answers she'd given Aron when asking him to attend. But a larger part of her wanted to see him in a different environment, literally. She'd been working with him for weeks, and they had fallen into a comfortable rhythm, moving seamlessly from colleagues to friends. But now, thanks to four simple words, her view of him had completely changed.

I like touching you.

Her gut clenched, just like it did every time she remembered those words and the blunt manner in which he'd said them. For the past week, an undercurrent had flowed between them even as they focused on work, making it more difficult to relegate him to client or friend status. Despite her intentions, her brain kept those four words on repeat with a down and dirty beat, and her imagination was working overtime drumming up scenarios that had nothing to do with character designs or accessibility standards and everything to do with different ways a desk could be used besides working.

"Sam?"

She blew out an exasperated breath. "He's coming because I asked him to."

"Really?" Max gave her epic side-eye. "Maybe the brownie points he wants to earn are with you."

A retort died on her lips the moment she made the attempt. Max was possibly right, even if only a little bit. Aron had said yes because she'd asked him to, because she'd be attending. She knew the event was out of his comfort zone, but he'd taken a huge step for her.

Sending him a selfie wearing this dress had been as much enticement as it was to help him identify her among the guests. She'd take a step too, because while he liked touching her, she liked touching him too.

"Sam."

The urgency in Max's voice snapped her out of her thoughts. "What is it?"

"Look to the left. Your CEO boyfriend's here."

"For the last time, he's not my . . ."

The words stuck in her throat, trapped by a sudden constriction. Like a scene from a movie or TV show, time slowed as Aron and Grayson rounded the dinosaur installation and headed toward them. Aron wore a black suit that had to be custom, it fit him so well. He wore his glasses, his hair falling in loose waves around his face, a scruffy beard shadowing his jawline, and hot damn, that look did it for her. Then he shoved one hand through his hair, combing it back from his face, and her brain short-circuited.

She really wanted to touch him then.

"Well damn," Max whispered. "Put the man in a suit and he becomes a thirst trap."

"Yeah." He was a total Man Crush Monday, Thirst Trap Thursday, Super Sexy Saturday, and every other day in the week. Aron Galanis was no longer categorized as a client, no longer a colleague in her mind. No, he'd definitely been upvoted to *man*.

"Your man too," Max clarified, "but I'm talking about the other one."

"Whaaaat?" Max's statement broke Sam's focus on Aron. She looked at Grayson, noted his tailored gray suit with black dress shirt, no tie, swept-back dark hair, then looked back at Max. The expression her friend wore was at once admiring and interested.

Before she could parse that, the men reached them. Aron stopped in front of her, his gaze sweeping her from head to toe. "Samara."

This close, the power of the suit was superhero strong. "Ah, Aron. You made it." She winced. *Way to state the obvious. Gather yourself, girl.*

He nodded, staring at her as if they were the only people in the reception area. "I promised."

"So you did." Her fingers itched with the urge to straighten his already straight tie, smooth his lapel, brush his hair back from his eyes, and *oh my god*, when did she start thinking of him that way?

Grayson cleared his throat, interrupting her thoughts and reminding her of where she was and what she should be doing. "You didn't get a chance to be formally introduced, but this is my friend Maxima Cargill. Max, this is Grayson."

Max stuck out her hand to Grayson. "Nerdy you is cute, but you're really working that suit, Mr. Bodyguard."

"Max!" Sam elbowed her friend.

"What? You're thinking the same thing about your gamer guy."

"I-I . . ." Sam broke off, unable to come up with a retort that didn't include another, sharper elbow to Max's ribs. She looked skyward to gather her calm and rein in her wayward thoughts. Looking back down, she found Aron staring at her in what was certainly not a professional way. Then he gave her a slow, shy, secretive, sexy, and sweet smile that was the equivalent of being ambushed by a fire viper in *Legendsfall*.

Luckily, Grayson came to the rescue, taking Max's hand, a huge smile wreathing his face. "Grayson Lee. It's a pleasure to officially meet you, Maxima Cargill. If your name is any indication, you must be the greatest."

Max laughed. "It's why my parents gave me the name, so I'd always remember to be great at whatever I do." She gave him an assessing look. "So you've got brains to go with that brawn."

"I'd like to think so. By the way, I'm not a bodyguard, but I do practice Muay Thai in my spare time."

"Really?" Max's expression lit up. "I do kickboxing for fitness, but I've been thinking about taking Muay Thai training."

"My gym offers beginner classes. I can give you more information if you're interested."

Sam's mouth dropped open as Max placed a hand on Grayson's arm with a flirtatious grin. "I'm definitely interested."

Oh no. "Can you guys excuse us for a moment? Thanks."

Smiling through clenched teeth, Sam grabbed Max's arm and dragged her a little distance away from the men. "What the hell do you think you're doing?"

"Colluding with the enemy," Max whispered back, then winked. "Or is it canoodling with the enemy? Either way, I'm going to pump Grayson for information on your guy."

Anticipation laced every word Max spoke, causing anxiety to spike Sam's gut. She needed to head this off, and fast. "For one thing, they are not the enemy. For another, are you sure information is all you wanna pump Grayson for?"

Max's smile widened. "Well, if all goes well, we'll be working out together, you know, pumping . . . iron and stuff like that."

"Okay." Sam shook her head with a sigh. "You're grown, and we're not related, so it's not like I can stop you doing what you're gonna do. Just . . . don't do this to get information out of Grayson. One, he's smart enough to figure that out, and two, what can he tell you that I can't discover from working with Aron in his house for the past several weeks? If I want to know something, I can ask him without playing a spy game."

"Okay, okay, I got it." Max leaned in. "Can I go back to having fun now?"

Sam made a shooing gesture with her hands. "Go. Go."

Max sashayed back to Grayson, linking her arm with his. "Where were we? Oh right—I have a ton of questions to ask you about Muay Thai."

"Hopefully, I can answer them," Grayson said with a laugh. "Can I buy you a drink while we talk?"

"You certainly can."

They walked away arm in arm, leaving Sam gaping after them. She turned to Aron, who looked as bewildered as she felt. He motioned after them. "What just happened?"

She shrugged. "I'm not sure, but I think they just instantly hit it off?"

"But they met at the con, didn't they?"

Sam shook her head, hoping the gesture would evict her from whatever parallel universe she'd been sucked into. "Maybe because we all had an agenda then that we were focused on, but now since we're not so antagonistic, they were able to notice each other this time?"

He nodded slowly as if processing the information. "I have to admit I'm very curious and want to follow them and see what happens, but what was it you said? They're grown, and we can't stop them doing what they want to do."

Oh god, he'd heard all that? Which meant Grayson had heard it too. Her face flamed. Where was a good portal to another map when you needed one? "Oh, umm, well . . ."

He leaned closer to her. "Like you said, there's no need to play spy versus spy. Ask me anything and I'll reciprocate. I've learned about professional you and gamer you, and I've seen peeks of private you. I look forward to learning more."

He smiled, and holy hot key, that smile combined with those glasses and that stubble along his jawline drove all professional thoughts out of her head. Yes, she had to be out of her mind to think the things she thought at that moment.

She pulled her mind out of the gutter with effort, then reached for his arm. "Next time, I'll move farther away when having girl talk. Why don't we go inside and I'll show you some of the projects being showcased tonight?"

He tensed, causing her to immediately drop her hold. She inwardly winced. "Sorry about that."

"Don't apologize." He deliberately took her hand and placed it on his bicep. "I like it when you touch me too."

A flash of heat burned up her throat to her face and ears. Well, damn. This man was lethal without even trying. She couldn't imagine what the effect on her would be if he actually tried to game her.

Chapter 17

"Still terrified?"

Aron pointed upward. "Of the gigantic skeleton towering above us, maybe. But these kids and their presentations? No."

"See? I told you they were harmless."

"If by harmless you mean not yet ready to do business with me head-to-head, okay. I need to start planning for the competition now."

"More than a few of them already have apps out there," she told him. "You might already be behind. Aren't you glad you came?"

"That raised eyebrow and that smile tell me that you're being snarky, and I deserve it." He leaned toward her. "But yes, I'm glad I came."

He looked around the main hall. A few people still lingered, staring at the massive dinosaur that dominated the area. The glass ceiling allowed moonlight to cascade in like a waterfall of light, outshining the man-made illumination and giving everything a magical, otherworldly feel that would be great inspiration for a *Legendsfall* map.

"Breathtaking, isn't it?" she asked softly, her head tilted back, staring skyward, her expression one of obvious joy.

Some of the white portions of her patterned dress glowed in the moonlight, making her look as magical as everything around them.

"Yes, it is," he answered, then felt compelled to add, "and so are you."

She dipped her head, and he wondered if she were blushing. "I think you've had one cocktail too many, Mr. Galanis," she teased, pressing her shoulder against his arm. "Still, I can admit that we both clean up very nicely. You wear that suit very well."

"Thank you." He made a mental note to thank Grayson for his fashion sense. Aron cared more for what his clothes felt like against his skin than what he looked like in them, but he'd wanted to look his best tonight, their first time out together since Game Night, a time that seemed more like a date than a work-related social function. "I think you're the one who's had one cocktail too many, Ms. Reynolds. Would you like to walk with me for a little bit?"

"I'd love to."

They walked slowly through the cavernous room, taking in some of the exhibits they hadn't seen. "Thank you for inviting me. I haven't been here before."

"You're welcome. I came here a couple of times on school field trips and enjoyed it so much that my parents bought a family membership. The planetarium at the science center was mind-blowing to elementary-school me, and you can even learn stuff on the nature walk through the woods. You haven't seen half of what's available."

"I like what I've seen so far. I think I'd like to come back."

"Then you should come for Fernbank After Dark. It's an adults-only cocktail party that always has a science twist. I've come with Max and Quinn a couple of times, but it's a very popular date-night thing."

"Is it? That's good to know." Especially since she liked the venue.

"Really?" She stopped for a moment, then nodded, turning slightly away from him. "Of course."

That "of course" sounded strangely deflated and at odds with the previous liveliness of her tone. He couldn't let it slide. "Of course, what?"

"Of course you'd bring a date here."

He moved until they faced each other again. "I don't understand. You just suggested this for a date night, and I agreed. If I had the time or the inclination, I'd bring a date here because of the science and tech aspect and because I wouldn't have to worry about networking or avoiding shaking hands."

"So you're not seeing anyone?"

"Have you heard me talk about seeing anyone?"

"Well, no, but—"

"You work with me up to twelve hours a day, and I work longer than that most days," he pointed out. "I think I mentioned that my brother comes over every other weekend and then I take him back home so we can have Sunday dinner with our mother. My family will always come first, and that's non-negotiable." A couple of exes had tried to challenge that, which was why they were exes.

They resumed their sedate stroll, making their way to the entrance. "Our family does Sunday dinners too," she told him. "There's four of us kids, but my oldest brother and sister have families, so it's usually me and my brother Mitchell, although he's in a committed relationship now."

"Sounds like family is important to you too."

"Absolutely. My parents are a big reason why I'm still able to safely do what I do, so attending Sunday dinners is the least I can do."

Her statement was a sobering reminder of why they'd met and why they were working together, but it also made him wonder if she'd had to face more than online trolls in her quest for gaming equality. The virtual stuff was bad enough. He couldn't imagine what she'd experienced in real life.

He didn't want her to have to talk about that tonight. He didn't want to talk about projects and presentations either. "Our Sunday dinners usually revolve around whatever my brother Benjy likes to eat. At the moment that means noodles— spaghetti, ramen, pad thai, pho—if it's noodles, he wants it."

"I like those noodles too." She laughed. "We never know what's for dinner until we show up, but it's grilling season now, and my dad's outdoor kitchen is his pride and joy. He makes a brisket so tender and juicy you swear you hear angels singing when you taste it. Next time he makes it, I'll be sure to snag you some."

"I'm already looking forward to it." He wondered if she knew it implied their continued association, at least to him. He'd already decided to do whatever it took to keep seeing her, whether it was work related, work adjacent, or not about work at all.

He focused on the second option. "I want to thank you again for inviting me to this event," he said as they made their way out onto the plaza. "If you learn of any other events like this, let me know. I'm going to make a personal donation to Girl Code and then work with my team to look into some internship and mentorship opportunities at Artemis."

"Really?" Her smile was a glorious thing. "The girls will be excited to hear that. You're awesome!"

One moment Samara was beside him. The next she'd literally done a happy hop to throw her arms around his neck. Something lurched inside his chest. Instead of his usual instinctive dodge, his arms circled her waist, pinning her against him.

He blinked at her, his brain sputtering with the need to parse what had happened and decide what to do next. Letting go didn't seem to be an option. Samara blinked back at him as if she'd just realized she was pressed from her chest to her thighs against him. She also seemed incapable of moving, and he found that he didn't mind at all.

The air between them thickened, as if staring at each other baked the space that separated their lips. Her lips. A sudden, incandescent need flared inside him, the need to know exactly how her lips felt, how they tasted. How she kissed. A need he knew he shouldn't have but couldn't suppress even if he wanted to.

Her gaze searched his, then dropped to his mouth, and that incandescent need went nuclear. He shifted forward, just a breath, just testing. She leaned in, looking interested, looking beautiful. Distance narrowing, closing . . .

"There you are!"

Samara jumped out of his arms as quickly as she'd jumped into them, whirling to face Max and Grayson. "Where have you guys been?"

"Talking on the terrace," Max answered. "What about you?"

"Yes, well." Samara took another step away from him, brushing at the front of her skirt. "We came out to get some air now that the exhibition and awards ceremony are done, trying to find you."

She looked and sounded flustered, and he wondered if the cause was the almost-kiss or getting caught by their friends. As for himself, he hovered somewhere between disappointment and resentment, both sitting like boulders on his shoulders.

Max folded her arms with a crooked smile. "I don't think you're going to find us by staring into each other's eyes like that."

Aron coughed. That answered the question of whether or not they had seen how close he and Samara were. Which wasn't close at all now since she took another step away from him.

"And I don't think you realize you're lit like a Christmas tree and just as likely to fall over right now," Samara retorted. "Good thing I'm your designated driver."

"Uh-uh." Max linked her arm with Grayson's with an exaggerated shake of her head. "We're going for dessert, aren't we, Gray?"

Aron blinked. Had he ever seen a smile that wide on Grayson's face before? Then again, he couldn't remember a time he'd seen Grayson even slightly unsteady on his feet. Did he go beyond his usual one-drink limit? Samara's friend certainly seemed like she could drive someone to drink. Still, if they were going for dessert, he and Samara could too as long as it was in the opposite direction.

"Nobody's going for dessert," Samara announced. "I think we're all going to our respective homes because we all have to work in the morning."

Resentment swung back to disappointment, which was ridiculous because relief should have been the only emotion in his mind. Just as Samara was the only levelheaded and correct one among them, reminding them all, and him especially, that business needed to come before pleasure.

"You're right, especially since we're getting into crunch time on the certification proposal."

He turned to her, wishing she would step closer again, knowing it was better that she didn't. "Thanks again for giving me a chance to take a break from work projects."

"Of course." She took a step toward him, then froze, glanced at Max, then took a step back. "See you tomorrow. Max, let go of poor Grayson and let's go."

They separated like pulling apart a chocolate chip cookie fresh from the oven, which, wow, why did his mind go there, and also, he was going to tease the hell out of Grayson the next day.

Samara wrapped an arm around Max's waist, turning to face him again. "Good night."

She and Max headed toward the parking lot, each step she made tugging at him. Only the knowledge that he'd see her in the morning kept him from going after her. But what could the morning bring other than work? They still had time on their contract, which meant they still had to be professional. He had to be professional. Too much was at stake to be anything but.

Now his brain just had to convince his body of that.

Chapter 18

"Hey, Aron."

He looked up from the documents he'd spread across the coffee table. "Yes?"

Samara grabbed a file folder, then rose. She opened it to read as she walked toward him. "Did you see this report on five-year pro—ah!"

Time slowed. He watched in horror as Samara tripped, then pitched forward, her head on a crash course with the table. Fear rose like bile in his throat as he sprang to his feet to break her fall. He managed to grab her, but her forward momentum sent him falling back. They landed on the couch, bumped foreheads, then lips.

Just a couple of seconds of their lips touching, but it seemed like more as she stared at him in undeniable shock. Then she scrambled backward and shot to her feet, rubbing at her forehead.

He stood too. "Are you okay?"

She put her left hand on her hip while still massaging her forehead with her right. "Other than falling into a rom-com situation, I'm fine."

What? He scrunched his eyebrows in bewilderment. "A rom-com situation? Is this something that happens often?"

"In a romantic comedy, yes. In real life, no."

His bewilderment deepened. "So that was supposed to be romantic?"

She dropped her hand. "No . . . well, I did discover that your eyes are even more gorgeous nose to nose, and your lips are damnably soft and kissable."

"Kissable?" He touched a finger to his mouth, still feeling Samara's lips against his. Her body against his. "Do you consider that a kiss?"

"Yes, albeit an accidental one, not a good one."

"I think I've just been insulted." He took a step closer to her with a smile. "I think I need to correct that."

She sucked in a breath, then spoke, her voice as soft as night. "Correct what?"

"That bad kiss. I can't leave you with that memory. I need to give you a better one. Is that reckless of me?"

She gazed at him, silently considering. He stared back just as long, longer, an eternity of waiting. Finally, she spoke. "Can it really be called reckless if it's something we've both wanted to do since that night with the dinosaurs?"

She—did she—did he hear her right? He had to make sure. "Can I kiss you right now?"

Her eyes softened. "How about we kiss each other?"

Somehow, he managed to answer her. "I would like that very much."

Instead of moving forward, she drew her hands up to frame his face. Her thumb brushed beneath his eye, a soft caress that burned him to his core. "I can finally touch you like this."

"Touch me all you want." Okay, maybe not all she wanted. He didn't need to pop off like a firecracker with a short fuse. "Just remember to kiss me."

"Oh, trust and believe, I won't forget that."

The low, husky laugh made his body tighten in ways that had to be obvious to her. Yet she continued to stroke his cheeks as if oblivious as she held his gaze. "I'm sure you've had lots of ladies tell you how beautiful your eyes are."

Maybe, but in that moment he couldn't recall a single one. "I don't remember," he confessed, bringing his hands up to mirror her gesture. "But you can bet that I'll definitely remember this."

He stared at her for a long moment, just drinking in the reality of having her with him like this. She'd talked about his eyes, but hers were deep pools of onyx with sparks of amber shooting through. He wanted to dive in headfirst and knew if he did, he'd never want to come back out.

"So much hidden here," he whispered, grazing his thumbs beneath her eyes. He raised his head, closing the distance between them until their mouths met, meshed. She hadn't reapplied her lipstick after dinner, and her lips were soft and full and wonderful against his. It was a sweet, exploring kiss that made his muscles tremble with the need to clutch her closer.

She drew back, dark eyes hazy. "Mm-hmm, pizza and cider and kisses. I need more of alla that."

They came together again, and this time, oh, this time it was game on. He turned, putting her beneath him, so that he could kiss her with all the bottled-up need he possessed. Her hands slid up his shoulders to clasp together around his neck, her mouth hungry against his.

It took a superhuman effort to pull away from her, but he managed. Barely. "I should . . . probably go home now."

She pushed her hair back, blowing out a breath. "You *are* home."

"Oh yeah." He looked around. "I forgot."

"So did I." She touched a fingertip to her lips with a soft smile that produced a shadow of her dimple. "But I do need to go. It's way later than I thought, and we both have work to do in the morning."

"I want to date you."

Chapter 19

Sam backpedaled, putting space between them. "What?"

"What do you mean, what?"

"Did you hear what you just said?" She narrowed her eyes at him. "You said you want to date me."

A frown crinkled his features. "Why do you sound surprised about that, especially after the kiss we just had? I'd like for us to start dating, so if you agree, let's do that. Let's date. After our contract ends, of course."

She took another step back, needing a clear mind. "You know, this is sounding very reminiscent of when you impulsively offered me a job. A total spur-of-the-moment thing."

"Hiring you turned out well," he pointed out. "Why wouldn't this?"

"Why?" she echoed. "Because dating shouldn't be a decision made in the heat of the moment."

"The moment was heated, but the decision is not."

Seriousness pulled at his features, lowering his brows as he stared at her, his hand gliding over the front of his T-shirt to smooth it back into place. The man was devastating in a suit, but the tight T-shirt revealed his muscular frame. It was obvious that he didn't spend all of his time sitting on that fine ass staring at a screen. She wondered what his workout was.

"There's nothing to work out," he said. "I've given it a lot of thought."

Damn, she'd said that out loud? Thank goodness he'd only heard part of it. She locked down her inner voice that really wanted to become an outie. "Since when have you thought about this? From the moment we kissed?"

"No. The almost-kiss last week after the Girl Code event was when I began to seriously consider asking you about the possibility of dating, but the thought has crossed my mind before."

"Really? When?"

"Every time we're gaming. Every time you laugh. Every time you walk in the front door and walk out again."

"I . . . umm . . . oh." How did he manage to completely defuse her upset with the blunt-force truth of his words? How was she supposed to respond to that besides going all melty? "Why didn't you let me know?"

"Several reasons." He ticked them off on his fingers. He was really forcing her to focus on his hands, leading her thoughts into side quests she had no business taking. At least, not yet. "First, we have a great working relationship, and I have no desire to ruin that. Second, I had no idea if you'd even consider dating me until our night out upped the probability."

She had to admit those were some pretty good reasons. "Is there a third?"

He nodded. "Third, I wasn't sure I'd be able to wait until our contract was over if you said yes."

The third reason eclipsed the first two and made her a little light-headed. The only response she could come up with was a weak-sounding "Okay."

"Okay, then." He clapped his hands together. "Dating would begin after our contract is finished, which will be soon. Everything is just about ready for handoff. Even though your contract will be done by then, I want you to come to NexCon with me as the representative for Rise Consulting, but after we're done we can go out on the town as a couple."

It would be interesting to see a convention through his eyes as head of a tech company. But she hadn't gone to a gaming convention with anyone other than Max and Quinn in years, and it would be jarring to do so now in a professional capacity. Even more jarring to leave the con as his date, which she hadn't agreed to yet despite what he'd assumed. "I'm more likely to go with Quinn and Max, if they can get time off," she told him.

"If they can't, will you go as my guest?"

"As your guest, yes," she answered. "Still a big question mark on the dating part. I'll give you an answer in three weeks, when the contract's done."

"All right." He fully faced her, his expression one of resolve. In the last few weeks, she'd become quite familiar with that look. It was one of near single-minded determination that clearly telegraphed that he'd do whatever was necessary for however long it took to achieve his goal. "What do I need to do to convince you to give this a try?"

"Why don't you do what you do best and make a risk assessment? At the very least, a pro versus con chart."

"You think I haven't?" he retorted. "Have you met me?"

"I have, which is why I'm wondering how your data crunching came back favorable for dating."

The tightening of his mouth told the truth. "Despite that, I still want to date you."

"And I want to verify your data," she said, because she wanted to make sure he was taking things as seriously as they needed to be taken. "Have you given thought to your company's rabid fan base? They're already complaining that you've become 'woke,' which is now more of an epithet than the good thing it used to be."

"Do I want a fan base that thinks equity and inclusion are curse words?" he wondered. "Or should our focus be on what I hired you for, widening our customer base and inviting in those who haven't had much opportunity to see themselves portrayed favorably if at all in the platforms they love?"

She was impressed despite herself. The man knew how to talk a good game when it was a subject he cared about. "I'll give you kudos for thinking of how our potential relationship might affect you and your company, but what about me?"

A frown of confusion dipped his eyebrows down. "What about you in what way?"

She gestured between them. "There's a chasm of difference between you, a well-off white guy heading his own company, future so bright you gotta wear shades and all that, and me, a Black woman in America."

His chin stuck out in a stubborn jut. "There's also an ocean of similarities."

"Like what?"

"Like a passion for gaming. A desire to do the right thing. A drive to make things better. Work styles." His expression softened. "A love for family. A mutual attraction that's harder to ignore with each day that goes by."

She wanted to deny it in pure self-defense but couldn't.

Truth dripped from every word, scalding her with undeniable fact. They had so much in common. Especially that attraction that was almost a living thing between them. Every day they worked together it beckoned her, tempting her to cross the line. But he had the luxury of living in a bubble that she couldn't afford, and she had to make sure that, if they took that step, he wouldn't back out when things got hard.

"You know what my platform is," she said, her tone slow as she thought through what she wanted to say and how to say it. "I've told you how that makes me a target for online trolls. What if some of the hate directed my way ricochets to you?"

"I promise you, I'll maintain your privacy. If you want to go to NexCon as ReyofSun, I won't stop you. I'd really like you to go as a representative of Rise Consulting. Tell the audience how Rise helped Artemis move forward. If you don't want to speak, I'll publicly thank you. Then we leave and tour the city as a couple. What do you think?"

"I think that's a lot to consider. You make a good argument, but I still have concerns."

"I'm more concerned about you being targeted by those online trolls," he told her. "If I could, I'd wrap you in silk and Bubble Wrap and keep you somewhere they can't reach you."

His intent touched her, but she had to say, "That would be a place without Internet service and probably without pizza delivery, so we'd have to fight."

He smiled as she'd intended, then immediately sobered. "I want to shield you from all that, but I know you don't want that, and short of staying offline, there's not a lot we can do. Because of that, I'm willing to step into the fire with you. All I need is for you to agree to let me walk with you."

Samara blinked rapidly. Damn it, she was not going to cry over being asked for a date. The man just had a way with words with her that punched all her buttons. "Are you going to bail when it gets too hot?"

"If the fire gets too hot, I'll bring the marshmallows and we'll have s'mores. Seriously, though, if they come for you, my lawyer will come for them. I haven't given her enough work lately anyway."

"Umm . . ." Sam pressed a fist to her sternum, unsure if heartburn or gratitude or something more dangerous was flaring in her chest. Every protest she made, he obliterated with facts, with assurances, with confidence that bordered on arrogant. She made a final try. "Maybe you should read some of the comments on my social media and streaming accounts before you make a final decision."

"I have," he answered, his tone heavy and serious. "That's some of the most heinous, racist vitriol that I've ever read. Some of them I had to respond to."

"No. Aron!" she exclaimed. "You can't do that! Think about your position."

"I used a couple of my aliases, untraceable back to me." A slight smile bowed his lips. "I will be your shield. I'll keep defending you and protecting you, and when we start to date, I'll do it under my own name."

"Aron . . ."

"I told you I was serious about this, about us. Now you know how serious." He stepped closer to her. "I want to date you, Samara. So why don't you want to date me?"

He winked. "After all, I'm a woke white guy."

She laughed because he wanted her to and because the whole thing was absurd. "I didn't say that I didn't want to date you," she pointed out. "I said I'd give you an answer in three weeks."

"Am I not woke enough?"

"God, please stop saying 'woke.'"

"If I do, will you agree to go on a date with me when our contract is up?"

"You are one persistent man," she said, shaking her head in admiration.

"I have to be, to be successful and to get what I want."

"And you want me?"

"Yes, dammit." He stalked away from her, then turned back. "That was the first reason in the pro column. The only reason I needed."

A reason that overrode every detriment. If she'd created a pro versus con chart of her own, her list of cons would probably be as long as his, if not longer. And like him, the first item in her pro column would have beat all the others: *I want him*.

Yet her fears for him, his company, and herself were real. She'd already lost a friend to the hatred, and a partner who couldn't handle the heat had ghosted her. She wasn't ready to share those stories with him, not yet.

"I hope you understand that this is something I should give all the due diligence that you did," she finally said. "I'll take the next three weeks to do just that and give you an answer when the contract ends. Besides, we have a lot of loose ends we need to tie up. Is that okay with you?"

"Yes," he confirmed with a nod. "It's important enough to me that I want you to have zero doubts. I can wait three more weeks."

Three weeks. That was plenty of time to engage her brain in making a decision her body already had. Till then, she'd give everything due consideration so that they could both go into it with eyes wide open. She'd also be her best professional self, ending their working relationship on a high. They still had a lot of tasks that needed to be completed on both the certification presentation and documentation and the final stages of the character designs.

Following their usual routine, Aron walked her to the front door after she'd gathered her belongings. He turned to her before opening it. "Tomorrow, we'll go back to our regular working selves, but I was wondering . . ."

"If we should cross the line one more time?" she guessed, since that was pretty much in line with her thoughts. "To make sure it's not the alcohol?"

"I know it's not the alcohol," he told her, his expression serious and intent. "Say yes."

As if she could say anything else. "Yes."

He slowly stepped closer, and once again the space between them became this charged, living thing that demanded closeness to appease its hunger. She took a step closer, then reached up to cup his cheek. His eyes slid closed as he covered her hand with his own.

"It's probably a good thing to institute a no-touching policy," he said softly. "When other people touch me, try to shake my hand or pat my back, it's this jangly, static sensation. But when you do it, do this, it just makes me hungry for more."

"Well, then." She reached her other hand up until she cupped both cheeks. "Let's see if this appetizer can help us hold out for the next three weeks."

He bent his head as she raised her chin, and the distance between them closed, and their lips met. Her body heated and her breath shortened as his arms encircled her waist, not to pull her closer but to hold her in place. Honestly, she needed that anchor because the man kissed with the same focused intensity that he brought to his work, and she very much liked it.

They parted bit by bit, their bodies reluctant to separate. She gripped his forearms to steady herself. "I think I'm actually drunk now."

"Same." He rested his hands on her shoulders. "I won't repeat an offer for you to stay here. I think it's safer to push you out the door."

Why did that dash of disappointment shoot through her? That had her taking a step back, and she was able to breathe again. "I should get going."

He opened the door for her, and she stepped out into the night. "Samara."

She turned to face him again. "Yes?"

"While you're deciding, don't just think of the reasons why you believe it won't work. Spend some time thinking about the reasons why it could. Good night."

"Good night."

He watched her until she got in and started the car, not closing the door until she began to drive away. She gave herself a stern talking-to on the drive home. She could do this. She could focus on the business at hand while minimizing the distraction of a potential personal relationship and all the possibilities that came with it. She could think about the collaboration and not the kisses. She was a professional, dammit. She could handle it.

But then she met Aron's mother.

Chapter 20

"Do we have the final interviews and feedback from the focus group?"

Samara scrolled through her files. "I transferred them to our collab site. I also cross-indexed each participant's responses from the initial interview through the final feedback with the final survey responses. There's also a hard copy next to your keyboard. It's that red folder there."

Aron sorted through the stack on his side of the massive desk. "Got it. Did you have a chance to look at the storyboard for the promo video I'm working on?"

"I did, but I feel like I should remind you that you have people on your payroll who do this sort of thing so that you can do other things."

"Of course, but I know the concept I want to convey better than anyone, except maybe you."

"Control freak." She smiled to take the sting out of her words. "You know we have a meeting with Dylan to review the storyboard. You can convey your concept to him then. If I recall correctly, you said Dylan was the obvious choice and you trust his abilities."

"He is and I do." Aron pushed his glasses back into place

with one finger, a classic anime move that was just as sexy in real life as it was on screen. Maybe even better because he was the one doing the IRL version.

She had done a good job so far of not thinking of personal things during work hours. She was also grateful that Aron hadn't mentioned dating again after that initial conversation, keeping true to his word to run the clock out on their contract. Good thing the work they needed to complete in the time they had kept them too busy to think about anything else.

The end of the workday was the hardest part. Whether Grayson was there or not, Aron walked her to the front door as usual. What wasn't usual was the look in his eye, the touch to her back, the soft good night. As if he wanted to remind her of that night, that kiss, that promise. As if she could think of anything else on the drive home.

A chime sounded through the house. "That must be Grayson coming back," Aron said.

"I hope he thought of us while he was having lunch with Max," she said, reviewing a checklist in her planner. "I'm almost at the hangry stage."

"Even if he didn't, we should stop for lunch. I don't want you passing out on me or flipping the hangry switch due to lack of nourishment."

"That sounds like a—"

"Aron?" a female voice called. "Sorry for dropping by without calling, but we were nearby and—oh!"

A beautiful older woman with dark brown waves and a bright smile stopped in the doorway. Aron shot to his feet. "Mom?"

Sam's eyes bugged as she looked at Aron. *Your mother?*

Before Aron could speak, a young man pushed past his

mother. He stopped when he saw Samara, clutched a portable game system to his chest, then skirted around her to head to the gaming chairs on the other side of the office.

Aron walked around the desk. He touched Sam's shoulder, and she rose to her feet. "Mom, this is Samara Reynolds from Rise Consulting who's collaborating with me on our diversity initiative and the certification process. Samara, this is my mother, Artemis Galanis."

Sam's gut clenched on a sudden case of nerves. One, she was meeting Aron's mother. Two, did the other woman know exactly how she came to work with Aron on this project?

Not knowing what else to do, she fell back on basic manners. "Mrs. Galanis, it's a pleasure meeting you." Knowing how Aron felt about touching, she didn't extend her hand.

"Ms. Reynolds." Mrs. Galanis extended her hand, and Sam took it. "I've heard a lot about you."

She had? That didn't settle her nerves at all. Sam turned to glance at Aron, whose expression was a study in neutrality. She turned back to his mother. "Oh, I hope it was all good."

"It was." The other woman gave her hand a hard squeeze before letting go. "He's very excited about the work you've been doing. I'm sorry we interrupted you, but Benjy and I were in the vicinity and decided to stop by."

"You mean Benjy wanted to play games," Aron replied, nodding to the other man completely ignoring their side of the room. He turned to Sam. "My brother can be just as single-minded as I am."

Samara laughed. "Considering how massive your game collection is, you can call me single-minded too. I'm still determined to play every single one at least once."

"That's going to take a while, even with your skills," Aron

said, then turned to his mother. "Samara's also a gamer, a very excellent one."

"Really? Sounds like a great match."

Sam tried hard not to fidget as his mother's attention swung her way again. Based on his mother's reaction, or lack thereof, it seemed as if Aron hadn't told her about how she'd been the one to initially call Artemis Games out. "Thank you. We've been working hard to make sure the projects are successful."

"We're just now taking a lunch break," Aron cut in, his body radiating tension. "Samara, why don't we—"

"I can go out to lunch, no problem," she said, gathering her planner and phone to shove into her bag. "I'll come back later."

"Absolutely not," Artemis cut in. "We're interrupting you, not the other way around. Did you order delivery or were you planning to make something?"

"We were counting on Grayson returning soon with lunch in hand," Aron explained, "but he's been delayed."

Mrs. Galanis pulled her phone out of her purse. "Why don't I order something, then, as an apology for barging in and stopping your work?"

"Umm . . ." Sam looked from one to the other, uncertain what to say or do. She didn't want to offend the other woman, but she didn't want to do anything that would exacerbate Aron's strange mood. She finally settled on a lame "If it's all right with Aron."

"Of course I have no problem with it," he answered, his tone tight as if he spoke through a clenched jaw. "We need to eat something to refuel for the rest of the workday. I'll call Grayson and let him know what's happening."

"Great," his mother said. "Will pizza be all right? There's a local place called Giorgio's that makes delicious gourmet pizzas, and Benjy loves it."

Seeing as how she and Aron had ordered food from them before, Sam didn't have a problem with it. It also proved that his family frequently visited his house. She was still reluctant to intrude on their family time, and she couldn't tell if Aron wanted her or his family to leave, but she didn't know how to extricate herself without offending anyone.

"That place does have great pizzas, so thank you." She turned to Aron, determined to make the best of things. "Why don't you introduce me to your brother?"

The look he gave her could have sliced concrete. "You don't have to do that."

Did he not want her to? He seemed to be hovering between protectiveness and defensiveness, neither of which she wanted to continue. "Come on, he's a fellow gamer. Of course I want to meet him."

A warm smile spread across his face, lighting up his eyes. "All right."

He led her over to his brother, who sat in one of the gaming chairs in front of the coffee table, then squatted down. "Benjy, I have someone I'd like you to meet."

Sam knelt beside him. "Hi, Benjy, I work with your brother. My name is Samara, but a lot of people call me Sam."

She laughed softly. "People sometimes mistake me for a guy when I'm gaming, but I don't mind. Sometimes it's helpful and I can just focus on playing games. Do you have a favorite that you like to play?"

She waited to see if he would acknowledge her, ignore her,

or want to get away from her. It surprised her when Benjy showed her his portable. "Of course it's one of your brother's games. I like that one too. Can I play it with you?"

Benjy dipped his head, then turned toward Aron, who appeared stunned. "He'll play with you."

"Excellent." She kept her voice low as she softly clapped her hands. "Set us up for the big screen, then go order the pizza. Don't let your mama pay for pizza in your house."

He looked at her as if she'd asked him to grow another head. Finally, he nodded and did as she asked as she settled on the floor beside Benjy. "All right, Benjy," she said as she handed him a controller before picking up the other. "Let's do this thing."

• • •

"Can you believe this?"

Aron sat next to his mother on the couch watching as Samara and Benjy launched into another round. They'd barely paused to devour a couple of slices of pizza each before returning to the game. If his chortles were any indication, Benjy was having a good time playing games with Samara. Her smile suggested she was having a good time too.

"No, I can't believe it," he answered, even with the proof in front of him. All of the apprehension he'd felt the moment Benjy and their mother had entered his office had evaporated as soon as Samara had knelt on the floor beside him to be introduced to his brother. The people who'd made the cut to be introduced to his family were few, yet none of them had done what Samara did. Her easy acceptance touched him in a way he couldn't describe. His heart wobbled even more. The end of their contract couldn't come soon enough.

His mother sat back with a sigh. "I already liked her just

based on what you'd told me about her. But this . . . this is wonderful."

It was the best possible outcome of Samara meeting his family, a meeting he wouldn't have considered until well into their personal relationship, a relationship that hadn't even been decided yet. The fact that Benjy and his mother seemed as taken with Samara as he was and that she seemed comfortable with his family gave him hope for their future.

"Are you sure you don't want to stay a little longer? I'm sure Samara won't mind if we delay work for an hour."

"I'm the one who will mind. She's here to work and has been playing games instead."

"Playing games is work for us, Mom."

His mother snorted. "Oh, did you put your brother on the payroll without telling me? Anyway, you have work to do, and I don't want you keeping her later than necessary. But I would love for you to bring her to dinner soon."

She stretched out her hand before he could respond. Not that there was a way he could respond that wouldn't count against him with both women. "Come on, Benjy, it's time to go home. Aron and Samara have to get back to work now."

Benjy frowned, clearly unhappy with this development, but he rose when Samara did. "It was nice to meet you, Benjy," Sam said with a genuine smile. "Maybe when you come over again, your brother will call me so we can play some more games. Would that be okay?"

In a move that sent a current of shock through him, Aron watched as Benjy bumped her shoulder with a happy grin. He'd never done that to someone he'd just met. As a matter of fact, Aron couldn't recall Benjy ever showing affection like that to someone not related to him.

He turned to his mother as Sam's delighted laughter rang out. His mother lifted her hands to her mouth, eyes wide and bright, then grabbed his shoulder. She knew as well as he did. This was huge. Benjy didn't accept everyone. There weren't many people he liked. And he certainly hadn't liked any of the women that Aron had introduced him to. Then again, it wasn't like there had been a bunch of women that he'd wanted to introduce to his family. Only one had made it to that point, and she'd walked out on him soon after.

But Samara . . . she'd actually gotten down on the floor with Benjy, curtailing a meltdown before it could begin, then offered to play a game with him. She hadn't turned up her nose, gotten impatient, or worse, ignored Benjy altogether. She'd gotten down on the floor despite wearing a dress and treated Benjy as the human being he was. Because of that, he would be forever grateful to her—and probably forever in the palm of her hand.

Samara and Benjy walked over to them. "It was a pleasure meeting you, Mrs. Galanis. I'm sorry we didn't have much time to talk."

"No need to apologize at all," his mother said. "Benjy had a great time. Thank you for that."

"Ah, you don't have to thank me for that." She lowered her head. Was she blushing? "Benjy's great and a terrific player. We definitely need a rematch."

"He obviously likes that idea. And feel free to call me Artemis."

"Oh no, I can't do that," Samara protested. "My mama would pop me upside the head for disrespecting my elders."

Her eyes widened as she waved her hands. "Not that I consider you elderly. You're not old at all. I mean, no one would think you have a son Aron's age. Oh god, I'm rambling and digging myself deeper, aren't I?"

Her discomfort was kinda endearing, but Aron kept that thought to himself. Instead he said, "No one thinks she's my mother when we're out together. They think she's a cougar."

"Aron!"

Both women called his name with a harmonious blend of surprise and indignation that made him laugh. "Well, it's true."

"That only happened once," his mother retorted, then smiled. "It was a nice compliment, though."

Aron turned to his brother. "You see that look in her eyes, Benjy? I don't trust that look in her eyes." Benjy grunted his agreement.

His mother laughed. "See? This is why I never tell you what happens on my girlfriend weekends."

She turned to Samara, who looked a bit shell-shocked. "You can call me Mrs. Galanis until we get to know each other better. Hopefully, we'll see you again soon, maybe have you over for dinner?"

"Oh, umm . . ." Samara's eyes widened again before she tossed a helpless glance to Aron. "Thank you for the invitation, but my contract with Aron is up in a couple of weeks . . ."

He could see her Bat-Signal loud and clear. "Mom, why don't I walk you and Benjy out? Samara, if you could cue up those character profiles, I'll be right back."

"Sure. Goodbye, Mrs. Galanis. Bye, Benjy."

Aron walked them out to the garage, then pressed the button to raise the door. His mother spoke as soon as he closed the house door. "Are you going to keep her?"

"Mom!" He darted a glance behind him to make sure the

door was closed, hoping the composite wood was dense enough to muffle their conversation.

"Don't you 'Mom' me," she retorted. "She's only the second one to make it to meet-the-family level, and the first one to pass with Benjy. If you don't keep her, I will."

Remembering how Samara had interacted with his brother as smoothly and easily as she did with him made his heart hurt. He had a sense that it meant the battered organ was trying to revive and regrow itself despite his every intention to keep it dead. "You don't even know her," he felt compelled to point out, playing devil's advocate with her, with himself, with his emotions.

"I'll tell you what I do know. I know Benjy likes her." Benjy nodded as he opened the front passenger door of his mother's sedan, then climbed in. "I know she didn't have to get on the floor with him. I know if she treats Benjy that way, she treats you well too. I also know that as protective of us as you are, you would have found some way for us to not interact when we showed up unexpectedly."

"I guess you do know a lot," he grumbled. "But your arrival caught me off guard. It's way too early to be talking about keeping someone or not, and it's definitely too early to talk about feelings and stuff like that. Right now we're work partners only. There's still a couple of weeks remaining on her contract with me. Nothing but business will happen until then."

"Sounds like you've given a lot of thought to someone you don't have feelings for."

He gritted his teeth, reluctant to share more of his plans with his mother when the idea of dating had yet to become reality. "I don't know what this is, Mom. I don't even know if she wants it to be anything other than what it is now or if it'll go sideways at some point. You remember Amanda."

His mother's expression soured. "Yes, I do. I also know that Samara is not Amanda. In just five minutes, I could tell they are polar opposites. Samara is far sweeter than that woman ever was."

"Does it matter?" he asked, trying to swallow the sudden bitterness that tainted his tongue. "I told her that I want to date after the contract is over, but she hasn't given me an answer. In fact, she gave me a whole list of reasons why it's not a good idea. As soon as our work is done, she may decide that she's going to move on with her life, and that will have to be okay. In the meantime, I'm trying my best to run out the clock without blurring the lines."

His mother clapped her hands. "I stopped listening after you said that y'all have talked about dating. Tell your mother what she can do to help make this happen."

"Nothing," he quickly replied. "Absolutely nothing. Samara's not one to be pushed, coerced, sweet-talked, or guilt-tripped into doing anything she doesn't want to do. She has a right to be wary and take her time deciding whether to date me or not, especially because the trolls have been out in full force since we announced the new initiative and upgrades. I have to protect her as much as I can from any speculation about us and our work, or she'll never give us a chance."

His mother touched his arm again, her expression serious. "I don't think Samara is the type who will appreciate you doing things for her sake while keeping her in the dark about them."

She was right, and it made him grumpy. Hiding things

from Samara was a surefire way for things to end before they had a chance to begin. "I'll figure something out, Mom. I promise."

"You always do." She offered her cheek for him to kiss. "If it matters, Samara's got my vote. Benjy's too."

"I can tell." He sighed. "But I have to be sure. We—I—don't need another Amanda." It had taken a while to get over that breakup, far longer than he'd admitted to anyone. It was just easier to be single, all the better to avoid scenarios in which potential partners rejected you, your family, and your gene pool.

He helped her into the car, then moved around to the passenger side. When Benjy rolled down the window, he held out his fist. "Glad you had a good time, bro. You want to game with Samara again, I promise I'll make it happen."

Benjy grinned, then bumped his fist against Aron's. His mom started the car, and Benjy rolled up his window before turning his attention back to his tablet. His mother blew Aron a kiss, then drove away.

Aron stood in the garage long after they'd left, happiness and guilt twisting in him. He shouldn't have promised his brother that Samara would game with him again because he had no way of guaranteeing that she would. Had no way of knowing that she wanted to, despite what she'd said. She could have just been polite for his sake.

Of course, there was one way to make sure, and that was to go inside and ask her. Yet he couldn't make his feet move. Couldn't take the thought that Samara would reject his family the way his ex had. Couldn't take the thought that he'd come to hate her for it too.

Chapter 21

It was taking far longer than Sam had expected for Aron to return. Acidic worry bubbled in her stomach, and she made her way to the kitchen for a glass of ice water.

Her mind roiled as much as her stomach as she contemplated various scenarios, none of which ended well. She hadn't been able to hear anything from the garage other than the outer door being raised, and not wanting to be caught eavesdropping, she had hurriedly made her way back to the kitchen to deal with the leftover pizza.

She'd thought meeting Mrs. Galanis and Benjy had gone as smoothly as any of them could have hoped. At the very least, she hadn't triggered Benjy to react negatively to her presence. Their mother seemed fine with her gaming with Benjy. What if she was only going through the polite niceties of meeting one of her son's coworkers? What if Mrs. Galanis wasn't as accepting of her presence as she'd seemed? A heated flush burned up her chest to her throat as she mentally reviewed every action she'd taken since Mrs. Galanis and Benjy had arrived. Had she been too casual with Aron? Too forward? Had she been too familiar with the layout of the house, his things?

Could his mother tell that they were thinking of being more than simple coworkers?

Groaning, she slumped onto one of the stools at the breakfast bar and dropped her head in her hands. Maybe she was overreacting, but Aron still wasn't back yet. That couldn't be a good sign, could it? Maybe it was taking him so long to return because he was apologizing to his mother on her behalf, and his mother wanted him to stop seeing her, work or not.

The idea of not seeing Aron again, even for work, settled like a stone in her stomach. Mrs. Galanis could have a problem with her being Black. Even worse, she could have a problem with Samara being the Black woman who put her son and his company on blast, threatening his livelihood.

"God." That was it. His mother had been all smiles to her face, and as soon as Sam was out of sight, his mother had let Aron have it about bringing her on as a consultant, bringing her into his house. And she, blithely unaware, had played games with Benjy.

Maybe she should leave. Get out before Aron could come back and tell her to go himself. It would happen, she knew. Aron was devoted to his mother and brother. If Mrs. Galanis wanted her out of Aron's life, Sam was as good as gone.

"Hey."

Sam jumped to her feet with a nervous squeak at the sound of Aron's voice. She'd been so deep in her wildly galloping thoughts that she hadn't heard him come in. Seeing the cold and irritated expression dragging at his features, it seemed she had good reason to speculate the worst about his conversation with his mother.

It definitely was time to stage a strategic retreat. "You

know what? It's later than I thought it was. Why don't we call it a day? I can take some of this home to work on and just see you and Grayson in the morning."

A deep frown drew down his features as he shoved his hands into his pockets. "Back to business already, I see."

Wasn't that what he wanted? Wasn't that safer territory than talking about her meeting his family? She tried for a joke. "Of course I'm getting back to business. Isn't that why you pay me the big bucks?"

His eyes widened, a split-second reaction before his expression shuttered. "Of course," he said, shaking his head and laughing softly. "How stupid am I to forget that?"

Sam paused, her Spidey senses tingling. Something was off with Aron. Would he react like this if his mother wanted her gone, or was something more going on?

She asked a feeler question. "Is everything all right with your mother and brother?"

"Do you care, since that's not a business-related question?"

The challenging tone pushed her back a step before indignation drove her a step forward. She had to remember that she'd done nothing wrong, and if someone had an issue with her for simply existing, that was on them.

"Of course I care," she retorted, her hands cocked on her hips. "I'm human, aren't I? I can make nice with people when I need to."

"Is that all it was?" he demanded. "Making nice?"

Her Spidey sense went nuclear. "What's going on here, Aron? It sounds like you want an argument. If that's what you're looking for, you should know by now that I'd be delighted to give you one."

He mirrored her gesture, pulling his hands free of his

pockets to settle them on his hips. *Oh, it's on now.* "What do you think of my mother?"

She frowned at the unexpected question but answered honestly. "If you want to know the truth, I like her. She's nice, easy to talk to, seems to have a good spirit, and obviously dotes on her sons. And if she was genuine, I'd be happy to game with Benjy again."

"What do you mean, if she was genuine?"

Did she have to spell it out? "If she suspects that we have any sort of personal relationship, she might have a problem with her son being with a Black woman. Sometimes people say one thing to your face and something completely different behind your back."

"My mother would never do that!"

Maybe the indignation was real and he spoke the truth. Maybe he protested too much. "All right, then I'll assume you guys had an unimportant but insanely long conversation in the garage. So what I want to know now is, what does your mother really think of me?"

"She likes you, thinks you're charming and funny and more than a match for me. And as an answer to what you said earlier, she really hopes that you'll come over for dinner one day soon."

"Oh." Relief swamped her, quickly chased by confusion. Then what had taken him so long? "Okay, then perhaps you can tell me what"—she waved her hands at him—"all this attitude is about."

He seemingly ignored the question to ask one himself. "What did you think of my brother?"

A genuine smile bubbled up as her mood shifted. "Benjy is a sweetheart. I had fun playing games with him. He's really good. I had to stay on my toes in every match, no matter what we played."

Some of the tightness leached from his expression. "He didn't bother you?"

What the hell kind of question was that? "How could he bother me when we bonded over playing games? He even showed me the game you developed just for him. He thinks you're pretty cool. Obviously, he's never seen this side of you."

He reached for her hands, and she reluctantly surrendered them. "I'm sorry for reacting like this. Not everyone is accepting of Benjy's differences. So I tend to be overprotective."

"Oh, Aron." She gave his hands a sympathetic squeeze. "I'm so sorry that someone subjected you and Benjy to something like that."

"It's why I do my own verification process with anyone I date before they meet my family, if they meet at all. The odds were favorable that you'd be accepting and not abruptly end things."

She threw up a hand. "Hold up. You think I was gonna ghost you because of Benjy? Is that what you think of me? What level of bullshit is this?"

A bleak expression crossed his features. "The truth is, I'm going to get custody of Benjy one of these days. The only reason he doesn't live with me full-time now is because my mother believes I should attempt to have a personal life. I tried having one, it didn't work, so it became a low priority."

Anger broke in bits off her like dandelion spores blown away by a child. "Until you met me."

"Until I met you." He shoved his hands into his pockets. "I saw your passion for equality and representation. I learned that your professional career is to help companies create a more inclusive environment. I heard how much you care about family. I've seen you interact with your friends, acquaintances, the Girl Code students. I saw your capacity to care, and I thought, maybe, maybe trying again would go better this time around."

He was warning her, she knew. Warning her of what the future could hold if she wanted to be with him, if she wanted to go beyond a kiss here or there. But he was also prepared for things to end between them, prepared to return to a strictly business relationship.

A big question mark hovered between them. A question not only of could they move forward but should they. They had their personal and professional reputations to consider. Having a relationship could overshadow the importance of their project, and it would definitely hurt her worse than it would him. That was before she'd learned of his concerns for his family.

"But you're doubting already, so I guess I have to ask again. Do you really still believe we should try dating? Last week you gave a presentation on why we should date, and this week, you're expecting me to bail on something that hasn't started because you got burned by an ex who has absolutely nothing to do with me. You've come to know me so you want to try with me, but you also doubt me. You're contradicting yourself, Mr. Galanis."

Dammit, her voice cracked, making her hurt painfully obvious even to someone who had difficulty picking up emotional clues. She turned her back to him so he couldn't see how deeply that fissure of hurt ran. Honestly, it was probably too late to pretend that the damage they'd caused each other hadn't occurred. Maybe there wasn't a way to reset things.

Maybe there wasn't a way to repair their relationship, nascent as it was. Maybe—

Suddenly, he spoke. "I need to cross the line."

"Seriously?" A watery laugh burst out of her. "I think that line got blown to smithereens repeatedly over the past hour, so it doesn't ma—oof!"

He wrapped his arms around her waist and shoulders, hauling her back against his chest. He tucked his chin into the crook of her neck and began to slowly rock back and forth. The unexpected act shocked her so much that she couldn't do anything but lean back against him. She could feel the pressure in her ears subsiding, her heart rate slowing, her breathing evening out.

"I apologize," he said after a long moment, as if he'd needed comforting as much as she had. "Everything was fine, my mother seemed thrilled with the idea of us dating, and somehow my last relationship was mentioned. Logic and emotion were on a collision course, and emotion won. Logically, I know—I know—that you wouldn't do any of the things my ex did, but emotionally, all I could feel was the need to protect my family from everything and everyone. I shouldn't have taken it out on you. I'm sorry."

The sincerity of his apology washed over her. She reached up to rest her hands on his forearm and leaned her head back against his shoulder, wanting even more contact with him. They stood like that for a while, the silence simmering between them, melting anger and assumptions away.

"Apology accepted," she finally said. "But you've got to stop making assumptions about me. I have a cousin who is nonverbal, and a couple more who are on the spectrum. We all grew up together, and my aunt, who has a doctorate in behavioral sciences, taught all of us how to interact with our cousins or anyone else on a level they're comfortable with. The way you feel about your brother is the way us kids felt about our cousins. We stomped more than one kid into the ground before they learned their lesson."

"I will never, ever, make another assumption about you again," he vowed. "One thing you can say about me is that I'm a fast learner."

"It's always a good day when you learn something new." She turned until she could embrace him. "We both learned something today."

"There's one more thing I'd like to learn," he told her. "Given this position and the fact that you're hugging me instead of pushing me away, what should we do for our first date? We can go to Italy for a dinner date if you want."

He said it so casually she had to believe he'd do it if she wanted. "I'm okay with something simpler than that, that doesn't require a passport or an overnight stay."

"Noted." He gave her a light squeeze. "So that's a yes, with our first date the end of next week?"

She reached up to cup his cheek, capturing his attention. "There's one more thing I need to talk about with you, because I want you to have full understanding of what could happen. But after that emotional roller coaster, I don't have the spoons to discuss it tonight."

"Fair enough." He sobered. "Can you tell me what it's about?"

"My friend Marquessa, and how she died."

Chapter 22

Samara hadn't mentioned her late friend again, and Aron didn't want to mention it either. It would obviously be a painful story for Samara to tell, and he wanted her to tell it only when she was ready.

The day before their contract officially ended, and after Grayson had left for yet another date with Max, Samara finally turned to him and said, "I'm ready to tell you about my friend, and in a way, about my social activism."

"Okay." He gestured to her cup. "Do you want something else to drink? Something stronger?"

"Do we have any of those IPAs left? If not, I can stick to the lemonade."

"I'll go check."

He made his way to the kitchen, extracted a couple of bottles from the beverage fridge, popped the caps, then returned to the office. Samara had moved over to the couch, staring blankly in the general direction of the TV, her hands interlocked. He placed one of the bottles on the coffee table in front of her, then sat down beside her.

She flexed her hands free, then rubbed her palms over her

thighs with a light laugh that held no humor. "Now that the moment's here, I don't know how to start."

He gathered her hand, interlocking their fingers in a loose grip. "Why don't I ask you a question, and you can answer it how you want?"

Taking an ample sip, she nodded. Given what she'd said before, he figured the answer to his question would eventually lead to where she wanted to go.

"What you do, your activism . . . I understand that it's needed, but what made you decide to do it? It can't be easy for you."

She rubbed her forefinger along the rim of her bottle, her expression cloudy yet thoughtful. "No, it's not easy," she finally said. "Anyone who advocates for change, for an equitable playing field, has to deal with backlash from people who are resistant to change, people who think making space for others means taking space from them, or giving something to others means stealing it from them. Then there are the people who are just sad and hate filled and miserable and want to spread that misery and hate to others so they can feel better about themselves."

Because he watched her so closely, he noticed the flicker of her lashes, the way her fingers tightened on his. "Like the pushback you got when you called Artemis out." It wasn't a question.

"Pushback?" A hollow laugh escaped her. "Pushback is too tame a word for the threats and vitriol I get whenever I critique a game for its lack of representation. Some of the comments left on my videos are . . . and then there were private messages and emails before I locked those down. People show their true selves when they're behind the relative safety of burner accounts and sock puppets."

He drew in a measured breath to quell a rising wave of worry and anger. "Have you been threatened?"

Again that empty laugh that hurt to hear. "Is it a day that ends in Y? Like I said, people are brave behind their screens when they can hide their identity. Most of the time it's just empty threats. I have a black belt in Delete and Block, and I employ several different bots to automatically block certain accounts that engage in hate raids."

"Hate raids?"

"I think I told you about it before. Basically, it's targeted harassment of marginalized users who are streaming their game play, which Max, Quinn, and I do a lot for fun and viewership and profit, most of the time from Game and Flame. These users barrel into our chats and inundate them with hate speech, then bots join in on the melee."

"God, now I remember." He was ashamed of how blissfully ignorant he was about the challenges facing marginalized members of the gamer community.

"If there's anything that seems as if they have specific, personal information about me and mine, those I flag and report. Sometimes, most times, nothing gets done. That's why I make sure I can protect myself."

"How?" he wondered, his voice hoarse with shock and rising horror.

"First of all, I never go anywhere alone during conventions. Max and Quinn and I always go to cons together and never go up to our hotel room alone if possible, or if we have to, we'll punch the button for a different floor than the one we're actually staying on. I've been followed a couple of times, and it's scary as hell. Once he found out about the threats I was getting, my father wanted me to get a concealed carry permit, if I insisted on going to cons. I was able to negotiate that to pepper spray, a Taser, and self-defense courses."

"God." He stared, then stared some more, taking in the heaviness of her expression. "Damn, you're serious, aren't you?"

"I wouldn't joke about something like this," she told him, her tone too even. "Or overexaggerate about it, if that's your next comment."

He was ashamed to admit that he'd thought it, but he was smart enough to keep that to himself. "I just . . . I can't believe that people are capable of this kind of stuff and make you have to protect yourself like this. It's gotta be exhausting."

"It is. Fanboys hate having their space encroached upon, especially by whiny women." She rolled her eyes. "I hope you can understand why I said you need to expand your knowledge. Take the gender blinders off. GamerGate got a lot of press, but it wasn't the first incident, and it won't be the last. It isn't easy being female in this industry on either side of the controller. You add being a woman of color to the mix, and guys lose their everlovin' minds."

White guys. She didn't say it, but he knew what she meant. He sat back, trying to understand, trying to empathize and put himself in her shoes. It proved difficult, and he realized how insulated he actually was.

He had a peripheral knowledge of what went down during GamerGate, but he silently admitted that he didn't know the details because he didn't have to. It only tangentially impacted him as a game developer. Artemis Games hadn't been directly involved, so he'd been able to focus his attention elsewhere.

"Having to go through all of this . . . I know advocacy is important to you, but daily threats and hate mail? Potential stalkers? Extreme safety precautions? Why do you do it? I mean, you've deliberately put yourself on the front line of this fight. Why?"

He wasn't asking to dissuade her, or even to understand, really. It felt as if there was a reason that drove her to be a lightning rod for change. He could see the struggle rolling across her features, indecision, anger, and a soul-deep pain that urged him to do something, anything, to erase it. The simplest thing he could do to ease her stress would be to stop pressing her for answers.

"We can stop talking about this if you want. I can see that it's difficult for you."

She carefully placed her bottle on the table, as if any sudden movement would cause it to shatter. Straightening her shoulders, she turned to face him. "Not talking about it doesn't make it go away. Sitting in silence doesn't make it less painful."

His muscles twitched with the urge to pull her closer, wrap his arms around her, and vow that everything would be all right. He settled for gently squeezing her fingers, then releasing her hand. "If you want to tell me, I'm here, and I'm listening. If you don't want to tell me, that's okay too."

"If I stop now, I might not ever start again." She drew in a soft breath. "I'll tell you about it. About Marquessa."

• • •

Sam stared at her bottle of ale, unsure of where to start now that she'd agreed to talk. A slice of regret and the ever-present guilt shafted through her, and she rubbed her palms on her knees again to disguise her suddenly shaky hands.

Marquessa's story was one she'd mentioned before in interviews as a call to action, and she could have easily pointed Aron to any number of the videos and articles posted online. Those articles only gave a highlight, though, glossing over what was a huge turning point in her life, an event that was the foundation of her advocacy. They treated it as just something that happened instead of the traumatic incident that left horror, sadness, and remorse percolating through her heart daily.

She didn't talk about Marquessa much these days, not to people who didn't already know of her. Talking about the incidents that led up to Marquessa's death, and her own inability to save her friend, meant reopening wounds that hadn't completely scabbed over yet. It meant being vulnerable in a way that she fought hard to keep hidden behind a facade of righteous anger, especially to con-goers and casual acquaintances. It took a level of trust to be voluntarily vulnerable with someone, a level she hadn't reached in years.

Aside from trust, it also took a level of intimacy she wasn't sure she should have with Aron. Then again, he was easy to talk with. They had clicked immediately, establishing what she'd thought of as the first forays into friendship until she'd discovered he was the CEO of Artemis Games. Even now, she never felt as if he was. Instead, their relationship felt more like friends collaborating on a project, a relationship transitioning into more. If she could talk about Marquessa to anyone outside of her nearest and dearest, Aron would be the one.

She jumped when his hand covered hers. Shaken, she

stared at their hands for a long moment before looking up at him. Concern shaded his eyes. "Your mind's racing, and you seem to be getting worked up," he explained, his tone tight with worry. "I thought you could use a distraction."

"Thank you," she answered, surprised and touched. Why his concern surprised her, she didn't know. She already knew that Aron had a deep capacity to care—she'd seen that first-hand when he'd promised that Artemis would do and be better, when he mentioned the accessibility certification that was his pet project. Those things seemed at odds with the commanding nature required to helm a multimillion-dollar company he'd built himself.

"Samara." He gave her a smile, soft and comforting. "You don't have to tell me. I don't need to know who Marquessa is or why her story causes you obvious pain. It's not my place to ask, and I apologize."

"God dammit!" The words burst out of her paired with something close to a sob, surprising them both. She curled her free hand into a fist on her knee but didn't try to retract the hand Aron held. "Why the hell are you so understanding?"

"I don't know," he answered, perplexed. His smile faded, and she instantly missed it. "I don't know why I feel comfortable with you, as if I can tell you anything and everything. I don't know why I want that to be reciprocal, why I want—no, I hope—that you can confide in me whenever you need to. You know I want to be more than friends, Samara. Even if that's not happening, I hope you at least consider me a friend."

She turned her hand over to clasp his. "I do," she confessed. "It surprises the hell out of me, but I do think of you as a friend."

His smile, brief as it was, animated his entire face. "I'm glad, but I'm also serious. While I feel like we can talk about anything, I never want you to feel pressured to share, okay?"

She nodded, sudden emotion clogging her throat. Aron was a sensitive man, and she wondered how many people got to witness the squishy interior that he showed her. Not many, she would bet, and somehow the idea that she had a private glimpse of him that no one else did helped to loosen her tongue.

"Marquessa was my best friend," she said into the quiet, then stopped again, unsure of how to tell this story.

Aron asked the question any reasonable person would. "She *was*?"

"Yeah." Her head bobbed as she swallowed, and she squeezed his hand in return to steady herself. "She . . . she died five years ago."

"I'm so sorry," he said, and even though the words were an automatic response, she could hear his sincerity. The next reasonable question would be to ask what had happened, but Aron didn't pose it. Instead, he waited, giving her the time and space she needed to continue.

"I met her in an online gaming forum, and we realized that we both lived in the general Atlanta area. She was my first gaming partner, but we clicked in real life too. We hung out all the time, doing the stuff that friends do. Mostly, though, we just gamed."

She rubbed her thumb along the back of his hand. "One day, someone began talking smack in the chat of a game we were in, really disparaging remarks about minorities. Okay, they were really racist comments and memes. Quietly complaining to the moderators did nothing, and the comments continued to escalate. Marquessa couldn't take it. I just wanted to bail instead of feeding the trolls, but Marquessa had a different idea. She let loose, revealing herself as a Black woman instead of the default male everyone had thought she was. We'd always used aliases as a safety precaution, being careful not to reveal our gender and definitely not our race, and she, she just ripped the curtains down. The attacks were a pile-on and became so obstructive they had to shut the server down and ban us.

"Marquessa was incensed. I was mad too, but ready to let it go and move on to something else. It was just par for the course and a reminder of why we used aliases. Marquessa, however, was filled with this awe-inspiring, fiery conviction that we'd been wronged. She created a video discussing the crap talk and then posted screenshots of the hateful comments that followed."

"I'm guessing that didn't go over well."

"That's an understatement. It blew up. Huge. The comments on her post . . . people are just awful. I wanted Marquessa to let it go; I even begged her to take the post down because no one should voluntarily subject themselves to all that bullying bullshit. Especially when our so-called allies ghosted us. They all fled like roaches when shit got real."

Anger surged through her. "Marquessa refused to back down, saying she didn't need performative allyship and that she wasn't going to let the trolls win. She seemed to be dealing with everything as best as could be expected, but one day she got doxed. Someone posted all of her personal information in different forums, her real name, her phone number, address, even where she worked."

She swallowed. "That's when things got really bad. Prank calls and massive food deliveries were the tamest. The scariest were the cars driving slowly by her apartment, the phone call to her job reporting that she was seen doing drugs in the parking lot. That's just the things she told me about, but I'm sure there were others. If I had known . . ."

Her voice faded, weakened by the weight of her words and her wounds. Wishing Marquessa was still alive. Wanting the conversation over with.

Aron reached over, wrapping his arm around her shoulders. The sudden contact startled her, but she didn't pull away. Right then, she needed the support, needed to lean against him. "She died, and it wasn't accidental, and they never found the person or people who did it. She died with her dream unrealized. And I, I felt so much guilt that I promised her, promised myself, that I would make her dream my dream, that I would do whatever it took to see her dream to fruition."

She swallowed. "This is the reason why I'm hesitating over dating you. Some of this could hit you too, could affect your company. It's hard. Some days it's just so damned hard to pretend to be strong and unaffected."

"Samara." He tightened his grip. "I sincerely hope that you won't receive any negativity from working with me, but I'm not naive. I just hope that, at least in this, you'll let me be your shield. Would you let me do that?"

His voice, so sincere; his expression, so earnest; his hand, so steadying. In that moment of weakness, she wanted to say yes, wanted to lean on him and ease her burden, even if only for a little while. She wanted to, but she couldn't.

"I know you want to help because you want to make amends, but I can't ask you to do that," she said, regretting every word she spoke. "It wouldn't be fair."

"What does being fair have to do with this?" he asked, his voice still soft and sincere. "This isn't about being fair."

"I'm used to taking the flak with stuff like this," she pointed out. "You aren't."

"Samara." A world of emotion weighted that one word. He leaned forward, capturing and holding her attention. "Just because you're used to taking the flak doesn't mean that you should, or that you should continue taking it."

She jerked as the words scored a direct hit. She'd heard different versions of those words from different people, but for some reason, coming from him they reverberated. Staring at him, she again felt the full force of his focus, as if nothing else mattered except her and here and now.

He raised his hand, hesitated a moment, then slowly reached out to cup her cheek. "I will be your shield, Samara. This involves me too, and I have the resources and the legal team to handle anyone who slanders and threatens you. Please allow me to do this."

Her throat tightened. Her last boyfriend had ghosted her because he couldn't handle the online attacks even when they weren't directed at him. Yet here Aron was, fully aware of the things she experienced and, instead of washing his hands at the contract's end, offering to shield her.

She blinked back tears so a smile could bloom. "Where should we go on our first date?"

Happiness dawned on his features, lighting and animating his face. "Don't worry, I have it all planned out."

She side-eyed him. "Like what?"

He rubbed his hands together in clear excitement. "We'll do a celebratory dinner tomorrow for the successful completion of our collaboration. Grayson will be there too, and he might invite your friend Max. I'd like our first official date to be Friday, if you're available."

The start of the weekend. Suspicious, she frowned at him. "Please tell me we're not going to Italy."

"We're not going to Italy," he promised. "I'm going to take you to the Jurassic instead."

Ah, he meant the cocktails at the museum event. A perfect setting for their first date. "I think that's a wonderful idea."

"Great. The only other thing I'd like to definitely put on your calendar is a fundraising event. The Emory Autism Center is holding a black-tie fundraiser at the Georgian Terrace across from the Fox Theatre. My mother is the fundraiser chairperson."

"Black tie at the Georgian Terrace?" A little frisson of alarm snaked through her. She'd been to plenty of fundraisers that required a cocktail dress and had a few stashed in her closet. But a black-tie event meant tuxedos and floor-length dresses. "That sounds fancy."

"It's a major event and takes up all three ballrooms. Tuxedos and evening gowns are required. If you need a ball gown, I'll buy it for you."

"I don't know if you know this, but I just finished a contract gig that paid me extremely well," she told him, knowing he meant nothing negative by the offer. "And I was financially in good shape before that. I can buy my own ball gown."

Firmness set his expression into hard angles. "Maybe I want to go with you. Maybe I want to see you try on all those dresses."

Whew. Her entire body warmed at the intensity in his words and in his eyes. Did she really think she had a chance of resisting this man? "Going clothes shopping with your girlfriend. You're really serious about this whole dating thing."

"I'm serious about you, Samara. Don't ever forget that."

Chapter 23

After contorting her arms to pull up the zipper on her gown, Samara turned a critical eye on her reflection in the full-length mirror, analyzing her front and side views. She'd cinched and pinched herself to within an inch of her life, but the results spoke for themselves. Her waist was snatched, her hips didn't lie, and her butt could stop traffic. The best part was that she'd even be able to sit down and eat an hors d'oeuvre or two.

Blowing out a slow breath, she placed her hand flat against her belly, where butterflies were currently doing their version of a drunken wedding line dance. Too many things were converging, ramping up her anxiety. A formal date with Aron, at a fundraiser for which his mother served as chairperson. A public outing where they could be outed as a couple. She wasn't sure she was ready for it, any of it.

Truth was, she wasn't ready to give up their anonymity. For the last three weeks, they'd just been Aron and Samara, hanging out and having fun. They'd done the museum, a double date with Max and Grayson, dinners out, and walked some of the nature trails around the city. Even after meeting up with her crew at Game Night, where no one had treated him as anything other than one of group, they had managed to maintain their blissful bubble of being themselves instead of being defined by their careers.

Here, though, he wouldn't be just one of the people hanging out. Here he would be Aron Galanis, president and CEO of Artemis Games. The gorgeous son of the gala's organizer. The very well-off bachelor. It would be foolish to hope that he could be incognito. Mothers would probably throw their single daughters his way, even though it was a fundraiser. No, she was pretty sure that people would have their eyes on him, which would make them curious about her.

That was the hard part, and that was why she'd checked into the hotel the night before, scheduled a session at a spa, and watched a crapton of YouTube videos to figure out how to contour her makeup. Neither she nor Aron had brought up how to introduce her to any of his or his mother's acquaintances at this event, and that needed to happen as soon as she met him downstairs. However they decided to introduce her—friend, business partner, or something more intimate— she was going to make sure she was her best self. Her standard operating procedure was to never look raggedy when she left the house, even for a grocery store or fast-food run. She certainly wasn't going halfway on how she presented and represented at this nearly two-hundred-plus-dollar-a-ticket fundraiser.

As she secured the second blush pearl stud in her earlobe, her phone rang, Aron's name flashing on the screen. "Hi, Sam. I just arrived in the atrium. Should I come up to escort you?"

She thought about it for a hot second before deciding against it. She had a reasonable guess of how he'd react once he saw her glammed up for the first time, and she didn't want the temptations of his kisses and more to delay their attendance. Especially since his mother was head of the event and would certainly be looking for them sooner rather than later. "No, I'll be down in a few minutes. I'll meet you in the atrium."

She disconnected, then retrieved the tiny beaded purse with a gold chain strap she'd found at a vintage thrift shop. It fit her phone, a gloss, and her ID and one credit card. Slinging it onto her shoulder, she checked her appearance one final time, then headed for the elevator. The bouncing butterflies in her belly intensified with each floor she descended until they became an all-out rave by the time she reached the lobby level.

The Grand Ballroom had already opened its doors for attendees, soft music filtering out into the lobby where dozens of glitterati awaited entry. She glided past them, making a mental note that her dress did indeed fit in with the attire other women had chosen, then began an earnest search for Aron. She caught a glimpse of him in a seating area in front of the main entrance but slowed her steps when she noticed other people with him. His mother and Benjy, and a petite brunette.

At that moment, Aron turned and caught sight of her. His expression blanked, then he began to walk toward her as if pulled by an invisible string, ignoring everyone else. The crowd parted like the Red Sea for Moses, giving them a clear view of each other.

Her heart stuttered. Aron was good-looking on a regular day. Tonight, in his midnight blue tux with his hair swept back and that intensely focused look in his honey-colored eyes, he was devastatingly handsome, secret agent suave, and sexy as fuck.

Her inner voice sang, *Girl, you in trouble* . . .

"Samara," he said, then stopped as if he couldn't speak. His gaze swept over her like a physical caress, a caress she felt to her core.

"Aron." She tried for something pithy to say, but with him this close, with him staring at her, with him being *all that*, her higher brain functions seemed to melt away, leaving only a base urge to claim him then and there.

"You look . . . you look . . ." He gestured between them, as if incapable of finding more words.

"So do you," she answered, wondering at the breathiness of her voice.

He shook his head as if clearing fog from his mind, glanced around, then gathered himself. "I wasn't ready. I mean, did someone sew this dress onto you?"

She struck a pose. "This is an evening gown, dahling, not a dress." She put a hand on his arm. "You don't need to worry about the process. Just be happy with the final result."

"I'm more than happy. I'm mentally turning cartwheels and acting like that wolf in those old cartoons. I am definitely appreciating this view. I just don't want anyone else to appreciate it."

Sam suppressed a smile. "Your Neanderthal is showing, sweetie. Should I enter the ballroom by myself?"

"Don't even think about it, especially since you just called me sweetie." He offered his elbow. "Before we go in, come say hello to Mom and Benjy."

"Sure." She curled her hand into the crook of his arm and allowed him to guide her through the throng to reach his mother, brother, and a young woman who stared at them in unabashed curiosity.

"Samara!" Artemis Galanis called out, then quickly followed up with a careful hug before grabbing both her hands. "I'm so glad to see you. You are stunning. I can see why Aron abandoned us so quickly."

"Mom," Aron protested, but it was a weak protest, as if he'd do it again in a heartbeat.

"We all saw you do it, son. It's okay."

Sam shared a smile with his mother. "Thank you, Mrs. G. You're looking absolutely gorgeous yourself. Planning to break a few hearts tonight?"

"Sam." A definite protest from Aron that time. He'd have to deal with it. Mrs. Galanis could be the perfect cougar if she wanted to be.

Mrs. G. lightly slapped Aron's arm. "Leave her alone. She's on a roll, and I'm enjoying every bit of it."

Sam gave him a so-there smile before turning to Benjy. "Hey, Benjy, look at you all handsome in your tux. Bet you're gonna break some hearts too."

She held up her fist for him to bump. He ignored it but leaned forward instead. "Oh, you want a hug?"

When he stepped closer to her, Sam leaned in to give him a quick and light hug. "I got to hug the entire Galanis family? I need to clean up more often."

"I haven't gotten a hug yet," Aron mumbled. "I'm suddenly the invisible man here."

"Good things come to those who wait," his mother said, beating Sam to the punch. "Samara, this is Beth Calloway, Benjy's assistant."

Assistant? A personal assistant like Grayson was for Aron or more like a helper when he went out without his mother? Either way, "assistant" was a good, professional way of describing her duties, Sam supposed. She stretched out a hand. "Pleased to meet you, Ms. Calloway."

"Call me Beth." The other woman shook her hand, then glanced between her and Aron. "So, you and Aron, huh?"

The blunt question from someone she'd just met had her drawing back like *who the fuck are you?* She drop-kicked her initial reaction into the ether and said a very polite, "Excuse me?"

"Don't mind Beth," Aron cut in. Maybe her tone hadn't been as polite as she'd thought. "Beth has been working with Benjy for about ten or so years now. She's basically the obnoxious sister we never had."

"Completely obnoxious, but Benjy thinks it's funny." Beth laughed. "I'd stick my tongue out at you, Aron, but it wouldn't look good with my outfit."

"Children," Mrs. G. said in that parent tone that made everyone stand up straight. "I think it's time to enter the ballroom. I'll go first with Benjy and Beth, and you two can follow. All right?"

They broke like a sports team after a time-out, then turned to the ballroom entrance, following the marching orders the Galanis matriarch had given them. Aron deliberately lagged behind the others until they were out of earshot.

"I feel happy and lucky tonight," he told her, his mood decidedly more upbeat than usual at these types of gatherings. "Maybe I should buy a lottery ticket."

"As if you need more money," she scoffed. "What's got you feeling so lucky and happy?"

"You, of course," he said, his tone indicating that she should have known his answer. "You on my arm. You being you. You being mine. How can I not feel happy and lucky?"

Floundering at his answer, she almost grabbed his arm in both hands and leaned against him, but stopped herself just in time. Their affection for each other was theirs and theirs alone. She didn't want to broadcast their relationship status to the entire gala, but did want this to be like a date for them. Settling for a demure grip on his elbow would have to do. For now.

Together they walked into the Grand Ballroom, chock full of people dressed in glittering gowns and tailored tuxes. More than one of the attendees stared at Aron, then at her, then back at Aron in a way that squeezed her stomach and shallowed her breaths. Many of these people probably knew his mother, and by extension, him. Some of them would surely want to speak with him. What was she supposed to do then? Go off by herself?

"It's okay," he whispered, and she realized she'd tightened her grip on his arm. "There are a lot of these events, but this is the only one I attend because of the cause and because it's my mother's fundraiser. Most of the people I know here even in passing also know that I'm . . . antisocial?"

He wasn't antisocial; he just had a limited amount of tolerance for bullshit discussions. "How about we say you're not fond of small talk?"

"That sounds better, so we'll go with that. I may have to talk to a few people at some point tonight, and I want you with me when I do. I'll follow your lead on how you want to introduce yourself, but my goal is to make the meet and greets as brief as possible. So, if you'll be my support human, I promise to be yours. Deal?"

How could she refuse? They were an unofficial couple. Backing each other was a given. "Deal."

"Aron, is that you?"

They turned together at the sound of the voice. A stunning brunette in a scarlet gown approached them. She was beautiful, and she clearly only had eyes for Aron. Fascinated, Samara stepped back to watch their exchange.

Aron shot Sam a look as if he knew what she intended and didn't like it. He turned back just as the brunette reached out to touch his shoulder, or maybe even hug him, Sam wasn't sure. But she was sure about his intentions when he stepped back out of reach, his body and expression stiff. "Ms. Conley."

Ms. Conley released a light laugh. "Oh, don't be like that, Aron. You know my name's Kaitlyn, so call me that, especially since we've been friends for so long."

"Our mothers are friends," he corrected. "I only interact with you when we're with them."

Ouch. Sam internally winced. Blunt truth was his usual communication style, but add to that his standoffishness in social settings and not-quite-friend Kaitlyn Conley had about thirty seconds before Aron walked away. Maybe things would have been different if they were having dinner with their mothers, but Sam had a feeling Aron had always been distant with the brunette. She wanted to soothe him with a supportive touch, but there was enough distance between them that she couldn't make it surreptitious enough.

Ms. Conley wasn't fazed. Obviously, she had encountered Aron's remoteness before and blithely ignored it as if it were her superpower. She turned her gaze on Sam. "I haven't seen you before," she said with the brightness of an atomic bomb, beautiful yet deadly. "Aron, did you get another secretary?"

Both Sam and Aron bristled. "If you're talking about my administrative assistant, Janet, she still has dominion over the executive section of our office," he said, his voice a cold front chilling the atmosphere. "If you're speaking of my personal assistant, Grayson still puts up with me. As for Ms. Reynolds here, she is—"

"Samara Reynolds, with Rise Consulting," Sam said with a nod. In this post-pandemic world, she didn't shake hands with just anyone, and it was a relief to no longer have to. "Mr. Galanis and I have been collaborating on a project together."

Kaitlyn assessed her, apparently assumed Sam wasn't a threat, then gave her one of those dismissive half smiles Sam usually received when people underestimated her. It was one of her greatest pleasures proving how idiotic those assumptions and estimations were.

"Really? And what have you been collaborating on?"

Kaitlyn's tone insinuated that the collaboration wasn't important at all. *Lady, you don't even know. We're about to collaborate on some bedroom games once this gala is over.* "Unfortunately, I'm not at liberty to share that information with an outsider," she said in the brightest sugar-dripping tone she could muster, with a sprinkle of Grandma Nina's bless-your-heart spice on top. "Unless you're . . . Aron?"

She turned to Aron, "Is she an insider?"

"She is not."

"Well, then." Samara turned back. "I'm sure you'll learn about it in due time." *Make an assumption about that, lady.*

She didn't have to. "It's been one of the best collaborations I've ever taken part in," Aron added, giving Sam a knowing smile. "I can't wait for the opportunity to collaborate again."

The other woman clearly didn't like that, given the brittleness of her smile. "Ms. Reynolds, was it? Do you mind if I steal

Aron away from you for a bit? There's something I'd like to discuss with him."

Seriously? Sam gestured to Aron, wishing she had some popcorn to watch the rest of this scene. "Shouldn't you be asking Aron instead of me? He's his own man."

Kaitlyn made two mistakes, and a true friend of Aron's would have known better. She invaded his personal space without permission, and she placed a hand on his forearm. "Aron, is it possible—"

"No, it's not." He stepped back from her, and Sam hoped she'd never be on the receiving end of the winter in his tone and posture. In stark contrast to his reaction to Kaitlyn, he took Sam's hand and curled her fingers around the crook of his arm again. She gave him a light squeeze of encouragement, letting him know she had his back.

He inclined his head in acknowledgment, then turned back to the other woman. "I am Ms. Reynolds's escort for the evening, and it would be rude of me to leave her alone to go off with another woman."

Sam stared into the distance, conflict facing off inside her. Womanly pride on one side that he'd chosen her over Ms. Conley versus womanly outrage on the other that he was leveraging her support–human capacity as an excuse to block the other woman.

Not that he needed her as a block. His voice dropped low, weighted by the ice in his tone, quite like the ice giant character in *Legendsfall* who smashed his way through anything and everything with an ice sickle the size of a high-rise. "You really believe you can come up to me like this and I'm supposed to pretend that everything's fine? I'm not that good of an actor."

The brunette huffed out a laugh, hands on her hips. "Come on, Aron, it's not that serious."

"It is. I am. We are." He wrapped his fingers around Sam's, then brought their entwined hands up to kiss the back of her hand. "Sweetheart, are you ready for a glass of wine?"

Shock drove conflict right out of her head. No one could mistake that gesture or that endearment as an unimportant thing between collaborators. Kaitlyn Conley certainly didn't, if her shocked and outraged expression was any indication. "Actually, I would love—"

She squeaked as Aron tightened his grip and pulled her away from the Conley woman, who, judging by the storm clouds in her eyes, seemed extremely upset about it. She quickened her steps to keep pace with him. "Would you mind slowing down? I can't keep up in this dress or these shoes."

He paused as his displeasure deepened. "How would you escape if you had to wearing all this?"

"I already scoped out all the exits, and I'd kick off my shoes and hike the dress above my knees so I could sprint. Maybe even use you as a human shield." She gauged his expression. "Are we escaping?"

"I wish." He blew out a breath. "We can't leave until Mom makes her speech."

That displeasure was definitely him being pissed now. She touched his bicep with her free hand. "Do you want a moment to yourself so you can take a breather? If you need quiet and solitude, I can give you my room key. It's okay if you want to be alone."

That had him fully turning around to face her. "I don't want to be alone. I want to be away from her."

That much was obvious. Without Grayson to run interference, Aron's people meter filled pretty quickly at public events. Even a handshake was one step too much sometimes, but still . . . "Do you have a history with her, like she's your ex or something? If so, I can understand being remote with her, and getting pissed when she touched you without permission, but wasn't that rejection with a side helping of PDA a little harsh?"

"No." His jaw jutted with justification. "She shouldn't even be here. She considers my brother and anyone on the spectrum to be an inconvenience who should be kept at home. As I told her then, there was no need to interact with her after that."

"What the hell?" That flipped her anger switch to full power. She turned to throw a glance into the crowd, hoping to catch sight of a red dress. "Benjy is a person, not an inconvenience!"

His fingers flexed, his grip preventing her from stalking the crowd. "You don't have to go defend Benjy's honor, although I appreciate that you want to. I took care of that. I also didn't tell my mother, because she's friends with Kaitlyn's mother. Mrs. Conley is a decent human being who treats Benjy with respect, but I refuse to interact with her daughter ever again." His harsh expression softened. "So you understand?"

"I totally understand." She did too. Aron measured every woman by how she treated his brother. Anyone who belittled or ignored Benjy had no chance of winning Aron's heart.

Not that she wanted to win his heart, right? That wasn't on the radar. It didn't matter that she'd known him for four months. She'd only been dating him for three weeks. They hadn't even had sex yet, but if his kisses were any indication, she was in for a world of trouble.

Needing to steady herself, she grabbed his elbow with both

hands. His intense stare almost made her loosen her fingers, but she held on and made a joke instead. "Do I have to be worried about any of your other exes showing up tonight, Mr. Galanis?"

"She didn't get the chance to become my ex." His voice dropped as he stepped closer. "The only ex I'm worried about is if the woman standing in front of me, looking like a golden goddess in her gown and who would cause wrecks on Peachtree Street if she happened to step outside, decided to no longer collaborate with me."

Whoa. At that moment every sound, every person, every *thing* faded away until only she and Aron remained. Thank goodness for the strapless bra and the gown's beaded bodice. She didn't need anyone to know that her nips stood at attention just from Aron staring at her. This was his superpower, his level up. She'd gotten so used to his formality and then his increasing casualness over the last few months that when he focused in on her with such intent it was like an electric jolt to her system, short-circuiting her reserve and jump-starting her heart.

"Samara. Don't look at me like that."

She blinked out of her stupor, trying to look him in the eyes instead of in the lips. "Excuse me?"

He leaned in, body closer, lips closer, losing-her-common-sense closer. "Keep staring at me like that and I'll be forced to abandon my carefully plotted timeline and disappoint my mother by disappearing with you for the rest of the night."

Determination burned through every word, heating her blood and making her flush. Since fanning herself with her purse would be too obvious, she opted for a deep breath in and out. Aron's gaze immediately dropped to her chest. Her heart immediately raced. Her libido immediately demanded satisfaction.

"Okay, then," she whispered, incapable of speaking louder. "The same goes for you staring at me, mister. You're not going to make me cause a scandal by tossing my panties at you."

He straightened so fast she heard his vertebrae crack, raising his hands to reach for her. Did he intend to grab her and make off with her? Now that sounded like a damned good idea. And with a room upstairs, she could throw her panties at him as soon as the door closed behind them.

"Yes, well." He cleared his throat, then tightened his tie. "What about that drink? Something with lots of ice?"

"Sounds good to me."

Chapter 24

Aron stood next to Samara at a high-top table, fighting the urge to adjust his tie yet again. Not even two hours in and he was already over it. His people meter was pegged to full, making him anxious to find a quiet and less populated spot, preferably with Sam next to him. He wanted to hold her in ways that he couldn't in this setting, especially after that panty-throwing comment.

She dazzled him, even unsettled him at times. Like tonight. Seeing her in that golden gown for the first time, it was as if a bright shaft of light illuminated her and faded everyone else. His body had moved toward her before his brain had caught on, just as it had when they'd walked away from Ms. Conley. Samara's role as just a collaborator had gone up in flames at that point.

Not that he minded, but he knew Samara did. He knew she was cautious about publicly acknowledging their relationship, knew she had a right and a reason to be. Normally, he was cautious too. Normally, he'd be guarding his emotions like a dragon in front of its hoard. Normally, he wouldn't display them for all the world to see, even at this gala where he knew half the people gathered. But Samara had a way of excavating everything he'd locked away before, bringing it all to the surface and turning it into something she treasured.

Discomfort wrapped around him again, making him shift his stance. At least the live band specifically chosen for this event soothed him. Soft music filled the air, accompanying two vocalists who didn't try to outsing each other. That wouldn't do tonight, where many of the attendees had different degrees of autism and couldn't deal with bright lights or loud noises. There were even people out on the small dance floor, quietly swaying close together to the smooth, jazzy song.

Close together.

He swore he heard an audible click in his brain a second before he turned to Samara. "Would you like to dance? With me," he added, in case it wasn't clear.

Her smile dimpled her cheeks in a way that he'd never get tired of. "I'd love to dance. With you."

Relieving her of her wineglass, he took her hand to guide her onto the dance floor. Dancing wasn't something he did; he felt all gangly like a baby moose taking its first steps. But he'd asked, she'd said yes, so he'd do his best not to stomp on her toes and pretend he was a suave secret agent out to win the girl and save the day.

Just as they hit the dance floor, the band launched into a song about love being king. No pressure there. He focused instead on the fact that Samara was in his arms at last, one hand on his bicep, the other wrapped in fingers he hoped hadn't gone clammy or sweaty.

"Aron."

He instantly stopped. "Are you all right? Should we go back?"

"Yes and no." She pulled her hand free of his grip and draped it over his shoulder. "Relax. We don't have to waltz or do the samba, thank goodness. We can just sway like this and talk. I firmly believe you won't step on my toes."

Relief flooded him, relaxing him enough so that he could joke with her. "Maybe I'm worried about you stepping on my toes. I have a pretty good idea of how high those heels are."

"Very." She sighed. "My feet will probably curse me out tomorrow, along with my calf muscles. But it was all worth it to look this good in this gown."

"Good is an understatement," he informed her. "Good isn't a decent descriptor for the . . . sheer magnificence that you are. When I saw you in the lobby, my mind actually went blank. My brain may short-circuit once in a while, but it has never gone blank. Until I saw you."

"Hmm," she said, drawing his attention. "Judging by your expression, I'm not sure if that's a compliment or a complaint."

Instead of a supposition he had yet to resolve, he went with a statement of fact. "You're beautiful. You must know that."

"I have to admit that I hit 'pretty' much more often, like when I'm dressed in business professional attire."

"No." He shook his head. "You're beautiful when you're working. You're beautiful when you're gaming. You're beautiful when you're with my family. But you're especially beautiful when you're happy."

She stared at him, her eyes shiny, her lips pressed tight together. Alarm swept him. Did he say the wrong thing? Was she about to cry? He couldn't apologize for telling her the truth, but maybe he should have waited until they were alone.

"Umm." She cleared her throat, her expression softening as she patted his bicep. "You have this amazing ability to say something about me that's so matter-of-fact for you but knocks me off my feet and makes me go all mushy inside."

"Is that good or bad?"

"It's good." Another dimpled smile as she carefully pressed her forefingers beneath each eye. "Actually, 'good' is an understatement. It's way better than good."

"I'm glad." Pleasure breezed through him. "Then I suppose now is a good time to make a confession."

It was her turn to stop their dance, the hand on his shoulder tightening. "What sort of confession?"

"So much wariness in those four words, as if you're always assuming the worst. You should know by now that I'm just as direct with good news as I am with bad."

"You're right, and I apologize." She squared her shoulders as if bracing herself. "Tell me what you want to confess."

He leaned closer. "I'm not a dancer. I only asked you to dance so that I could use it as an excuse to hold you like this."

That liquid smile of hers washed over him again. "Then I suppose I need to make a confession too," she told him, her voice low and soft.

Curiosity poked him. Did her confession align with his or was it something else entirely? "What do you need to confess?"

She stroked her thumb across his bicep, a small movement that sent a big shock through him. "I actually wanted you to ask me to dance because I wanted you to hold me like this."

He splayed his hand low on her back to pull her just a little closer. "Do you think we could make it through three consecutive songs before people realize we're something more than business collaborators?"

She made an adorable face. "I think we kinda spoiled that with your former friend. Who, by the way, is currently glaring daggers at me behind your back. She needs to learn that God don't like ugly, as my grandma always says."

"If she's bothering you, I will speak to her." *Tell me she's bothering you.*

"We don't need to cause even more of a scene tonight." She gazed up at him, her expression serious. "Do you want this to be our official coming-out party?"

"Why not? It's as good a time as any. Besides, your Game Night friends posted a lot of photos of us all over social media."

"Those were all group shots, though, and we weren't tagged in any of them," she reminded him. "Other than the fact that we sat next to each other, it would take a giant leap to infer that we were on our second date."

"And this is the third date—or fourth if you count that dim sum place we went to last Thursday. Or the twenty-second date if you count all the evenings we've spent eating and gaming since the contract ended. Doesn't that many dates mean we're dating?"

Her smile seemed part admiration and part annoyance. "Railroaded by your infallible logic yet again. I suppose attending this event together, three outside dates, and at least one more scheduled, does indeed mean we're dating."

Yes! "Then I see nothing wrong with making it official. Is it possible that you have some reservations that you have yet to disclose?"

Hearing the stiff formality of his words caused him to mentally cringe. He hadn't done that since the day he'd given the presentation on why they should date. He didn't want to fall back into those old defensive patterns with Samara. He didn't want to be defensive with her at all. What he wanted was as simple as holding her hand in public and as major as sharing a hug or a kiss without worrying about who saw them.

She squeezed his arm again. "Believe me when I say that I have no reservations about you or about us being together. But I want our relationship to just be, without a press release or public declarations or any other sort of grand fanfare. I'm dating Aron Galanis, not the CEO of Artemis Games. Does that make sense?"

"Yes, it does, and I sure as hell am not going to issue a press release announcing our relationship," he assured her. "I enjoy my privacy and my private life too much. Business and personal are separate, and I'd like to keep them that way. But if someone asks either of us if we're dating someone, I'd like us to be able to say yes."

"I can do that." She stopped swaying and gave him a wink. "By the way, that was the third song we danced to."

They had danced through three songs? He hadn't noticed, so focused was he on Samara, but he wondered if other guests had. "I guess we've done it now," he said as he stepped back, already missing holding her.

"Aron. Samara."

He turned in answer to the soft call to see his mother, Benjy, and Beth approaching them. "Hey. Have you been in here for a while? I didn't see you."

"That's because you only have eyes for Samara," Beth said. "Which I totally understand."

Aron took an instinctive step in front of his girlfriend. "Should I remind you that you're very married, and your wife has a jealous streak Mississippi River wide?"

"I call them like I see them, Mr. Blunt Truth," Beth retorted.

Samara's laughter stopped whatever comeback he was about to make. "You guys really do act like siblings. Benjy, do you have to put up with this all the time?"

Benjy gave her a smile and an affirmative grunt, and damned if Aron's heart didn't do the same little hop it did every time Sam engaged with Benjy, and every time Benjy showed how much he liked her. The logical side of him had no chance when it came to her, leaving him to wonder if he was already in too deep.

Their mother gave him a look, and he knew Samara already had a permanent place in her book. "Benjy has to referee them all the time, poor angel. As for you, Aron, I don't think you would have noticed me even if I didn't wait until the song ended. You seemed to be having an important conversation."

A very important conversation, but he saw no need to share it. His mother would go over the top with joy, drawing the attention that Samara wanted to avoid. "Have you finished your official hosting duties?"

"I have a break until it's time to give my thank-you speech," his mother answered. "I was hoping that we could take a photo together. There's a designated area past the silent auction that's been set up for posed photos."

"Sure."

He turned to Samara to offer his arm, but she drew back. "I'll wait for you over there," she said, pointing to the table they'd used before.

"No, you won't." His mother locked arms with Samara. "You're included in my photo request. We cinched ourselves into these gowns within an inch of our lives. We should have photographic evidence of all this fabulousness together, don't you think?"

Samara tossed him a half-pleading, half-flustered look. They had just settled things between them, agreed to acknowledge their relationship without fanfare. Having Sam take pictures with his family, witnessed by anyone in the vicinity, would be akin to renting a billboard near the highly traveled Spaghetti Junction highway intersection. Torn between humoring his mother and placating his girlfriend, Aron tried to thread the needle.

"Samara, would it be all right if we take a picture together to commemorate our night? And maybe one with all of us together? I promise that I won't post it anywhere, nor will it be on the front of the Galanis family's Christmas cards."

She laughed, just as he'd hoped she would. "Well, there's that at least. I guess it wouldn't hurt."

"Excellent. Let's go." His mother all but dragged Samara away, leaving him to follow with Benjy and Beth.

"Talk about being between a rock and a hard place," Beth said with a snort. "Your mother never takes no for an answer when she wants a yes. She gets her way no matter what. You're going to have to make it up to poor Samara somehow."

"Trust me, she's probably already thought of something."

Beth laughed, then sobered, her stare heavy on him. He braced himself for whatever she was about to say. "If I can put on my big-sister hat for a moment, I just want to say how thrilled I am that you're dating someone. Especially someone like Samara."

He swallowed down sudden discomfort. "You don't even know her."

"I know she's smart, funny, and puts up with you," Beth retorted. "Besides, she makes an excellent first impression, doesn't she?"

His mind instantly raced back to the convention, listening to her panel, talking in the food court, facing her righteous anger at his okay-maybe-it-wasn't-small deception. "Yes, she does."

"Wow." She punched his shoulder. "I wish I'd had my phone out so I could have taken your picture right now. You're slobbering down your chin."

Like an idiot, he actually raised his hand to check, and Beth's peal of laughter inflamed an urge to yank her ponytail. He turned to his brother. "Come on, Benjy. We probably shouldn't leave Samara alone with Mom for too long."

They made their way to the area cordoned off for photography with the event's logo emblazoned on a backdrop, catching up with their mother and Samara. A volunteer greeted them with a smile. "Chairwoman, are you here to get your event photo taken?"

"I am," his mother answered, keeping a firm grip on Samara's arm. "I've brought my family with me."

"What?" Samara tried to pry herself free of his mother's grasp. "Mrs. Galanis, I still don't think it's right for me to be a part of your family photo."

"Of course it's right," his mother insisted, waving her hand as if to dismiss Samara's protest. "You've helped Aron tremendously over the last few months, and Benjy adores you. That makes you family in my book. Now, come on. It looks like we're next."

Samara's expression sent panic crawling up his chest. Any moment now she was going to bolt and probably never talk to him again. He couldn't let that happen.

"Mom." He touched her shoulder, then leaned in. "You're making Samara uncomfortable."

"Really?" His mother turned. "Am I making you uncomfortable, Samara? I don't want you to feel pressured."

Which actually was pressure, Aron knew from having been on the receiving end of his mother's ferocious good intentions for the last thirty years. He might have been used to it, but Samara was not. Samara could also free herself of his mother's grip and walk away. "Mom," he warned, preparing to free Samara and deal with his mother's feelings later.

"Aron." Samara briefly touched his arm. "It's okay."

He wanted to—not argue, not really—relieve her pressure, but all of the scenarios he thought of would only pressure her further. When he nodded, she turned back to his mother. "How would you like to arrange us?"

His mother beamed, then proceeded to arrange them as she liked into four consecutive photos, because of course one wasn't enough. "Benjy needs a break," she announced, "so I want this last one to be you and Samara, okay?"

And that's how he found himself doing the very last thing he wanted to do, standing with Samara against a fake backdrop in front of bright lights, basically confirming what their dancing and "family" photos had hinted at.

"I'm sorry," he whispered to her as the photographer readied her camera. "I know this has been uncomfortable for you. I'll make it up to you somehow."

"You're worrying," she whispered back. "I'm beginning to accept that your mom is going to out us whether we want her to or not. I'll just pretend it's prom night and I'm taking pictures with my guy."

He liked that she'd called him her guy, no matter how reluctant she'd been to make it official. "Prom night?"

"Yeah, remember in high school, toward the end of the

year, how we got all dressed up with our classmates, went to fancy restaurants and had our pictures . . ." She wrinkled her brows at him. "You didn't go to prom, did you?"

"I didn't see the point, so I never went."

"Well, then, let's pretend like this is prom night," she said as she shifted her pose. "Even though you didn't bring me a corsage."

He made a mental note to learn about corsages as Samara deftly guided him through a pair of poses. Finally, they rejoined the rest of his family and left the photo area. He was ready to spend some more time with Samara, maybe have a real meal in the hotel's restaurant, away from all the festivities.

His mother had other plans. "Samara, do you mind if I steal Aron away from you for a moment? There's something I need to discuss with him."

What could his mother possibly want to discuss with him that was important enough to interrupt his date night with Samara? He gave her an assessing glance, trying to determine her mood from her body language. Her relaxed posture and bright smile indicated that she was far from upset or irritated with him, thank goodness.

"Of course, Mrs. Galanis, we can trade." She turned to Benjy and Beth. "Do you want dessert, or did Beth bring your tablet so we can play some games?"

"Of course I have his tablet," Beth said, patting her beaded tote. "Never go anywhere without it."

Benjy smiled as he bumped her shoulder, then turned in the direction of the dessert tables. "Well, it looks like we're going to do both," she announced with a grin. "Benjy, do you mind if I hold your arm right here?"

Aron watched as Benjy gave his affirmative grunt and allowed Samara to slip her hand into the crook of his elbow. "I like this brother better anyway."

Aron stood in stunned silence as Samara smiled, blew a raspberry at him, then walked away with Benjy and Beth without giving him a chance to respond. Not that he knew what sort of response he should have given, seeing as she didn't even say goodbye. Watching her sway away, he could tell that her earlier reluctance and discomfort had evaporated as if it had never been. She seemed happy. Happy to be away from him?

"You're staring so hard, you're going to burn a hole in her back," his mother admonished.

He blinked, then turned to his mother to ask her what she wanted to discuss. But what came out was, "What just happened? Is she really glad to be away from me?"

"Son." His mother gave a reassuring pat to his arm. "She was joking with you, having fun."

"Oh. Okay, then." He'd misread her. Probably wouldn't be the last time either. "I suppose I'm still not good at reading a woman I'm dating."

"I hope you're not trying to compare Samara to that other woman." Reprimand colored her tone. "Or any of the part-timers who came after."

"I'm not comparing Samara to anyone, especially not Amanda."

"Good to know." His mother gave him a sidelong glance he immediately distrusted. "Now tell me. When are you going to propose?"

He tripped over his own feet. "Mom!"

She kept walking, blithely unbothered that she'd just

launched a missile at him. "I know my boy. You've already mapped out a timeline for every major event of your relationship, haven't you?"

He bit down on his bottom lip to block a reply. Yes, of course he had a road map for how he believed his relationship with Samara would go, but he certainly wasn't about to confirm that to his mother, and definitely not to Samara.

"Your heart's in the right place, Mom. I know that. Samara does too. But pushing her—pushing us—isn't going to help. In fact, it'll have the opposite effect. Let me handle things, okay?"

"Okay." She gathered herself, and he fought to not feel like an ungrateful son as she drew in a fortifying breath. "Why don't you go back to them while I finish up my hosting duties? Even though he's with two of his favorite people, I'm sure Benjy's at his social limit."

Aron certainly was. He was sure Samara was too. He found the trio in a quiet seating area. Samara stood, giving him such a welcoming smile that his heart stuttered. When she held out her hands, his body moved forward of its own volition, as his need to be with her overrode everything else.

She met him halfway, and it took a massive amount of effort to not sweep her into his arms and haul ass out of the fundraiser. He managed to keep his tone casual. "Mom's going to give her speech soon. She and Beth will take Benjy home after that. We should have dinner when they leave." *Then I get you all to myself.*

Her laugh, soft and knowing, hit him in the gut. "Is dinner what you really want?"

He went with blunt truth. "I want you to myself, by myself."

"Good." She placed a hand on his lapel, close to his heart,

and glanced up at him with a teasing glint in her eyes. She leaned up to whisper in his ear. "I think that can be arranged, if you want."

"I very much want." He turned his head, his lips grazing her ear. "Is it wrong of me, Samara? Should I not want you to myself, by myself?"

Her soft intake of breath careened straight to his hind-brain. She looked up at him, dark eyes darker, lips parted, breath coming fast, a tremble going through her hands as she gripped his biceps. *She's as excited as I am.*

He knew he'd guessed right when she licked her lips, then whispered, "Upstairs now?"

"God, yes." He grabbed her, turned toward the lobby, then stopped short. "My mother's speech."

She groaned in dismay. "Waiting until after would be the polite thing to do."

Frustration swarmed over him. Polite was the last thing he wanted to be, but this was his family. "After we say goodbye?"

"Immediately after."

Chapter 25

Each floor they rose heightened the tension in the oh-so-tiny elevator car, tightening Sam's stomach even more than her shapewear. She and Aron had been alone together before. They'd even been alone together before, during, and after their dates. This was different though.

Different than him dropping her off at her apartment after a night out or sharing toe-curling kisses in his home office before she headed home. This time had intent stamped all over it, underscored by them entering a room dominated by a king-size bed so that he could honor her request to help her out of her dress.

Then after she was unclothed . . . game on.

Anticipation had her fumbling open her tiny clutch for her phone so that she could use the hotel's app to unlock her door. Her neck prickled with the awareness of Aron following behind her. That awareness did little to warn her. As soon as the door closed, he swooped down on her, snatching her by the wrist. She yelped as he swung her around and pressed her against the door. Before she could protest—was she going to protest?—his mouth descended on hers with a hot, hard, and heady kiss.

The only reason she didn't melt into the floor was because he'd pinned her wrists with his hands, her body with his chest, her mind with his sensual attack, like being overwhelmed by a tidal wave. Her brain desperately tried to send a proper signal to respond to the ferocity of his kiss but then it softened, slowed, as if now that his hunger had been appeased, he could take his time to savor.

He might have been an expert at making games, but Aron was also an expert at making her lose all common sense when he kissed her. Releasing her wrists, he settled his hands on her hips to draw her firmly against his body. As if pulled by invisible strings she went, wrapping her arms around his neck, needing an anchor to maintain her balance under the sensual barrage. A wave of heat washed over her, Kilauea awakening as their tongues tangled.

She wouldn't need help to take off her dress. Her body heat would burn it off for her.

He let her go only to slap his hands against the door on either side of her head. Then he slowly eased back, breaking their kiss, then resting his forehead against hers. "I have wanted to do that for hours, from the moment I first saw you walking toward me in this dress. Do you have any idea how many times I said to myself, 'I'm a fucking gentleman,' just so I wouldn't create a scandal by throwing you over my shoulder and stalking off?"

The raw huskiness of his voice scraped over her senses along with a healthy dose of shock. "But . . . you're always reserved, especially at public events like this one."

"Before you." He drew back to lock gazes with her. "Plans and timelines get ripped to shreds because my body overrules my brain and I say or do impulsive things. I'm not an impulsive man, Samara, but when it comes to you, I leap before I look."

His apparent upset about that moved the needle on her own attitude meter. "And somehow that's my fault?"

"No." He leaned in, his lips grazing her jawline until he reached her ear. "Yes."

She couldn't remember what question he was answering, but he sounded conflicted, "So what are you going to do about it?"

The warmth of his breath against her cheek almost made her wobble again. "To hell with timelines and carefully plotted plans. If I'm going to leap, I might as well go all the way. Are you gonna take the leap with me?"

His words and his rough tone obliterated every awkward thing that had happened during the gala. All that mattered was him and her, here and now. "Get me out of this dress."

After that kiss and his confession, Sam fully expected Aron to get right to it like in those romantic movies when clothes start flying. Thank goodness he didn't—her gown wasn't exactly off the rack. Instead he stepped behind her, taking his time pulling the zipper down, then helping her step out of the champagne-colored gown.

"I can't believe how heavy this thing is," he said, draping the gown over the back of the chair before turning back to her. "What is that? It looks like tights and underwear had a baby."

She pulled at the waistband. If this was a mood killer, she'd think way less of him. Then again, she probably should have headed for the bathroom to remove the rest after he'd loosened her zipper. "It's called shapewear, and it's the reason your jaw hit the floor when you first saw me tonight. It's also the reason why it took me thirty minutes to come up here to go to the restroom."

"Then why wear it? It's not like you need it."

He wasn't even trying to earn points, but she gave him some anyway. "I had to keep my poufy belly in check to wear that dress."

"I like your poufy belly."

That prompted a smile and more points. "You haven't seen my poufy belly. Yet."

His whole face lit up as he smiled. "But I've felt it. A lot. Seeing it will be the icing on the cake."

A shocked laugh escaped her. Usually, she was the one teasing and flirting. It was nice to uncover this facet of him. Better than nice. "Then let's double-team this contraption. My belly needs to breathe."

"Teamwork makes the dream work." He curled his fingers into the waistband at her sides. She would have thought there was nothing sexy about this undressing other than it would be faster than if she did it alone, but the feel of his knuckles dragging across her skin as he pulled the shaper down called her a liar.

Belatedly, she realized that she'd forgotten to remove her strappy heels. Aron surprised her yet again by kneeling in front of her. "Put your hand on my shoulder."

She obeyed without thought, and he carefully lifted each foot to slip off each of her shoes, then the shapewear. A relieved sigh lifted her shoulders. She hoped it would be a good long while before she had to wear that torture device again.

"That thing left indentations in your skin," Aron grumbled as he looked up at her. She had a pithy retort at the ready, but her thoughts scattered when he slid his fingers over the indents, leaving fire in his wake.

She tightened her stomach muscles to control the sudden shiver of need. A smile that would have been arrogance on anyone else curled his lips. "By the way, now that I see it with my own eyes, I adore your poufy belly even more." Then he kissed her right below her belly button.

Thank goodness they'd already removed her shoes because she was suddenly thoroughly unsteady and about to fall head over heels. He steadied her by gripping her waist, then unsteadied her by kissing her again. "You should have told me that this would be a quest to free the princess," he grumbled as he rose to his feet. "I would have done some hand exercises or brought a pocketknife. Maybe some baby oil."

Laughter burst free as she grabbed onto his lapels. It should have been awkward standing in the center of a hotel room in nothing but her bra and undies while Aron still wore his tux. "Did you just call my vagina a princess?"

A lopsided grin accompanied his hooded gaze as he answered her. "I mean you. The whole you. You were trapped in restraints from head to toe."

"Not anymore." She stepped back, her arms spread wide. "The handsome prince freed me. Do you think he should be rewarded?"

He muttered something under his breath. She frowned. "What?"

"I was repeating tonight's mantra." He clenched his jaw. "I'm a fucking gentleman."

"You could be if you wanted to."

His turn to frown. "What?"

"Let me ask you a question." She folded her arms across her

chest. "I know that you probably have a timeline of major relationship milestones mapped out in your head, and deviating from that makes you uncomfortable. Where did you plot 'sex for the first time' on your timeline?"

"Next week," he answered. "On our one-month anniversary."

"Then it's a good thing we're here now, since I'll be on my cycle and grumpy as hell next week."

He nodded. "I made my best guess based on my observations but assumed an error of plus or minus a couple of days. I decided the risk was worth the reward."

"Of course you did." She snort-laughed. "I'll let you know the exact day so you can refine your calculations. Another question for you. A little while ago you said to hell with timelines. You said you'd go all the way. Was that a lie?"

She could see his mind weighing his response and decided she'd give him about four seconds before she reached for her sleep shirt and sent him on his way. She'd never had to persuade anyone to sleep with her, and she wasn't about to start now.

"No. It wasn't a lie."

He placed his hands on her shoulders, then slid them down to unfold her arms, gathering her hands in his. With a gaze as warm as his fingers, he spread her arms and took a long, lingering look at her and her champagne-colored bra and panties. Then he unzipped a slow, possessive smile that caused her spine to tingle and her nipples to harden. "You are a goddess. And now I finally get to have you."

Yes!

They collided together like two trains on the same track, cupping each other's cheeks as their mouths met, meshed, melded. One hand slid down her bare back, leaving fire in its wake as he urged her closer.

"Take this off," she demanded against his lips, angrily snatching his jacket open. He immediately complied, jerking the jacket off and tossing it away with less care than he'd done with her evening gown. Need swept through her like a hundred-year flood, the decadent kisses drowning out everything other than the need to be skin to skin with him as soon as possible.

Her fingers clawed at his tie and then his shirt buttons while he reached behind her to unclasp her bra. Their hands tangled as he slid the bra straps down her arms and she yanked the shirt down his. A quick movement, then finally, finally, her hardened nipples met the hard planes of his chest and the sensation was everything.

His grunt of satisfaction thrilled her as much as his kisses did. She had to revise that thought the moment his mouth moved to her jaw, her throat, her collarbone. Her turn to groan as she clutched his shoulders, craving more, craving everything. "The rest," she gasped. "Take off the rest."

They parted long enough for him to jettison the rest of his clothing. Then, in a move that had her hormones harmonizing a hallelujah, he hoisted her up. Legs around his waist, arms around his neck, she stared at him, mesmerized by the hungry expression he wore. Yes, the gentleman was gone, and Sam was immensely grateful for it.

"Kiss me," he ordered with husky command. "Kiss me like you mean it."

Wasn't she doing that already? Guess she needed to level up. Locking eyes with him, she cupped his cheeks, then used the tip of her thumb to trace the curve of his bottom lip. "My boyfriend is gorgeous," she whispered, then gave him the hottest open-mouthed kiss she could muster, a kiss brimming with all the want, all the need, all the hunger boiling inside her.

A shudder went through him as he tightened his hold and began to walk them to what she hoped was the bed. He stopped, and there was a sideways lean as he yanked the bedcovers down. Then she fell backward, Aron falling with her, restraint falling away. With her legs still around his waist, she could feel him hard and heavy and insistently pressing against her panties.

Oh no, those have got *to go.* She squirmed, about to ask him for help—he was in the way, after all—when he stopped kissing her. The burgeoning request morphed into a protest that spontaneously combusted the moment his lips grazed her throat and his hand—goodness, his hand—traced a heated path down her breastbone to her belly. She bowed up, her hands flailing with the need to touch, to tease, to torture him the way he tortured her, but somehow he captured her hands and pinned them above her head.

Hot damn. Her body burned from the simple power move, burned from the meandering kisses at her throat, yearned for that decadent mouth to move down to her poor, distressed breasts. *Please, oh please oh please . . .*

He obviously realized how much she wanted it because instead of taking her nipple and giving her much-needed relief, he hovered just above it, his breath bathing it, teasing it, denying it. It was too much. "Aron, if you don't suck my nipple *right now*, I swear I will—glurgh!"

Her words cut off with a gargled moan as he flicked the bullet-hard nipple with his tongue. *I'm going to die. He's going to send me to the great beyond, and all the female saints will high-five me as I go.*

Aron continued his sensual assault on her breasts, open-mouthed kisses and licks on one while his skillful fingers tended the other. Of course a gamer would be good with his fingers. Wait, when did he release her hands? No clue, but she reached down to clutch his head, to clutch his shoulders, and to clutch the covers in alternating waves of needing to hold him and needing to hold back.

She couldn't pop off like this. It didn't matter that each tug of his lips tugged at her sex and she was so close to the edge al-damn-ready. Gathering the scattered remnants of her will-power, she tried to slow her breathing and her craving so that she could endure this delectable devastation longer.

Then the evil man had the audacity to drag his hand down, fingers gliding past her navel to hook into the lacy waistband of her panties. *Finally.* She lifted her hips to help hurry the process so they could get to—

"Shit."

Hearing his voice after so long startled her out of her sensual haze. What was he talking about? She'd taken care of that before her shower, so why? "What's wrong?"

He raised his head, his expression filled with regret. "I didn't plan for this, so I didn't bring any condoms."

Oh. She suppressed a giggle as she relaxed. "I guess it's good that my plan included seducing you. There's some on the bathroom counter, in the little red toiletry bag."

"Thanks."

He sprinted to the bathroom, giving her a good view of his amazing backside. He quickly returned, giving her just enough time to appreciate the front view before he climbed into bed, bracing his hands on either side of her head. "Samara." The low, gravelly tone scraped across her senses, as did the stark hunger on his face. "I don't know how much longer I can hold out. I really want this. I really want you."

"Thank goodness." She reached up to touch his cheek, then stroked his chest. "Your quest is over, my prince, and your reward awaits. Get on with it."

"As my princess commands."

The air between them electrified with built-up passion and pending satisfaction as he quickly donned the condom, then returned. Then he slowly reached between them, and she felt the tip of him brush against her clit and then her entrance, once, twice, three times, each movement zipping tiny shocks through her body. His gaze locked to hers, and as he leaned down to kiss her, he slid inside her.

They groaned against each other's mouths at this first oh-so-intimate connection. Each point of contact of their bodies stampeded through her senses. Breathing heavily, she ran her hands down his back on either side of his spine. He groaned again, louder this time, his hips flexing involuntarily. Damn, that felt good. Craving more, she wrapped her legs around his waist, settling him deeper.

That small action flipped a switch inside him. He pulled back like a roller coaster reaching its zenith, then crashed down with the same exhilarating force. She thrust her hips up and he plunged down. Again and again, driving her higher and higher, the pleasure almost too much.

Without warning he rolled, and Sam found herself on top. He gave her a strained smile. "Got a little too close too fast." He settled his hands low on her hips. "Besides, you should come first."

Sexy and thoughtful, truly a gem of a guy. She placed her hands flat on his chest. Helped by his grip on her waist, she rose, then sank back down on him, down to the root of him. So good, she did it again and again, increasing her pace until she bounced. Caught up in a delectable daze, she rode him until her thighs protested and her pace faltered. She switched to slow undulations of her hips that allowed her to feel all of him. It probably wasn't doing much for him, but it sure was doing a lot for her.

Aron didn't seem to mind though. He reached up to cup her breasts. She hissed with pleasure as his thumbs brushed over the distended tips. Before she could voice a request, he lightly pinched both nipples. White-hot sensation bolted through her, causing her inner muscles to clamp down on him. He dropped his hands as his hips bucked up and *oh my goodness*, she could see a galaxy of stars behind her eyelids.

Desire swept her up as she leaned her head back, chasing that spark of pleasure that would ignite an inferno if she could just reach it. Again, as if he could read her mind, Aron reached between their colliding bodies to stroke her clit. The spark flared into bright, burning pleasure, blazing a climactic path from her sex and up her spine. She pressed her lips together to keep from crying out, her body bowed with the bliss rolling through her.

"Fucking beautiful."

Breathing heavily, she lowered her head to see Aron staring up at her, his gaze one of heated admiration. "Beautiful fucking," she countered softly, then leaned down to kiss him. "Now claim your prize."

She found herself on her back again with Aron rising above her, lust glowing in his gaze. Fitting himself to her again, he plunged down, burying himself deep, so deep her sex spasmed around him. "Yes," he hissed out, his tone guttural. "Let's do that again."

He thrust deep again and she clamped down again. Repeating the push and pull, thrust and grip, the delicious friction building up pressure, building up pleasure in an increasingly frenetic pace she couldn't match. She wrapped her legs around his waist, giving him free rein, giving him passion, giving him—

He stiffened, biting his lower lip, eyes closed in bliss, lower body fused with hers. She hummed in delight as she felt him pulse inside her. Then he collapsed, his forearms flanking her shoulders to keep him from crushing her, his forehead resting against hers. She reached up to cup his cheeks, rising high in an orgasmic haze that left her incapable of doing more than that small gesture.

He turned his head enough to kiss her palm, then her forehead, and finally her mouth for a slow, sweet kiss that was the perfect finishing touch and made her entire body sigh in satisfaction.

She was in so much trouble.

Chapter 26

When Aron returned from the bathroom, Sam rolled out of bed, snagged his shirt from the floor, then made her way to the bathroom, where she happened to glance at herself in the large mirror. The proof that she'd just finished having very good sex was written all over her face. Smeared makeup, puffy lips, curls slipping free of her bun. Mostly, though, it was the ridiculous, loopy smile on her face that telegraphed clearly that she'd had a damn good time in the sheets.

She pulled out a makeup-remover towelette to do a cursory cleaning so she wouldn't look as thoroughly fucked as she felt. God, she hadn't expected their first time together to be so good. Yeah, she knew Aron would bring his single-minded focus to the bedroom, but she'd been completely unprepared against those weaponized kisses and teasing touches. And the way he'd read her body with expert precision left her utterly and happily wrecked.

She was in for it now.

She returned to find that instead of getting dressed—minus his shirt, of course—Aron had gotten back in bed. He faced her, his head propped up with one hand. "What is it about a woman wearing a man's shirt that's so damn sexy?"

"It's probably a possessive hindbrain thing." She shed the shirt, draping it over the chair before sliding into bed beside him. "Something like *my woman in my shirt, mine mine mine*, like scent marking."

"I agree with you up until the scent-marking thing." He gave her the same loopy grin she'd worn earlier. "Now I want to set aside all my dress shirts for you to use every time you come over."

"Like a sex uniform?" she teased, stroking her hand across his chest. She was glad that he hadn't immediately left, gladder still that he seemed as blissed out as she was.

"No." He pulled her into his arms, giving her a squeeze. "A getting-out-of-the-pool uniform. A late-night-fridge-raid uniform. A lying-on-the-sofa-watching-a-movie-together uniform."

"Okay, I get it. You want to see me in your shirts. You're lucky you can't fit into anything of mine."

"I'm lucky in other ways too."

Even though it was a totally cheesy line, the soft way he said it, and the happiness in his tone, had her squeezing him in return. She liked this relaxed, adorable side of him, especially after he'd been so tense down at the gala. "I'm happy to be your stress reliever at any time."

Soft laughter rumbled from his chest. "I like your method of relieving stress. It's the best health kit ever."

It was her turn to laugh. "How else could my prince keep his strength up?"

"Motivation to keep up with my princess." He pulled her closer. "I like this. So much that I don't want to leave."

She didn't want him to leave either, didn't want to burst this quiet, comfortable, cozy afterglow. They should have come up to the room earlier in the evening. His mother probably would have cheered them on.

Tossing that thought quickly, she said, "I don't want you to leave either, but you can't walk out of this hotel in the morning wearing a wrinkled tuxedo. If you don't care what people will say about you, consider what they'll say about and to your mother if they find out you stayed overnight."

"I wasn't expecting you to be the logical one here," he grumbled, propping himself up on one elbow so he could look at her. "I also didn't expect you to kick me out so soon."

His pout was made all the more adorable by his puffy, over-kissed lips. While she had no idea what time it was other than late, she didn't want the night to end so soon either. None of her people were expecting to see her until late Saturday. If she wanted, she could spend more time with Aron so they could explore this new dynamic of their relationship.

She very much wanted.

"Well," she began, drawing a finger across his chest. "I'm scheduled to check out tomorrow morning, but there's no reason I can't leave now."

She saw the exact moment her words registered. He leapt out of bed and grabbed her suitcase off the stand where she'd done some preliminary packing, then plunked it on the bed.

"Umm, Aron?"

He turned his head to see her, one of his hands in the dresser drawer. "What is it? Do you want me to stop? Because we're going to have to debate that."

"No. I want you to think about finding your briefs. Purely for safety reasons." She wriggled her eyebrows. "I might want to use that after we get home."

A slow smile spread across his face like dawn rising. "You make a very good point. Maybe I should let you do it?"

She shook her head. "And deprive me of this view, even after you put your briefs on? No, sir. I guess you really do use all that exercise equipment at your house."

"They're not just for drying clothes." He grabbed his underwear and stepped into them with a casual gesture, as if it were no big deal being naked in front of her for the first time. "Also, I now have this smart and sexy girlfriend, so I'm going to have to step up my workouts and up my game."

If he upped his game any further, she'd need oxygen and an IV drip. "You don't want me to have to take a trip to the urgent care after every bedsheet smackdown, do you? I might not be able to get out of bed in the morning as it is."

He emptied the dresser. "Then I guess I'll have to offer massages, breakfast, lunch, and dinner in bed, and whatever else you might need."

Wow. That was a tempting lure she couldn't resist. She slid out of bed, then rummaged through the chaotic contents of her luggage for a pair of panties. "You weren't kidding about being all in, were you?"

"You're the one who pushed me into the deep end," he reminded her. "The water's great and I want to swim for a good long while."

"That metaphor is painful, but because you look so cute in your undies, I'll let it pass." She went to the closet and found the outfit she'd worn when she'd checked in, her version of business casual. It was a sartorial suit of armor that wouldn't have people questioning why she was walking out with a man in a tux. Not that she cared, not really, but she was in a great mood and didn't need ugly stares to harsh her mellow.

Soon enough they were dressed, her bags were packed, and they were ready to leave. Aron had broken his tux down to the shirt and pants and had even rolled up the sleeves to match her business casual look. "Do you have everything?"

She snorted. "I think you packed everything I brought with me and some of the hotel's property too." She pulled out her phone. "It'll just take a couple of seconds to check out."

"I should have paid for your room since you did this for Mom's gala."

"Like that wouldn't be weird or set up some sense of expectation or obligation even if you didn't intend it that way?" She shook her head. "I would have refused anyway. I decided to splurge on a rideshare and a room, I decided to pamper myself with a spa day, and I decided to invite you up. All of which were very good decisions on my part."

"I hear you and I can't argue with that." He took her suitcase from her. "May I escort you one final time tonight? Your carriage awaits."

"Yes, you may." She draped her gown's garment bag over her arm with more calm than she felt. They really were a couple now. Every moment at the fundraiser, every minute together in her hotel room, and now spending the night at his house proved that.

Which meant she needed to tell her parents about her new relationship status. And hope they wouldn't flip their collective lids when they found out.

• • •

Aron awakened at his usual six a.m. start time. The sun had a little more time before it rose, but the bedroom's nighttime setting provided enough muted illumination to see that Samara was still in bed beside him, still asleep.

Samara beside him in bed. He savored the thought and the reality of it. There were moments during the gala when he'd been certain that Samara would pull the plug on their nascent relationship, but instead she'd claimed him as her boyfriend and invited him to her room . . .

Heat drenched him, and he carefully extracted himself from the bed while he was still able to empty his bladder. After he'd taken care of business, he stood in the doorway to the bedroom simply staring at her curves beneath the covers. Having her here was ahead of the timeline he'd diligently plotted in his mind, but for some reason it didn't bother him. Samara had that effect on him. She came in like a tornado, uprooting every thought and feeling and carefully laid plan, churning them up and then spitting them out, leaving him in a chaotic debris field.

He didn't like chaos. Disorder made him uncomfortable. So did the thoughts and actions he'd taken when she'd decided to come home with him. He didn't like acting and reacting on impulse, yet that had quickly become standard operating procedure with this woman. Maybe it was because he was relationship rusty, but this all-consuming, bone-deep need for Samara wouldn't allow him to act in any other way.

Sighing, he scrubbed his hands through his hair. He couldn't go on like this, he knew. Order and logic were the lynchpins to his ability to run his company, to interact with people, and to basically function. He still had a gaming empire to run, a certification to achieve, and a major update to roll out, not to mention new titles at various stages of development. All he could think about, though, was how good their first time had been at the hotel, how awesome the second time had been in his bed, and discovering how good sleepy morning sex would be before making her the promised breakfast in bed.

Yeah. He laughed to himself. He was way too deep already, but only wanted to dig in deeper. Things were good. They were good. He knew Samara worried about potential fallout, but he didn't. He'd promised to be her shield, and he would keep that promise.

"Aron?"

The soft, sleep-filled tone instantly called to him, pulling him out of his head. "It's still early. You shouldn't be awake yet."

"Neither should you, Mr. CEO," she scolded, then yawned. "We haven't been asleep that long."

True. "My brain woke me up."

She stretched out a hand. "It's time for sleeping, not thinking. Come back to bed. I need to snuggle you so I can fall asleep again."

She needed him. He went as if he'd been caught in a tractor beam. She welcomed him with wide-open arms and a soft, warm body. To hell with logic. He'd jump again and again if it meant more nights like this.

Chapter 27

Samara woke up to the best aroma in the world: fresh-brewed coffee. Stretching her worn-out muscles, she opened her eyes to find Aron sitting on the bed beside her, holding a cup of steaming goodness. She sat up, slightly more perky, making sure the sheet covered her. Which was really silly considering the night they'd just enjoyed. "Please tell me that's for me."

His eyes lit up in amusement as he handed it over. "Your morning fuel."

She took a careful sip, then glanced at him with surprise. "It's just the way I like it. Are you a mind reader?"

"No." He gave her a long look that woke her up faster than the caffeine did. "I just pay attention."

Lord, did he. Heat singed her cheeks. The way he paid attention to her during that second round—because how could they climb into his bed together for the first time and just fall asleep?—made it better than the first, as if he'd remembered every move and touch and kiss that left her breathless. If he paid any more attention, she'd be walking crooked for days.

Flushing again, she took note of his navy shorts and white tee with the company's logo on it. "Did you pay attention to the fact that you're fully dressed and I'm fully naked?"

"I did, but I don't mind." He made a slow perusal of the sheet covering her body that had her temperature rising. Maybe she should have been self-conscious and awkward this morning after their first and second time together, but how could she, given that neither of them had died of embarrassment when he'd helped her out of her shapewear?

"Have you been up long? Did I oversleep?"

"You didn't oversleep. I had to do a quick run on the treadmill before taking a shower."

She'd slept through all that? She must've been more exhausted than she'd thought. And he wasn't.

"Had to?" Lifting her cup, she gave him a sour look. "Maybe you should work off some of that energy over here."

"I hit the treadmill because I knew you were in here naked and sleeping, and I didn't want to wake you up the way I really wanted to wake you up. You needed the rest and I needed to get a hold of myself."

A flush of memory burned through her. She was gonna die of heatstroke and it would be all his fault. The words were so bluntly spoken that she couldn't decide if they were a compliment or a complaint. "I'm fully rested now."

"Don't tempt me." He lifted her hand, kissed her fingers. "But I do need you to decide between a shower and a bath. It's a deep soaker tub with jets, and the shower has multiple sprays and a steam setting."

She was pretty sure she was gaping at him, so she lifted the mug to hide her expression. "You're going to spoil me."

His smile dropped into seriousness. "I would if you'd let me."

Before she could process that, he brightened. "I put your suitcase in the closet, it's to the left there, and your toiletry bag is on the counter in the bathroom. Feel free to take your time. I'll go see what we can have for breakfast."

She watched him leave because she liked looking at him even if it was his back. Then she slid out of bed, her muscles protesting every movement as she made her way to the bathroom. She vaguely remembered it from last night, but she'd had sexier things on her mind.

Stifling a yawn, she stepped over the threshold, then stopped short. Was it possible to fall in love at first sight with a bathroom? It looked like something from one of those TV shows where one partner grew microgreens and the other hosted paint-and-drink parties and they had six figures to spend to remodel their bath. It had a luxurious spa feel in shades of sage and bright white, with a large soaker tub that could easily fit two, and—

Oh. My. God.

The shower was a dream come true. Straight out of one of those high-end decor magazines, it had a rainfall showerhead, a wall-mounted showerhead, multiple sprays, two seating ledges, and color therapy and steam shower option. It was the king of showers and she wanted to live in it.

She hurriedly took care of business, then returned to the split marble vanities. As promised, her toiletry bag sat on the vanity on the right, along with a fluffy towel set and a pale blue men's dress shirt.

Laughing, she shook her head as she held it up. "Subtlety is not your strong suit, Mr. Galanis," she said aloud. "But that's part of your charm."

Donning her shower cap, she made her way to the glass and stone enclosure. She played with the levers like a handheld game until she found a setting she liked. Feeling the jets hitting her body made her want to break out into that "Hills are alive" meme. There was certainly enough room. The opulent space certainly fit the amenities a CEO was expected to have, but Samara couldn't help but wonder again about one man in all this space, alone. Did he get lonely after his mother and brother left every other weekend?

Would he be lonely anymore, now that their relationship had taken another, deeper turn?

That thought tagged another. Did he have any friends? Did he consider Grayson a friend? In their conversations over the past few months, Aron hadn't mentioned any. Granted, they had been working professionals during that time, so it wasn't like she would ask personal questions like that. Not at the beginning anyway. He didn't like to "people" unless he had to, but surely he had others he could hang out with if he wanted?

He'd enjoyed hanging out with her friends at Game and Flame. Maybe her friends could be his friends. She and Aron had gone from adversaries to collaborators to friends, and now more. If he needed someone to be a close friend, a confidant, she would happily do that for him.

She reluctantly shut the shower off, dried herself with the fluffy towel, then returned to the vanity to finish her morning ritual. She glanced in the mirror as she slipped the dress shirt on. Okay, wearing Aron's shirt did make her look cute, but she needed to at least do the bare minimum on her face so she didn't look as tired as she felt.

More presentable, she went to find the closet. It was larger than her bedroom, obviously meant to be used by two as each side mirrored the other, with one starkly empty and the other sparsely used. She stepped inside to take a closer look. Three suits and six dress shirts hung on one rod, three pairs of dress shoes: matte black, brown, and highly polished black wing tips. She'd known that Aron cared little for formal business attire—and the circumstances that required it—but this was extreme. The tux he'd worn the night before was carelessly tossed onto a bench as if he had been in a hurry to—oh yeah, he had been. She hoped it wasn't a rental, then stopped short. Of course it wasn't.

The next rod held a few pairs of casual trousers and shirts of a style that seemed as if he'd found a brand and fit that he liked and had purchased one in every color. The shoe cubby here held a pair of high-tops, a pair of sneakers, and a pair of loafers. His expansive collection of pop culture T-shirts and shorts must have been tucked away in the drawer units.

Her boyfriend was definitely a minimalist. The sparseness here contrasted with the well-lived-in office and with the *Architectural Digest* look of the remainder of the house all reflected aspects of Aron's personality. He liked what he liked, tolerated what he could, and did the minimum required when necessary. Still, it made her wonder if it was preference or defense mechanism.

She found her suitcase open on a bench in the empty side of the closet, and her garment bag hanging in one of the cubbies. Why bring that in? Best not think about how that seemed like an invitation to fill up the vacant space with her belongings. Which she certainly could if she wanted to.

Okay, so her mind obviously wanted to think about it. It was healthy to fantasize, right? In the silent safety of her head, she could easily imagine her and Aron in this space, talking about their plans for the day as they got dressed, or their plans for each other as they got undressed. There would be laughter. There would be kisses. There would be more warmth here and in other areas of the house that seemed in stasis, as if waiting for someone to revitalize them.

Okay brain, time for a time-out. She shook her head as she retrieved a pair of light blue lacy panties from her suitcase. After freaking out over Mrs. Galanis and her efforts to push their relationship forward, Samara couldn't very well do the same thing without being a hypocrite, even if it was just her imagination, right?

With that thought, she grabbed her mug off the night-stand, then made her way to the kitchen. He stood at the stove making breakfast magic. "Good morning," she called out before pressing her cheek against his back and wrapping her arms around his waist. "Something smells delicious."

"That's either the coffee or the bacon." He squeezed her hand before turning to face her. "Both of which are . . ."

His voice faded as he took in her outfit. "Well." He cleared his throat. "That's just as good as last night's version. Is sexy-cute a good description?"

"I'll accept it." She twirled in a slow circle so that he'd get the 360-degree view. With only two center buttons fastened, she knew he'd get a flash of her panties and a hint of her cleavage. Not that she was ready for anything other than breakfast, but it wouldn't hurt to prime the pump.

"If you think I'm sexy-cute when I'm not all glammed up like I was last night, I'm going to have to give you brownie points."

His eyes lit up. "What can I redeem these brownie points for?"

"Hmm." She strutted over to the coffee bar, putting extra swing into her walk. After selecting the pod flavor she wanted, she turned back to him. "I'll give you special prizes."

"Special prizes, huh?" He tossed a sexy smile her way. "What sort of quests do I have to complete to earn these prizes?"

"You're racking them up already, with your random acts of thoughtfulness. The coffee in bed, making breakfast—I'm not sure you need to earn any more points, at least not for the next few weeks."

Acting on impulse, she crossed back to him and wrapped her arms around his waist. "By the way, you can't renege on being my boyfriend now. I'm in love with your shower."

He laughed as he returned her hug. "If that was all it took, I should have shown it to you a couple of months ago. Also, I'm not doing things for you to earn brownie points. I'm doing these things because I like doing them and they make you smile."

"Aron." Overwhelmed, she headbutted his chest. She was in danger of falling hard for this man, not because of the material gifts he gave her, but because of the nonmaterial things, the warmth, the respect, the things that were worth so much more to her than anything he could buy.

She thought about his sparse closet. "Okay, then, I'm gonna take you on a shopping spree, buy some things that I think would look sexy on you. Or I'll just shower you with gifts that you can't refuse."

"I don't care about that stuff. And I'm not doing stuff so you'll give me stuff in return. If you're thinking like that, you're going to make me uncomfortable."

"Equal opportunity, sweetie." She smacked his cheek. "We'll just have to spoil each other."

"You could spoil me with one of your kisses," he suggested. "A real one, not the smack-on-the-cheek kind. I haven't had one yet this morning."

"Poor baby," she teased. "Let's fix that."

He wiped his hands on a towel, then cupped her cheeks. The look in his eyes, teasing, caring, warm, and hungry, stuttered her breath. His slow, sexy smile tugged at her heart, then a part far lower. A staccato rhythm jacked up her heartbeat as he slowly lowered his head, stopping just before their lips met. "Good morning," he softly said, then kissed her.

Her eyes slid shut along with her other senses as her awareness focused on the sensation of his mouth against hers. She had the presence of mind to grab the front of his T-shirt, then fell into his kiss.

Soft and sweet at first, soon surging to sensual and scorching, as if he'd been holding back with all the kisses before the gala. Her body cheered as he dragged her closer, especially when she realized without a doubt that he was having a very good morning. Heat swept her body as she wrapped her arms around his neck to get even closer to him. Need flared, burning through her, scorching her synapses—

Setting off the smoke alarm.

Chapter 28

All the bonus points he'd earned burned up with the bacon.

Not all of the bacon. He'd cooked some before Samara had entered the kitchen, before his brain had become as scrambled as the eggs he'd made after almost setting the kitchen on fire.

So much for being calm, cool, and collected. Every time they kissed, he lost his damn mind. What he'd intended as a sweet good morning kiss had devolved into this hunger that had nothing to do with food and everything to do with her. At least he'd managed to salvage breakfast, taking their plates out to the covered patio and turning on the heater and some music. Despite their breakfast conversation turning safely to online gaming, losing his bonus points still rankled, so much so that he had to address it.

"I can cook," he insisted as he stabbed at his eggs.

"I know," she said, her voice as smooth as the butter she spread on her toast. "The eggs are deliciously cheesy."

That didn't make him feel better. Awkwardness had come with the morning sun. He didn't know if Samara would stay after breakfast, didn't know if she'd spend the day with him. He had a regular routine that he followed on weekends, depending on whether or not Benjy came over. Veering from his routine usually made him antsy, and he wondered if the feeling in his chest was from deviating from his schedule or from Samara seeing him dispose of burning bacon and rip the smoke alarm off the wall.

"I can redeem myself with lunch or dinner," he declared. "I'm not helpless."

"I didn't say a word." She returned her mug to the table. "But I looked in your refrigerator. There's nothing to feed two people in it."

Not wanting her to think he was a total loser, he felt he had to defend and possibly redeem himself. "I have a thing about leftovers and frozen foods. My housekeeper only stocks enough fresh food for me for the week and some of Benjy's favorites when he comes for the weekend."

"And if it's not a Benjy weekend?"

"I work. I eat when my smartwatch tells me to. Unless I'm working on something important and can't be bothered."

A frown marred her features before clearing. "All right, then, if we're going to eat again this weekend, we'll have to go get groceries or have some delivered."

He froze, certain that he hadn't heard her correctly. "You're staying the weekend?"

Her eyes widened before she dropped her gaze to her plate. "I guess not."

She looked up again, her smile too bright, her shoulders too tense. "Sorry for making assumptions. I know you have routines you like to stick to, and running a company isn't a Monday through Friday job. It makes sense that you have stuff you've already planned to do and this"—she gestured between them—"definitely wasn't part of your agenda. Honestly, I should have already left."

A strange feeling blossomed in his chest as he heard the odd note in her tone. Belatedly, he realized she'd misinterpreted his question. "Samara."

Impulsively, he reached across the table to capture her hand, preventing her from leaving. Was she going to leave? He wasn't sure, but he didn't want it to happen. "I want you to stay. I was going to ask you to spend the weekend with me after breakfast, but then I attempted to burn the house down and figured you'd want to escape while you still could. I was surprised, that's all."

"Okay." She squeezed his fingers, and this time her smile was genuine. "I'm not going to escape."

The weird feeling in his chest melted beneath her smile. "I'll ask Mrs. Jeffries to add some of your favorites to her shopping list." He rattled off her top five.

She blinked at him. "How do you know what my favorites are?"

Why was she surprised? "I just made a list of things you've ordered for lunch or dinner and some things you've mentioned before."

"You weren't kidding when you said you pay attention." She came around the table and surprised him by sitting on his lap, then kissing his nose. "I like that."

Brownie points restored. It wasn't a bad idea to take on a bonus challenge. He slid his arms around her waist. "Is there anything you want to do today? Anywhere you want to go?"

Her features scrunched. "Do you really want to go out?

There are people out there, you know. Wasn't yesterday enough?"

"A little." Just the thought of being in a random crowd was enough to make him fidgety. "But we deserve some time out without dealing with relatives or torture devices disguised as clothing, don't you think?"

"Something a little less stressful for both of us?"

"Your favorite restaurant and a movie? Or anything else you'd like to do. We can go back to that museum. You said it had a nature trail, right?" Whatever she wanted to do, crowded or not, he'd happily handle. He'd be with her, and she'd be all he could focus on anyway.

"If we go anywhere, I'd like to go to Game and Flame. I think I want to stay in though." She stretched like a cat, flexing her entire body down to her toes. Thoughts scattered as he focused on her movements. He hadn't kissed the inside of her left wrist yet, had he? He needed to right that wrong.

"Aron?"

He tore his gaze away from her hands and back to her face. "Yes?"

"It's our first weekend together. Tomorrow you're having dinner with your family and I'm having dinner with mine, which means we've got about twenty-four hours or so left to spend together."

A glance at his smartwatch told him she was right. A glance at her hands told him that kissing her wrist was his highest priority. "It wouldn't be right to celebrate our first weekend together with other people, would it?"

"No." She stood, gathering the dishes. "Why go to Game and Flame when you have a game museum in your home office? Why go to the movies when you have all the streaming services?"

True. "Why go out to dinner when we have . . ." Oh yeah. The cupboards were bare and slightly charred . . . "Access to delivery services?"

"Exactly." She spread her arms, making the shirt gape in ways he found highly fascinating. "Why go out when we have all this fantastic space to ourselves? Let's go to the living room after we're done cleaning up."

• • •

Some time later he found himself sequestered in the living room beneath blankets draped over the furniture and pillows stacked around them, Samara beside him, a bowl of popcorn between them, and some movie he knew nothing about playing on the flatscreen over the fireplace. "This is different."

She eyed him. "You never built a blanket fort in the living room when you were a kid?"

He thought about it for a moment. "Not that I remember. Then again, my form of play was rebuilding computers and playing and designing games and apps. Back then, Benjy didn't like things over his head. Not even umbrellas."

He glanced around him. "Since this was your idea, I'm assuming this is something you did often?"

"Not all the time, but it's something Mom let us do once in a while." She wrapped her arms around her knees. "I'm the youngest of four, two boys and two girls. We're pretty close in age, so there were a whole bunch of years when the house was nothing but noise until our parents kicked us out into the backyard. When it rained, they let us build forts in the living room with blankets, pillows, and the kitchen chairs. We'd play storming the castle or capture the flag, boys versus girls but mostly older versus younger. My brother Mitchell and I learned to be really sneaky to win against Jarrod and Olivia."

"This . . . is interesting." He and Benjy usually crashed in the video chairs in his office in the middle of a game. The living room had never been used like this before, but he found that he kind of liked it. "Are we going to play storming the castle?"

"Haven't you stormed my castle enough for the time being?" She grinned as she patted her lower belly. "Ol' girl needs a rest."

"That last time was your fault."

"My fault? We were cleaning up after breakfast!"

"You were dancing around the kitchen in a shirt and panties," he pointed out. "And then you held your hands out to me and asked me to dance and somehow I ended up on my back on the patio love seat."

She arched her brows. "Are you complaining?"

"Since I'm the one who pulled you down onto the love seat, I'm not complaining one bit."

He'd never be able to step out there again without thinking of her. Or any other room she'd been in. "As much as I like going out there alone to decompress from work, I really enjoyed having breakfast out there with you. And everything else too."

"Me too." She leaned against him. Silence wrapped around them as warm and cozy as the blanket over their heads, and he decided that they'd build as many blanket forts as she wanted.

When she didn't react to an outrageous scene in the movie,

he gave her a concerned prod. "Are you tired? You should go take a nap. I can distract myself with emails or something."

"I'm not tired, and we already had a work break while we waited for our lunch delivery, remember?"

She wasn't tired, they weren't working, and they usually didn't go that long without talking to each other. He took a guess. "What are you thinking about so deeply? Are you worried about something?"

"No, not really." She tightened her hold on his bicep. He wondered if she realized it. "Your house seems like an awful lot of space for a bachelor, even with your brother staying over. You could probably make double your money back in this market."

"I don't care about that. Benjy likes it and I hadn't considered how attached my mother is to the house we grew up in, the house that Dad died in. She said her most precious memories lived in those walls, and she couldn't stand the thought of someone else having them."

"That's so beautiful," she whispered.

He nodded. "I should have thought the purchase through better than I did. Lucky for me, Benjy loves the place. Since he's going to live with me permanently at some point, I decided to keep the house. But it's yet another reason why I don't act on impulse."

"I can understand that." She paused. "The decor doesn't seem like you, though."

"It's not, except for my office."

"That's definitely you." She nodded against his shoulder. "I bet that couch is practically a family heirloom."

"It is." Like his mother couldn't give up his childhood home, he hadn't wanted to part with the sofa from his father's home office. Sitting there, he'd learned so much about running a company, being a man, and handling any adversity.

She fell silent again, and this time it seemed awkward. Aron reviewed everything they'd said and how they'd said it, trying to get to the bottom of it. The worry she did or didn't feel. The house too big for him. The reason he kept it. The decor not to his taste.

Oh. "Amanda never lived here."

She jerked upright. "No, that's not what . . . Okay, maybe that is what I wanted to know."

If she wanted an explanation, he was happy to give it to her. It was all in the past anyway. "I bought the house before I began dating her. She stayed overnight at times, but I . . . Trying to share space with someone was an adjustment I was ill equipped to handle."

He tried for a less formal tone. "Anyway, an interior designer did all the rooms except the office before I moved in, and I had him redo the main suite after she left. If I'm being honest, it was a relief to have the quiet back. I guess I'm just weird that way."

Samara shifted until she faced him. "One person's weird is another person's normal. We are the way we are, the way we're made. Anybody who can't get with that can suck it."

He barked out a laugh, surprising them both. "I really like the way you look at things, Samara."

"Good to know." She pulled out her phone, held it up. "How about looking at the camera to memorialize our first blanket fort and our first weekend together?"

"Let me do it. My arms are longer."

"Okay." She handed the phone over, then leaned against him. He took the photo as he looked down at her.

"Hey!" she protested. "You're supposed to look at the screen, not me."

"I wanted to look at you."

"Fine, then." She pouted, then smiled. "Let's take another one."

He obliged her, except this time, she looked at him as he took the picture. "I thought you wanted us to look at the screen."

Her smile widened. "I wanted to look at you."

Did she get the same little hop in her stomach when he'd said the same thing? "Do you want to take one more?"

"Yes, please."

Again, he held up her phone. This time, they both looked at each other. A mischievous smile lit her eyes, popped her dimples, drew him in. He wasn't sure if the image would come out correctly, but in that moment he didn't care about order, didn't care about perfection. What he cared about was Samara, here in his space, and how much he liked having her in it.

He handed the phone back to her. "Send me all of them. Don't edit or delete them."

"I won't." She quickly sent a text with the images. "Thanks for asking me to do it instead of sending them to yourself."

"It's your phone. Why would I?"

"Aron . . ." She leaned against him again, squeezing his arm. "You're amazing."

He was reasonably certain that was a good thing and she meant it, at least in that moment. "I think you're amazing, too."

"Even when I'm being loud and dancing around your kitchen to old-school R & B?"

"Given where we ended up, yes, even then."

A quizzical expression crossed her features as she studied him. "I'm not sure if you're joking or serious."

"Serious. I like having you here. Even before this, when we worked together, I liked having you here. Even when you're not here I can feel you, if that makes sense."

It was the truth, a truth he couldn't explain to his satisfaction. Even with Grayson as a buffer, he only tolerated a handful of people outside of his company. Of those, even fewer had been invited to his house, and fewer still were invited back. Somehow, Samara had made the cut even when all he'd known about her was what he'd gleaned from social media and a few short conversations.

"Thank you. I like being here with you too, and I understand what a gift that is." She wrapped her arms around her knees again. "I know sensory overload from peopling too much is a real thing for you, a thing I don't want to add on to. Being the youngest of four, it was hard sometimes to have space to myself, which is a big reason I gravitated to video games, because I could put my headphones on and close out my siblings. And even though I live with my two best friends, we're not interacting with each other all the time. Sometimes we're in our own spaces, and sometimes we're just silently together."

She reached for the remote, shut off the TV. "All of that to say this: When we're together don't feel pressured, and if you need space you should make it. Even if you don't need space, we can be silently together. All right?"

He pulled her closer, wrapped his arms around her. "All right."

Silently together or not, being with her like this, holding her like this, feeling the heat of her body sinking into his like this were a comfort, a gift, and a need he never wanted to relinquish.

Throat suddenly tight, he rested his chin on her shoulder. "Thank you."

"You don't have to thank me for this," she whispered, giving him a quick smack on his cheek. "And aren't we supposed to be in quiet time right now? Don't make me put you in time-out."

"That's not what I meant." He gave her a light squeeze instead of the possessive grab his muscles demanded. "If I stepped out of my comfort zone, I know you did too. Thank you for being my date for the fundraiser. Thank you for taking everything with my mother, Beth, and other guests in stride. I realize it wasn't easy for you and that you could have walked away at any time, but you didn't. So thank you for last night, and for today."

"You're welcome," she replied, her voice as soft and warm as her body against his. "I know they're coming from a good place, and when I thought about it, your family's enthusiastic approval of our relationship is nice when it could have easily gone the other way, especially since your mother has ample reason to be wary of any woman who tries to get close to you."

True. Which was why his mother had surprised him with not only her approval, but her attempts to hurry their relationship along. Which begged a question. "Do you think your parents will enthusiastically approve our relationship?"

"I don't know," she said with a sigh. "'Enthusiastically' might be too strong a word. They'll probably have some of the same concerns I did. At the end of the day, though, I'm a grown woman. They trust my judgment. Either way, I'll talk to them about it tomorrow, and you'll be the first person I talk to after."

"Okay." He trusted Samara's judgment. He wouldn't hyper-focus on any possible negative reactions, nor would he develop any talking points to counter them. He wasn't going to worry. Not at all.

Still, it was better to be prepared than not, right? Right.

Chapter 29

Samara was so not prepared for this conversation.

While her planner was never far from her hands, whether paper or digital, and she could prepare a presentation in any format in her sleep, she had never had to prepare to talk to her friends and family, had never strategized what she would say or how she would say it. She was more of a rip-the-bandage-off type of girl than one who carefully chose her words, especially with the people she'd known her entire life.

Lucky for her, only Mitchell had made it to this Sunday dinner. He was only a year ahead of her, and they had often teamed up against their older siblings. Having him at the dinner table would be a great buffer.

The smell of her father's smoker hit her nose before her feet hit the doormat. If Dad was in his outdoor kitchen, he'd be in an even better mood. It was her mother she was worried about. Well, not her mother, but the president and CEO of Rise Consulting.

Samara had had to work harder and longer than anyone else to prove that she deserved her spot in her mother's firm. She didn't want to do anything that would taint her mother's reputation. If her mother disapproved of her relationship with Aron . . .

No. She shook her head for emphasis. *Don't borrow trouble.* She'd deal with whatever happened when and if it happened. She couldn't deal with fallout if she hadn't caused the storm yet.

Instead of ringing the doorbell, she went through the side yard and opened the gate leading into the oasis her parents had built that she and most of the neighborhood kids had grown up in. Her mother de-stressed from her job with her garden, and her father de-stressed from tax season and quarterly filings by cooking in his outdoor kitchen every chance he got, even in winter. The result was a beautiful backyard that the neighborhood people and animals flocked to.

As expected, she found Mitchell and her parents on the deck, glasses of sweet tea in their hands. It was a perfect day for being out, in the short but perfect time between the pollen of spring and the heat of summer. "Hey, y'all."

"Hey, baby girl." Her dad waved tongs in her direction as her mother gave her a quick hug. "You got here just in time. I'm about to slice the brisket."

"Funny how she always does that," Mitchell said behind the rim of his glass.

Sam raised her chin in challenge. "I learned it by watching you."

"Sure would be nice if my youngest children would set the patio table for dinner instead of fussing with each other," her mother said.

Her father checked his meat thermometer. "Especially if they wanna eat."

"Okay, okay. We got the hint." Mitchell took a last sip of his tea before rising to his feet. "Let's set the table, sis."

They passed through the sliding doors into the kitchen and fell into their years-old routine of gathering plates and flatware to set the table. "I'm glad you're here, little bro," she said as she opened a drawer. "I need to tell Mom and Dad something, and I could use a buffer."

"Stop calling me little bro since I'm older than you." He pulled the everyday plates from a cabinet. Their mom kept their great-grandmother's china in a special cabinet and only took it out when all the kids came over for dinner, which was getting rarer even at the holidays with their older brother and sister adding to their families. "Are we doing good cop, bad cop, hype man, or boxing coach?"

"You want me to call you 'second brother'? And I think I need the coach today."

"'Second brother' sounds like you're ranking us, and everyone knows I'm your favorite brother. And if you need the coach, that means you're about to drop some serious tea. This should be good."

"I'm regretting this already," Sam muttered as she returned to the patio. She and Mitchell set the table while their parents brought over the food: sliced brisket, baked beans, and homemade coleslaw.

They held hands while her father said grace, then passed the food around to load their plates. It was a long moment before her brain reminded her there was another reason besides food for this visit.

Pushing away her plate with reluctant hands, Sam faced her parents. "Mom, Dad, there's something I need to tell you."

Her parents looked at each other, then back to her. "This sounds serious."

"It is, but it's not a bad thing. At least, I don't think of it as a bad thing, and I hope y'all don't either."

She shifted in her chair, took a deep breath, then made the plunge. "It's about Aron Galanis, the CEO of Artemis Games."

"What about him?" her mother asked. "Your contract with them ended a month ago. Is there a problem?"

"No. I just wanted to let you know that we've been dating for the past three weeks."

"Whoa." Mitchell whistled. "You're dating that dude you put on blast, the dude who became your boss?"

"Mom is my boss, he was a client, I was a consultant, and we started dating after the contract ended," she shot back. "And it's not like you have room to talk, Mr. Dating the Boss's Brother."

"Children."

They both sat back when their father spoke. "Yes, sir."

Their mother leaned forward, nailing Samara with a stare. "Are you sure your personal relationship with Aron Galanis didn't start until after the contract ended?"

"Yes, ma'am." She decided not to tell her mother about that first kiss that almost went too far. They technically hadn't been in a personal relationship then. "Like I said, we didn't go out until after the contract was over. We've been together for three weeks."

"I suppose that explains this, then."

Her father pulled out his phone, made a couple of swipes, then turned the phone so she could see the screen. Shock radiated through her like a mushroom cloud. There on the local newspaper's home page, in color, was a photo of her and Aron at the fundraiser, dreamily staring at each other. If there was any doubt that they were a couple, the headline blared the news:

Game On:
Gaming CEO and Diversity Consultant Level Up at Fundraiser

Crap. This wasn't one of the posed photos, but a candid shot someone had snapped while they'd danced. The cringe-worthy title was bad enough, but the lead paragraph was all about how one of Atlanta's most eligible bachelors was finally off the market, and there was her full name spelled out for the world to see, making things even worse. She swallowed a hard lump of concern. "Wow. We made the home page?"

"Apparently, your love life is big news," Mitchell cracked.

"So not helping," she hissed at him.

"So not trying," he whispered back. "This is too good."

Realizing she was on her own, Sam turned back to her parents. "We had no intention of announcing our relationship like this. Matter of fact, we had no intention to announce anything at all. We certainly didn't want it digitized in living color for the entire city to see."

Her father frowned. "Is he wanting to hide the fact that you're dating?"

"It's not Aron, it's me. And it's not that I want to hide it, I just . . . I want to protect it, protect us, for as long as possible. Avoid any negative public perception for him, for his company, and for yours, Mom."

"I appreciate you thinking about that, baby, but we're thinking about you right now. Do you want to keep dating him?"

"Yes." The answer flowed easily. "But no one's connected Samara Reynolds of Rise Consulting to ReyofSun, game critic yet. I just . . . I worry about the trolls when all of this comes to light."

"You're always worried about the trolls," her mother said.

"You know why."

"Of course we know why." Her mother gave her a hug. "But we also know you've got to live your life fully, and that means not caring what anonymous assholes online think."

"Mom!"

"I said what I said."

"You're as protected as you can be from getting doxed," her father said. "It'll take some effort for your private info to come out, and even then it'll point here instead of your apartment. I just hope this Galanis guy is as serious and protective about your relationship as you are."

"He is." She sat forward, eager to tell them more about Aron. "He's very analytical, and our collaboration went smoothly because our work styles meshed so well. He can seem standoffish and cold, but that's because interacting with strangers is outside of his comfort zone. Once we got to know each other and bonded over playing video games, I learned that he is warm and funny and kind and generous and loves his mother and brother more than anything else. He named the company after his mother, who's really nice. In fact, he does Sunday dinner with them just like we do here, and Benjy stays with him every other weekend. Benjy's autistic, nonverbal, but he loves video games, and man, can he kick my butt in . . ."

She trailed off, worried about her parents' matching expressions. "Did I say something wrong?"

"Well, that depends," her father said, folding his arms across his chest, displaying his sleeve of tattoos. "This sounds like it's gone on longer than we thought."

Alarm flared through her. "I swear it's been less than a month. You know we don't tell y'all about dating someone unless it's serious."

Her father snorted in disbelief. "And yet you've already met his family while we're just learning that you're dating him. I call that pretty damn serious."

Crap. "I'm sorry, Dad. I didn't meet them on purpose. What had happened was—"

Her phone chimed. Thank goodness! She dug it out of her pocket to read the text. Sure enough, it was from Aron.

CAN YOU TALK?

"It's Aron," Sam told her parents. "He wants to talk. I bet he just found out about this photo too."

"Then call him," her father said. "I, for one, want to hear what he has to say."

"Me too," Mitchell chimed in.

Her mother swatted his arm. "Boy, if you don't hush . . ."

Sam wrinkled her nose. "Don't you have somewhere to be or a boyfriend to see?"

Mitchell planted his elbows on the table, then cupped his cheeks. "Nope."

Sam barely resisted the urge to bop her brother on the head because doing that would only hurt her hand. This revelation was not going the way she'd hoped it would and was heading into worst-case-scenario territory. But if she couldn't handle the scrutiny from her parents, how could she handle it from the outside world?

• • •

"How did this happen?"

Aron stared at the ridiculous article and its ridiculous title with equal parts shock and dismay. His mother had hit him with the news as soon as he'd stepped over the threshold, souring the end of what had been one of the best weekends ever.

"That's what I'd like to know." His mother paced beside him, a frown pulling at her features. "I want to know who took this photo and who gave this society reporter this information. At my event."

Aron studied the photo again. Based on their posture, the way they looked at each other, it wouldn't take a body-language expert to reveal that he and Samara were a couple. Despite the night being a fundraising event, their dancing together had been a private moment, the moment he'd gotten Samara to acknowledge that they were a couple—and he'd promised to be discreet about it.

"I want to know how this happened as well, but I need to talk to Samara before we do anything else." He clenched his phone tight. "I'd promised her we wouldn't announce our relationship to the public, and I've broken that promise before the weekend ended."

"This isn't your fault, son," his mother exclaimed. "Surely, Samara will know that."

"I hope so." If not, their relationship was over before it had a chance to begin. He sent her a text, hoping he'd caught her before she'd made it to her parents, wishing that he could be beside her while she talked to them. He'd willingly take any censure if it meant he'd protect her from it.

His phone sounded with Samara's ringtone. He quickly answered it and wasted no time. "Samara, there's something I need to tell you."

"About the article?"

He closed his eyes, unease churning in his gut. "Yes. I don't know who took the photo or identified you, but I will find out."

"We both will," his mother chimed in.

"I believe you."

Those three words were exactly what he needed to hear, and they nearly did him in. "Thank you."

"I'm here with my parents," she told him.

He could hear the tension in her tone. "Are you okay?"

"It's fine. They want to talk to you. Is it okay if I put you on speaker?"

His stomach tightened, but he gave the only response he could. "Of course."

"Okay." A short moment, then, "We're here."

"Mr. and Mrs. Reynolds, I apologize for speaking to you for the first time like this and under these circumstances."

"These circumstances being this photo online?"

That deep baritone voice undoubtedly belonged to Samara's father, and Aron sat a little straighter. "Yes, sir. I'm not sure how this happened since there were only supposed to be photographs taken in designated areas, but I wanted to talk with Samara so we can decide how to handle this."

"I know how that brain of yours works," Samara said. "You already have a couple of suggestions, don't you?"

"I do. The way I see it, we have three options. One, we have my lawyer issue a strongly worded demand to take down the article, citing violation of your privacy. Two, we issue a joint statement announcing the relationship."

"Hmm." That noncommittal sound told him all he needed to know of her opinion. "And the third option?"

"The third option is that we ignore it altogether. Neither confirm nor deny."

Muffled discussion on the other side, then Samara asked, "Which option are you leaning toward?"

Based on their conversations since the gala, he had a good idea of which one she preferred, which made his choice easy. "The take-down demand."

An identifiable hard edge filled her father's tone. "Are you telling us that you don't want people to know that you're dating our daughter?"

"Dad!" Samara protested.

Aron waved his mother away. "Sir, if it were up to me, I'd rent a billboard at Spaghetti Junction announcing that I've won the relationship lottery. Samara is more circumspect than that, and I respect her desire for discretion. All of that to say, I want you to know that I'm very serious about dating your daughter."

His mother silently clapped her hands. Several different sounds emanated from the phone including a soft "Aron" that made him smile. He'd never get tired of hearing her say his name.

A cough diverted his thoughts, then her father spoke. "That's all well and good, but—"

"I agree with Aron," Sam interrupted. "For both our sakes, we need to get this scrubbed as soon as possible. The last thing I need is for professional me to become a subreddit like gamer me experienced."

Concern churned in his gut. He'd promised to protect

Samara, and leaving up that article would do anything but. "All right. I'll call my lawyer as soon as we disconnect. The article should be gone by Monday morning at the latest. Mr. Reynolds, Mrs. Reynolds, I apologize for interrupting your dinner, but I wanted to make Samara aware of the article and make sure that she was all right."

"Apology accepted, especially since it gave us the chance to talk to our daughter's boyfriend," her mother said. "So there's that."

"There's that and the fact that she's already met your mother and brother while we're just learning about your relationship," her father added, his disapproval apparent.

Aron waved his mother away before she could speak. "It was an accidental meeting, but if it's okay with you and Samara, I hope to meet you in person someday soon."

"Then how about two Saturdays from now?"

"Dad!" Samara protested. "Aron's got a lot on his plate right now."

Her father grunted. "If he's got enough time to take you for a date, he's got enough time to make a date with your parents."

"Of course, Mr. Reynolds." Like he wouldn't clear his calendar for Samara and her family. Even his mother gave him an enthusiastic two thumbs-up. "Whenever is convenient for you."

"All right. We're having a cookout in two weeks. You should come with Samara."

"What?" Another male voice sounded from Samara's end. "You inviting him to the cookout right out the gate? Like for real for real?"

Aron had no idea what that meant, but meeting Samara's parents was a big deal, and he was glad they'd made time for him. "I look forward to it. Since it's a cookout, is there anything you want me to bring?"

A chorus of voices answered him. "Ice."

Chapter 30

"Did you leave any ice for the rest of Atlanta?"

"I took my assignment seriously," Aron said as he wrangled the massive rolling cooler from the back of the SUV. "I want to make a good impression on your parents, even though this still feels like showing up empty-handed."

"So what's in the box?" she asked. "Is it a cake?"

He lifted the box and handed it to her. "Yes. It's not for the cookout, though. It's a gift for your parents since this is our first in-person meeting. It makes me feel a bit better about just supplying ice."

"Seriously, don't stress yourself." Discomfort scrunched her features. "A cookout, especially the ones my parents host, will always need plenty of ice. Second, there's a hierarchy when it comes to who can bring what to a cookout or family dinners, especially at the holidays. You have to be vetted before you can bring anything more involved than condiments. If people don't know you, they're not going to eat your food."

He nodded. "So it's like leveling up in a game, which makes me what? An Ice Master?"

"More like an Ice Apprentice," she answered with a smile.

"Maybe an Ice Squire. Remember, here you're at entry level, even if you're dating the princess."

A bubble of concern formed in his gut. "I'll confess that I researched cookouts on the Internet so that I wouldn't make any mistakes today, but I didn't see anything about a cookout hierarchy."

"Okay. Clear your mind because I'm about to do a major data dump."

They began to walk up the long driveway. There were an alarming number of vehicles in the drive and lining the street in front of the sprawling two-story house. "The hierarchy goes like this. For the cookout edition, the Grillmaster has the top ranking. That's my dad since we're at my parents' house. The Grillmaster only has the top ranking during cookouts. Every other gathering, especially holiday meals, the Queen of the house is at the top."

"Which is your mother," he guessed.

"Exactly. Back to the cookout hierarchy. After the Grillmaster and the Queen, you have the uncles. We'll call them Knights of the Grill. Friends and relatives who would be masters at their own place, they keep the master company, usually by offering advice that gets ignored. The uncles will also jockey for position, and anyone trying to step on the Grillmaster's toes will get hit by the Tongs of Death."

"This sounds like a game I should be developing, especially with masters and knights and death tongs."

"It's the *Game of Thrones* of cookouts, except people just get bloodied instead of killed off for no reason," Samara confirmed. "Okay, next up you have the aunties, who have dominion over the side dishes. Don't for a second think they're all sweetness and light. The side dish game is cutthroat. Side dish duels have been fought, but it takes a lot to upset the order. Some have tried and failed miserably. Trust me when I say that engagements have ended because people thought they could buck the system."

Whoa. "So basically, you saved my life by putting me on ice duty."

"Yes. There are relatives who don't speak to each other to this day because of a side dish incident twenty years ago. It's as serious as a game of Spades."

"Well, now I'm very glad I didn't make potato salad with tzatziki sauce."

Samara tripped. He dropped the cooler handle and caught her before the cake could go flying. "Do you want to get me disowned?" she demanded.

"I'm joking, I swear."

"We don't joke about food for the cookout. I'm stressed enough about the number of cars in front of the house as it is." She blew out a breath. "Okay. Okay, just be yourself and everything will be fine. Don't worry about anyone but my immediate family. Especially Mitchell, since he's a master-level shit-stirrer and lives to tease his siblings as often as possible."

The way she shifted back and forth, biting her bottom lip, gaze darting from him to the house to the yard, clearly telegraphed her nervousness. He touched the small of her back before stepping away to grab the rolling cooler's handle again. "It's why I had you create that family org chart, remember? I reviewed it again last night. I know the names of all your immediate family members and their children. I won't embarrass you or make your parents regret inviting me, so don't be nervous and don't worry."

"Aron." She stepped closer until they were nearly nose to

nose, then reached up to push his hair out of his eyes. "This would be nerve-racking to any couple. I just want them to like you as much as I do, and I don't want you to be disappointed if their reaction to us isn't as enthusiastic as your mother's."

His shoulders slumped as the weight of worry sloughed off him. "I don't think anyone can top my mom's reaction. I'll consider a 'he seems nice' to be high praise from your parents."

"I'm positive it will be better than that. They trust my judgment. Besides, no matter what, at the end of the day, I'm going home with you."

And just like that, just under the brilliance of her smile and her words, he felt impervious, ready to take on the world by her side. "Samara, I—"

"Hey, don't be doing that stuff out in full view," a male voice called. "My kids are here."

"That's the eldest, Jarrod," Samara whispered before turning to the other man pulling toys and athletic equipment out of the back of a minivan and into a cart. "Quit complaining when we know that all my nieces and nephews have seen much more than this from you and Debra. Speaking of PDA, where is your better half?"

"Throwing our kids into the pool," he answered. "Can't you hear their screams of terrified delight?"

He shut the van door, then joined them, his assessing gaze landing hard on Aron. "This him?"

Samara took his free hand, giving it a gentle squeeze before releasing it. "Aron, this is my oldest brother, Jarrod. Jarrod, this is Aron Galanis, my boyfriend."

Her brother stuck out his hand, then immediately retracted it, making Aron wonder if Samara had informed her family about his aversion to handshakes. "You got some more important titles than boyfriend, don't you, Mr. CEO?"

"I don't know if they're more important, but 'Samara's boyfriend' is my favorite one."

"Slick and quick on his feet," her brother noted with a nod of what Aron hoped was approval. "It's a good start. Let's see if you can keep it up."

Aron had no idea what that meant, but judging from Samara's smile, it was a good thing. "I'll do my best."

"That's my baby sister. You gotta do better than best." He gestured up the driveway. "Come on around to the backyard. Everybody's waiting on your ice."

They walked up the drive to the wooden gate that opened onto a stone path and a lot of noise. He could hear music, laughter, children. The first thing he noted was the size of the backyard, which could have comfortably fit another house. A firepit seating area, a fenced-in in-ground pool and lounge area, a badminton net setup in a lush grassy area with more seating, and a multilevel deck that led up to what looked to be the Grillmaster's domain.

People were everywhere, occupying all those spaces. Adults, teens, and children, laughing, talking, listening to music, staring at their phones. Way more people than he'd expected, so many more that he froze in place.

He wasn't aware that he'd stopped in his tracks until he felt Samara's hand on his arm. He turned to her, seeing concern blooming in her eyes. "This . . . is a lot of people."

"Yeah." She didn't sound happy about it. "It was supposed to be a family thing."

Jarrod shrugged. "You know how it is when word gets out that Dad's on the grill. I swear at least one of the neighbors peeps his groceries and tells the whole street, then suddenly we got cousins we never knew we had."

"You don't have to worry about the cousins," Samara told him. "Let's get the ice up to the kitchen, and I'll introduce you to my parents."

They made their way up to the top level of the deck. Long tables had been set up, groaning under the burden of food they held. The outdoor kitchen could make some restaurants jealous, and one granite counter held a mountain of foil and storage containers, probably for leftovers.

A tall, imposing man with a sprinkle of gray in his close-cropped beard looked up from grilling what looked like a hundred chicken quarters, then broke into a smile. "There's my sunshine," he exclaimed, handing his tongs off to a man who could have been his brother before coming around to pull her into a huge bear hug. "It's been forever since I've seen you."

Samara managed to hand the cake box off to Aron before it tilted too far. "It's been six days," she corrected her father with a grin and an equally large hug. "I was here Sunday for dinner."

"That's weeks in parent time," her father said, then turned to give Aron a head-to-toe assessment while keeping an arm around Samara. "So, you're Aron. I'm Eric Reynolds, your girlfriend's father."

Aron tried to parse the other man's phrasing, but it seemed crucial to shake the older man's hand after that introduction, so Aron stuck his out. "Yes, sir."

"Let's get a drink and go inside so we can hear ourselves talk." After a very firm handshake, Samara's father turned to a set of French doors leading to a sunroom. "Vannie, baby girl's here!"

Samara slipped her hand into Aron's and led him through the sunroom and into the kitchen. An older version of Samara wearing a tropical printed sundress waved as they entered. "Come on in. I'm Vanessa, Samara's mother. Oh."

She took note of the box he carried. "I thought you were bringing ice."

"He did," Eric Reynolds confirmed. "I don't know what that is."

"Umm . . ." Samara began, anxiousness tightening her tone.

"It's a coconut cake from Barduk Bakery," Aron said, holding the box out. "Samara told me that it's one of your favorites. I picked it up yesterday, so it's still fresh."

"I mentioned that once, in passing, like a month or two ago. How did you remember that?"

"I remember all the things like that that you tell me," he explained. "That's why we have ciders instead of beer at the house, and that brand of dark chocolate you like, and we only get molcajetes from Raul's."

Samara stared at him so long that he wondered if he'd made a mistake. Her parents wore equal expressions. "Did I say something wrong?"

"Not wrong at all," Mr. Reynolds said. "You pay attention to my daughter. That's good."

Mrs. Reynolds reached for the box with a smile. "Thank you for this. You're right, it's my favorite. Let's have some while we talk, okay?"

They took their drinks and slices of cake and followed Samara's parents to a formal dining room away from the noise and bustle of the cookout. Samara's father sat at the head of the table, her mother on one side, he and Samara on the other. The cake was as tasty as its reputation promised.

"Samara told me about your outdoor kitchen," Aron said to break the silence, "but words don't do it justice."

Mr. Reynolds beamed. "After my wife and kids, that setup is my pride and joy. Took me six months to decide on the equipment and layout I wanted, and another six to build it. Feeding my loved ones is a joy." He laughed. "Besides, it makes sure that at least one of my kids visits."

"Home-cooked meals are the best," Aron agreed. "I get one every Sunday when I visit my mother and brother. But thanks to Samara's needs, I've been more mindful of what I eat and when."

Mrs. Reynolds frowned. "What do you mean, Samara's needs?"

Samara dropped a hand to his thigh, but he wasn't sure if it meant stop, go, or support. "Samara had a low blood sugar incident while working late because we'd skipped lunch. It bothered me, so I took steps to make sure it wouldn't happen again."

Fingers dug into his thigh. Knowing that warning signal, he searched her expression, then her parents. All wore a blend of expressions that he couldn't categorize. He leaned closer to her. "Should I not have mentioned that?"

"It's okay," she whispered before turning to her parents. "It was no big deal. I ran out of glucose tablets, but Aron gave me juice and helped me with my readings without freaking out. He even stocked supplies for me in the guest bathroom, and I appreciated his thoughtfulness. He does random acts of thoughtfulness like that all the time."

Mr. Reynolds grunted, and his wife gave his hand a pat. "That thoughtfulness says a lot about you and your character,

Aron. We appreciate it, and it brings us to the main reason why we invited you here today."

Here it comes. Aron dropped his hand to cover Samara's, needing that extra connection. "Yes, ma'am?"

Mr. Reynolds leaned forward, his gaze piercing. "We have a rule in the Reynolds family that you don't bring your partner to a family event until you're serious about the relationship. We're making an exception for you today."

Aron frowned. Did they still think after their call two weeks ago that he wasn't serious about being with Samara? He'd have to convince them just as he'd convinced her.

Eric Reynolds raised a hand, halting Aron's protest. "I'm sure you can understand that our main priority is to protect our daughter. While we trust our children and understand that they know their hearts better than we do, I don't relinquish the right to protect my kids to anyone, even the ones who are married now."

That . . . didn't sound like a positive for him. His mind raced through a dozen possibilities and counterarguments that would get him the results he hoped for, but he needed more information first. "I understand and respect that."

Mrs. Reynolds smiled at him. "Then I'm sure you also understand that while we support Samara and the choices she makes and what she believes in, we will always worry about her safety."

His stomach sank as he finally understood their primary concern. "You mean her advocacy."

Samara shifted beside him as her father nodded. "You seem like a nice enough young man. Samara likes and respects you, and that weighs heavily in your favor. In all honesty, if you were just a random guy, we would have no problem with you dating our daughter. But you're the CEO of Artemis Games, and Samara is ReyofSun, the gamer who criticized your company and its product. She's already been attacked online since her critique was posted, and a lot of that has been from your core audience."

He turned to Samara, who sat silently, chin down, staring at the tabletop. He'd seen some of those enraging online attacks, but he wondered if there were more that she hadn't told him about. "I'm aware of that, sir."

"Then I'm sure you're also aware that both of you could face criticism from the gaming communities you both depend on," Mrs. Reynolds said, her words no less heavy for their softness. "They already come for her. They get worse after a convention or a live stream. She may not have told you this, but sometimes the viciousness spills over into real life. She lost a dear friend of hers because of retaliation, and we've vowed to never let that happen to our daughter. It's why her town house is listed under her father's name. It's why her cell phone is billed to my company."

A wave of surprise rolled over him. Samara hadn't told him that. It made him realize that he'd never truly know what it was like to endure the things she did. The comments that had been directed at him and Artemis Games were paltry in comparison. Even the most vicious ones had died off after a couple of weeks.

He clasped her cold hand in his. Although he spoke to her parents, he only looked at her. "Samara told me about Marquessa. I'm so sorry she had to go through that, just as I'm sorry that Samara had to lose a friend that way. My lawyer got the photo and article taken down. We can have a meeting with her to discuss different methods we can use to ensure Samara's safety. I'll do whatever it takes so that Samara doesn't regret dating me."

Samara looked up, eyes wide with surprise. He squeezed her hand with a smile of reassurance before turning back to her parents. "Samara made sure I understood what she's been through and any trouble that could come before she would agree to go on a date with me. I understand and I promise to do my best to shield her."

Her parents looked at each other. "Are you sure you want to do this?" Mrs. Reynolds asked. "Both of you?"

Aron turned to Samara. She stared back at him with calm certainty and expectation that brought a hopeful smile to his lips, one that she returned. When they spoke, they spoke together. "We do."

Two weeks later, their world became a dumpster fire.

Chapter 31

"Is this how you want it?" Aron asked.

Sam reviewed the location of her camera and light in relation to her gaming setup. "That looks great, thanks."

"Good." He gave her a quick kiss before handing her the headphones. "Go kick some digital ass, beautiful."

Her heart fluttered from the quick combination of his kiss and his hand on her back. It had been doing that more and more in the last couple of weeks. Aron had a way of making even the simplest of things seem special.

Now that they were firmly in the post-contract, physical intimacy stage, she missed seeing him daily even more. Aron must have felt the same because he'd suggested she come back to his place on Thursday nights after Nubia's Shield had their weekly live stream at Game and Flame so they'd have one more night together on the weekends that Benjy didn't stay over. Aron had bought hangers for the empty side of his walk-in closet, a move that practically invited her to claim "her side," although she only left a few pieces there. Aron had also made room for her toiletries without saying a word, so she now occupied her own vanity as well. If these moves were on his timeline, she wondered if he'd removed a few steps. If so, she definitely approved.

After settling into the gaming chair, she slipped her headphones on, then logged in. As usual on Game Night, she switched to ReyofSun mode, donning her curly wig and red glasses. Aron always dressed as Hoodie Guy. Now it was time to start their live stream. The game they decided to play each week was chosen randomly, and she'd warned Aron that one of his games could be chosen. Luckily, that hadn't happened since she'd put *Legendsfall* on blast.

Sam's good mood lasted for all of fifteen seconds into their live stream. Then the comments started.

> I noticed you haven't played or commented on any Artemis games. Don't want to critique your boyfriend anymore?

> Must be nice, sleeping with the enemy. Course, money makes everything better.

> Talk about a come up. Make a problem, get hired to fix it just so you can f*ck your way into money?

> Gold digger n—

It got worse from there, becoming a full-on hate raid, with each one of the bombs thrown at her causing damage. Shock kept her from putting up any kind of defense, taking any kind of action. Somehow they'd connected her online handle to her legal name and her mother's company. How? How could that have happened?

A hand covered hers. "Close it down, Samara. I already stopped the video. Don't look at it anymore."

Her chair swiveled. Aron gently pulled her headphones off. Although his tone and his touch were gentle, his eyes blazed with an anger she'd never seen before. "Let's go home. I'll call my lawyer and your parents. I'll find out how this started and I'll deal with it. Okay?"

She could barely register the words. If the commenters knew about Samara being ReyofSun, they had to have gotten that information from somewhere.

She looked at her friends, whose expressions ranged from concerned to enraged. "I hate to ask y'all this, but no one tagged Aron or my professional name on any Game Night group photos you posted on social media, right? You didn't post any pictures of Aron by mistake or without his consent, right?"

"We wouldn't do you like that," Janelle, one of their friends, told her. "I don't know about the rest of the people who come here. Maybe someone recognized Aron and put two and two together."

"Dammit." Why hadn't she considered that?

Janelle gave her a reassuring smile. "I'm willing to create some bots to crawl the Internet for information." She patted her boyfriend's knee. "Dev can help too."

"Absolutely." Dev nodded. "This seems a little more serious than the last time, so be sure to follow the plan we gave you before, okay?"

"Okay." Sam breathed deeply. "I'm sorry, everybody. We probably won't come to Game Night for a while."

"I. Am. Pissed." Max packed her equipment away. "I'm ready to slap a bitch. This is going too far. They could hurt Aron's company or your mother's."

Sam flinched. Aron wrapped an arm about her waist, and she leaned into him, grateful for the support. "You're right. I have to tell Mama about this. But I don't want any of you to get hurt by association. Scrub me off your social media, maybe even lock your accounts down for a couple of days."

"Samara, let me take you home," Aron said, sliding a strap of her tech backpack up onto her shoulder. "We can coordinate in the group chat, but we should leave here now. We're drawing attention."

Acid bubbled up to her throat. She'd dropped her guard. Kenya and Cam got the most attention since their cosplay competition had aired. Even with her friends calling her Rey, no one had confronted her as ReyofSun. That didn't mean that no one knew who she and Aron were. Their live streams had always gathered a group of fellow gaming enthusiasts to watch the play. Game and Flame also held individual and group tournaments, so there was always a crowd. Now, many of them were crowding close, and more than a few had their phones out.

Drawing attention was the last thing either of them needed, but she knew it was going to get worse before it got close to better. "Let's get out of here."

. . .

"You need to issue a statement."

Aron rubbed his forehead instead of answering Mark. His anger and worry were on a permanent simmer, and he didn't want to take it out on his head of communications. Five days into the crisis and the fire showed no signs of dying out. If anything it seemed to increase in hostility, threats, and vulgar innuendos, most of them directed at Samara. And now, gaming sites, internal and external message boards, and even gaming magazines had picked up the story, which was why Mark currently stood in front of his desk throwing a fit.

"I don't recall discussion of my private life being the subject of company press releases," Aron said. "I'm also pretty sure discussion of employees' personal lives is not in the employee handbook."

"It doesn't matter that it's not in the employee handbook," Mark told him. "Our Slack channels are on fire with speculation."

He'd seen some of it, enough to know that he'd end up firing a bunch of people if he kept poking around. Instead, he'd authorized his best and most trusted IT security staffer to have administrator rights to internal and external forums, looking for anything and anyone suspicious.

There were very few people that the company employed that could have connected him, ReyofSun, Artemis Games, Samara Reynolds, and Rise Consulting. And considering how passionately their families and friends protected their privacy, none of their nearest and dearest would have exposed them. Which left only one real option.

Someone at Artemis, someone at the executive level.

"Human Resources is handling our internal communications," Aron pointed out. "They'll deal with anything that violates our code of conduct."

Mark nodded. "That will take care of things internally, but what about externally? You're the face of Artemis Games."

"Only when necessary."

Mark sighed. "Aron, you need to think about how this looks."

Aron tilted his head. "How do you think it looks?"

"The company gets called out by this woman and it goes

viral. After meeting her at a convention, you offer her a job. After working together for three months, you're suddenly making moon eyes at each other at a fundraiser. Then you were spotted together last week at that game bar." Mark threw a hand out. "You don't think that's something that people will talk about?"

"People should have more important things to talk about than who I'm dating or not dating," Aron said flatly. "Besides, saying that Samara and I are dating is pure speculation. Neither of us has publicly mentioned it."

"Of course they should, but you know how the gaming community is. They're going after her with a vengeance. They're going after you, personally, not that you care, from what I've seen."

Mark splayed his hands on Aron's desk, then leaned forward, two moves he absolutely hated. "Most importantly, they're trying to go after our bottom line. DDoS attacks on our servers and our store almost took *Legendsfall* out. We had to disable commenting on the *Legendsfall: Mythica* promo we have running on YouTube and our home page. They're also trying to gather momentum for a large-scale boycott of Artemis. If you're not concerned about you or your girlfriend, you should be concerned about the value of the company you named after your mother."

Aron gritted his teeth as anger spiked. Mark had no idea how very much he cared about the damage being done, and a lecture from him was the absolute last thing that Aron wanted or needed. Instead of saying so and giving his anger an outlet, he very deliberately opened a drawer, pulled out a container of wipes, then proceeded to wipe down his desk's surface, leaving Mark no choice but to move.

He took a seat in one of the guest chairs. "How is your girl-friend doing, by the way?" he asked then, his tone brimming with sympathy. "This can't be easy for her."

"Of course it isn't." That was the worst part, seeing his Samara suffering. He did what he could to lift her spirits, but short of locking up all their electronics and sequestering her inside a pillow fort for however long it took, they had no choice but to wait for the hate to die down.

Problem was, it seemed to be ramping up, with some of the posts skating the edge of being terroristic threats. Calls to doxx her and her friends. Complaint calls to the consulting firm in an effort to get her fired. All of it was taking a toll on Samara. He could see it clearly but felt powerless to do anything about it. The only thing that helped him sleep at night was that they both lived in gated communities.

"This really isn't fair to her," Mark said then, surprising him. "She felt that she was doing the right thing, yet she's been hounded every step of the way. She wanted to help you, help the company, and was met with resistance. Then you started dating, and things got worse for her. I can't imagine what she's going through."

Guilt kicked him solidly in the teeth, forcing him to swallow a sudden lump of pain. He didn't have to imagine. He saw it every day.

Mark shook his head. "I can't imagine what you're going through either. I have a suggestion, but you may not like it."

Aron glanced at Mark, surprised that he'd spoken his thoughts aloud. "What do you suggest?"

"That statement I mentioned earlier . . . you release it, acknowledging Ms. Reynolds as gamer ReyofSun, then praise the work she's done for Artemis, praise her professionalism.

Then you can deny that you were ever in a personal relationship."

"No." His answer was immediate and resolute. "I'm not going to deny Samara. You can delete that option right now."

"Then your only other choice to save the company is to break up with her," Mark told him, his words earnest. "Let the statement say that you have mutually decided to end your relationship and you wish each other the best."

Mark sighed again. "Look, I know this is hard for you, but you're both sad and upset. Releasing a statement praising her work and adding that you've parted ways is the fastest way to take the pressure off her. People will leave her alone, and everyone will be able to bounce back. And who knows? Once some time has passed you can quietly get back together."

He stood. "You don't have to make a decision about it right now. Just think about it. Think about what's best for her, especially with this hitting mainstream media here. Let me know what you decide, and we can work on the statement together."

Long after Mark left, Aron sat staring out at the Atlanta skyline. Thick clouds pregnant with rain hung heavy on the horizon, a visual representation of his mood. He didn't want to make this decision. He didn't want to even think about it. Yet more than that, he didn't want to see Samara hurting anymore. He would give anything to take that from her.

Anything.

Chapter 32

"Mama."

"Baby, how are you holding on?"

Samara gripped her phone so tightly her hand shook. *Barely* was the answer. She was barely holding on. Day six and the harassment showed no signs of abating. It had even expanded out of the online gaming community and onto other social media platforms, even resurrecting and corrupting the LegendsFoul hashtag.

"I've been better." She blinked rapidly, took several breaths. "I'm actually calling to ask you for a favor."

"Of course, baby. What do you need?"

"A leave of absence. It may just be two weeks that could be called vacation, but I might need a month. It wouldn't be lying for Rise Consulting to announce that I'm on leave, and that will be a believable reason for pulling me off the Nelson project."

"Baby."

"It's the best damage control, Mama. And it shows the company being proactive while taking care of our clients."

"But—"

"Don't worry." She blinked rapidly to staunch her tears.

"My last contract paid me well enough that I don't have to worry about working for a while. And who knows? When I return to work you can use it as your opportunity to get me into management like you always wanted."

"This isn't the way I wanted it to happen, but if you're sure, then I'll agree."

"I'm sure." It was hard to focus on anything other than the dumpster fire that was now on par with the eruption of Mount Vesuvius. "I might even go on vacation. Out of the country sounds nice. Somewhere without Internet."

"Baby . . ."

The concern in her mother's voice almost did her in, but her parents worried about her enough as it was. She couldn't add to it. "I think Tiya would be a good choice to take over Nelson. It's similar to a project they worked on last year, and I think they would be a good fit for the client."

"See, you're already thinking like a manager," her mother said with a light laugh before sobering. "I think a vacation is a great idea. Your mental and physical health should be your priority right now. You don't have to be in the trenches fighting the good fight all the time. Sometimes retreating is the right choice."

"You're right." She lifted her chin skyward, blinking rapidly to staunch threatening tears.

"I have to ask . . . what about Aron?"

"I've been staying over at his place the last few days," she answered. "I feel bad for leaving Max and Quinn at the town house, and Aron's going into the office most days, but it still feels better being here. He's doing his best, but he's got to focus on Artemis."

Silence from the other end. Either her mother didn't know

what to say or didn't want to say what she wanted to say. "It will all be fine, Mama. It will burn out soon enough, and we'll all be able to get back to our lives and looking forward to Dad's next cookout."

"You're right, baby. Remember to take care of yourself. Tell Aron I said hi. Love you."

"I will. Love you too. Bye."

Sam disconnected the call, shoved her phone in her back pocket, then surreptitiously blotted beneath her eyes. She needed to go get a cool cloth for her face so Aron wouldn't notice how many times she'd been at or close to the point of tears. The last thing she wanted to do was add to his burden.

"Samara."

Arms encircled her waist, and Aron pulled her back against his chest. She wanted to turn to face him, but that was a move that would surely drag tears to the surface. Instead she pressed back against him as much as she could, allowing his body heat to warm her, his arms to anchor her.

She wasn't sure how long they stood there before he released her. She turned to face him, steadier, able to bear his searching gaze, the soft stroke to her cheek, the softer kiss to her forehead.

"I heard you talking to your mother," he said then. "I think you're right. You should go away for a while."

She fought the urge to flinch. Not take a break, not go on vacation, but go away as if she were a pest disturbing his peace.

"Go away," she repeated. "Like get out, disappear, go anywhere but here instead of staying here and fighting?"

"Yes." His voice was heavy. "I don't believe this is going to work."

Sam stepped back, concerned by the heaviness in Aron's voice. "What's not going to work?"

He sighed, then gestured to the space between them. "This."

Intuition whispered to her that "this" didn't mean sharing the office. She didn't want to jump to conclusions, though. Besides, if what her intuition had whispered was right, she needed him to have the balls to say it out loud.

"This what?" she prodded when he remained silent. "What is the 'this' that isn't working? I need to know what has you concerned so I can fix it. My reputation's on the line here too, you know."

He winced as if her words were axes tossed at his torso. "It's your reputation I'm worried about," he blurted out, then winced again.

"Huh." Dread and distaste bubbled in her belly, but she refused to give either one free rein. Instead, she bunched her hands into fists, then turned to fully face him. "I'll ask again. What is the 'this' that isn't working, the 'this' that you think is damaging my reputation? Which 'this' out of all the 'this'es that have happened is making you think this way? Just spit it out, Aron. Say it with your whole chest."

He began to pace as if stalking a hole in the carpet would give him the power he needed to say what he wanted to say. She sat and began to seethe, hoping that folding her arms across her chest would hold in the emotion that threatened to strangle her.

Finally, he stopped in his tracks, then turned to face her, expression locked down to nothing. "We haven't publicly announced that we're dating, so maybe . . . maybe we should release a statement to our social media accounts stating that we're not a couple, just friends. We could even separate for a while."

There it is. "Why?"

He startled, his expression cracking into surprised. "What do you mean, why?"

She barked out a laugh. "Have you forgotten who you are? Aron Galanis, who has flowcharts and decision trees and pivot tables for every decision he's ever made? The man who convinced me to date him in the first place by showing me a pro versus con presentation?"

She tightened her self-hold. Yelling would only make him shut down more, and she really needed him to talk to her at that moment. "Yes, I definitely want to know why you think our relationship needs to end, especially since it seemed to work extremely well last night."

If possible, his expression grew even more remote. "I promised you and your parents that I would keep you safe. I weighed all the possibilities, and this seems to be the most effective method."

"What?" She climbed to her feet, needing to do something to bleed off the energy coiling inside her. "You thought that you could just say, 'Let's separate to protect you,' to me and I'd just accept it?"

"I should have given thought to what you would feel about this," he said then, his tone and demeanor growing more robotic with every word he spoke. "I didn't do that, and for that I'm sorry."

He was sorry that he didn't consider her feelings, not for breaking up with her. "How could you have not thought about what my reaction would be? Did that lame-ass statement work on your previous relationships?"

He actually thought about it. "This is different."

"Why?"

She could see a debate in his eyes that his body didn't reveal, as if there was something he was reluctant to say. Aron was honest to a fault, and he'd never lied to her. She used that fact to her advantage. "Is there something you're not telling me?"

"Yes." The answer was immediate, and so was his regret, if his eyes were any indication.

"What is it? What happened?" Intuition whispered again, and this time she listened. "If you want to break us up because of something that concerns me, I have a right to know."

He swallowed as if that would keep the words in. She settled her hands on her hips. "Aron, you need to tell me. Now."

He hesitated for a moment, then plunged ahead. "Since rumors of our supposed relationship began to spread, the company's forums are a shitshow, but lately there's been escalations and threats and DDoS attacks on our game servers. When I talked to Mark about this—"

"Hold up." She threw up a hand to stop his words. There was no fucking way she'd heard him right. "Did you say that you talked to *Mark* about this, about us?"

"Yes. He's the one who suggested a couple of different options, including this one."

Yeah, I bet he skipped and sang all the way to your office. "Do you consider him a friend?" She hoped the hell not.

Aron shook his head. "He and his team monitor the company's social media accounts. Even our internal communications hub has been overwhelmed. So he and I discussed some options to combat the negative surge."

Sam rubbed at her temples, fighting to rein in her temper

while trying to make him understand. "You talked. To an *employee*. About our private relationship. Before talking with me?"

"Things escalated quickly. We had to take decisive action."

A "we" that didn't include her, the other fifty percent of the relationship. "So you didn't think it was important enough to talk about with me first. That *I* wasn't important enough."

"That's not true!"

"I don't believe you." She huffed out a laugh. "You can't say this isn't fair to me without deigning to ask me what I thought about it. Mark hasn't liked me from the start, yet you thought he was a better person to discuss what action you should take about *our* relationship. I would have thought the opinion of the person you regularly have sex with would carry a little more weight than your fucking employee!"

"Protecting you is important! Finding a solution as soon as possible is important," he insisted. "Artemis would release a statement acknowledging gamer ReyofSun as consultant Samara Reynolds. We'd highlight your unique viewpoint and the professional job, high-quality work you did for us and how we'd work with the firm again. The press release would end with the announcement that our partnership has come to an end and that we wish each other the best. You can take the vacation you and your mother were talking about so that it seems like we actually are only friends. We can meet again once the madness ends."

The details of the statement told her that he and Mark had talked about the plan for more than a couple of minutes. "First of all, neither you nor Artemis have the right to out me as ReyofSun. Second, I've been wondering—no, I've been worried—that being with me would cause some harm to you. That your board or your investors would make being with me difficult for you. I've been trying to find the right time to bring this up to you so we could figure it out together, then decide what to do, together. I thought you had to have seen the same things I've seen and heard, but since you hadn't brought it up, I thought it meant that you either didn't know or didn't care."

Her voice began to wobble, and she had to pause to reach for a calm that was nowhere to be found. "You promised you could handle any blowback we got from being together. You promised that you'd be my shield. I didn't realize that was a limited-time offer. I should have known better. I should have known not to . . ."

Not to give my heart to you. Her throat closed up. She wouldn't give him those words. He didn't deserve those words. "I trusted you. You've been open and honest with me all this time, but now you're lying and making life-changing decisions about me without me."

"I'm not lying—I'm trying to protect you!"

"From what, the crap I have to deal with every damn day? I'm going to guess that Mark struck again and said that you're the one who should initiate the breakup, right?"

The flush to his cheeks gave her all the answer she needed. "You know why he said that, don't you? It was to make you look better and make me look guilty, evil, like I did in fact seduce you for your money. People are going to think you came to your senses and escaped my evil influence."

"That's not true!"

"You think the truth matters in the court of public opinion?" She huffed out another sour laugh. "You want the truth? Here's your truth."

She ticked them off on each finger. "You said you want to

break up with me. You said you and your employee Mark concocted this idea as the best solution. You at no point deigned to consult me on something that would have a major impact on my life. Did I get that twisted?"

She threw up her hands. "You know what? Never mind. I'm going to be the bigger person here. I am too angry to continue this conversation. I don't want to say something irretrievable. One thing I will say is that if this is what you think being a shield for me means, you failed."

Regret splashed red pain across his face. He lunged for her hand. "Samara, I—"

She marched closer until she was eye to chin with him. "What you need to recognize and understand is that I'm not angry because you want to break up to protect me, as ridiculous as that is. I wouldn't be mad if you wanted to break up because your company couldn't afford the hit to your bottom line. No, I am furious with you because you stole my agency, and I will never, ever, allow anyone to do that to me."

She snagged her bag as she stalked to the door. "By the way, the only one happy about this is Mark. You should think about why that is while you're lying in bed alone."

She left without looking back.

Chapter 33

"Aron, is something wrong with Samara? I wanted to see how she's doing, but I can't reach her. It seems like her phone is turned off. I'm worried about her, especially with everything that's going on."

"There's nothing wrong with Samara." He glanced around his empty, silent office. "There's something wrong with me."

"You haven't said that since high school," his mother said sternly. "I will not hear you say that about yourself again."

Right. He focused, tried again. "I made a mistake. A big one."

"Is it fixable?"

He rubbed at his chest, trying to smooth out a sensation that felt like he was slowly burning to death. "I don't know," he whispered, suddenly unable to speak louder through the burning sensation that had crawled up his throat, charring his vocal cords and his eyes. "The data . . . it doesn't look good."

"Are you in a condition to drive, or should Benjy and I come there?"

"I'll come there." He didn't want to stay home where his favorite rooms, the office and bedroom, were dominated by memories of Samara, and the other parts of the house felt too cold, too lifeless without Samara there to liven them up.

Twenty minutes later, Aron glumly stepped over the threshold into his mother's house, feeling like three-day-old crap warmed over.

She gave him a hug that almost broke him. "There's my son. I was worried about you driving over. Samara still hasn't reached out to you? Is your relationship in trouble?"

"How did you know?" He stumbled forward, clasping her forearms.

"Considering that she's not here with you and you look as if you haven't slept in days, it's not hard to jump to that conclusion."

She patted his cheek. "Why don't you go into the living room with Benjy, and I'll bring you something to drink. Then we can talk."

Aron shuffled into the living room. Benjy was already there, plopped down on the floor in front of the big-screen TV, game controller ever present in his hand. He looked up as Aron entered, gave him a welcoming smile, then looked behind Aron as if expecting someone else. As if expecting Samara.

"I'm sorry, bro. She's not coming today." Probably not ever again.

The disappointed expression on his brother's face shredded his gut. He hated to disappoint Benjy more than anything, and he knew that once he talked to his mother, he'd probably disappoint her too.

What the hell was he going to do? Samara had yet to respond to any of his texts or return his numerous phone calls. He wanted to talk to her, to explain to her, to apologize to her.

He wanted to see her. The only reason he hadn't shown up in front of her town house again or her parents' house was because he didn't want to be labeled a stalker. There was no coming back from a restraining order.

"Here," his mother said quietly, holding a glass of red wine out to him.

"You're giving me alcohol?" He took it, cradling it in both hands. The only time he drank alcohol in front of his mother was the rare occasion when she attended events with him. This would be his one and only exception.

"I'm sure chugging beers is what guys would do in circumstances like this when they're clearly miserable, but I don't have beer, so this will have to do." She sat beside him, then reached over to brush his hair off his forehead. "What happened between you and Samara? It has you looking as if your world is ending."

"That's because it is." Aron looked at her, then down to the glass, as if he could find the secret of what to do in its burgundy depths. Maybe if he drank it he'd find the answer.

He downed half the glass, then carefully placed it on the coffee table. He appreciated his mother's comforting touch more than he could say, especially since he knew it would be withdrawn soon enough.

"We broke up," he finally said. "I broke us up."

"All right. Tell me what happened."

"She said I stole her agency."

His mother sat back. "That means you made a decision that impacts her without even consulting her about it."

"Mom . . ." He started to protest, then backed down. "There's been a lot of . . . negative commentary about our relationship, things posted and whispered that I hope she never discovers. Things she'd warned me about, but I believed I could handle them even when they became very direct attacks and threats on her."

He sank his head into his hands. "But I didn't think about the toll it would have on her. She's been so sad. She . . . lost her light. I wanted to do anything I could do to protect her and make her smile again. Mark and I came up with the idea that it would shield her if I praised the work she did for Artemis while stating that our partnership has ended and we wish each other the best in future projects. I didn't want to disavow our relationship, which meant that the only other option was to end things. We could get back together after things cooled down. That . . . didn't go over well."

"You and Mark came up with this idea?" His mother frowned. "Did you discuss this with Samara beforehand?"

"No." He rubbed his chest. "She got furious, then said she needed some time and that she'd never forgive me for stealing her agency. I can still hear the sound of the door closing. And now my chest feels like I'm on fire and I don't know how to stop it."

"Oh, Aron." A deep sigh lifted his mother's shoulders. "You remind me so much of your father right now. He kept his cancer diagnosis a secret because he wanted to protect me. I almost hated him for that. Almost hated the man I'd loved for nearly all my life. The man I still love."

He felt a glimmer of hope. "But you forgave him, right?"

She ran her hands down her thighs, another sigh escaping her. "I understood why he did it. I even understood why he thought he was doing it to protect me. He wanted me to focus on taking care of you and Benjy, and he wanted to build up as many happy memories as he could. I know all that."

She pointed to her temple, then folded both hands over her heart. "But he . . . he broke my heart when he denied me the right to stand beside him at the start and fight with him and for him until he couldn't hide it anymore. He carried that burden alone for months instead of allowing me—his wife, his partner—to shoulder some of that burden because that's what couples do. So, while I moved past it because I love him and I stood beside him until the end, I never forgave him for making that decision without me, taking that choice away from me."

The quaver in her voice crashed through him. He hugged her, guilt stabbing him. Those months preceding his father's death had been gut-wrenching. If watching his larger-than-life father lose his fight had been unbearable for him, he couldn't imagine the devastation his mother had felt. He'd witnessed most of her grief, or so he thought. Now he had to wonder. "I'm sorry, Mom."

"I'm not the one you should be apologizing to," she said, gently pushing him away before delicately dabbing at her eyes. "I shared this so that you could understand how Samara is feeling right now."

"I'm figuring it out." He finished off his wine, wishing it was something stronger. "I don't think she's a liability to me or the company. I have never thought that. I don't care what trolls say about me anymore. But I—some of the things they're posting about Samara because we're together—I don't want her to have to see that, deal with that. So I thought if we broke up she wouldn't have to worry about comments like that anymore. But I miscalculated. I didn't consider her feelings, and I hurt her."

It hurt to confess that, to say that, especially to his mother.

If she never forgave his father, he knew Samara would never forgive him.

"You need to apologize to her. Immediately."

"I've tried. She's not answering my texts or calls. She said she needed some time."

"When did this happen?"

He glanced at his watch. "Thirty-two hours, forty-six minutes, and thirteen seconds ago."

His mother smiled. "I think she'll need a little more time than that. Give her the weekend. But it wouldn't hurt to send her a bouquet and an apology note."

"I delivered it in person yesterday," he confessed. "Her roommates said she wasn't there, but I saw her car in her designated parking spot."

"Did you accuse them of lying, get mad, pitch a fit, or demand to see her?"

"And make her even more angry with me?" He looked at his mother, frowning. "Should I have done that?"

"My sweet boy." His mother cupped his cheek. "No, thank goodness you didn't do that. She's mad at you right now. You don't want that to deepen into something else, something worse."

He suppressed a shudder. He'd clearly made a mistake with Sam, one his mother seemed to think he could repair. He didn't want to do anything to make it worse. If she wanted time, he would give her time. That was the least he could do.

"Is it all right if I crash here tonight?" He didn't want to go home, not when he could still feel Samara's presence in every corner.

"As if I'd let you drive home like this." She squeezed his

hand. "Get some rest. I completely believe you'll have a Win Samara Back plan ready to go in the morning."

He hoped his mother was right. If he knew anything, it was that he needed Samara. Needed her smile, her companionship, her intelligence. Her body next to his. Through the stupidity of a noble gesture, he'd lost all of that, lost her. But of all the things he'd lost of hers, losing her respect cut the most.

• • •

"Got a moment?"

Sam looked up as Quinn poked her head into her room. Any distraction from her own problems, especially one that had her mind and heart trapped in a tangled mess, was welcome. She sat up, rubbing at her eyes. "Sure. Come in."

The door opened fully, revealing Quinn and Max and a tub of salted caramel chocolate chunk ice cream. "What is this, an intervention?"

"No, it's an ice cream social." Max sat on one corner of the bed while Quinn sat on the other. Max handed Sam a spoon. "Okay, it's mostly an ice cream social, with a bit of an intervention thrown in."

Quinn squinted as she pinched her thumb and forefinger together. "Just a tiny bit."

They had a code for these things. Liquor and Lizzo for the FU breakups. Bey and Bacardi for the sad ones. Ice cream interventions happened when one of them was on the verge of doing something stupid.

"Fine." She stabbed her spoon into the creamy goodness. "I'm surprised y'all didn't do this yesterday."

"You weren't ready yesterday," Quinn told her, then nodded

at the giant bouquet on her dresser. "Considering that isn't currently in the trash made us think you might be ready."

"Besides, I had to go buy the ice cream," Max said around a spoonful.

"Thanks." Sam stabbed her spoon into the frozen treat again. "I'd rather have a sugar rush than be drunk and depressed right now."

Quinn peered at her. "So does that mean that you've gone from wallowing in emotion to thinking things through?"

"I was not wallowing," she protested, glaring at her friend. "I was . . . processing."

"Okay, processing." Max rolled her eyes. "Have you moved to step two yet?"

"Trying to."

"Ready to share?"

"Yeah." Sam gave them as honest a recap as she could of her argument with Aron, hoping that her friends could understand her thought pattern. They had been her best friends forever, and they'd understand why she'd reacted the way she had. They'd also be honest enough to call her on her bullshit if it was warranted.

She had a feeling it was warranted.

"You ready to hear what we have to say?" Max asked.

She snorted. "Even if I say no, you're going to give it to me anyway."

"You're right. We just want to make sure you're listening."

Sam barely refrained from rolling her eyes at Quinn. They were trying to help, and getting different perspectives would only assist her in figuring out what she needed to do. "I'm listening."

Quinn nodded at Max to start. "Okay, first of all, you're

completely justified in getting pissed at Aron talking to that Mark guy instead of you. I don't care how long they've been friends—"

"Aron says they're not friends. He's just an executive at the company, over marketing."

Max blinked, then blinked again. "He talked. To an *employee*. Instead of you?"

"That's what I'm saying!" She squeezed the pillow. "He just made a decision about me without me, as if I was an employee he needed to fire. Then had the nerve to say he didn't consider how I would feel. He apologized for not thinking about my reaction, not for wanting to end our relationship."

Fuck, that hurt. The cold disregard for her feelings, her thoughts, her agency, hurt worse than the fact that he thought breaking up would protect her. "I thought I understood the way he parses data. I thought he understood what's important to me. And why the hell did his superior analytical skills deduce that breaking up was the best solution?"

Quinn pulled her spoon out of her mouth. "I don't think he really wanted to break up with you. And I don't think he was actually using his brain to come to that decision."

Sam gaped at her. "The King of Decision Trees not using his brain? Please."

Quinn gave Max a questioning look. Max nodded, then turned to Sam. "He wasn't using his brain when he said all that. His heart was in control."

"His heart?" she echoed. "So his heart was telling me to go away and that our relationship wasn't working? And here I thought you guys were trying to cheer me up, not make me feel worse."

"I'm basing it on what you told us. You said he was very

remote when he told you that, but got more agitated the an-
grier you got, and he tried to stop you when you were ready to
walk out."

"Not to mention that he said it was all to protect you from
the trolls," Quinn added. "That's why his heart made the decision his brain refused to do."

His heart made the decision? Sam dug her spoon deep into
the softening ice cream, scooped out a mountainous portion,
and began to devour it as her mind careened from one thought
to another.

In the time that she'd known Aron, she'd had a close-up
view of how Aron processed data, considered options, then
decided. At no time had she witnessed him using his emotions
to help him reach life-changing conclusions. Despite what
Quinn and Max believed, the facts couldn't be ignored.

Since their association was made public, he and Artemis
Games had been gouged on social media, and she'd been ha-
rassed and threatened, and had her moral integrity questioned. Artemis Games and Rise Consulting had both been
subjected to negative reviews and distributed denial-of-
service attacks that flooded their servers with traffic that kept
actual customers from accessing their accounts. Anyone
would recognize that she was the liability.

"What are you going to do, Sam?" Quinn asked, her face
pinched with worry.

"Head to the airport." She glanced at her watch, having
turned her phone off on the second day after the breakup. "I
told him I needed some time to think; he told me I should follow my mother's advice and get out of town. So, I'm going to
think while sitting on the deck of a gorgeous beach house,

sipping a fine wine. I paid for a week, so you guys should come down for the weekend."

She stabbed her spoon into the remaining ice cream. "And if Aron puts out that lame-ass statement, let me know. It'll make my thinking a helluva lot easier."

Chapter 34

"Are you going to make a statement?"

Aron looked over the top of his monitor to where Grayson sat. "Did Mark reach out to you to convince me, or is this coming from Max?"

"Both." Grayson pushed his glasses higher on the bridge of his nose with a sigh. "I'm getting double-teamed, and let me tell you, it's not pleasant."

"You don't work with or for Mark or for the company," Aron pointed out. "Feel free to delete any email he sends you and hang up on him if he calls you. As a matter of fact, block his number. You don't need that negativity in your life."

"I will very happily comply," the other man said, pulling out his phone. "But you don't need that negativity either."

"Don't I deserve it, though?" Aron pushed back from his desk. "I'm sure your girlfriend thinks so."

"She doesn't," Grayson surprised him by saying. "Besides, aren't you punishing yourself enough?"

He pointed to the other side of the room, a stark contrast to the office area. The couch was now his bed, the coffee table became the pizza-eating location, the gaming chairs were where he'd built a miniature Stonehenge out of empty energy drink cans.

"I can't sleep in the bedroom," Aron muttered. "It doesn't matter how long I've been up or how tired I am. Besides, it's easier to take a quick time-out on the couch while I'm working. There's still a lot of work to do."

He could barely stand to be home without Samara there. Before the Game Night blowup, she'd stayed over at least every other day, so even if she wasn't there, he knew she soon would be. Now he wondered if she'd ever come back. The only reason he hadn't completely lost it was because she hadn't agreed with that stupid breakup idea, and just needed time. Now he just needed her to answer her phone.

"I knew it." The other man shook his head. "I had a feeling you go right back to work after I leave for the day."

"There's a lot to do." Aron rubbed at his temples, headachy, grumpy. Lonely. "I'm wrestling it back, but it's taking longer than I'd hoped."

"Which is why Mark is foaming at the mouth to get a statement from you, I'm guessing. I'm surprised he hasn't done an end run around you."

"I personally told the PR team that no statement goes out without my signature." It had been necessary to go to the office and stare each team member in the eye as he gave that order, especially after looking at the copy Mark had wanted to send out on his behalf. "My company, my messaging."

Grayson held up his hands. "Not that I'm trying to channel my inner Mark or anything, but have you thought of what your messaging is going to be?"

"For the company? Business as usual. Focusing on *Legends-fall: Mythica* and finalizing marketing plans for NexCon."

"You're making a distinction," Grayson noted with a sly smile. "Does that mean you have some other messaging to do?"

"If voice mails and texts don't work, I have to do something to make up for my colossal mistake. I now go to her parents' house every day to beg for forgiveness, and I'll keep going until they forgive me or chase me off for good."

He swallowed, then looked to Grayson, hoping he'd hear the words he wanted to hear, even if they were a lie. "Do you think she'll come back to me?"

"As my girlfriend would say: you gonna give her a reason to come back to you?"

Aron snorted. "That does indeed sound like something Max would say. But yes, I plan to give Samara a reason to come back, if I can get a message to her. Does Max know where Samara is?"

"Samara rented a beach house on the coast. Max and Quinn are planning to go down there this weekend. They say Samara's waiting for you to make a statement before deciding what to do."

Hope stirred in his chest for the first time since Samara rightly walked out on him. "Can I tell you how glad I am that you're still dating Max?"

"You can, but you can also give me a raise. My baby and I love buying each other presents."

"Done. As for the statement, I have an ultimate move to play, but I'm still trying to perfect it."

Grayson sat forward. "What ultimate move? Can I help?"

"I've been working on a video statement. A statement to an

audience of one that leaves no doubt of where I stand so she'll never doubt me again. Think I can workshop this with Quinn and Max?"

Grayson pulled out his phone. "Absolutely. They've been waiting for your grand gesture."

Aron shot to his feet, feeling better than he had in days. "Let's do this."

* * *

Sunsets and solace and sangrias could only do so much.

Sam sat on the deck, wineglass in hand, looking out to the ocean. The late afternoon greeted her with a tangerine sun hanging low in the sky, a warm breeze sweeping in off the water, and the soothing susurration of low tide. It was beautiful. It was peaceful.

It was lonely.

She hadn't ever lived alone, she realized. She'd gone from her parents' house, to a dorm room, to an apartment with her friends, and then the condo. Even when she'd had a few moments of me time, sequestered in her room, she knew her roommates were there or on their way. That alone time hadn't lasted more than a handful of hours.

As serene as it was, being alone with her thoughts in the beach house was an exercise in self-flagellation. Since walking out on Aron, her anger had dissipated the first day, sadness the next couple of days, then regret after that. Regret that she hadn't answered his calls or texts after her anger had receded.

All that was left now were answers that only he could provide. He'd said he wanted to end things to protect her, but that made no logical sense. Their association hurting his business, his reputation—those were logical reasons she could see and understand. But to break up to protect her? That didn't seem logical, which was why it was unusual for him to not have reasons prepared.

She was beginning to believe that Quinn and Max were right, that protecting her by letting her go was an emotional decision on Aron's part. He'd promised to be her shield, a promise he'd made to her and her parents because of their concerns that what had happened to Marquessa might happen to her. Maybe he'd thought that ending things would end the hate. He didn't realize that they would just hate on her for something else.

It was time to contact him, so they could talk it out. She needed to know why he thought breaking up was the best course of action. And if he answered with some self-martyrdom bullshit, she was gonna have to check him on that.

For the first time in days, she powered on her phone. It came alive in her hand with notification after notification, text, email, voice mail. Before she could call Aron, the phone rang in her hand. Unfortunately, it was Quinn calling instead.

Quinn dived in as soon as Sam answered. "Did you see Aron's message?"

Sam made her way back into the house. "I haven't seen anyone's messages. I just now turned my phone back on."

"Okay, then ignore everything except the last message that Aron sent you."

"Why?"

"Because that's the most important one," Quinn told her, her voice brimming with excitement. "That's the one you need to read right now."

Sam didn't understand the urgency in Quinn's voice. "Is

this about the statement he planned to put out about our work together?"

"Not even close."

"Oh." Her heart sank. "So this is something else about me that everyone else knows before me."

"Dammit, Sam." Quinn spoke with uncharacteristic heat. "If by everyone you mean your friends and your fam, then yes, everyone knows because everyone helped him put this together."

Everyone did? "What are you talking about?"

Quinn said a few choice words under her breath. "Girl, if you don't hang up right now and check your boyfriend's message, I swear 'fore God that I will kick your ass from the beach house to the town house."

Neither swearing nor threats were part of Quinn's vocabulary. For her to use both meant Sam needed to pay attention. "I will, I will! Hanging up now."

After ending the call, Sam curled up on the love seat and opened her messages. As she'd expected, dozens of texts greeted her, most of which she'd delete unread. Curiosity faded on a pang of guilt as she saw how many texts and voice mails Aron had left. That had to mean that he wanted to apologize and reconcile, right?

Precariously balanced between hope and dread, Sam scrolled to Aron's last text, noting that the attachment was a video file. The accompanying text was only three words: **PLEASE WATCH THIS.**

She ran her fingers lightly over the still. He had on his glasses and a hoodie, hair falling over his forehead, his back to the shelves of games and gaming consoles in his home office.

His attire was a deliberate callback to their first meeting, Benjy the Hoodie Guy and ReyofSun. Behind the lenses she could see fatigue engraved in his features, but she also saw his smile, a smile that caused her heart to beat faster as she tapped to start the video.

"Samara. You are the most amazing woman I've ever met."

The view suddenly changed to what looked like an 8-bit side-scrolling game. The character looked very much like a digitized version of Hoodie Guy. As she watched, the character walked forward through a green landscape, stopping at a colorful frame that held a digitized version of her ReyofSun persona. Rey pulled out a mallet, struck the side of the frame, and freed herself. Avatar Rey then joined Hoodie Guy.

The voice-over continued. "You blew into my life like a fire and brimstone whirlwind, urging me and my company to do and be better."

Both characters were caught in a fiery tornado and metamorphosed into their professional personas. Together they moved forward past a frame showing the Artemis Games logo and one showing the Rise Consulting logo. The pair then stopped in front of a frame bearing the WeCAN logo. "Thanks to your passion and professional expertise, not only is Artemis better, but we were awarded the WeCAN certification."

A surge of joy had her yelling, "Yes!" at the top of her lungs as game Aron removed the WeCAN logo from the frame. She was so happy for him and what that certification meant to him and Artemis. No matter what happened, she was proud of her contribution in winning the certification.

The game scrolled forward again, their characters moving past other frames that held personal photos. Them at Game Night. The Girl Code fundraiser. Deep in discussion in his home office. "I've enjoyed every moment that we've spent together, Samara. The quiet ones and the loud ones. The professional ones and the personal ones. The good ones and . . . the not-so-good ones."

The posed photo from the gala. Him partnering with Mitchell for a game of horseshoes against her father and Jarrod. "I want more of those moments, Samara. The comfortable ones and even the uncomfortable ones. I believe we can be together, we should be together."

The characters stopped in front of a gap that looked like an ocean. Aron confirmed it when he said, "Remember when I said we had an ocean of similarities? I think we've proved that. We love gaming. We love our families. We have a passion for the work we do for others and for our careers."

A photo of a younger Aron at a desktop computer floated down, enabling them to hop onto it. The next photo was a younger version of herself, also at a desktop computer. They hopped onto that one too. It was followed by a picture of them with her parents and a picture of them with his mother and Benjy. After hopping on those photos, they made it to the other side.

"You know my family adores you almost as much as I do. And your parents . . ." He cleared his throat. "It took a lot of pleading to get them to forgive me, and I would have done more. Of course, their forgiveness is contingent on you forgiving me."

Aron's avatar remained still, becoming shrouded in twilight as her character walked away, taking the sunlight with her. "I understand why your father called you ReyofSun, because you lit up my world in ways I didn't know I needed, ways I don't want to lose. I know . . . I know I disappointed you. I know I didn't protect you in the way you needed me to. You had every right to walk away. I've learned my lesson, Samara. I know we should stand together, work together, and face together whatever the world wants to throw at us. I swear, that will be the last time I take your agency away."

The Aron character pulled out a heart symbol that grew bigger with each step into the sunlight, back to the Samara character. "You are smart, funny, passionate, loyal, dedicated, and kind. I can say with certainty that you are the best thing that's ever happened to me, and I will do whatever it takes, whatever you want to make sure you're safe and happy."

The game faded to black as the real Aron reappeared onscreen, wiping at his eyes. "Samara. If you can forgive me, I will be forever grateful and happy. I want you to be my Player Two for life. I love you." The video faded to gray-white, then blurred. She gasped for breath, then gasped again, finding it hard to catch her breath. That's when she belatedly realized that she was crying and had been for a while. And if her runny nose was any indication, it was an ugly cry too.

Aron had made a statement, all right. The grandaddy of statements that left no doubt of what his feelings for her were.

She needed to call him. Needed to talk to him, because this wasn't something that could be discussed via text. How long would it take her to drive back to Atlanta? She had to pull herself together so she wouldn't be crying and snotting and emotionally all over the place when she called him.

Rising to her feet, she unsteadily made her way to the kitchen for paper towels to clean her face. Her skin protested every swipe. "I'll pamper you later. Right now there are more important things to do."

Her hands shook so violently that it took her two tries to hit the call icon. He answered immediately. "Samara."

"Aron." Her voice wobbled. She swallowed, then tried again, but all she could say was his name before her throat clamped tight.

"Did you see it?" he asked, his voice rough and scratchy. "I meant every word. Please tell me you saw it."

"I miss you. Where are you? I'll go there right now."

"I'll come to you. Hold on."

The doorbell rang. "Open the door, Samara."

She dropped the phone and raced to the door.

Chapter 35

The thick oak door flew open, bounced against the wall, then began to swing back until Samara blocked it. "You're really here."

"There's nowhere else I could be," he answered, throat tight. "Nowhere else I want to be than wherever you are."

"Aron." Tears drenched her cheeks. "Catch me."

Finally.

He dropped everything to open his arms wide. She launched herself at him. He caught her, hugging her tightly as she wrapped her legs around his waist. She threw her arms around his neck, and they both touched forehead to forehead, remaining silent except for breaths suddenly turned ragged. Joy and relief and need crashed through his system. Then they were laughing and crying and hugging and kissing and his world finally began to right itself.

Kisses slowed, deepened. Desire flared, burned. There were so many things he wanted to ask, to tell her, to show her, that they all jumbled in his brain like a massive traffic jam. One question stood out from the others, and he asked it both as a request and a demand. "Bedroom?"

She interspersed her answer with kisses, which was all right with him. "On this level, the second door on the right."

Locking his hands beneath her bum, he followed her directions, carrying her through a door. He didn't have any idea nor did he care what the room looked like, except for the king bed. He set her on her feet, and then it was a race to shed their clothes as quickly as possible. But once the last piece of clothing fell away, they paused.

She reached up to cup his jaw, her thumb brushing along his cheek. "I'll take that hollow look from you and bring you brightness again."

He covered her hand. "I'll take that sad look from you and bring you happiness again."

Heart pounding, he scooped her up and gently settled her on the bed before joining her. His emotions somersaulted in his chest, flipping from happiness to apology, to desire, to love. He needed to show her all of those.

He kissed her slowly and thoroughly, forehead, cheeks, lips lingering, savoring each one. He kissed his way down her throat, along her collarbone, happily rewarded by her soft moans. But when her hands curled over his shoulders, he quickly pulled them away, pinning her hands to the bed. "You can't touch me right now. I need to focus on you so I don't lose control."

Hazy heat filled her gaze. "What if I want you to lose control?"

His focus wavered for a moment, and he had to breathe through it, his fingers tightening on hers. "Later," he told her. "I need to do this now."

He resumed his slow exploration, reacquainting himself

with every dip and rise of her body. It seemed like yesterday but also forever ago that he'd been able to do this, to kiss his way down to the juncture of her thighs. All his senses reveled in her, the sight of her up close after so long, the silky touch of her thighs, the scent of her excitement, the sounds of her gasps and moans as she responded to him.

Then she ripped her hands free of his grasp, digging them into his scalp as she arched against his mouth as if shocked by a defibrillator. He kept going until she tugged at his hair again with a throaty "Come here" that he had to obey.

He rose above her, taking in her heavy-lidded gaze, her chest rapidly rising and falling, the satisfied smile, and warned, "I'm going to lose control now."

She gave him a husky laugh, then opened her arms. "You damn well better."

He fell into her arms, into her gaze, into her, heart and body and mind racing. With his thoughts in shambles, his body took over, remembering what to do and how to do it, fast and frenzied strokes driving them higher and higher. Dimly, he was aware of saying something, harsh gasping whispers of declarations, apologies, or promises. One or all, he wasn't sure which. All he knew was that the words needed to come out just as much as his body needed hers.

She wrapped her arms around his neck, her legs around his waist. Her hips thrust up to crash against him, her breath hot and heavy in his ear, her movements almost frantic. He knew the signs and quickened his pace, giving her everything he had, everything she wanted. Then her inner muscles clamped down on him, launching him into the stratosphere, stars exploding behind his eyes.

He returned to earth slowly, his muscles giving out as he

collapsed against her. He felt exhilarated, euphoric, even as he realized he was finally back where he was supposed to be.

• • •

Sam wrapped her arms around Aron, racked and spent. It hadn't been that long since they were last together, but it felt as if her heart and her body had gone into panic mode, and the only way to reset was that wild physical intimacy that couldn't be denied.

Aron still lay atop her, head nestled between her breasts. He should have been heavy, but he wasn't. He was just right, the perfect weighted blanket to soothe her. She held him tightly, irrationally afraid that if she loosened her grip he'd somehow disappear. "Thank you for coming down here for me," she whispered on a shaky breath.

"I couldn't not come for you," he mumbled against her breastbone. "I needed you to see the video, I needed to convince you to give me another chance, I need, needed—"

"I know." She stroked a hand down his back. "Me too."

Now that the kiss-and-make-up step had been successfully completed, it was time to clear the air between them. "I saw the video. It was—it was beautiful and moving and perfect. And somehow you got here right after I saw it. I'm assuming my roommates told you where I was?"

"I hit the road right after I sent it to you. And yes, Quinn and Max and Grayson all pitched in. They and your parents also helped me with the photos." His head dipped. "I came down here because I figured you might still have your phone off and I might be able to convince you to look at it. I didn't realize that you'd turned your phone on."

"I was done thinking and wanted to call you to talk things

out," she answered, snuggling against him. "While my phone was seizing, Quinn called me and told me to look. I can't believe you made a video game apology."

"I wanted to make sure you would see it to know how I feel, and just saying the words wasn't enough."

"It was perfect. Beautiful, funny, sad, and loving. Perfect."

"I almost lost you. That won't happen again. You walked away in every dream. No matter what I did, no matter what I said. You walked away. No words, no curses, just sad eyes and a softly closing door. It was easier to just stay awake and work."

"Aron." She cupped his cheeks. "I didn't break up with you. I just needed some time to get over my anger and think things through."

"It felt like you left, and it was my fault you walked away," he told her, his voice hollow. "I thought I was doing the right thing, and it was too late when I realized how seriously I'd messed up. I began to believe that you had put together a stay or go chart and found more reasons to go than reasons to stay."

"Do you understand why I was upset though? Do you know how much you hurt me? The man who promised to be my shield thought breaking up with me would hurt less than reading comments from people I'll never meet in real life."

"Yes, I promised to be your shield, no matter what it took. My miscalculation was that in trying to shield you from one pain I caused a greater one, and for that I will be forever guilty. But I wasn't thinking, I was only feeling. Feeling that I needed to defend you from anything that might hurt you. Feeling that I needed to protect you from anyone who might attack you.

Feeling like a grenade ready to explode on anyone who looked at you wrong."

The intensity in his words told her just how emotional and illogical he'd been, how much his heart must have hurt for her that prompted him to take the nuclear option to protect her. "I understand now what you went through and why you made the choice you did."

"Samara, I need you to understand. I know you don't need me to protect you, but I'm gonna do it anyway. I'm always going to have your back, and if you ever need me to tag in, all you have to do is say."

"Are you saying you did all this because you love me?"

"Yes."

"This is what you should have said," she told him, her voice cracking. "This I can understand."

She turned away, not wanting him to see her hurt, the brimming tears. Yet she couldn't smother the gasps emanating from her throat, her attempt to swallow the emotion that surged like bile up her throat.

Then he was there, wrapping his arms around her, pulling her tight and hard against his chest. Breath swooshed out of her, but she fought to hold in the emotion and desperately tried to move past the lingering hurt.

He rested his chin on her shoulder, his embrace like a vise she didn't want to escape from. His words were shaky when he spoke. "I am sorry, Samara, for making you feel like this. I am sorry I hurt you. I am sorry I made a decision about you without talking to you first. I'm sorry I didn't consider how much this would hurt you. I also thought any pain I would feel would be negligible. I was wrong about that, too."

A shudder swept through him. "I never once thought of you as a detriment. Not to the company, not to me. I wouldn't have offered you the contract otherwise. I value your skills, your intelligence, your everything. I value you, Samara, and it's not just because of the work you've done. And because I value you, I need to do whatever I can to ensure your well-being. But I promise you that from now on, I'll never make a decision that impacts you without discussing it with you, just you and no one else."

"Okay, I'll trust you to keep that promise." She turned in his arms until she faced him, her heart tugging at his pained expression. She reached up to wipe his cheeks, then attempted a light tone. "Mark better be a nonfactor in our private life going forward, or someone is gonna catch these hands."

"You don't have to throw your hands. I promise you, Mark will have nothing to do with us from now on."

His fingers tangled with hers. "I'm glad you called Artemis out. Changes obviously needed to happen, but it also brought you to me. It's definitely in the top three of the best things to happen to me."

She swallowed a lump of emotion before speaking. "What are the other two?"

"The successful launch of Artemis Games, and you agreeing to date me."

"Oh." She blinked rapidly. Being two of his top three both humbled her and turned her emotions to mush. "Thank you."

"You're welcome. I'd like to ask you something," he continued in that same serious tone.

Her stomach twisted. He'd just told her he loved her. Surely, he wasn't going to ask her *that*. Not while they were still naked in bed all sex tousled instead of walking the beach at sunset, having dinner at an elegant restaurant, or even while gaming in his home office. Still, she plastered on a smile and said, "Go ahead."

He took her hand. "Samara, will you go to NexCon with me?"

That wasn't the question she expected. "Say what now?"

"I want you there as my partner in every sense of the word. I want you beside me at the panel when we introduce *Legendsfall: Mythica*. I want to acknowledge the work you did with the company culture and the WeCAN certification. I want you to talk about the process and how you worked with me to make it happen. I would also like to introduce you as our director of equity and inclusion."

"Whoa." She sat up. "This is definitely not a conversation I can have naked."

"Oh, right." He released her hand. "That's understandable. Why don't you go take a shower while I go get my bag and see if your dinner is salvageable? I can order something else, then jump in the shower myself. Then we can talk again."

After showering and having more food delivered, they sat down at the dining table to eat and continue their earlier conversation. Sam picked up a hush puppy, then pointed it at him. "First question: did you logically and methodically think this through or is it one of those spontaneous ideas you get while talking?"

He pointed a clam strip back at her. "Me wanting you on-stage was an 'in-your-face' idea that I then thought through so that I could convince you it's a good idea."

She munched on the hush puppy. "I'm guessing that the

whole offering-me-a-job part was totally off the top of your head when you mentioned it a little while ago."

He winced. "Is it really that obvious?"

"I've been literally face-to-face with you for nearly five months now," she reminded him. "I've learned a thing or two by observation. But I must respectfully decline your offer."

"Why?" He jerked his head up, surprise flooding his tone. "Yes, I came up with the idea, but it's not like I called up the head of HR and told them to get your packet ready. You and I are talking about it now, so it's not like I made a decision without your input."

"Baby, I realize that. My input is that I can't come work for you because I work for my mother. She's been talking about having an early retirement and wants me to learn the management side of the business so I can take over the company when the time is right. I can't do that and be your equity director too."

"You're right, and if I were in your shoes, I'd do the same thing. I just want us to be on that stage together. You've made tremendous contributions to Artemis Games, which is why I wanted to introduce you to the crowd. But keeping you safe is more important. What do you think about waiting backstage, and after I'm done talking, we run out of there and take a couple of days elsewhere? We're at the beach now, so maybe a mountain cabin?"

"Hmm, I like that option a whole lot better. There's no need to give them ammunition."

"See?" He raised her hand to plant a kiss on the back of it. "I think this was a good demonstration of how I learned my lesson about making decisions about you without you."

She gave his hand a squeeze. "You can decide things without me like picking up dinner or maybe a surprise weekend away, but not life-changing things like moving to another country or setting our relationship on fire."

"Understood." He held out a hush puppy for her to bite into. "Can we agree that if we get to a 'think things over' point that we call a twenty-four-hour truce, then come back together to talk things through instead? Flowcharts and presentations optional."

"I can agree with that." She laughed. "Hey, look at us being all grown-up and stuff."

"Speaking of grown-up . . . when are our grown-up friends supposed to get here?"

"Tomorrow afternoon," she answered. "I think Max and Grayson will come first. Quinn has to wait for her girlfriend to get off her shift at the hospital, which I think is early afternoon. Why?"

"I wanted to know how much alone time we're going to get. I also want to know if there's a hot tub. Maybe we can we kiss and make up in there?"

"Do you know what sex in a hot tub will do to my coochie? No, sir. All the nopes."

He laughed. "I can guess what a coochie is, and hell no, I don't want to damage the pretty princess."

"Okay, if you're going to call her the pretty princess, I guess I'll have to call him the very proud prince."

"I like the sound of that." He stroked his hand down her arm, leaving shivers in his wake. "As long as we don't share these names with anyone else. If you tell Max, then Grayson will know, and I'll have to fire him."

She raised a hand, barely keeping her smile in check. "I

swear these names will be a secret between you, me, and the sheets."

"Speaking of sheets, are you done with dinner? I'm feeling a need to cuddle in a blanket fort, if you know what I mean."

She burst into laughter as he wiggled his brows suggestively. "You have the best ideas."

Chapter 36

To say that the Artemis Games panel was packed was downplaying it. Standing room only, it seemed to be filled with a combination of curiosity seekers and gamers who really wanted to know what was up next from the company.

Standing just offstage, she was able to watch in unabashed appreciation as Aron shone in full CEO mode, his tone ringing with conviction as he thanked Rise Consulting for its work with Artemis Games; walked the audience through a presentation of what WeCAN was and how the partnership would not only provide opportunities for Artemis Games to hire more neurodivergent people in a wide swath of positions, but also create inclusive content. Then he launched into the behind-the-scenes designing and planning for *Mythica* and thanked everyone, including a diverse group of gamers as focus groups, who offered valuable input into the development of the new expansion.

"I'd also like to announce that *Legendsfall* and all games developed by Artemis going forward will offer an extensive modification panel for all characters. We want all our customers, all members of the Artemis family to be able to create and play characters that reflect them."

Sam bounced on her toes, grinning and clapping as applause greeted that statement. That was what she'd wanted the most from her collaboration with Aron, until she realized she wanted the man himself. She was definitely living her best life.

"And now, the moment you've been waiting for. Let me introduce you to some of the new playable characters in *Legendsfall: Mythica*!"

The hall darkened, and voices fell to hushed, excited whispers. A thundering hero soundtrack echoed through the large room. Although she'd seen the character reveal numerous times, it was nothing like feeling the booming music beat against her heart as a cinematic voiceover announced each character. She knew what the crowd was about to see and waited with tightly clasped hands for their reaction.

The audience exploded into cheers, screams, and applause. Sam covered her mouth with both hands. The new characters had won them over. No, Aron had won them over.

Sam made her way to the backstage corridor. She blew out her nerves on a woosh, walking in a circle and shaking her hands to relieve the last of the tension.

Emotion welled up, pushing a smile to her lips. Once the trailer for *Mythica* ended, Aron would thank the audience, then leave, which meant he'd be all hers soon. Her boyfriend was an amazing guy, and she needed to tell him and show him how proud she was of him, how happy she was for him, how happy she was to be with him. Maybe during the celebratory dinner. Maybe after dinner back in their suite. Or maybe she should wait until they returned to his house, a place that felt more and more like her home too.

"Are you happy now?"

Her lips twisted as she looked up at Mark waiting for her. From what she understood, he and his team were supposed to be with the marketing group staffing the Artemis Games booth, not hanging backstage of Aron's panel.

Her defenses immediately went up. She'd tried to tolerate Mark for Aron's sake, and for the fact that she was a professional in a professional setting, but Mark was the sort of toxic person you didn't allow onto the elevator, especially when you were the only one in it.

She made to go around him with a muttered "Excuse me," but he stepped into her path.

"How does it feel to be labeled as the bed-warming house wench responsible for bringing down not one, but two companies?"

There were times to retreat and times when you needed to bless someone's heart. Sam held her ground. "You fixed your mouth to say this, like I'm going to be bothered by old news that isn't true? Artemis is fine and so is Rise Consulting. This lame tactic didn't work on Aron, and it's certainly not going to work on me."

His jaw worked as he searched for another arrow to launch. "It's obvious you're too dazzled by being with a CEO."

This time she laughed. "Both of my parents are CEOs of their firms. That's all out in the open too. How could I be dazzled by your one CEO when I grew up with two?"

"You don't have the common sense to be concerned about yourself when you should be."

Concerned about herself? "Is this . . . Are you threatening me? And insulting my intelligence?"

"Am I?" Mark's smile was the equivalent of the razor-sharp edge of a blade about to stab her in the back. "I'm just asking a question. Testing a theory, if you will. Or maybe it's a proven fact that you're coming off as two-faced to your devoted following. It will be difficult for you to sell your 'poor, mistreated Black women' schtick when you're reaping the benefits of being in Aron's bed."

Sam settled a hand on her hip. "What benefits are those exactly?"

Mark sneered. "Do you really need me to spell it out for you?"

"Yes, please." Sam gave him the best wide-eyed-innocence, saccharine-laden smile she could muster. "And if you don't mind, use small words. I want to make sure I understand."

"You know he's just using you, right?" Mark stepped closer. "He's going by the playbook that I designed and gave him."

"Really? Your playbook included him making a video game–like confession to me and driving four hours to the beach to make sure I saw it?" She grinned at him. "That means I have to thank you. I should also apologize to you."

"You're apologizing to me?" His eyebrows shot up. "What for?"

"You're obviously the product of a failed school system. I'm sorry that you didn't learn that multiple things can be true at the same time and not contradict one another. Facts are facts. For example, it's a fact that Aron is a brilliant and generous man. It is also a known fact that you are a racist asshole."

"Why, you little bi—"

"Fact: I am not little, a bitch, or intimidated by you. Fact: if you touch me, I will mace you until you cry for your mama. Fact: I can love Aron and continue championing the visibility and inclusion of Black women in gaming while doing my job creating inclusion programs for a variety of clients."

"Love? You say you love him when you don't even realize that Aron's just using you. It would be funny if it wasn't so tragic."

"What's tragic is you believing that dye job is covering your bald spot," Sam replied, her voice dripping with bless-your-heart honey. "What's tragic is you believing I'm too stupid or naive to understand what's going on between me and Aron. I could go on, but my daddy taught me it's uncharitable to speak ill of people who open their mouths and prove themselves a fool."

Mark's face shot from pale to lobster red in a blink. "You think you're better than me?" he demanded. "You?"

"No." She shook her head for emphasis. "To do that I'd have to think you're somebody worth comparing myself to. My mama taught me to be more discerning than that."

She raised a hand. "So let's recap, shall we? One: Aron brought me on as a consultant to help identify the lack of representation or problematic representation in the company's games. Choosing me, given my track record of speaking on this subject for the last few years at cons and online and my profession as a consultant on those very same issues, was, if I may say so, a good business decision. Two: Announcing my consultancy is what I would expect any company to do that wants to shore up its public image and gain new ground. Three: Putting action to words and actually walking the walk to make his products better? That's why Aron is who he is and why Artemis will continue its upward climb. Four: I have no doubt that that man loves me, and I love him."

"Now I know you're lying," Mark said with a snort. "Aron only loves two things, his family and his company. You're deceiving yourself. Like I said, tragic."

"How can she be deceiving herself when she's part of my family?"

They both turned as Aron joined them, his expression implacable. He glanced to her. "Mind if I join this conversation?"

She gestured between them. "Be my guest."

"Thank you." He turned to Mark. "What's tragic is that I have a company executive overstepping his bounds by attempting to interfere with my personal business. It's also tragic that you hear but you don't listen. That's been the point of the past few months, and if you can't understand that, then you're part of the problem."

"You're the one who hasn't been listening! You're so busy chasing clout and skirts and being influenced by social justice warriors that you're forgetting about the audience that made Artemis Games what it is today!"

Aron frowned. "Weird, because I just talked to Cecily, you know, our chief financial officer? According to her, new subscribers exceeded our projections thanks to the *Legendsfall* expansion pack. And if you had been at the panel instead of laughably trying to intimidate my girlfriend, you would have seen the audience reaction to *Mythica*. I have no doubt that our preorders are going to go through the roof. Who would have thought that inclusion would be good for business?"

Sam hid a smile. Aron's bless-your-heart honey was almost as good as hers. Then he turned that honey into pure poison. "By the way, you're fired."

Mark gaped. "Fired? You can't fire me. I have a contract!"

Aron shook his head. "Funny thing about contracts. There are always some clauses that can be enacted if either party does something outside of the agreement. After presenting information to Legal and the board, they agreed that I have the right to fire you because of the damage you've done to Artemis."

"Damage? How have I damaged the company? She's the one who did that!"

Aron stepped forward, closing the distance between him and Mark and blocking him from Sam. "I would have happily paid out the remainder of your contract for what you just tried to pull with Samara. But because of your actions against Artemis, I can tell you that my last act as your boss was buying the plane ticket waiting at the hotel's front desk for you to leave tonight."

"I have done nothing but protect this company. You can't fire me for that!"

"You seem to have a habit of insulting people's intelligence." Aron's tone could have frozen fire. "Did you really think I wouldn't discover that you've been the one trolling in our public-facing forums? Since you want to insult someone's intelligence, how stupid are you to use your company-issued laptop to spread rumors and hate?"

It was Sam's turn to gasp. Mark had been behind that? How much hate did he have to do that to Aron?

"I-I-it's not me!"

"It is you. I privately gave a special assignment to a member of our IT team, and he gave me all the evidence I needed. All of it has been turned over to Legal. Aside from firing you, there may be charges in your future."

He stepped back, then took Sam's hand. "Don't mess with me, my company, or my woman. You will always lose."

He raised his other hand, and one of the security guards he'd hired approached them. "This gentleman is no longer a part of my team. Please escort him to his hotel room so he can pack, then make sure he gets his plane ticket from the front desk."

He turned his back to Mark, whose expression seemed to be a mix of shock, guilt, and remorse, then stepped in front of her, blocking her view. "Samara?"

She pressed her face against his chest and wrapped her arms around his waist, needing to anchor herself while she shook off the adrenaline rush. "That was . . . rough. Thank you."

"You don't have to thank me for that."

The terse tone had Sam scrunching her shoulders. He sounded angry, and she wasn't entirely sure if he was mad at her, Mark, the situation, or the fact that he'd just fired his communications vice president. "Are you mad?"

"Yes."

Ouch. Maybe he needed some time and distance to cool off. She shouldn't be hanging on to him like a damsel in distress anyway. "I'm sorry," she mumbled, trying to pull away.

"Samara." He tightened his grip a moment before easing his hold, sending a soothing stroke down her spine. "I didn't clarify. I'm not mad at you. I'm frustrated that I can't go Level 42 Berserker Mode on my former head of communications."

That startled a short laugh out of her, but she quickly sobered. "Normally, I can swallow it down and be unbothered, but he kept pecking and pecking at me and I just . . ."

Her fingers trembled as she grasped his lapels, and she had to take a deep breath before continuing. "My defenses weren't working as well as they should have been today, and I needed to unload on him. I shouldn't have done that."

He gripped her shoulders hard enough to hurt. "Are you apologizing? Don't you dare apologize for standing up for yourself!"

His anger on her behalf was a balm soothing her jangly nerves. She wanted to return the favor, burrowing her hands beneath his jacket to circle his waist. "Okay."

"You said what needed to be said. I did too. I should have released him from his contract a while ago. Not saying he's the only source of toxicity in the company, but he is the most visible face of it."

"Is there going to be fallout from firing him?"

"That depends. Jamilla, his deputy VP, has been waiting for an opportunity to show off her skills. I've decided to give her that chance. I'll have a conference call with the head of Human Resources and all the team members to let them know what happened and why. Everyone needs to know that if I won't tolerate that behavior from an executive, I won't tolerate it from anyone."

She shook her head in awe, overwhelmed. "I'm getting makeup on your shirt."

"Like I care about the shirt." He ran his hand down her back again, and she leaned into it, into him. "I care about you. Are you all right?"

"Almost." She tightened her grip. "This helps."

"Good." She felt him nod. "I'll keep doing this, then."

And she would have happily stayed in his arms like that for an hour, for life. That independent streak that ran down her backbone wouldn't let her. She drew in a fortifying breath, straightening her shoulders. "I can fight my own battles, you know."

"I know. Believe me, I know." He slid his hands down her arms, capturing her hands instead. "I didn't think of it as fighting your battle for you, but with you."

"Aron." Emotion clogged her throat. He knew the right

words to say. She knew they weren't empty words. Rocked by her surging heart, she looked down at their clasped hands, then back up at him. Emotion broke free with three simple words. "I love you."

"What?"

The surprise and hope that widened his eyes humbled her. Surely, she'd told him that before? She cupped his face, making sure she had his attention. "I love you, Aron Galanis. Probably should have said that a while ago, but I do love you."

She saw the exact moment her words hit home, his eyes incandescent, his smile a thousand miles wide, his arms lifting her up to spin her around as he laughed with unabashed joy.

"Samara." His voice roughened as he placed her gently back on her feet. He cleared his throat. "I think I wanna marry you."

She gave him an epic side-eye to keep from bursting into joyful tears. "Think?"

"Know. I *know* I wanna marry you."

His expression sobered as he took her hands. "I want to marry you, Samara. And just in case you're wondering, yes, it's an impulsive emotional decision that my pivot table–loving side heartily endorses. I love you. I know I haven't said it out loud a lot, but I've said it hundreds of times here." He touched his forehead. "And thousands of times here." He touched his heart.

That adorable puppy-dog look always made her smile, but she felt secure enough, loved enough, to not let him off the hook that easily. "I'm going to need a better proposal than that."

"I can code a game that ends with a marriage proposal. Or do you want a big production proposal that includes a highway billboard or a Jumbotron? I could make a video proposal, or do you want something smaller?"

She wrinkled her nose. "Maybe not something that screams publicity stunt to people still cynical about our relationship. Something that's just us."

"We started our relationship at a convention. It seems right that we move to the next level at one, too." He took her hand, then dropped to one knee. "Samara Reynolds. There's a spot in my heart that only you can fill. I want to spend the rest of my life with you, I want to make you smile every day, and I want you to never doubt what I feel for you. Will you marry me?"

"For a practice run, that was pretty damn good," she said, her voice thick. What an amazing man, and how lucky was she that he wanted to be hers? "Yes, I will."

He literally leapt to his feet. She didn't know people could actually do that. "Let's go ring shopping tomorrow. No, let's go tonight."

He squeezed her hands, his eyes like sparklers. "Even better, let's fly to Vegas, get married, then come back home and plan a huge formal event."

She laughed. "You think either of our mamas will be happy if we do that?"

"No, but I don't want you to change your mind."

"I won't change my mind." Her cheeks hurt from smiling, but she didn't care. "I'm your Player Two for life."

"I wouldn't have it any other way."

Game on

SERESSIA GLASS

READERS GUIDE

DISCUSSION QUESTIONS

1. Samara and Aron are both very interested in video games, both personally and professionally. What is your relationship to video games?

2. Were you surprised when Aron offered Samara the consulting job at Artemis? If you were Samara, would you have accepted the job? Why or why not?

3. At the start of the story, Aron didn't know the meaning of misogynoir or how dangerous it is online for Black female gamers. How does Samara help change his preconceived ideas? What did you learn from her experience and Aron's evolution?

4. Samara has a strong community of friends and fellow gamers that gives her support and feedback as a gamer. Are you a part of a community formed around a shared interest?

5. Aron and Samara are both fiercely protective of their friends' and families' safety and comfort. How do you see those character traits appear in their relationship together?

6. The job at Artemis requires Samara and Aron to fully play through all of *Legendsfall* in order to check the content. Would you like this job? What talents does someone need to have to successfully complete a project like this?

7. Samara has a day job as a consultant in addition to her on-line gaming persona, but working at Artemis allows her to combine the two. Do you have a passion that you follow outside of your career? What would a job blending it and your career look like?

8. What did you think of Aron's video game–themed grand gesture at the end? How did he consider Samara's feelings and interests when creating it? Has anyone ever made a grand gesture for you?

9. If you were to look five years into the future after the end of the book, what do you see Samara and Aron working on professionally? How do you think their relationship would have evolved?

Bonus level unlocked!
Read on for an excerpt from

THE LOVE CON

by Seressia Glass, available now
from Berkley Romance!

"Welcome back to *Cosplay or No Way*. Our three remaining contestants are fighting for the opportunity to make it to the final round where one of them will win $100,000 and the chance to work in costuming for a major motion picture!"

Kenya stared at Mark as the host recapped the competition so far. Being in the final three had her mentally bouncing with excitement. She'd read enough online comments after last week's show, the first to broadcast live, to know that a lot of people thought she was there simply to mark a diversity checkbox. *Please.* She'd worked her ass off to stay in the competition.

"As you know, this round's theme is cosplay mashups. Kenya, tell the judges about your cosplay."

Kenya smiled as she stepped forward, buoyed by the audience's applause. "For my cosplay mashup, I chose Dora the Milaje Explorer. In my vision for this, Dora's mother is a powerful warrior who instilled in her daughter all her skills and a desire to explore, learn, and grow. Dora's prized possessions are her digital helper Boots, her mother's gauntlets, and a map to Wakanda."

Based on the audience's reaction, she'd done an excellent

job on her mashup. Using the fabrication skills her best friend, Cam, had shown her, she'd recreated Shuri's panther-headed gauntlets, complete with blue glow-lights to simulate energy beams. She'd sewn her battle costume in General Okoye's style but with Dora's pink and yellow colors. A black panther–shaped backpack holding a map of Wakanda and Dora's signature brown bob completed her look. Everyone had instantly known what she'd done. When you didn't have to explain your cosplay, you were already a step ahead. That didn't stop the anxiety fluttering in her stomach.

"Thank you, Kenya." Mark turned his good looks to the panel. "Judges, do you have any comments you'd like to make about Kenya's cosplay?"

Kenya tightened her hands in her gauntlets, almost wishing she could bite her nails. This was the part she hated most, facing the judges. Not because she didn't want their opinions—they were some of the best in their fields—but because one judge seemed to have it out for her.

On cue, Rebecca leaned forward, concern drenching her features. "Kenya, do you really feel that you *embodied* the blending of Dora the Explorer and a Dora Milaje?"

She bristled at Becky's use of the word *embodied*. Throughout the competition, Rebecca had taken issue with her size, her race, and her assertiveness, but Kenya hadn't made it anywhere in life by being anything other than true to herself. Today was not the day to change.

"It's plural, not singular."

"Excuse me?"

"It's *the* Dora Milaje, not *a* Dora Milaje. They are a group, a sisterhood, never alone. Like Dora, who has many adventures and discoveries with the help of her friends. Neither Dora nor the Dora Milaje apologize for who they are or what they do. They simply are, and people accept that and move, or they will be moved."

Applause washed over her. She lifted her chin. She'd refused at the start of the competition to wear the Angry Black Woman mantle, and she wasn't about to cosplay that caricature now. That didn't mean that she wasn't going to stand up for herself.

"You've been a dark horse this entire competition," Rebecca said. A murmur rose from the audience. Rebecca had made herself the judge people loved to hate, with good reason. "Your cosplay choices have been extremely risky, considering your limitations."

Dark horse? Limitations? Kenya fixed her face in the automatic flat expression that all Black women perfected before puberty. She had no idea if Becky meant her size, her color, or her skill, but she'd be damned if she would consider any of those limitations. She was fat, Black, and had been cosplaying since she'd first dressed as Sailor Moon for Halloween as a kid. She knew what she was, but she also knew what she was capable of. Her parents hadn't raised her to be ordinary.

Knowing she had nothing to lose at this point, Kenya squared her shoulders. "With all due respect, Rebecca, I don't know what you mean by limitations. I believe I've met every challenge with grace and ingenuity. I refuse to limit myself so someone else can be comfortable." *Including you. Especially you.*

The crowd applauded in support, and Kenya nodded at them, gratitude welling in her chest. Their opinions mattered the most, since they could boost her popularity at cons and help her costuming business get off the ground.

"That's what I like about you, Kenya," Leon said, a ghost of a smile curving his lips. "You don't allow anything, or anyone, to hold you back. I've enjoyed your unique spin on each of the cosplays you've presented to us over the last two months, especially today's. I know you have a lot of people who see you as a role model and who are rooting for you. I look forward to seeing what else you have up your sleeves. You have my vote."

"Thank you," she mouthed. *One vote in my favor. I only need one more.*

All eyes focused on Rebecca. Kenya knew her vote before she opened her mouth. "I'm sorry," Rebecca said, her tone declaring she was anything but. "I think Amanda delivered the better cosplay this week."

Amanda had chosen the Cat in the Hat Woman for her cosplay. She'd had another meltdown on set because she'd run out of glue for her glue gun, as if it was someone else's fault she didn't have extra glue sticks in her supply kit. The crying jags had become a daily occurrence; they just didn't know what would set her off. Kenya hadn't minded giving the other woman support, but she wasn't there to help someone else win. The longer she stayed in the competition, the more exposure and publicity she received. During the brief times they'd been allowed to use their phones, she'd discovered that she'd gained tons of new followers (along with some new trolls) on all her social media streams, but that wasn't all she wanted. The winner would get the chance to work in the costuming department of a big-budget live-action fantasy film. She hadn't come to the show to be runner-up, and she sure as hell hadn't come to be number three.

Kenya's stomach bubbled as she focused on the last judge, Caroline. The perky blonde flailed her hands. "Oh my God, I can't believe it's up to me! Both of you have done an amazing job week after week. I've been so impressed with how each of you have risen to every challenge we've thrown your way."

Mark stepped forward. "Unfortunately, only one can move forward into the *Cosplay or No Way* final round. So, Caroline, who will it be? Will it be Amanda, or will you choose Kenya?"

Dramatic music swelled as the audience chanted both their names in a muddled cacophony. Caroline looked at them each in turn. Kenya reached out to clasp Amanda's hand, awkwardly squeezing the other woman's trembling fingers in an effort to steady her own. The other woman had already started the deep breaths that presaged tears.

"This is so hard . . . and I'm really sorry that I have to do this," Caroline began.

Silence fell, thick enough to choke on.

"Kenya."

Her eyes flew open as ice raced down her back, her shocked gasp echoed by the audience. Surely that didn't mean . . . ?

Caroline stared at her for a long moment before finally breaking into a smile. "Welcome to the final round."

"Oh God." Relief nearly buckled her knees as the audience rose in a standing ovation. She covered her open mouth with her gauntleted hands, smothering the gasp that wanted to become a scream. She had the presence of mind to turn to hug Amanda before the other woman sprinted from the stage. Blowing out a breath, she pulled back the panther on her left gauntlet, then straightened her shoulders to face the judges.

The host set up a commercial break as Ben, the other finalist, returned to the floor. He gave her a smile and a hug before joining her in facing the panel.

"And we're back with our two *Cosplay or No Way* finalists, Ben and Kenya!"

The audience cheers washed over Kenya. Euphoria zapped through her, nervous energy making her bounce on her toes as she vacillated between disbelief and elation. The final round! She was in the final round! She almost pinched herself as the reality of being a finalist began to settle in. The grand prize was close, so close. Just one more cosplay away.

Mark turned to them with a smile. "Congratulations, top two. You've fought long and hard to make it here, and each of you deserve your place in the finals. However, there's no time to rest on your success. In fact, in this final round we want to see how you design and create your cosplays on your home turf."

She and Ben exchanged glances. Home turf?

"That's right. The next part of the competition will follow the two of you as you return home to make your final-round costumes. A production crew will film you in your element. We want to see how you craft your creations in your personal space!"

Excitement and anxiety faced off in her nerves, ready to duke it out for the top spot. Her personal space was her bedroom in the apartment she shared with Cam, her best friend. She couldn't imagine trying to fit a camera crew in there. Besides, it was her bedroom, and she tended to be a bit messy during the design phase, creating several sketches as she finalized her concept. Maybe Cam would agree to let her use their dining area since they usually ate at the breakfast bar or in front of the television.

"I'm sure everyone is wondering about the final-round challenge. For that, we turn to our judges. Leon?"

Leon regarded them, his smile stuck somewhere on the

road between heaven and hell. "Contestants, you've consistently brought your A game for every week of this competition. Now, we want to see your A-plus work. Your final challenge will be iconic duos."

Duos? After they'd just finished mashups week? If that's what they wanted, she wasn't going to complain. She could do a gender-bent Two-Face, or one of the gem fusions from *Steven Universe*.

"That's the good news," Caroline said, "but you know we have to step it up for this final round. With that in mind, your iconic duo must be a pairs cosplay."

"What?" Ben whispered, looking as confused as Kenya felt. Did that mean making two costumes?

"That's right." Rebecca surveyed them. "Not only do we want to see how you juggle cosplaying with your normal life, we want you to create two costumes: one for you, and one for your cosplaying partner."

Kenya's mouth dropped open. Two costumes? Cosplay partner? Her mind raced. Did they need to create them from scratch or could they source parts? Most importantly, how much time did they have to create two costumes?

Caroline leaned forward. "We all know that cosplayers do everything from making their own cosplays to commissioning full costumes from someone else. You're probably wondering what's allowed for you in this final-round iconic duo cosplay challenge. So here are the parameters.

"First of all, both costumes must be at least fifty percent handmade. Of course, the more handmade the costumes are, the more points you can score. Secondly, we know there's a lot of pressure to make two costumes, so you're allowed to have help from your cosplay partner. However, seventy-five percent of the work has to be yours. You'll also need to recap your work at the end of the day with a video diary entry."

Rebecca gave them a smile Kenya instantly mistrusted. "This is all about being the best, which means testing and stressing you. That's why you and your partner will have four weeks to complete your costumes before you return here to cosplay for the live audience."

The shocked murmurs of the audience echoed the shock that swept through Kenya. There was no way they could expect two costumes to be finished in four weeks, especially with that fifty-percent-handmade requirement. And with one person doing the bulk of the work?

She looked at Ben, who looked as floored as she felt. "What?" he whispered. "Are they serious?"

"We're very serious," Leon answered. "Just as you should be, especially about who you'll pick as your cosplay partner. Remember, your partner can do up to twenty-five percent of the build, and they'll need to cosplay with you in the finale."

"Who will our finalists pick as their cosplay partners?" Mark asked the audience. "We'll find out—right after this."

Kenya's mind raced as everyone waited for the commercial break to end, imagining and discarding all the duos that immediately came to mind. With four weeks to work, it would be nearly impossible to do any costume with a great deal of detail work, and certainly not two.

Then there was the matter of picking her cosplay partner. Who could she get to help her? Her mind instantly went to Cam, but her best friend had his hands full running the fabrication shop, especially since she wasn't there to handle logistics and order intake. Her parents were out. Neither one understood her obsession with the geekery of anime and gaming or adults running around in costumes outside of Halloween, and even then they deployed maximum side-eye.

Besides, they'd been against her doing the show from the start. They wanted her to "give up this foolishness" and use her engineering degree they'd paid for. Her brother was off in the air force and her sisters were busy with their families and their careers on opposite sides of the country. Janelle might have been willing, but her other best friend didn't even own a sewing kit. Bringing Janelle on board meant Kenya would wind up doing one hundred percent of the work. What was she going to do?

"Welcome back to *Cosplay or No Way*," Mark announced as he was counted back in from the commercial break. "Let's recap the parameters of the final round."

Dramatic music and lighting rolled across the stage as the jumbo screen lit up, bold white letters spelling out FINAL ROUND RULES on a purple background. "First, conceive of an iconic duo cosplay that you and your partner will showcase during our live finale. Second, at least fifty percent of each costume must be handmade. Third, your cosplay partner can help you, but you must do seventy-five percent of the work. Each of you will have a production crew following your progress, and of course we want to continue seeing those video diaries. Judges, anything else?"

Leon spoke. "You're going to have your hands full in this challenging round, but overcoming challenges is part of what being a *Cosplay or No Way* champion is all about. I would suggest you choose your cosplay partner carefully."

"Ben," Mark said. "Who will you choose to partner with to help you become the *Cosplay or No Way* champion?"

Ben, who'd done an excellent mashup of The Stay-Puft Michelin Man, smiled. "My husband, John. He's as into cosplay as I am."

Crap. She knew from their conversations that Ben's husband was an active cosplayer and did set design for their local theater. Acid churned in her stomach. The choice gave him a huge advantage. She needed to level the playing field, which meant she needed someone who not only cosplayed, but could help make their costumes without Kenya having to supervise every step.

Her thoughts returned to Cam. They'd been best friends for half their lives and had cosplayed together since they first attended Dragon Con during their senior year of high school. He also knew his way around a 3-D printer and an X-acto knife. But she couldn't take him away from the shop. Yes, Mack and Javier were there, but since she ran the project management software, she knew just how lean the shop ran. Taking her off the schedule was a pain, but manageable. Taking Cam out of production . . .

He would do it, she knew. Cam was the reason she'd heard about the competition. He'd helped her prepare her audition video, sent encouraging texts and a good-luck video with their game night friends. He'd supported her every step of the way. This . . . this might stretch the bonds of their friendship to the breaking point.

"Kenya, it's now your turn," Mark said, his voice snapping her out of her spiraling thoughts. "Who will be your cosplay partner in the final round? Who will you choose to help you create an iconic duo cosplay that will win you $100,000 and the title of *Cosplay or No Way* champion?"

The musical tension increased as the audience fell silent.

Kenya was sure they could hear her gut churning. She glanced at the judges, trying not to let Rebecca's smug expression get to her. She was pretty sure the snotty judge doubted she had anyone close enough to meet the qualifications to help her.

"Well, Kenya?" Rebecca raised an eyebrow. "Do you have a significant other who can help you in this final round, like Ben does?"

Kenya carefully blanked her expression so they wouldn't notice she was internally seething. She'd broken up with her last boyfriend months ago for good reasons, but she'd be damned if she'd give Becky the satisfaction of knowing that. "I do."

Rebecca tilted her head in surprise. "Really. Who might that be?"

"There's only one person who's been with me all through my cosplay journey," she said, her voice quavering as nerves stretched tight. "The one who believes in me the most. The one who helped me get here, who's cheered me on from the start. The one person who's encouraged me to push myself, to be more and do more. My best friend, Cameron Lassiter."

"Ah." Rebecca's expression reminded Kenya of the shark in that movie about the missing clown fish. "That's your friend, right? I hope that won't put you at a disadvantage, considering Ben is working with his spouse."

Does this heifer think I can't get a man? Kenya unzipped a smile. "Cam is my best friend and my partner. Trust and believe I'm not disadvantaged in the least."

"You go, girl!" someone in the audience shouted, causing the crowd to explode with laughter, then applause. Vindication swelled in her chest, and she gave them a genuine grin and wave before giving Rebecca the same smug smile she'd received earlier. *Take that, Becky.*

"There you have it, folks!" Mark boomed. "Two couples going head-to-head to create iconic cosplay duos. Which team will come out on top to claim $100,000 and a chance to work on a major movie? We'll have to wait and see. Tune in next week as our finalists return to their home turf and begin the build of their lives on *Cosplay or No Way!*"

Thrills shot through her like fireworks. There really wasn't anyone else she wanted with her in the final round. That was the truth. Maybe she'd split hairs on the whole partner thing, but they really were partners, given her tiny stake in his shop. Their friendship had lasted longer than a bunch of marriages. Surely it wouldn't be a problem to fake that their relationship was more than just friends.

Now all she had to do was convince Cam to be her cosplay partner—and her significant other.